W9-CAE-749

TOUCH

TOUCH

Book Two of *The Queen of the Dead*

MICHELLE SAGARA

DAW BOOKS, INC.

DONALD A. WOLLHEIM, FOUNDER

375 Hudson Street, New York, NY 10014

ELIZABETH R. WOLLHEIM

SHEILA E. GILBERT

PUBLISHERS

www.dawbooks.com

First Printing, January 2014
1 2 3 4 5 6 7 8 9

DAW TRADEMARK REGISTERED
U.S. PAT. AND TM. OFF. AND FOREIGN COUNTRIES
—MARCA REGISTRADA
HECHO EN U.S.A.

PRINTED IN THE U.S.A.

This is for the teachers:

Carol Morgan
Manjit Virk
Lisa Adams
Carolyn Watt
Sara Cheng
Eric Chellew
Ashley Marshall
Ed Hitchcock

Because you chose to see all difficulties as challenges, and you worked to meet—and even exceed—them. Teaching is a vocation; it is an incredible gift, and it's given day-in and day-out.

ACKNOWLEDGMENTS

This was possibly the hardest book of my career to write. I thought, going in, it would be the easiest. This is the occupational hazard of the writer's life. Usually, though, my hazards don't cause quite as many problems for my publisher. DAW has been, as always, fabulous. I'm sure there was hair-pulling and teeth-grinding in New York—but it stayed in New York.

So. Sheila Gilbert & Joshua Starr, *thank you, thank you, thank you.* You let me take the time to start this book *four times* from the beginning, to figure out where and why it didn't work, and to ultimately make it work, even though it messed up the schedule terribly.

Inasmuch as this book is any good, it's due in large part to that understanding and that space.

Also: my family put up with an increasingly stressed and depressed writer for way too many months—which is generally what happens when I keep dashing my head against the wall of writer competence. So they deserve your sympathy.

NATHAN

WHEN YOU SLIDE INTO THE CAR, it's empty. Stuffy. You roll down the windows, sit for a minute in the garage. It's quiet, in the car. It's like a bubble world. You're in it; it's your space. It's your space until you park, turn off the engine, and get out.

Sitting in the garage won't get you anywhere you want to be, and you want to be somewhere, but you're not in a hurry, not yet. You start the car, back out of the garage, think about where you're going.

Radio says there's an accident on Eglinton you want to avoid. You're not the only one to take that advice; traffic is slow.

Here's a thing about cars. In the summer, when the humidity is 98%, you might as well be in an oven if your dad's air-conditioning is dead. Intersections are not your friend. Windows are. Still air becomes breeze, and breeze becomes wind—but only when the wheels rotate.

Here's another thing about cars. They have history.

Some of the history is in rust and nicks and dents and the taillight that's sketchy. Some of it's in stains on the vinyl; some of it's wedged between the seat back and the bench. Some of it, though, is memory. Where you went. More important, with who. You can think about the empty passenger seat on the hot, humid drive, and you can imagine that

Emma is sitting beside you, hair trailing back in the cross-breeze, elbow on the doorframe.

You can remember the first time you kissed her, when she got out of the passenger side and walked around to where you sat, behind the wheel, looking for words. Words have never come easily to you, but Emma gets that. She doesn't make you say anything you're not ready to say.

It was dark, but her eyes looked so bright. You didn't even get out of the car; you looked up to tell her you'd see her tomorrow, and her face was inches from yours; she was leaning into the open window, into where you were. And then you didn't want to start the car at all.

And maybe you didn't.

When you're on the inside of a car in motion, you're not really thinking about physics. When you're behind the wheel, you pay attention to red lights, green lights, stop signs, walk signals. If you don't, you've got no business being behind that wheel. But there's room for Emma in that, and you think about her when you're waiting for lights to change. You want to see her. You're going to see her.

But here's the big thing about cars: They're a couple of tons of metal and extraneous bits. Add wheels, and you get momentum. It's pure physics. You get momentum even if your car isn't moving, because the car that *is* moving doesn't stop until half your car is crushed between its SUV hood and the wall of a building.

The front half.

You see the SUV.

You see the SUV a dozen times.

You see it a hundred times. You're trapped in a loop where time slows down or speeds up randomly. You can see the license plate. You can see the driver. You can see his passengers, and you can count them. He's not much older than you are. They're not much older than he is.

You can see the front grille getting closer and closer. You know the license plate number by heart; it's burned into your memory. You can feel the car crumple around you, can see the windshield crack and shatter. You don't feel pain. It happens too fast for pain.

And you don't feel heat. It's summer, the sun made the car seats too hot to touch. Now it's cold in the middle of July. Cold, dry, endless July. It's still a bubble world, and you know you're trapped here until you can open the door—but you can't. There's not enough of a door left. Not enough of you.

You are dead.

You come to realize you are dead. It only happened once, the dying; this stupid looped repeat has nothing to do with life. Nothing to do with you, except you're *in it*. You don't know where you are. You know that people talk about heaven—or hell—and this is hellish, except you feel no pain. Only confusion and anger and cold. You don't know how many times their car has hit your car. You can't begin to count.

But until you realized what it *meant*, you had to live it over and over again.

Now you know.

Now you can leave the car. You don't even try to open the door. You just slide to the left of the steering wheel, and you pass through the car door. You're out.

Your car still gets crushed against the wall, but this time, you're not in it.

Your ears are ringing. You can see the street. You can see pedestrians, freezing, turning; you can hear the sound of a woman screaming. That grabs you, makes your blood freeze, but you don't recognize the voice, and you can move again.

The thing is, you can't see very well. You know people are here, but they're blurs. You shout. They can't hear you. You stand in front of them. You jump up and down like a four year old, but nothing changes. They're still blurry. Some of them move. But they move past you, around you, as if you're not there. As if they're not here.

There's no sun here. No heat.

You spend an hour screaming. You can scream forever. No one hears you. You jump up and down, you try to throw things. You go nuts. You haven't gone nuts like this since you were five. There's no reaction. No one sees you. You can barely see them, they're so fuzzy. It's like you died and you suddenly need glasses. Or worse.

You need to get out of here. You need to leave.

You can go home. That's what you should have done. You should have gone home. You didn't even think of home. Why?

Thinking of home. Mom. Dad. Gotrek the hamster. You'll go home.

You don't recognize the street you're on. You don't recognize the intersection. You *know* how to get home. You know this part of the city. But . . . you don't. The streets are too long. The buildings are the wrong shape, the wrong size. You can see them more clearly than the blurred smudges that are people—but they make no sense.

You've had this nightmare before. You leave school, exit by the front doors, and stare out at a totally unfamiliar neighborhood. It's as if the entire building had been teleported to some other borough while you were in history or math. In those nightmares, you end up wandering the streets, lost, until you wake up.

But you can't wake up here. You've never been lost like this.

When it gets to be too much, you sit down. Just sit, in the middle of the road, staring at nothing, wondering where the hell the sun is. Wondering why there's no blood on your clothing, no dirt on your hands. Wondering why you're even here at all. This isn't how death is supposed to work.

You have no sense of time, because time makes no difference. You have no idea how long you've been sitting on your butt in the middle of this street. You are cold, you are silent. You don't scream anymore. You don't move. The world moves around you, leaving you behind. You miss

Emma. You miss Emma, but you're terrified because you don't remember what she *looked like*. You don't remember sunlight.

So when sunlight comes, it's almost too much. You curl in on yourself, because it's too much. But it gets stronger and brighter. It's not going away. You stand, you turn, you face it; it is so bright and so warm and so close you can almost touch it. And you can *hear* it. If you can reach it, you know you will never be cold again.

You won't be lost, either. Maybe this is why you couldn't find home when you tried: you can't live there anymore. You can walk toward the sun. You don't need the road. You can run, and you do.

Scattered throughout your childhood are memories: *Cover your eyes. Don't stare at the sun. Do you want to go blind?* Different voices, different ages, same advice.

So you know this isn't the sun because there's no pain. Your eyes don't water. Your vision doesn't blur. The light doesn't become a spread of painful brilliance; it takes shape and form. And you have no words for the form. It's not round; it's not square; it's not flat. It's not person-shaped, but . . . it's alive. You are certain it's alive. It's alive the way home is alive: it promises warmth. It promises what you need—what you've always needed: quiet space, and company in which you can be entirely yourself.

No defenses. No shields. No prescriptive behavior. No need to define yourself by other people's desires, by other people's approval or disapproval. No need to talk if you've got nothing to say, no need to shut up if you've got too much. People are waiting there, on the other side: people who see you and know you and accept everything about you until your fear of the things they can't accept becomes meaningless.

You can't see that—how could you? You're not even certain what it would look like, if you were still alive. You've seen glimpses of it in Emma. In your parents. In moments of time. You can't put a shape to it. But it's solid, and you understand that you only have to reach it, touch it, and you will be fully, finally, home.

But as you approach, you hear wailing. It is the most distinct sound you've heard since your car collapsed around you.

You can hear it as if it's your voice; it's inside you, inside your mouth and your ears. Your hands freeze with the strength of it because it is loss. It is loss; it is death.

You thought you were dead. No, you *knew* you were dead. But until this moment, you didn't understand what that meant.

The light is where you belong. It's where you want to be—it's the only thing you want. But you can't reach it. No one—you understand this as the screams take shape and form—can.

You can see shadows moving in the light. You know what they're doing: They're trying to touch it. They're trying to reach it. You want to do the same. You don't. You don't because you know you'll be up there screaming with the rest of them if you try and you fail.

And it's true. You would be. You'd scream for years, and you'd feel every passing second as if it were a century. It's what the dead do. This is their birth, their rebirth; this is when they come, at last, to accept their eternity. Like any birth, it's painful and of interest only to parents—but, of course, yours aren't here.

If they knew what awaited the dead, would they have children at all? It's a question that no one has asked. The living who can speak to the dead don't care, after all. The dead are dead, and they serve at the whim of their Queen, when they are at last presented to her.

Rare indeed is the dead boy who does not need to journey to the city to greet her. How many times do you think she has left her palace within that city and walked the paths the living walk to find the newborn dead?

Ah, but you *are* newborn. You don't know. You have no idea of the honor done you.

You know only that there is a light that reaches for you, a light you can touch. In form and shape it is familiar: human, only slightly taller than yourself. But it casts no shadow, and it offers warmth—the only warmth you've found in the land of the dead.

Is she beautiful? To you, yes; you are dead. You see what lies beneath the surface of life, and you see it purely. No age, no experience, no prior vision blurs your sight. You would kneel, if kneeling made sense; you are immobile, instead, staring; you are afraid to blink, because in blinking, you might lose sight of her. Thus do all of the dead who understand their state stand before her: transfixed. Helpless.

Here. Take the Queen's hand, and she will lead you to the only real home you will have for the rest of eternity.

Some people cry in public. They're champion criers. They cry when they see a familiar name in a phone book, or when they're signing yearbooks, or when they're talking about anything more emotional than grocery shopping. It's as though all of life is a big box of tissues.

Nathan's mother has never been one of them. Nathan's never *seen* her cry. Maybe her mother did, when she was a kid; if she did, she never shared. Nathan learned about crying from his mother, but it took him longer.

Maybe that's why he fell for Emma. Emma was a total failure as a crier. She wasn't like his mother in any other way, except gender. Which is also why he liked her.

But she and his mother had this in common. It wasn't that they didn't *want* to cry; it was that they chose not to and made it stick. No tears in public. Nathan never understood why.

"If it's the way you feel, why hold back?"

"If I feel like punching Nick in the face," Emma replied, "I don't see you encouraging me."

"Your fists, his face. Not practical. Get a tire iron." He shrugged. "It wouldn't bother me if you cry."

"It would bother *me*."

"Why?"

She kissed him instead of answering, which was a cheat. But it was a *good* cheat.

He knows the answer now. He knows, and he should have known it then, would have, if he'd known how to think about tears the same way he thinks about circuit boards. He is standing in his house. He is standing in his room. His room hasn't changed. Transistors, wires, solder, tweezers, in neat boxes, like a wall at the back of his desk. His clamps, his light, his computer. It's been three months.

He knows because the date is marked on his calendar, the calendar that hangs from the corkboard to one side of his bedroom window. Someone's been marking the date. He watches as his mother puts a neat, red line through a square box in October. She doesn't need it; her calendars exist in the ether.

But she puts the pen on his desk, draws his curtains shut. Stands behind the closed curtains, her shoulders curving toward the floor, her arms bending at the elbows until she wraps them around her upper body. They're shaking. No, she's shaking. Her head drops. Nathan stands frozen for one immobile moment, and then he reaches out for her back in a kind of terrified wonder.

She cries.

God, she cries. It's a terrifying, horrible sound. No quiet tears; it's like someone is trying to rip the insides out of her, but they've got nowhere to put them. It's paralyzing; it's worse than walking into his parents' bedroom when the bed was heavily occupied. He feels like he's violating her, just standing here in his own room.

And then the guilt and the paralysis break, and he's reaching out for her, he's trying, *trying*, to put his arms around her—from the back, he's not an idiot—but he *can't*. He can't. They don't *go* anywhere. He calls her. He shouts. He shouts louder than he's ever shouted—and she hears nothing, and her knees give, and her forehead is pressed against his goddamn desk, and it is the worst thing he's ever seen.

Worse than an SUV driving toward the side of his car.

He can't *do* anything. He knows, watching her back, that no one can. She's here, in his room; his door is closed. She *isn't* crying in public. There's no public here, because no one lives in his room anymore. And he knows she won't cry like this outside of her own house. Because it would have to practically kill anyone who could see her and hear her; a sound like this could burn itself into your brain, and the only way you could avoid it would be to plug your ears and run screaming.

You couldn't help her. You couldn't do anything to make the pain go away—and you'd *want* to. You'd be immobile, your own helplessness and uselessness made clear. You couldn't escape it unless you avoided her, avoided any hint of her grief, and let what you witnessed fade.

She doesn't cry in public because of what it would do to everyone *else*. It's not because of what other people will think of her—that's what he assumed, once—it's because of what they'll think of *themselves*, afterward. He knows because he *hates* himself, now. He hates himself for dying. He hates the people who killed him—first time, for everything—and he hates that he can't *touch* her, can't *reach* her, because if he could, it would stop. Or change.

This is the first time Nathan's been home since he died. He wants to flee. He almost does. But he waits it out, because in the end, he has to know that it does stop. If he leaves now, he won't believe it; every other memory of home will be buried beneath this one.

It does stop.

It stops. The rawness of grief peters into an echo of itself—but the echo speaks of pain as if pain were an iceberg, a colossal structure beneath surfaces that hide nothing if you know how to look. When it's once again submerged, she stands, slowly and awkwardly, as if she's spent months living on her knees, her forehead propped up against the edge of his desk.

Her father died when Nathan was a child. He remembers it clearly, now. He remembers the phone call; he remembers her eight-hour absence. He remembers arguing with his dad about bedtime because he wanted his mother. His mother did not come home that night. When she returned the next day, she told him his grandfather had died. He wanted to know why, because death made no sense. Death had no impact.

He asked her if his father was going to die.

"No," she told him softly. "Not for a long time. But, Nathan, everyone eventually dies."

She didn't cry. He didn't cry because she didn't. He asked her if she would miss Grandpa, and she said, "Yes, very much."

She carried him—at five years of age—for most of her father's funeral. He thought it strange, because babies were carried and he was a Big Boy. But she still didn't cry. For the whole, long day, she didn't cry.

People came up to talk to her. He recognized some of them; some were strangers—but not to his mother. They told her they were sorry (But why? They hadn't killed him). They told her he'd had a good life. A full life. But some of them told her stories about her father, instead, and they made her smile.

No one tells his mother stories in this room. He knows. No one can tell her that her son had a full life, or a good life. There is nothing to make her smile, here. Seeing her gaunt face in the evening light, he wonders if she's smiled at all in the last three months. He thinks she must have—but he can't make himself believe it.

She straightens her clothing. No one can see it, but she straightens it anyway. Then she turns, walks to the door, opens it, and turns again. Into the darkness that contains her son, she says, "Good night, Nathan."

She closes the door.

Nathan has learned a few things about being dead.

He's learned, for instance, that the dead don't eat. They can't. They don't feel hunger, and physical pain is beyond them. They never get thirsty. Snow, hail, storms, and blistering desert heat don't bother them. He assumes that bullets won't hurt; knives don't.

He's learned that the dead have their own version of sleep. It doesn't involve beds, and it doesn't hold dreams—or nightmares. It's a kind of darkness and stillness in which even memories fade. It's the ultimate silence. The silence of the grave.

It's not boring, this sleep. It's not confining. It's . . . nothing. Just nothing. But sometimes, nothing is good; right now, he's not keen on the alternative.

Because tonight, he's learned that the dead are useless. They can't touch anything. They can't change anything. In any way that counts, they've got no voice. They can speak—but no one can hear them.

Not no one.

I want you to go back to your home, Nathan.

"Why?"

Because there, you will find an opportunity that most of the dead will never have.

He didn't ask what the opportunity was. Even the first question had been a risk. The Queen of the Dead doesn't like to be questioned.

Go home. I will give you no other orders yet. Just go home. Watch your family, watch your friends. Her smile was winter, her eyes sky blue. They were wide, and looked, in the radiance of her face, like windows. Beyond those windows: clouds, lightning, destruction. As if she were the only thing that kept the storm out.

Promise me, when we're old, you'll let me die first.

What kind of a promise is that, Em?

The only one I want. I don't want you to die first. I don't want to be left behind again. Promise?

*   *   *

Emma's house is half lit. Her mother's office lights are on on the second floor, but her mother's probably working—as she usually does—in the dining room. Emma's bedroom is dark. Nathan stands between two streetlights, looking up. He wants to see Emma. He wants more than that, but he'll settle for what death has left him.

The moon is high. The night sky is a different shade of gray. Nathan slides his hands into his pockets and waits. He's got nothing but time, and he hates it. But he hates it less when the front door of the Hall house opens and Emma steps out, surrounded by Petal, the rottweiler who refuses to stand still. Nathan can't take his eyes off her; for one long moment, she is the only thing he sees.

He watches her lead Petal toward the sidewalk in silence.

Nathan joins her, stopping when she stops and moving when she moves. He can pretend, for a few minutes, that he's still alive, that this is a normal night, a normal walk. He doesn't have to fill the silence. Silence has never bothered Emma.

There's a difference between being alone and feeling lonely. Emma is alone. Nathan? Doesn't want to think about it.

The breeze lifts Emma's hair. Petal's name leaves her lips. She keeps walking. Nathan watches her go. He wants to talk to her. He doesn't try.

The problem with death—this version of death—is that it feels pretty much like life, at least to the dead people. He's not dragging bits and pieces of corpse around, because he's pretty sure that's what he'd be doing if the manner of death defined him. He's not spouting blood. He's not a poltergeist.

He's Nathan. She's Emma. They haven't seen each other for three months, and the last thing Nathan did was break a vow. He left her. He left her behind.

It was a stupid promise. He knew it was stupid before he made it. But she was there, lying in his arms, curled against his chest, her hair tangled, her eyes wide. She wasn't joking. She wouldn't *let* him make a joke of it.

He promised. He promised because to him it was just a different way of saying *I love you*.

And he does. He meant every word of it. She knows—she *must* know—that dying wasn't his choice. It wasn't his fault. She must know that he'd be out here by her side, walking her half-deaf dog, if it had been up to him.

He shakes himself, hurries to catch up with her, and stops when he finally realizes where she's going. The cemetery.

Emma. Oh, Em.

Nathan has no desire to see his grave. He'd had no idea, until he followed Emma from her house, where he'd been buried. But he knows now, and he almost leaves. He doesn't want to see Emma cry. He doesn't want to see her go to pieces the way his mother did. He can't comfort her. He's got nothing to offer her at all.

But when she slips behind the fence, he walks through it. He keeps her in sight. The night sky is clear. If there's a breeze, he can't feel it; he can feel the cold, but it's always cold now. He doesn't read the head stones. He doesn't read the markers.

To his surprise, Emma does. She reads them. She lingers. But she doesn't stop; she hasn't reached the gravestone with his name on it. Petal's tongue is hanging out of his mouth as he trots back and forth between the markers. He's happy. Emma is silent. She's not in a hurry.

Emma finds a standing wreath of white flowers before one marker. She kneels in front of it, picks up a petal, blows it off her fingers. Tucking her legs to the right, she sits; Petal flops down to her left and drops his head in her lap. She scratches behind his ears.

She doesn't speak. She doesn't weep.

Nathan listens to the ever-present sounds of passing cars. Mount Pleasant isn't a small cemetery, but it's in the middle of a city. He looks up, as Emma does, to see the stars. To see the moon in the night sky. To know that they're seeing the same thing.

He's never minded waiting for Emma. He could wait for her forever. He doesn't interrupt her. He doesn't talk. He knows she'll come to him in her own time.

She picks up Petal's leash as she unfolds, straightening her hair and brushing petals off her legs. Her head is bent as she walks back the way she came; Nathan knows, because he's standing there.

But she lifts her chin, and as she does, she slows. He can see her eyes so clearly, even though it's dark. He can see their shape, the way they round; he can see the edge of her lashes. Her mouth opens slightly as she approaches. Her eyes are brown. They've always been brown. But they're also luminescent. It's not an exaggeration: They glow; they're alight. He's seen light like that twice since his death. Only twice.

And he knows, then, that Emma can see him. He knows how to hide from the sight of anyone but the Queen of the Dead; if she's looking for someone among the dead, she'll find them. But he can make himself so still, so quiet, that no one else who can see the dead will see him.

It never occurred to him to worry that Emma might see him. It doesn't occur to him now. If he's afraid at all, it's of the sharp edge of ridiculous hope. He has never loved anyone the way he loves Emma. When she lifts a hand, palm up, it's the most natural thing in the world to reach out to take it.

It's the most natural thing in the world, but he's dead, and she's not. She can *see* him. He can see her. Touching doesn't happen, for the dead; it's too much to hope for.

He feels the shock of her palm beneath his. His hand doesn't pass through hers. Before he can withdraw, she closes her fingers around his, tightens them. And, god, she is so *warm*.

"Hello, Nathan," she whispers.

"Hello, Em."

There's so much he wants to say to her. So much he wants to explain. There's so much groveling to do, for one. Maybe he'll start with that.

But the words stick on the right side of his mouth, and as he stares into her eyes, his gaze drifting to her parted lips, they desert him.

He hugs her, instead. He reaches out, pulls her into his arms, tucks her head beneath his chin. He's dead. He's dead, but he can *feel* her. She smells of shampoo and soap.

He wants to apologize. He doesn't. He holds her instead, amazed at the warmth of her. But he always was. They stand together in the darkness until Emma begins to shudder. He thinks she's crying, but he pulls back to catch her chin, to pull her face up.

She's not crying. Oh, she *is*, but she's not weeping. She's shivering. She's shivering as if it's winter and she's caught outside without a coat.

He lets go of her. He feels the loss of her touch as a profound physical pain. He feels cold again, but this time, the cold is harsh. Isolating. And he understands, as her eyes widen, as her brows gather in the way they do when something confuses her, that the warmth he feels—he's stealing it.

Emma . . . Emma is like the Queen of the Dead. Like her, and nothing at all alike.

I want you there, Nathan. You have an opportunity that very, very few of the dead will ever have.

Nathan is afraid. Three months ago, Emma was his quiet space—one of the few in which he could be entirely himself. She knew him. He knew her. He thought he knew her. But the Emma Hall he fell in love with couldn't touch the dead.

Emma is a Necromancer.

Petal whines, and Emma glances at the wet nose he's shoved into her palm. She feeds him a Milk-Bone, but she tries not to take her eyes off Nathan, as if she's afraid he'll just disappear. Nathan knows the look.

Emma is a Necromancer with a whiny, half-deaf dog. She goes to school. She lives alone with her mother. She visits her dead boyfriend's grave. She lives *here*, among the living. And her eyes are still round, and she's still shivering. And grieving.

"You promised," she whispers. She's not smiling. There's no humor in her voice.

"This is the best I can do." He almost hugs her again, but balls his hands into fists instead.

Her face is wet with tears, shining with them. He always hated making her cry. Being dead hasn't changed that. He can't stand so close to her without touching her. He wants to kiss her. He wants to cup her face in his hands.

He heads toward his grave instead. The wreath of standing flowers is new. The petals that adorn Emma's legs—the few she hasn't managed to brush off—are scattered across the ground in ones and twos, but the flowers themselves haven't wilted or dried. He recognizes his mother's hand in this. His mother. He closes his eyes.

When he opens them, Emma is standing by his side. She's still shivering.

"Does my mother come here often?"

"Often enough. I don't see her. I think she must come after work."

"You?"

"It's quiet, here. Good quiet."

Which isn't an answer. He doesn't press. It's never been hard to talk to Emma before. It's hard now. What can you say to your girlfriend when you're dead? Apologies won't cut it, but beyond apologies, there's not a lot he can offer.

She holds out a hand. Nathan keeps both of his in his pockets. When she says his name, he shakes his head. "I'm making you cold. I'll walk you home."

"I'm not sure I want to be home right now."

Home, for Nathan, is where Emma is. God, he wants to touch her. He finds it hard to look at her; she's always been beautiful, to him. Now, she's luminescent.

CHAPTER
ONE

"GET YOUR FEET off my dashboard."

Chase, slumped in the passenger seat, grinned. "What? My boots are clean." The skin around his left eye had passed from angry purple to a sallow yellow; it clashed with his hair. In Eric's opinion, everything did. "And I'm wearing a seat belt."

"Seat belts," Eric said, sliding behind the wheel and adjusting its height, "are supposed to be worn across the hips, not the ribs. What did the old man say?"

"Long version or short version?"

"Shorter the better."

"Tell me about it." Chase's grin sharpened. "But I had to sit through the long version. No reason why you should get off easy."

"I'm driving. Don't make me fall asleep at the wheel."

"Couldn't make your driving any worse."

Eric pushed a CD into the player.

"You bastard." Chase was flexible enough to remove his feet from the dash and hit eject before more than two bars had played. He wasn't fond of perky singers. Gender didn't matter. Eric ignored them, but Chase couldn't. They were fingernails-against-blackboard painful to him. "You know I'd rather you stabbed me. In the ear, even."

"I'm driving or I'd seriously consider it. What did the old man want?"

"We've got a problem."

Eric reached for the CD again. Chase grabbed it and threw it out the window, barely pausing to open the window first.

"We've got three Necromancers, just off the plane. Old man thinks there's a fourth." Chase appeared to consider throwing out the rest of Eric's collection as well.

"Thinks?"

"Yeah. He can't pin him down."

Eric grimaced. "Why does he think there's a fourth?"

"Margaret insists."

Shit. "She recognized him."

"I wasn't the one questioning her. The old man was in a foul mood. You want to tell him he's wrong?" Chase fished in his pocket and pulled out a phone. Eric glanced at it.

"Driving, remember? When did they get in?"

"Yesterday. We had two addresses; neither was good."

"They take a cab?"

"Yeah. They were careful," he added.

Eric swore.

"He also reminds you we've got two midterms tomorrow."

"Midterms? Are you kidding me?"

Chase dangled the phone under Eric's nose again.

"This is getting unreal."

"Tell me about it. I've got the same midterms, and apparently my marks are crap compared to yours." Chase slid his feet back up on the dashboard. "We've got two addresses. Margaret supplied them. We're supposed to head over to the first one tonight." He frowned as he glanced out the window. "Is that Allison?"

Eric glanced at the side mirror. Allison Simner, in a puffy down coat, head bent into the wind, walked through the crisp November air beside another classmate. "And Michael."

"Stop the car and let me out."

"Chase—"

"What? She took notes."

Allison walked Michael home after school, as she had done for most of their mutual school life. It wasn't that he needed the company or the implied protection of another person, although he might once have. Now it was just part of their daily routine, and it was almost peaceful.

But Emma usually joined them. For the past two days, she hadn't. She'd explained her absences to Michael, and Michael—given his natural difficulty recognizing subtle social cues, such as white lies—accepted her yearbook committee excuses at face value. Allison tried. She wasn't her mother; worry was not her middle name, maiden name, or, on bad days, her entire name.

But her mother's best friend hadn't developed the ability to see the dead. She hadn't been targeted by Necromancers. She hadn't almost died in a fire that no one else could see, let alone feel, in an attempt to save a child who was *already* dead.

Allison's best friend, Emma, had. And it wasn't just that Emma could see the dead; if Emma touched ghosts, everyone else could see them, too. They'd learned that the hard way, at the hospital: Emma had grabbed onto her father's ghost because she didn't want him to leave.

And who could blame her? She hadn't seen her dad for the eight years he'd been dead.

But Allison had seen him, that night in the hospital. Michael had seen him. Emma's mother had seen him. And Eric. Eric had seen him as well. It had been disturbing, but—being able to see your dad, when he wasn't dangerous and he didn't look much different from the last time you'd seen him—wasn't inherently scary.

All the stuff that had happened after was.

Well, not Andrew Copis, the child who had died in the fire. And not his grieving mother, because if Emma wanted or needed to see her dad, Maria Copis was a hundred times worse: She *needed* to see her son. Emma was willing to walk through fire—literal fire—to help that happen, and Allison got that. She understood why.

What she didn't understand were the parts that happened directly afterward: the Necromancers. Two men and one woman, armed, had stopped their car outside of the house in which the child had died, gotten out of it, and pulled guns. Allison had been carrying Maria Copis' youngest child, a son. They had pointed the gun at the *baby*, and they had dragged Allison to Andrew Copis' burned-out house—in order to threaten Emma.

To threaten Emma, and to—to kill Eric and Chase.

Eric and Chase had survived. The Necromancers hadn't. But it had been so close. And the death of the Necromancer in charge, Merrick Longland, if he hadn't lied about his name, had been anything but fast. Chase had been covered in blood before he'd stopped stabbing and slashing at him.

Allison didn't watch horror movies. She found the violence in most of them too intense. She knew people who loved them, and she'd never understood why. Now she felt as if she were living on the edge of one. Predictably, she hated it.

She hated it because Michael was trapped on the same edge, and Emma was at the center of it. Allison could step away. She could turn her back. She could hide under the figurative bed with her hands over her ears. But if she did that, she was walking away from Emma. And Emma was no better prepared to be the star of a horror movie than either of her friends. Allison's fear was intense, and it made her feel so guilty.

Michael didn't know how to walk away. Michael didn't talk about the Necromancers—but Emma had asked him not to. Allison didn't talk about them because to talk about them, she had to think about them.

Then again, when something wasn't actively distracting her, it was hard not to think about them.

There had been no new Necromancers, but Chase had made it clear that it was only a matter of time—and at that, not a lot of it.

Allison usually walked Michael to his door, where she would wait to say hello to his mother. As a much younger child, she would then give his mother a report of the school day; as a teenager she'd continued more or less out of habit. She filled Mrs. Howe in on the positive or outstanding things, upcoming field trips, or perturbations in Michael's schedule.

Allison had avoided that at-the-door conversation for the past couple of weeks.

Michael's mother, being a mother, was worried about her son, because she knew there was something wrong. Michael didn't lie, so he'd told her he couldn't talk about it. His mother was not an idiot; she was pretty certain that Emma and Allison had some idea what was going on.

Allison wasn't Michael; she could—and on rare occasions did—lie. But she'd never been great at it, and it left her feeling horrible about herself for weeks afterward. She did the next best thing—she avoided the questions.

It was only as she was scurrying away from Michael's driveway, like a criminal, that Chase caught up with her.

Chase was almost a head taller than Allison.

Allison had never been tall. Emma was taller and more slender, with straight hair that fell most of the way down her back. On bad days, Allison envied her and wondered what Emma saw in her. Emma had a lot of friends.

Stephen Sawoski, in eighth grade, had answered the question. "Pretty girls don't want to have pretty friends—they hang around the plain girls 'cause it makes them look better." He'd sneered as he said it. Allison could still see his expression if she tried. She didn't really avoid it, either, because of what happened next: Emma had taken her milk, in its wet, box container, opened it, and then poured half of it into Stephen's lap.

The expression on his face then was *also* one Allison never forgot.

"If I wanted to hang around ugly people just to look better," Emma had said to Stephen, while Allison gaped like a fish out of water, "I'd spend more time with you. Come on, Allison, Michael's waiting."

Allison was plain. It was true. Emma offered, every so often, to help her change that if she wanted to do the work. But she didn't. No amount of work would make her look like Emma. Stephen was obnoxious, but he wasn't wrong—about the being plain. He was wrong about the friendship. She held on to that.

She glanced up at Chase.

He smiled. "You took notes," he said.

"I did. I can email them, if you want them. Biology?"

"And English. You're heading home?"

She nodded. "I have a pretty boring life."

"Not recently."

"I *like* having a pretty boring life." She started to walk. Chase shortened his stride and fell in beside her, hands in his jacket's pockets. Fire had singed his shock of red hair, and he'd been forced to cut it—but even short, it was the first thing anyone noticed.

"You really do," he replied. "Look—things are going to get crazy."

She didn't miss a step. "When?"

"Does it matter? You're not cut out for this shit. You, Michael, the rest of your friends—you've never lived in a war zone."

She had a pretty good idea of where this conversation was going: straight downhill. Allison didn't like confrontation. She didn't like to argue. Usually, there wasn't a lot to argue about. "None of us are cut out for this."

"Eric and I are."

Allison nodded agreement and stared at the sidewalk. She was three blocks away from home.

"Emma's part of this."

She shoved her hands into her pockets, which weren't really built for it, and lowered her chin. Chase had saved her life. She had to remember that Chase had saved her life. He'd almost died doing it. What had she done? Nothing. Nothing useful. "Emma didn't choose to be part of it."

"Choice doesn't matter. She has none."

Allison started to walk more quickly, not that there was any chance of leaving Chase behind if he was determined. He was.

"But you do. You've got the choice that I didn't have."

She stopped walking, her hands sliding out of her pockets to her hips. "And I am *making* a choice."

It was clear, from his expression, that he thought it was the wrong choice. "You think you can just duck your collective heads and the bullets will miss."

"No, I don't. But I know Emma."

"Really? I haven't noticed she's spending a lot of time with you recently."

That stung. "I'm her friend, not her cage."

"You don't understand how Necromancers work. You don't understand what they *become*."

"I understand Emma. Emma is *not* going to become a monster just because you're afraid of her!" Straight downhill. Like an avalanche.

"Why don't you ask her what she's been doing the past couple of days?"

"Because I trust her. If she wants to tell me, she'll tell me."

"And will she tell Michael?"

She could see him switching lanes. She let him do it, too; she was angry.

"If you're capable of making the decision to put your life on the line, is he? Are you willing to let him make the same choice?"

"Michael. Is. Not. A. Child."

"That's why he needs an entire clique of babysitters?"

"If Michael hadn't been at Amy's party, Emma would already be lost. In case you've forgotten, Merrick Longland had us *all* ensnared. None of your party tricks saved either you or Eric!"

". . . Party tricks?"

"Training. Whatever. Michael wasn't affected by Longland—but *you* were. And Michael knows it. We all know it. I get that you don't understand how we work—but if you try to break it, I'll—"

He folded his arms across his chest and stared pointedly down at her. "Yes? We're finally getting to the good part. You'll what? Scream at me? Cry?"

She wanted to punch him. Sadly, she'd never punched anyone in her life; if she'd thought she had any chance of landing one, she might have tried.

Chase saved your life. He almost died saving your life. "Probably both."

He looked down at the top of her head, and then he laughed. It was almost rueful. "You understand that I don't want to see you hurt, right?"

She did. But she also understood that there were all kinds of hurt in life, and he didn't count the one that she was most afraid of: losing her best friend. "I have to go. My mom's staring out the window."

"And she's not going to be happy that her daughter's shouting at a stranger?"

"No." She took three deep breaths, because deep breaths always helped. Chase made her so angry. She'd never met anyone who could make her so angry. Stephen Sawoski had made her feel ugly, invisible, unwanted—but never angry. Not like this. He'd made Emma angry though.

And maybe that made sense. Allison wasn't much good at sticking up for herself. She never had been, not when it counted. But she could stick up for her friends. She trusted her instincts where they were concerned.

"Your mom just disappeared," he told her.

Allison exhaled. "You might as well come to the house," she told him. "Because if you don't, she's going to come out."

"I really don't need to meet your mother."

"You should have thought of that before you followed me home."

Chase could be friendly. He could be charming. Allison had seen both. He had a genuine smile, a sense of humor, and a way of turning things on their side that mostly suggested a younger brother. Someone else's younger brother. Allison, however, was full up on younger brothers, given Tobias, the one she had. She searched the windows of the upper floor with sudden anxiety. If he embarrassed her in front of Chase, she'd have to strangle him. No Toby was visible from the street.

Allison headed toward her front door. Chase lagged behind, losing about three inches of height at the top of the driveway. She looked back at him. "Don't even think of running."

"Is it that obvious?"

"You smile when you're facing armed Necromancers. You charge *into* green fire. Compared to that, meeting my mother is terrifying?"

"I don't meet a lot of mothers."

"No, you don't, do you? Mine doesn't bite. Mostly. I'd suggest you drop any discussion of Emma, killing Emma, or abandoning her, though. I come by my temper honestly." She put her hand on the doorknob and added, "She also approves of Michael."

"Everyone does."

"Not really. But Michael's a kind of litmus test. People who see Michael as a person are generally people you can trust. People who dismiss him or treat him like he's a two year old, not so much."

"I don't follow."

"People who treat him as if he's a child see what they want to see; they don't see what's there."

"Me being one of those people."

"Not sure yet. You might have been trying to be manipulative."

"And that's not worse?"

"It's bad—but it's not worse. Not really. I know how to handle guilt."

Chase laughed as she opened the door. Her mother was buttoning up her coat. "Mom, I'd like you to meet Chase Loern. Chase, this is my mother."

Her mother held out a hand; Chase shook it. "I'm one of the new kids," he told her. "Allison finds me when I get lost between classes. I'd have built an impressive late-slip collection without her."

"He's lying," her daughter added cheerfully.

"Lying? Me?" The slow smile that spread across his face acknowledged a hit with a wry acceptance and something that felt like approval.

Allison's mother took her coat off as Allison removed her scarf. "Chase is behind on assignments," she said. "And he hasn't figured out how to use the electronic blackboard—yet." The last word was said in a dire tone. She took off her coat as well, reaching for a hanger to hand to Chase. He stared at it.

"You're not wearing that jacket in here—my mother will turn the heat up twenty degrees if she thinks you're cold, and the rest of us will melt."

He slid out of his jacket. Allison noticed that his eyes were sharper; he surveyed the hall—and the stairs and doors that led from it—as if his eyes were video equipment and he was doing a fancy perimeter sweep. She should have found it funny. Or annoying. She didn't.

She wondered, instead, what Chase's life was actually like. She didn't ask; her mother had headed directly for the kitchen, and Allison was about to drag Chase up to her room, which was the one room in the house in which her younger brother was unlikely to cause *too* much embarrassment.

Chase followed, looking at the staircase the same way he looked at the rest of the house: as if it were alien, and hostile at that. She didn't know a lot about Chase. Except that he made her angry and that he'd saved her life.

She headed straight for her desk when she reached her room and counted her pens. "I don't really need a brother, do I?"

Chase laughed. "What did he do?"

"He seems to think that he's working in an office, and stealing office supplies is a perk. This," she added, pointing to the penholder, "would be the office supply depot."

"He's younger?"

"Yes, or he'd already be dead."

"None of you seem to use pens much."

"It's the principle."

He laughed again. He had an easy, friendly laugh. Hearing it, it was hard to imagine that he'd killed people. But she didn't have to imagine it; she'd seen it. She took her tablet out of her backpack and plunked it on the desk, plugging it in before she opened it. "Biology and English. You'll actually get these? I notice you didn't bring your computer with you."

"I'll get them. I don't have much study time in the queue tonight." And there it was again: the edge, the harshness.

Wouldn't you be harsh? If your entire life was devoted to killing mass murderers, wouldn't you? But . . . he'd come to kill Emma, and Emma was not a mass murderer. And maybe he was staying to find proof that she would never become one. That was the optimistic way of looking at it. The pragmatic version was different: He was staying until she did, at which point he'd kill her.

Which meant he'd be here a long time.

She turned around; Chase was standing in the middle of the room, staring at the walls. The walls in Allison's room were not bare. She had posters, pictures, and one antique map, which had been a gift from her much-loved grandfather, covering everything that wasn't blocked by furniture. Even her closet door was covered; the one mirror in the room was on the inside of the door.

"This is a scary room," Chase finally said, staring pointedly at the *Hunger Games* poster to one side of the curtained window.

"Scary how?"

"If that bookshelf falls over, it'll kill you in your sleep. Who thought it was a good idea to bolt it into the wall *above* your head?"

She raised a hand.

"Have you read all of these?"

"Yes. Multiple times. I don't keep everything, just the ones I know I'll reread. My brother knows better than to touch my books," she added, as he reached for the shelf.

He grinned. "I'm not your brother."

"No. You're a guest, so you get to keep your hand." She smiled as she said it, but he wasn't looking at her; he was looking at *Beauty*.

"So . . . you come home, you do homework, and you read a lot."

"Mostly." Her phone rang. She fished it—quickly—out of her bag because she recognized the ringtone. It was Emma. Or someone who had stolen Emma's phone.

"Hey, Ally—are you doing anything after dinner?"

"Studying a bit."

"Want to come walk a deaf dog with me?"

"Not a random deaf dog, no—but I'll come for Petal."

Emma laughed. "He's the only one I have. Is something wrong?"

"No. Nothing. Want to come pick me up or should I meet you at your place?"

"I'll head over there. Mom's not home, so I'll make something to eat here." She paused. "I have something to tell you. It's not a bad thing," she added quickly, because she knew Allison came from a long line of champion worriers. Petal started to bark in the background. When Petal set up barking, it never stayed in the background.

"I'll talk to you later," Allison said.

Chase was apparently still perusing her bookshelves, but Allison wasn't fooled. "That was Emma?"

She almost didn't answer. *Chase saved your life, but he also probably saved Emma's.* "Yes. She wants to talk—later. You've met her dog."

Chase nodded, putting the book back on the shelf and withdrawing.

"We're going to walk him. Look, can you sit down? I don't care where. It's hard to talk when you're standing there looking down at me."

He sat on the edge of the bed—probably because it was the farthest away.

She turned to her computer and found the Biology and English notes he'd asked for. She wasn't sure they'd do him much good; Chase didn't really understand how to study. But she sent them to him anyway before she turned.

He was sitting absolutely still, watching her, his elbows on his knees, his hands loosely clasped between them. "I don't hate Emma," he said.

"No?"

"Let's pretend that I believe you. That Emma—the Emma you know—is never going to become another Merrick Longland. She's never going to learn how to use the power she has. It's never going to define her."

This was not a surrender, and Allison knew it; the tone of his voice was too measured for that. But she nodded, waiting.

"They're not going to leave her alone." He exhaled, running his hands through his hair. "They know—roughly—where she is. They'll know exactly where she is, soon."

This, Allison believed. "How do we stop them?"

He stared at her, his eyes rounding, as if he couldn't believe the stupidity. "Eric's spent his entire adult life trying to do just that. So has the old man."

"Yes, but you're hunting proto-Necromancers, if I understand anything. You're stopping their numbers from growing. How do we stop them, period?"

"Kill their Queen," he replied. He might as well have said, *kill their god*, given his tone.

She stared at him.

"It's complicated. I'd say it's impossible."

"If we kill their Queen, it stops?"

"If we kill their Queen, the dead are free," he replied. "Wherever it is the dead go, they'll go."

"Andrew Copis—"

"Yes, there'll always be some who get stuck or trapped. But they won't stay that way forever, and they won't be able to hurt anyone who isn't a Necromancer by birth. But it's not going to happen."

She swallowed.

"I don't think you have it in you to kill. Not yet. Probably not ever. It's not a problem the Necromancers have."

"I noticed."

"Good." He lifted his chin, exposing his Adam's apple. "Emma might not have it in her, either. But they won't stop. So let's go back to that: Emma is in danger here."

"And because she's in danger, I'm in danger."

He tensed; he heard the edge creep into her voice. She tried to stop her hands from balling into fists, since she wasn't going to use them anyway.

"If you can't step away, yes. I know you don't want to do it. If you were the type of person who could, I probably wouldn't be here. I mean, here, in this room, in this house. I wouldn't be having this moronic conversation. I wouldn't be—" he fell silent, and his expression was so raw, Allison had to look away.

CHASE WITH DOWNCAST EYES was probably for the best; the door—which was ajar—swung open, and her mother walked into the room carrying a tray. "I didn't ask what Chase drinks," she said apologetically.

Chase shook his head. "I don't drink when I'm working."

Her mother laughed, because Chase was grinning. "And I don't serve alcohol to minors." She set the tray on the desk beside Allison's computer, which was conveniently open at a screen full of biology notes.

"I'm going to walk Petal with Em after dinner," Allison said.

"Make sure you wear a heavier coat. It's not getting any warmer out there."

Allison reddened but nodded, and her mother left. "It's hot chocolate," she told Chase. "And bagels; there's jam. And apples."

"I can see that." He took his phone out of his pocket. Allison hadn't heard it ring. He glanced at the screen and grimaced dramatically.

Allison laughed.

"I'm disappointed," he said, with mock gravity. "You didn't strike me as someone who mocks the pain of others."

"You laughed."

"I did not. And if I did, it's gallows humor." He took the mug she handed him and held it cupped in the palms of his hands—something Allison couldn't do, because the mugs were too hot. He also took the snacks and ate them. He was not a slow eater.

"You didn't eat lunch?"

"I did. All of mine and half of Eric's." He looked around the room again, his expression shifting into neutral. "If it gets bad, we're going to have to run." Before she could speak, he said, "Yes, 'we' includes Emma."

Allison was silent. She didn't want to be left behind. But the future as Chase painted it was grim. If they had to leave the city on short notice—and short could mean none—where were they going to go? What were they going to do?

"I want to go with you, if you go."

"I know. I don't want to take you. If it were up to me, we'd already be gone."

"Where?"

Chase shrugged. "Wherever the old man sends us. He has the wallet. He doesn't normally hang around for this long—and he doesn't trust Emma, either."

"Did the old man train you?"

"Yeah. He and Eric."

"Could he train us?"

To her surprise, Chase didn't sneer; he didn't dismiss the idea out of hand. But he did empty his mug. He was tidy; he placed it back on the tray, along with the empty plate. Allison suspected he would have taken the tray back down to the kitchen if she'd finished as quickly.

She couldn't. She'd never been good at eating when upset.

Chase didn't have that problem—but he wouldn't, would he? All of his life, seen from Allison's vantage, was nothing *but* being upset. Any uneasiness Allison felt was probably trivial in comparison. And any pain. "Chase?"

"Yeah?"

"Promise you won't leave me behind?"

"I can't. I can promise I won't kill your best friend unless she deserves it. I can promise to be polite to your mother. I can promise to ask the old man about training you on really short notice. I don't know *why* I'd promise any of this—but I will. I can't promise to drag you out of your home and away from your family just so you can be a fugitive until the day you die." He ran his hands through his hair again and stood. "Don't ask.

"In return, I won't ask you to promise me that you'll keep your distance from Emma. I won't ask you to promise that you'll warn me when—if—things with Emma start to go downhill."

"Promise you'll stop nagging me?"

He sucked in air. "That's a borderline case. I can only promise to try." He exhaled again. "If Emma cared about you at all—"

Allison's expression tightened. "If she cared about me at all, she'd stay as far away from me as possible, is that it? She'd leave me because that was safest for me?"

"Yes."

"And if that wasn't what I wanted?"

"If you knew what we face pretty much continuously, you *would* want it."

The conversation was, once again, going straight downhill. "Chase, what's the worst thing that's ever happened to you?"

He stared at her for a long moment and then looked down at his phone. "I've got to run. Hopefully I won't see you tonight." He headed toward the door, then turned back, his brow an oddly broken line across the bridge of his nose.

"The worst thing that's ever happened to me? Not dying."

Not dying.

Allison saw Chase to the door and even saw him out; after he left the house, she watched him from the window, as if she were her mother.

His hands were in his pockets, his shoulders hunched slightly against the brisk wind.

She brought the snack tray down to the kitchen, set the table, and ate dinner with her family while Toby grilled her about the redhead she'd brought home.

"Is he your boyfriend?" he asked, in the highly amused, singsong tone that annoyed older sisters the world over.

"No."

"Mo-om, is he Ally's boyfriend?"

"Eat your dinner, dear."

"Allison's got a boyfriend! Allison's got a boyfriend!"

"Tobias," her father said, coming—in one word—to her rescue. He did give Allison the careful once over, but asked none of the questions he was probably thinking.

"Allison is about to be minus a brother," Allison told the brother in question, through gritted teeth. This had the predictable effect—none. But aside from Michael, which boys had she ever brought home? Nathan, but he'd come with Emma.

She finished dinner in slightly embarrassed silence and retreated to her room. She even picked up a book, but her mind bounced off the words instead of sinking beneath them.

Not dying.

Emma had said that, once, two weeks after Nathan's death. She hadn't used the same words, but it didn't matter. What Chase saw when he chose his words was what Emma saw when she looked into a future that, now and forever, had no Nathan in it.

There had been nothing she could do for Emma, and she'd hated it—fluttering helplessly to one side, uncertain whether or not any comfort she tried to offer would be intrusive or make things worse. She understood Emma's loss, she understood Emma's grief—but she'd never known how much room to give. When did giving someone space become abandoning them or ignoring them?

What saved her was understanding that it was Nathan, not Emma, who had died. Allison knew she couldn't fill the empty, collapsing space that Nathan had left in Emma's psyche—but Allison wasn't Nathan. She didn't *have* to fill it. She just had to make sure that the space she did occupy in the same psyche was a safe one. It was best-friend territory, not love-of-life territory, but it was important.

Allison had watched Emma withdraw. It wasn't completely obvious to begin with; Emma went through all the motions. She took care of her appearance, she did all her schoolwork, she spent time at school with her friends, she watched as their relationships began or fell apart. But none of it mattered anymore.

Michael mattered. Allison mattered. Petal mattered.

Why? Because the three of them needed Emma, and she couldn't just turn and walk away from them.

Nathan was a shadow that could fall, unexpectedly, over any conversation. A line of a dialogue. The punch line to a joke. A piece of familiar clothing on an entirely unfamiliar body. Snatches of music. Even food. Emma would flinch. She always withdrew when it happened, but she didn't always leave.

Both of Allison's parents were still alive. So was her brother. The Simner family didn't have pets, except goldfish, and while burying goldfish had seemed enormously heartbreaking in kindergarten, she knew it didn't and couldn't compare. The only death she'd experienced had been her grandfather's, and she had been younger. Death hadn't seemed real. Her grandfather hadn't lived with them. She had come to understand that death meant permanent absence—but it hadn't shattered her.

She could sometimes hear the echoes of his voice, and pipe smoke pulled his image from her memories, because she'd liked his pipe. Her mother, not so much.

Emma had lost her father and her boyfriend. She'd had eight years to recover from the loss of her father. She'd had less than four months to recover from Nathan. And Allison didn't lie to herself: Those months were *not* a recovery. They were a tightrope act, an effort to find and maintain emotional balance when you'd just lost half of yourself.

Now, Emma could see the dead.

She could see the father she'd missed and longed for for half her life. And she knew that if she waited long enough, she could see Nathan as well. There was no balance in that. She could see Nathan. The fact that he was dead and she wasn't wouldn't matter. Not yet.

Maybe not ever. Emma's dad had told her that it took two years for the dead to find their way back to their old homes and old lives. Allison knew Emma. Emma would wait.

The wind was loud beyond the windows, but Emma would be here soon; Allison headed downstairs to get ready.

She was worried. She hadn't told Chase she was worried, because he wouldn't understand, and it would only make his suspicions more unreasonable.

Petal came to the door, dragging Emma behind him; he'd never been clear on the concept of leashes. When he approached a door from the outside, he wagged his stump and bounced up and down, but he didn't bark. Allison wasn't Michael; she didn't have a ready supply of doggie snacks in the house. Petal liked her anyway.

Emma, dressed for the cold, looked nervous. Nervous but happy.

It was a kind of happy Allison recognized, although she hadn't seen it for four months. She stepped outside, closed the door at her back, and smiled as they headed down the driveway.

I haven't noticed she's spending a lot of time with you.

Allison had noticed. Seeing Emma's expression, seeing the way her gaze slid to her right—Allison was on her left and Petal, as always, was in the lead—she knew why. She knew exactly why. It wasn't the first time she had come second to Nathan.

But she also knew it hadn't been two years.

Chase was already suspicious. The old man—Ernest, if she remembered correctly—was suspicious. If Nathan was here only four months after his death, what did that say about Emma?

She bit her lip. It said nothing bad about Emma. Necromancers used some essential part of the dead—Allison hesitated to say "soul"—for power. There was no way Emma would do that to Nathan. Even if she knew how, and she didn't, Nathan would never become that source.

But he was here. He was here, by her side, and he shouldn't be.

Well, where should he be? she thought, in some disgust. Emma was happy. It was the troubled happy of early love—anxiety mixed with euphoria. Allison braced herself for Emma's news, and was surprised when Nathan's name wasn't the first thing out of her mouth.

"I don't understand my mother."

"My mother gave me a lecture about wearing warm clothing in November. In front of a guest."

Emma laughed. "It's different when someone else's mother does it."

It always was. Mercy Hall could worry at Emma like a pit bull, and Allison never found it embarrassing. Mercy Hall could worry about Allison, and she still didn't take it personally.

Petal took offense at a raccoon, which diverted Emma's attention. But she had something to say, and she came back to it, slightly sideways. "Have you talked to your parents?"

Allison was certain her eyes looked liked they were about to fall out of her face.

Emma laughed. "I'll take that as a no."

"My mother would never let me out of the house again. Ever. Why? Have you?"

The reply took longer. "I tried to talk to my mother. About my dad." She glanced at Allison. "She saw him, Ally. We all saw him, the first time."

"What did she say?"

"The first time? That she had an early morning meeting."

Mercy Hall was so not a morning person.

"The second time, that she had work to do. It was after dinner. The third time she came right out and said she didn't want to talk about it because she had nothing to say."

"She didn't ask you about . . ."

"Being able to see the dead? No. She asked me nothing. And I don't understand. I don't understand why."

Conversations with Chase went straight downhill. Sometimes they started at a very steep incline. Conversations with Emma were different. They went off the map. But not all terrain off-map was safe. It's not that Allison and Emma had never had a fight; they'd had a few. But fighting wasn't what they did. Allison could see the direction this conversation might take. She wanted to avoid it.

"Why doesn't she want to know?" Emma almost demanded.

"Is she pretending she never saw him?"

Emma frowned. "More or less. She won't out and out deny it. She just won't talk. It's like—like she doesn't care. Like she doesn't *want* to see him." She shoved her hand—the one that wasn't holding Petal's leash—into her pocket and lowered her chin against the wind, in a frustrated, moody silence.

"She doesn't know about the dead." Allison spoke because the silence was growing uncomfortable. Most silences with Emma were peaceful. This wasn't. Allison had known her for long enough to pick up on the difference. "She doesn't know why she saw her husband. You know. I know. And honestly, Em? Sometimes even I find it disturbing."

"But—if she listened. If she listened to me, she could *talk* to my dad. He's right there, Ally. He still keeps an eye on both of us."

"Have you asked your dad?"

Emma was silent. It was still not the good silence. Petal made enough noise for two. Toronto had a *lot* of garbage-raiding raccoons.

"Do you know what I would have done?" Emma asked.

Allison looked at her best friend's face in the streetlight. The outer shell of socially adept, polite Emma had cracked.

"I would have done *anything*. If it'd been me—if I'd been my mother and I'd seen Nathan at the hospital—I would have done anything just to be able to talk to him again."

"Em, your dad died eight years ago."

"And that's all it takes to forget him? Eight years? He wasn't just a grade school crush, Ally. He was her husband. It's been eight years for me, too, but *I* wanted to see him. I wanted to talk to him again."

When a conversation was going straight downhill, you could still control your descent. You could just stop talking. Going off-map sometimes revealed surprising cliffs in the conversational landscape. Allison felt the edge of one beneath her feet. She wasn't certain how steep the drop would be.

"He's dead. Even if your mother could talk to him again, he'd still be dead. She can't touch him without freezing. She can't talk to him without you. If you're there, she can't say any of the personal stuff."

"It would still be better than nothing."

Allison wasn't so certain.

"Chase, pay attention."

Chase frowned. He didn't argue; Eric was right. He wasn't paying attention. Not to the streets and the dwindling stream of people getting in the way of their stakeout. Not to the cars that were parking on the street, and not to the ones that had slowed to leisurely crawls in search of parking.

He wore three rings, all etched with symbols; one was solid silver, and two had iron cores. He passed his hand through the air; nothing wavered. There was no visible distortion. He slid his phone out of his pocket.

"What's with you?"

"Checking to make sure you got the right address." He slid the phone back into his jacket pocket, because nothing had changed. They'd been sent to midtown to check out two addresses. "We're up," he added, as the door to the apartment building swung open.

*   *   *

There were multiple ways to get into a building. Chase had been an electrician, an apprentice plumber, a cable technician, a phone technician—in short, one of the invisible people who kept things running. It was easiest, when necessary. In countries like this, it was mostly necessary. Money opened doors—but only figurative ones.

He vastly preferred to hunt—and kill—Necromancers in the streets of the city. Any city. Buildings were too easy to trap, too easy to bug, too easy to monitor. The Queen of the Dead didn't care much for modern life—and modern life was therefore their best advantage.

But they didn't catch all of the proto-Necromancers, as Allison called them. And some of the ones that slipped through their fingers were also part of the modern age. Given that most of them were teenagers, their understanding of the finicky bits of modern life only scratched the surface; most of them didn't know how their phones worked or where their internet connections came from.

Then again, Necromantic magic was generally more useful than cell phones when it came to communication.

They entered the apartment. "Number significant?" Chase asked, nodding at the door.

Eric shook his head. "I don't think they had the time." He nodded toward the kitchen and the dining room beyond it. Chase headed that way; Eric headed to what were probably bedrooms and closets.

The living and dining area was clean. Eric whistled, and Chase headed to the bedroom. "Got something?"

"They're here." There was a mirror in the room, on the desk; Eric had already covered it.

"All of them?"

"Two." He lifted passports, tossed them to Chase, who frowned. One of the two was twenty. One appeared to be in his thirties. "Not high in the upper echelons of the Court."

"Good. They didn't leave much."

"You think they've already gone hunting?"

Eric nodded. "Grab their passports."

"Cash?"

"Some. Not much. They didn't leave wallets here."

"Robes?"

Eric shook his head. "They're either wearing them or they don't intend to grab and run."

"You think they're going to kill her?"

Eric frowned. "Emma opened the door," he finally said.

"She'll know."

Eric nodded. "Every other Necromancer alive might have missed it, but the Queen will know. She won't know how Emma managed it, but she has to suspect."

"The lamp."

"The lamp. If Emma dies, she won't get her hands on the lamp." Eric was examining the phone. He swore.

"What?"

"Car. Now."

The only person Chase worried about was Chase Loern. That had been his truth for a long time now. Eric was his equal—or, on a bad day, his better; he could take care of himself. So could Chase. Anyone who couldn't was dead and buried in some unmarked grave somewhere.

Chase wasn't afraid of death—he just wanted the bastards to *work* for it. So far, they hadn't worked hard enough. Rania had called him suicidal, back in the day. She'd been a lot like Eric—proper, well mannered, well educated. Unlike Eric, she'd become a casualty.

Chase had no illusions about death. Death was not a peaceful end. It wasn't a release into the great, happy beyond. There was no heaven waiting, no divine presence. Only the Queen of the Dead. If she found Chase, he'd be a figurative lamppost in her city—if he was lucky. Rumor had it she held a long grudge.

Then again, so did Chase. But he wasn't a Necromancer. His grudge wasn't worth much; he made it count by killing Necromancers. But it was a stalling action. Sooner or later, they were all going to end up in the same damn place.

"My mother's not like yours," Emma said. "We don't talk about important things in the Hall house. I don't know if that would be different if my dad hadn't died. I kind of doubt it, though. But she talked to me about Nathan. After he died. She talked about my dad. It was the first time I'd really thought of him as her husband. I mean, I knew—but he was my dad first.

"He was her husband. She lost him. She had me—but it wasn't the same. I have Petal," she added, with a wry smile.

"You're more important to your mother than Petal," Allison said. "Sorry, Petal."

Emma smiled. "We had that in common. The loss. The way we understood it. I knew she'd survived. So I knew I could." Her smile faded. "On some days, I didn't want to."

Allison knew.

"Maybe Dad wasn't as important to her as Nathan is to me. Have you ever noticed that people seem to love less as they get older? I don't want that to happen to me." She swallowed. "If I forget him, Ally, if I reach a point where talking to him, seeing him, isn't important enough— what was the point?"

"Emma—"

Emma smiled. "Hold this?" she asked, handing Petal's leash to Allison without waiting for a reply. Allison took it in gloved hands; they were numb. It was a cold night, even for November.

Emma removed her right glove; Allison held her breath as Emma held her hand out to the night air. She held her breath when Nathan materialized beside her best friend. He wasn't dressed for November; he was dressed for summer. The cold wouldn't touch him now. Aside from Emma and people like her, nothing could.

"Hey," Nathan said. It was dark enough she couldn't see the color of Emma's eyes, although she knew they were a lighter shade of brown. She couldn't see the color of Nathan's, either.

For a long moment, she said nothing. And then, exhaling, she said, "Hey, Nathan."

The problem with being Emma's best friend was that Emma understood her. Allison smiled. She *did*. But the expression was half-frozen; it was like a mask. Emma knew. Emma needed Allison to be happy for her, and the best Allison could do was try.

But it was November, it was cold, and Allison knew that touching the dead sucked warmth and heat out of Emma. "We should—we should go inside," she suggested. It was a compromise.

Emma's smile was fragile, and it broke. Her hand—her bare, glove-less hand—twined with Nathan's, tightened.

"It's cold," Allison said again. "And you're not going to get any warmer if you—if Nathan— " She shook her head. She had Petal's leash, but Petal was no longer tugging at it; he'd doubled back. Allison watched as he headed toward Nathan, whining anxiously. His stub of a tail was still. He wasn't growling. But he wasn't happy, either—and he'd always liked Nathan.

They all watched as he walked back and forth through Nathan, as if he were a particularly solid shadow. He whined, and Emma eventually tried to feed him—but for once he wasn't interested in food.

Allison took the leash more firmly in hand and began to walk; Emma followed, Nathan held just as tightly.

It was quiet. It was the wrong type of quiet. Emma said nothing, but Allison knew the look. She wasn't happy, but she didn't want to start an argument about Nathan in front of Nathan. Allison didn't want to start an argument at all.

But she understood why Mercy had no desire to see her dead hus-band again. She was certain that Emma wouldn't see it the same way—

and who could blame her? Ghosts didn't age. They didn't change. Their touch was cold enough to numb. They couldn't work. They couldn't eat. They couldn't *live*, or they wouldn't be dead.

Emma wasn't dead, but she stood in death's shadow—and she wanted to stay there.

You don't understand, Allison thought, because she knew that's what Emma wanted to say to her. And maybe it was true. But Nathan was dead. He was always, and forever, dead. She was afraid that Emma would join him.

And she couldn't say that. Not now. Maybe not ever. *Who is it hurting? You, Emma. It's hurting you.*

But Emma would tell her she'd lived in a world of hurt since last July, and this was the first time she could see an end to that pain. There weren't many things you couldn't say to your best friend—but Allison was facing one of them now.

Emma's phone rang. Emma fished it out of her pocket without letting go of Nathan's hand, which was awkward; she was trembling with cold. Nathan watched her as she fumbled and then looked past her to meet Allison's eyes.

Allison wanted to talk to him about Emma—but that couldn't happen now. Anything Nathan heard, Emma would hear by default; she was his only conduit to the rest of the world. He knew she was worried. He probably even knew why; Nathan had never been stupid.

And he'd never been selfish, either.

"Em," he said, as she brought the phone to her cheek. "Let go. Ally's right. It's cold."

She ignored him. "Hello?" To Allison, she mouthed, *Eric.* "We're just out walking Petal. I'm with Allison. No, we're near the ravine, why?" Her eyes rounded. The phone slid from her face as she turned.

"What's happened?" Allison asked, voice rising.

"Eric says—Eric says we have two Necromancers incoming. He wants us to head to the cemetery. Now."

"Why the cemetery?"

"It's closest to where he and Chase are. They'll meet us there."

"I don't understand what the Necromancers want," Allison said, short-ening the leash and picking up the pace.

Emma was silent for half a block. One phone call from Eric had turned quiet night shadows into dangerous omens. "Ally, I want you to go home."

Allison stared at her.

"They're not—they're not after you. If you go home now, you should be safe."

Allison felt a pang of something that was like anger. Or hurt. Hadn't she just had this argument? Coming from Emma, it was harder. Her hands were shaking. Her throat was dry. Speaking over the fear took work. "Don't."

"I don't want you hurt."

"Don't say it."

"If they're here, they're hunting me or Eric or Chase—"

Adrenaline made Allison's hands shake; it wasn't just the cold. The last time they'd seen Necromancers, they'd had guns. Allison never wanted to see them again. "If I go home and something happens to you—"

"Ally, what are you going to do if you don't go home and the Necro-mancers find us?"

"I don't know. We'll figure that out if it happens." Her eyes, made much larger by her glasses, narrowed.

Nathan reached up to touch Emma's cheek; his hand stopped an inch from skin and fell, curling into a brief fist. "Em, listen to Ally. She's right more often than she's wrong."

"You shouldn't be here, either," Allison told him. "You're dead. Nec-romancers use the dead for power—and if they don't have enough, they'll grab whatever they can reach."

Nathan shook his head. "I'm not in danger. I'm already dead. There's not a lot they can do to me to change that. There's a lot they can do to you—but you're staying." He hesitated, and then said, "If the dead have power to give to the living, I'm willing to give all I have to Emma."

Allison couldn't argue. She didn't tell Nathan that Emma didn't know how to take that power, and didn't know how to use it. Emma believed that—but Allison wasn't certain. Emma had walked into the phantasm of a fire that no one else could see unless she touched them. Emma had walked out again, hair singed, clothing black with soot.

Emma had given Maria Copis the ability to see her dead son—and the ability to pick him up and carry him, at long last, out of the fire that had killed him. If Em wasn't trained in magical, Necromantic magic, she could still do things that Allison couldn't explain. And could never hope to do herself.

But Emma's question hung in the air between them. Nathan at least had the sense to stand on the far side. *What can I do? If Necromancers come, what can I possibly do?*

They picked up the pace in the uncomfortable, heightened silence.

Emma didn't have to drag Petal with her; he hunkered down by her side, like a portable, living tank. The streets were dark; the streetlamps were high and unevenly spaced, and there were no houses on this side of the street. There were graves just beyond the fence that bounded the cemetery, and moonlight, although the background of city lights caused stars to fade from view on all but the clearest of nights.

Petal's growling grew deeper.

Allison stopped walking. In the street ahead, in the middle of a road that cars traveled on shortcuts, stood two men.

Had they just been walking, she wouldn't have noticed them. They wore normal winter coats, hats, faded jeans; one wore boots, the other, running shoes. One of them seemed to be about their age; the other was older.

They weren't walking, though. They were waiting. Their hands hung by their sides, and in the shadowed evening light, Allison saw that they wore no gloves. Emma slid her gloved hand out of her pocket and held it out to Allison who understood what she intended; she pulled Emma's glove off and shoved it into her own pocket for safekeeping.

"The dead are here," Nathan told them.

Emma knelt to let Petal off his leash and rose quickly. The rottweiler was growling now as if growling were breath.

"Emma Hall?" One of the two men said, after a long pause.

Emma nodded.

He lifted his hands, palm out, as if in surrender. Or as if he was trying to prove that he meant her no harm. As if. "We've come a long way, looking for you," he said. He took a step forward.

So did Petal.

"You're in danger, here," the younger man added. "We've come to bring you to safety."

"Why am I in danger?" Emma asked, as if meeting two strange men who knew her by name in the middle of the night near the cemetery was a daily occurrence. Allison heard the tremor in her voice, because she knew Emma so well.

Her own throat was dry.

"You're special, Emma. *We're* special, and you're like us. You're gifted. People won't understand what you can do. They'll fear it. If they can, they'll kill you. We're here to make sure that doesn't happen."

Allison was stiff and silent. The two men said something to each other; it was quiet enough that the feel of syllables traveled without the actual words. Emma swore. She let go of Nathan's hand, lifting hers as if to surrender. Nathan seemed to disappear. But Allison knew Nathan. He wouldn't leave Emma. Not now.

Neither would she.

"They have the dead with them," Emma whispered to Allison, although she faced straight ahead. Her voice dropped. "Four."

Allison wasn't Emma. She couldn't see the dead. But she didn't need to see them to understand what Emma meant. Necromancers derived their power from captive ghosts. Four was bad.

EMMA'S HANDS WERE SHAKING; one was numb.
Allison had been right about one thing: Touching Nathan was no different from touching any other dead person. It leeched heat out of her hands, numbing them.

There were four ghosts chained to the two men who now approached. Two of them were women, one only slightly older than Emma or Allison and the other older than Emma's mother. The two boys, however, were exactly that: boys. One looked as if he could pass for six on a good day. The other she guessed had been nine or ten at the time of his death.

The dead, to Emma's eyes, looked very much as if they were still alive. There was one significant difference, though. She could never tell, looking at the dead, what color their eyes were. It didn't matter if she knew what the color had been before their death, either. Her father's eyes—and, more significant, Nathan's—were the same as the rest. They seemed slightly luminescent in the dark of night, but that luminescence shed no color; it was like an echo of the essence of light. Maybe it was pure reflection. Her father had told her that there was a place to which the dead were drawn and that, for roughly two years, that place was all they could see.

All they wanted to see.

Eye color wasn't the only thing the four dead people were missing. They lacked any expression at all as they stood silent, still, unmoving. In that, they looked like corpses. Emma knew she could scream at—or to—them, and they would hear as much as an actual corpse, and respond the same way. She thanked whatever god existed that Allison couldn't see them.

Nathan, however, could.

"Stay back," she told him, voice low. "Stay with me."

With the dead as escorts, the two men began to move; they walked slowly. Nathan started whistling the theme song to an old Western his dad used to watch. Emma wanted to laugh. She also wanted to run.

One of the two men gestured; white fire rose on either side of the road. It stretched from a point just behind the men to a point well behind where Emma, Allison, and Petal were. They now stood in a tunnel.

Allison's sharp intake of breath made it clear that the fire, unlike the ghosts, was visible.

"So," Emma said, backing up. "This is supposed to make me trust you?"

"No," the taller of the two men replied. "It's supposed to keep us safe." His eyes were now the color of a dead man's eyes, he'd absorbed so much power.

Emma stopped moving.

Eyes narrowed, she could see the delicate strands of golden light around the Necromancers' hands and wrists. If she were closer—and close was *so* not where she wanted to be—she would see those strands as chains, like the chains of a necklace or a delicate bracelet. Unlike jewelry, the chains ended in the figurative heart of a person—a dead person. If she could grab those chains, she could break them, depriving the Necromancers of the source of their power.

Petal was growling nonstop. Emma felt the hair on the back of her neck rise; she felt the howl of a sudden, arctic wind and turned, leaving her dog to keep watch.

The road behind her back was gone. In its place, rising up past the boughs of the old trees that lined the street on the wrong side of the fence, was a standing arch composed almost entirely of the same fire that blocked escape on two sides.

"We don't have time to explain things here," the tall man continued. "So we've arranged a little trip." He frowned, said something to the man beside him. Emma reached out and caught Allison's hand, pulling her close. As she did, strands of white flame shot out from the right side of the road and wrapped themselves around Allison. The fire was *cold*.

"Stop it!" Emma shouted. "Let her go!"

The taller man shook his head. "I'm sorry," he said, in a calm and reasonable voice. "But she's seen us, and she's not one of us. In future, you'll understand why it's important to leave no witnesses behind."

Emma grabbed the white strand that was tightening its grip on Ally's throat. It was bloody cold; ice would have been warmer. Contact with it numbed her fingers instantly.

This is why I wanted you to run! she thought, struggling—and failing—to get a grip on the tendril of fire. Ally was turning purple; her knees buckled. Petal leaped at the man who'd been doing most of the talking, and Emma couldn't even watch; she was trying—and failing—to force the fire to let go of her best friend's throat.

"Em," Nathan said. He caught her hand in his; his hands, like the hands of all the dead, were cold. She didn't try to pull away; she knew that Allison's only hope lay in Nathan. In his hands and in hers. Nathan was dead. Emma was a Necromancer. If she could use his power, she could save Ally.

"I'll go with you," she told the Necromancers. "I won't fight—but you've got to let her go."

"You'll go with us anyway," the younger of the two said.

The pressure of the strand didn't let up. Emma swallowed and began to pull the only power she had access to: Nathan's. He offered it; he offered it willingly. As she took it in, her hands began to tingle. No white glow gloved them; it wasn't that kind of binding. But it didn't matter. Emma could now see how the strand was connected to Allison, and she could—and did—melt it off. Allison was gasping for breath as Emma turned. The men were closer now; the younger of the two looked both annoyed and surprised.

The older just looked weary.

"It was the least painful way for her to die," he told Emma, in a gentle voice. "But there are others, and they are more certain." He gestured again, and this time—this time she recognized the fire that lay in his palm, like a roiling ball. It was green. Chase had called it soul-fire.

It had almost killed him—and it would kill Allison if it hit her.

Emma didn't know what to do with the power she had. She didn't know how to use it, how to defend herself—or anyone else—with it.

"Please," she said, voice low and shaking. "Just let her go. I'll go with you. I won't fight. Just—let her go."

The taller of the two shook his head, although there was a weight to his expression that hadn't been there before. "I can't," he replied. "It's against the law."

"Everything you're doing now is against the law!"

"Mortal law doesn't concern Necromancers, Emma Hall. It doesn't concern you anymore, although you don't understand that yet. You have a gift—"

"It's the same as yours," she said quickly, her hands now warm in Nathan's because she was drawing power from him. "It's the same as yours—and this is *not* how I want to use it!"

"You'll learn. All your friend loses is a few years. A few years, in the existence of the dead, is nothing."

"She's not dead—"

"She will spend far, far more of her existence dead than she will alive, even if she lives to see old age. Come, Emma. If you feel you must, in the decades to come, you can return here and find her; if you grow in power and stature within the City, you can command her, and she will come to where you wait."

He threw the fire.

He threw it, and Emma reached out and caught it with her arm; it splashed, as if it were liquid, and spread instantly across the whole of her coat. Real fire wouldn't have done that.

The Necromancer's eyes widened in either shock or horror. He was still too far away to tell.

Allison was nearer, and she started to reach out, but Nathan barked at her, and she stopped. She could see Nathan now. Emma was holding onto him.

Emma was doing more than that. The fire wasn't hot, but it wasn't cold. It burned, but it didn't burn hair or skin; it burned something beneath it.

"You fool!" the Necromancer shouted. Power spread out from him in a fan; it was distorted by the rising waves of green.

She reached for Nathan almost blindly, and she set what he gave to her, his very presence, against the spread of the fire itself. She didn't tell Allison to run—there was nowhere to run to. She didn't look to see if her dog lay dead in the streets, because there was nothing at all she could do about him now.

Where Nathan's power surged through her, the fire stopped its painful spread. But it didn't bank; it ate away at what he'd given her. She could take everything he offered—everything—and she might extend the fight with the flame for long enough to put it out. And then? He'd be here, unable to talk or interact or do *anything*.

But she couldn't stop herself; she couldn't disentangle their hands; she took what he offered, fighting every step of the way.

She wasn't prepared for the way the green fire suddenly guttered, and she stumbled, still holding Nathan's hand. She was surprised that his weight supported hers, but she didn't have time to think about it:

Looking up at the Necromancers, she saw that the one who had thrown the fire had fallen to his knees. His eyes were wide; she could see their whites from here.

Behind him, she could see Chase.

Eric swore. Chase heard the words at a distance because he left them behind at a sprint. Two men stood side by side in the street. Beyond them, Emma and Allison were backing up. Emma appeared to be talking; she'd lifted both of her hands, as if in surrender.

Allison was silent.

Chase saw the white-fire corridor spring up to either side of the two girls. He saw the hazy swirl of visible light behind them, and he swore himself; he knew what it meant. The Necromancers didn't intend to head back to their apartment for passports and plane tickets; they intended to walk home, with Emma between them.

Allison would be a footnote. Allison, who stumbled. Emma stopped immediately, huddling at her side; she lifted her face. He was close enough to hear her words. Close enough to see the white filament around Allison's neck as it melted. He sucked in air, picked up speed, lightened his step as much as he could; he wouldn't have much time before the Necromancers became aware of him.

But he wouldn't need it.

He gave up on stealth the minute he saw the green-fire globe form in the Necromancer's hand. He wasn't going to make it in time. He wasn't going to be able to drop the Necromancer before he threw the fire.

"Allison!"

Necromancers didn't spend years learning how to throw; aim, when it came to soul-fire, didn't matter. Blindfolded, they could still hit their targets. There was only one certain way to douse soul-fire: Kill the Necromancer. There were less certain ways—but Chase knew whom the soul-fire was meant to kill. And he knew that Allison had no protection against it.

No protection but Emma and Chase. He knew which of the two counted.

He threw one of his two knives; it struck the man cleanly between the upper shoulder blades. He made it count, leaping to grab the handle of the knife as the Necromancer's arms windmilled. Chase twisted the knife.

He yanked the blade out as the man fell forward, blood spreading across the new gap in the back of his jacket. Chase looked up, then, to see that Allison was not on fire. Emma was—but the fire, like the Necromancer, was dying. He grudgingly revised his estimate of Emma's usefulness.

The second Necromancer turned. The white walls on either side of the street faded as he pulled his power back. He made no attempt to help his partner; he had no hope of saving him, and they both knew it.

Instead, he ran. If he could make it past Allison and Emma, if he could make it to the portal, he'd survive. He thought he had a chance. As Eric leaped past Chase in the night streets, Chase grinned.

Allison's skin was red where the white filament had twined round her throat. Her fingers, on the other hand, were blue, and her hands were shaking. She'd managed to half-knock her glasses off her face.

"Ally?"

"I can breathe." Not without coughing, though; her voice sounded hoarse.

"Allison!" Chase had saved Allison's life. On television, rescue usually came in the form of someone a lot less blood spattered. Chase was, once again, wearing a variant on the world's ugliest jacket.

Allison lifted one hand; it was shaking. "I'm alive," she said. "We're both alive. Where's Petal?"

"Here," Eric's voice came from somewhere behind Chase; Chase was close enough it was hard to see around him. Petal was whining, which meant he wasn't dead.

"We need to get out of here," Eric told them. He was staring down the road, and Emma turned to look that way as well. The arch was slowly fading, its cold light giving way to the night of streetlamp and road.

"Where did it lead?" Emma asked.

"To the City of the Dead," he replied, without looking at her. Petal's tail started to move, and he set the dog down. The Necromancers hadn't killed him. He glanced at the two dead bodies that lay in the middle of the street. "Chase, give the old man the heads up."

Chase, however, was kneeling beside Allison. Allison felt dizzy and nauseated, but she knew, looking at his expression, that this wasn't the time for either. She smiled. She forced herself to smile at him.

He grimaced and rolled his eyes. "Don't even try," he told her. He practically shouldered Emma out of the way. Allison caught only a glimpse of Emma's expression before Chase's shoulder covered her face.

"It wasn't Emma's fault," she said, between clenched teeth.

He slid an arm beneath hers and lifted her to her feet. "I didn't say it was."

"Chase—"

"Not here," he told her. "Not now."

She would have argued—she almost did—but she realized that part of the trembling she felt wasn't her own. The fact that Chase, spattered in blood, was shaking, silenced her.

"Emma?"

Emma smiled wanly. "I'm fine."

Eric's brows rose. "I haven't known you long," he finally said. "But 'fine' in Hall parlance doesn't mean much."

"No?"

"No. You're just closing the door in the face of external concern."

She grimaced. "I'm *fine*, Eric. Allison was the one—" She exhaled.

She couldn't see her best friend; Chase's back was in the way. Pointedly in the way.

"I'm okay," Allison said. Her voice was shaky. No surprise, there. The Necromancers hadn't tried to kill Emma. Just Allison. Because Allison had been stupid enough to join Emma while she walked her dog.

Her dog bounded toward her, and she felt a surge of both guilt and gratitude. She knelt and let his wet nose leave tracks across her face. People were often put off food by danger; Petal proved that in some ways, he was all dog. She offered him a Milk-Bone, and he ate it.

"Eric's worried about you," Nathan said. Emma startled, which was embarrassing. She ran her hands through her hair and then turned toward Nathan. He didn't *look* different.

"He's like that," Emma replied. "Chase—the redhead with the broad shoulders—doesn't care if I die."

"I wouldn't bet on it. He was worried about Ally, though."

"It's why I can't hate him," Emma said, speaking quietly so Allison wouldn't hear her. "He's attractive, he's confident, he's—I don't know. A guy. But he does like her. He didn't even notice Amy—and I can't think of another living male who hasn't."

Nathan smiled. "It's hard not to notice Amy. If most women are bullets, Amy's a nuclear bomb—overkill on all levels."

Emma didn't even feel a twinge of jealousy; she would have, once. Eric glanced at Nathan.

"Oh, I'm sorry." She was. She'd forgotten that Eric could see the dead. Eric, who wasn't a Necromancer, who wasn't suspicious, and who Chase had not come to Toronto to kill. "Eric, this is Nathan. Nathan, this is Eric."

"Pleased to meet you," Eric said. He didn't hold out his hand.

Neither did Nathan; they stood sizing each other up in an almost painfully obvious way. Emma cleared her throat. "We were going to leave?"

Eric nodded. "The old man's coming to clean up. But you're not going home yet."

"Where are we going?"

"Our place."

Chase was pissed off. Emma wasn't in the best of moods herself, but she wasn't angry with Chase; he, however, was clearly annoyed with her. He inserted himself firmly between Emma and Allison and made clear by the direction his shoulder was turned—toward Emma—that that was where he was staying, period. Ally didn't notice; Chase had his *arm around her shoulder* and she wasn't saying anything. She was white as a sheet.

Nathan walked on the other side of Allison, glancing at her from time to time. He made no attempt to touch her or speak with her—it was pointless—but seemed to take comfort from offering her his entirely invisible support.

Petal stuck like proverbial glue to Emma's side. He did attempt to eat a Milk-Bone through her pocket; she shoved his nose aside—his wet, warm nose—to save her jacket from saliva and teeth marks.

For a group that had survived death by Necromancy, it was pretty grim. The blood really didn't help. Eric's hands were still red; his shirt, his coat, and part of his face were sticky with blood. It wasn't his—which did help—but it was disturbing. Mostly, it was disturbing because he didn't appear to notice or care. Both he and Chase acted as though this sort of thing happened every day. Or every night.

"Eric," Chase said, "I'm taking Allison home."

Emma stopped walking. "No, you're not. Not looking like *that*."

Chase bristled. "Would you like to keep her here so someone else can try to kill her?"

Allison made a strangled sound and ducked out from under Chase's arm. "Don't say that!" She was trembling, she was white, and she was—

and this hurt—frightened. But she was also angry, and that added a bit of welcome color to her cheeks.

Chase grimaced. "Allison—"

"Don't ever say that again. Emma didn't want me to stay—*I* wanted to stay."

"And now you know why it's a very bad idea. Look, Allison, I know the two of you are friends—"

"Best friends."

"Whatever. But she's a Necromancer. You're *not*. Even if there's something you could in *theory* do, you don't have the training, you don't have the experience. The best you can do is die painlessly. The Necromancers don't always aim for best case. They don't care about you. They care about Emma because they think she'll become one of them. But they don't spare friends or family. Trust me."

Emma's throat tightened. Chase was right. She knew he was right. Forcing herself to speak lightly, she said, "If you take her home right now, her mother will see you, covered in blood, and have a coronary. If you're very lucky, she won't call the police. And I know you—you're never going to be that lucky."

Allison winced and managed a strained laugh. "She's right."

Chase swore. "Fine. Come with us to Eric's and hope that we don't get traced."

"Emma," Allison said, in a much more subdued voice, "I'm sorry."

That was the worse of it. She apologized and she *meant* it.

"Why?" Emma said, wanting to grab her by the shoulders and shake the words so far out of her they never came back. She was surprised by the anger, by how visceral it was.

"Chase is right. I didn't do anything. I couldn't do anything."

"Ally—neither could I." Emma glanced down at her hands. At the hands that both Allison and Nathan had grabbed. "I couldn't do anything, either. I thought you—" she stopped speaking; it took effort. "It's not you who should be apologizing. It's me. I—I should have at least as much power as they do—and I couldn't do anything, either. If Chase and Eric hadn't arrived, you'd be dead, and I'd be god only knows where.

"But I'd never, ever, forgive them."

NATHAN

NATHAN'S SURPRISED AT HOW MUCH Chase seems to hate Emma, and how much Chase seems to care about Allison.

Most of Emma's friends at Emery are like Emma. They're comfortable in crowds; they fit in; they find energy talking about similar things. Clothing. Boys. Music and Drama. They go shopping in packs, roving the malls with bright eyes and easy laughter; not all of that laughter is kind, but it has an energy that's fascinating at a distance.

None of those girls is Allison. Allison wanders into bookstores and paper stores. She sits to one side of the group, buried in words that she didn't write and won't have to speak out loud. She's moved by things that are imaginary. Her head, as Nan once said, is permanently stuck in the clouds.

What Nan doesn't see is where Ally places her feet. Yes, her head is in the clouds, but she's rooted, grounded; when she can be pulled out of them, what she sees is what's there. Maybe, Nathan thinks with a grimace, that's *why* she likes clouds.

There are no clouds for Allison now. Her eyes are dark and wide. There's a livid bruise around her throat, and her hands are shaking. She snaps at Chase, Chase snaps back. Emma flinches with each exchange, although she stays out of it.

Allison feels guilty. Nathan recognizes it; it's twin to his own sense of guilt. She was there. She was *right there*. And she couldn't do anything. She couldn't stop the Necromancers. She couldn't even protect *herself*. She was dead weight. Worse. She was terrified.

She was afraid she'd die. That part's simple. But the fear itself has branches. Death is frightening to the living. Hell, it's no walk in the park for the dead either. But it's not just that. Ally knows what her death would do to Emma.

Because Ally's seen what Nathan's death did.

Nathan's seen it as well. He's spent days watching Emma at school, like some kind of crazed stalker. She's still Emma—but she's quieter. She still talks to Amy and the Emery mafia, and they still talk to her—but it's different. No one mentions Nathan's name. They're careful not to talk too much about boys or boyfriends when she's in the group; they wait until she's gone.

As if she understands this—and she probably does—she drifts away. She doesn't want to be a wet blanket. She doesn't want to pretend that Nathan never existed. She doesn't want to force her friends to acknowledge him the way she did, because they didn't love him the way she did, and she's fine with that.

But Allison almost never talked about boys. She talked about books, and with the same happy, riveted intensity. She talked about Michael and his friends, about schoolwork, about stray thoughts brought on by too much Google and not enough time outside. None of that has changed.

Nathan is afraid that tonight, it has. Allison feels guilty.

And Emma feels guilty as well. Because Emma is a Necromancer, and if it weren't for Chase and Eric, Allison would be dead. Being a best friend has suddenly become a death sentence. She didn't *need* company, tonight. She had Nathan.

But she wanted company. She wanted to tell Allison that Nathan had returned.

Allison was not happy about his reappearance. Emma was surprised. Hurt. Allison recognized that. So did Nathan—but Nathan weighs Allison's unhappiness differently. She's worried. She's worried *for* Emma.

And she should be.

"You can drive us home after you change. And shower. Get the blood out of your hair and your hands."

They're still arguing. Chase, in the overhead light above the door, is the color of chalk; his red hair makes him look even worse.

"Fine. Eric can drive us home. My mother will never let me out of the house again if she sees you looking like that!"

"And that's bad how?"

If Chase could see Nathan, Nathan would tell him to stop. He can't. Allison always seems meek and retiring to people who don't actually know her. She's uncertain in social situations. She's afraid she's just said the wrong thing even when she hasn't said anything.

But once she's made a decision, she doesn't bend, and she is not bending now.

Emma, arms wrapped around her upper body, is exchanging glances with Eric, who looks as much of a mess as Chase but without the red hair to top it off.

Eventually, they enter the house, where eventually means Chase shouts, "Fine!" and opens the door and slams it shut behind him. Allison is practically shrieking with outrage; Nathan laughs. He can; she can't see him.

"I always liked her," he tells Emma.

Emma gives him a shadow of a smile. But she's not with him right now; she's in Allison's orbit. When Allison yanks the door open and marches in—a sure sign that she's angry—Emma apologizes and follows her.

That leaves Eric on the porch.

*　　*　　*

Nathan doesn't want to talk to Eric. He avoids Eric where at all possible. But given tonight, given Allison's reaction both before and after the Necromancers, he knows it's time to stop.

Eric folds his arms across his chest; Nathan lets his hang loose by his sides. There's nothing Eric can do to harm him. Not directly.

Eric gets straight to the point. "Why are you here?"

"I could ask the same question." Nathan shrugs. "Did you come here to kill Emma?"

Eric's a tough audience. He doesn't even blink. "Yes."

"She's not dead."

"I changed my mind."

"Why?"

Eric's gaze never leaves Nathan's face. "Your girlfriend isn't a Necromancer."

"That's not what Chase thinks."

"And I'm not Chase. I've been doing this a lot longer than he has. Long enough to know you shouldn't be here."

"Allison knows I shouldn't be here?"

"She knows you're here?" He exhales, loosens his arm, and runs a hand through his hair. "Never mind. Of course she knows. She's Emma's best friend."

Nathan chuckles. He can't help it. He's not much of a sharer; it took him a while to get used to the fact that there were no secrets between Emma and Allison. Something about the chuckle loosens the rest of Eric's expression.

"Why are you here?" He asks again, in an entirely different tone.

Because he does, Nathan can answer. "I don't know."

Eric glances at the closed door. "Walk with me," he says. He moves—rapidly—away from the front porch, and Nathan follows.

"It usually takes the dead time to recover," Eric says, as they walk. The chill in the air is lessened by the start of snowfall, but it's a gentle fall.

Flakes cling to Eric's jacket and begin to dust sidewalk and road. "Two years, give or take a month. Sometimes it's longer."

"But never four months."

"No. You want to tell me why?"

"Not really. I will, though. I—" he glances at Eric. "I don't know how much you know."

"About the door?"

"Is that what you call it?"

"It's what Emma called it, when she saw it."

Nathan stops walking, frozen for a moment at the idea of Emma lost there.

"Emma hasn't told you this?"

"I haven't asked." But the answer is no, and they both know it. He stumbles over words; it's not like he can stumble over anything else here. "I was there. I don't think of it as a door. It's a window—a solid, bullet-proof window. You can see through it. You know what's waiting. But you can't ever reach it."

Eric nods.

"She came to find me there."

He stiffens. "Who?" he asks, but it's clear he already knows the answer.

Nathan gives it anyway. "The Queen of the Dead."

Eric says a lot of nothing for a few blocks. "Why did she send you here?"

"I don't know."

"What did she tell you?"

"She told me to go home."

"That's it?"

Nathan hesitates. Eric catches it instantly. "No," he finally says. "She also told me I'd be safe from her knights."

"Her . . . knights?"

"That's what she calls the Necromancers."

"*Knights?*"

"Sorry. Now that you mention it, it's kind of stupid. She summoned her Necromancers to her throne room."

Eric is quiet. It's a controlled quiet, a veneer of stillness over something so large it might burst at any moment. "Does she spend all her time in her throne room?"

Nathan says, more or less truthfully, "I don't know."

"How much time did you spend there?"

"I don't know." He exhales out of habit, Nathan's version of a sigh. "You know where I was when she found me."

Eric nods. It's a tight, leashed motion.

"She was the only other thing I could see. She's like a bonfire. I'm like a moth. She's terrifying—but she's *there*." He hesitates, then doubles down. "I see Emma the same way, except for the terror. She's luminous. When I'm near Emma, I don't think about what I can't have or where I can't go. I don't think about an exit. I just think about Emma. And that's natural, for me."

"How do you see the others?"

"The others?" For a moment, Nathan thinks he's talking about Allison. Michael. Even his mother.

"The rest of the Necromancers. Do you see them the same way?"

"Only in comparison to my friends. They're brighter, sharper. They catch the eye—but they wouldn't have been able to catch my attention in the beginning. Not the way the Queen did."

"And Emma would." It's a question without any of the intonation.

"Yes," Nathan replies, voice softer. "But I can't be objective."

Eric's brow rises. "I don't believe that."

"What do you see when you look at Emma?" Nathan strives for casual, now. For objective observer. Eric can touch Emma without burning.

Eric closes his eyes. "I see a naive, bleeding heart with a collection of scrappy friends, a deaf dog, and a dead boyfriend." He exhales, opens his eyes, and adds, "I see what you see. Tell me what the Queen of the Dead said to her . . . knights."

"She introduced us, more or less. She told them that if they touched me, if they mentioned me at all in any capacity, they'd be serving her in a 'less advantageous way' for the rest of eternity."

"She meant for you to come to Emma," Eric says, voice flat.

Nathan doesn't argue. He wants to, but it's the only thing that makes sense.

"Have you spoken with the Queen since you arrived home?"

"Yes. Once. She summoned me." He slides hands into his pockets and regards Eric for a long moment, trying to decide whether or not to say what he's thinking.

Eric knows.

"She's waiting for you," Nathan tells him. He's not sure why.

Eric slows; eventually he comes to a dead stop. Nathan's not surprised to see that they've returned to the cemetery. There are no corpses in the street, no obvious signs of blood. No dead that Nathan can see.

"Did she tell you that?" Eric asks, hands in his jacket pockets, balled in fists.

"No."

"How do you know?"

"There are two thrones in the throne room. They're identical, at least to my eyes. I don't know what the living see—the only living members of her Court are Necromancers, and it didn't seem safe to ask. The Queen sits in the left-hand chair, if you're facing her—and no one stands at her back."

"The chair on the right is empty?" When Nathan fails to answer, Eric turns.

"Yes. And no."

"Which is it?" Eric asks, hands in pockets, eyes on the sidewalk just ahead of his feet.

"It's empty. But you can see an image—like a storybook ghost—seated in the chair. It's her magic," he adds softly.

"You can tell that?"

"Yes. By the light, the quality of the light."

"Whose image?" he asks, his voice dropping, his breath a small cloud of mist.

"Yours."

Eric turns and walks away.

Nathan drifts to his grave. It doesn't feel familiar, but it bears his name, and it's where Emma was waiting for him. He touches the headstone, or tries; his hand passes through its marbled surface. Beneath his chiseled, shiny name, there are flowers.

Eric eventually returns, as if Nathan is actually alive and can't be deserted. "It's not my image," he says.

"No. He's not dressed the way you are."

"Please don't tell me I'm wearing a dress."

Nathan laughs. "No. You're not wearing armor, either. You are wearing a crown, though."

Eric snorts. "A crown."

"A big, heavy, ornate, impressive crown. There's less blood and more gravitas."

"I bet. We'd better head back. Chase and Allison probably need a referee by now." He starts to walk, stops, and says, "What have you told Emma?"

Nathan follows, borrowing part of Eric's silence. "Nothing," he finally says. "When I'm with her, I can almost forget I'm dead. I don't want the reminder. I don't want a Queen. I don't want to remind Emma of what the Necromancers represent." It's all true, but there's more, and it's harder. "I don't want to think that my presence here is a plot against Emma."

"If you found out that it was, could you leave?"

"Yes. But I'm not you. I don't think there's anywhere I can go that the Queen can't find me." He lays out his fear. "If I left, if she knew, she'd send me back. If I couldn't, or wouldn't, stay, she might even come here in person."

"She won't leave her city."

"Why? She left it to find me."

"No, Nathan, she didn't. Her city is the only place she's built where she feels safe."

"You probably understand the Queen better than anyone. Why am I here, Eric? What does she want from me?"

Eric says nothing.

There's a question Nathan wants to ask, but he doesn't, because if Eric answers, Nathan will know—and if the Queen thinks to ask, Nathan will tell her what Eric said. Maybe not immediately.

He contents himself with thinking it as they walk back to Eric's house.

Could you kill her, Eric? Could you kill the Queen of the Dead? Could you kill someone who loves you so much?

Eric drives Emma and Allison home. Nathan hitches an uncomfortable ride in the front seat. He still doesn't have the hang of sitting. He passes through chairs and seats. A lifetime's gravity habit is apparently hard to kick.

Nathan missed the beginning of the conversation, but he's not concerned. He can read a lot in their physical closeness. Allison has obviously shared information that's upset her—but the sharing, the spreading of that pain across two sets of shoulders, diminishes it. It's something he's often envied about girls: Talking actually makes a difference to them.

"Chase didn't mean it," Emma says.

"He meant some of it. The part he did mean is still—"

"Making you angry."

Allison nods. Anger isn't her natural state; most people find it hard to believe she has a temper. "I hate it when he talks about killing you—about killing anyone—so casually."

"Amy does it all the time."

"Amy's never killed anyone." Allison gives Emma the Look. "Chase has."

"Good point." Emma concedes with grace whenever she's in a losing position. "But I think he's genuinely worried—about you."

"He's worried about my safety."

"Same thing."

"It's *not*, Emma. He doesn't care about anything *but* that. Do you know how I'd feel if I just walked out on you, now? Let's pretend you're not you. Or you're not involved. You're some other, random Best Friend I've known since we were five years old."

"Okay."

"He's not asking me to walk out on my Best Friend; he's asking me to walk out on my own life. He's asking me to be so afraid for my own safety that I'm willing to just leave you behind. And I could," she adds. "But it would change what friendship means—to me—forever. I could never, ever throw my whole heart into it, because if things were too dark or too scary, I'd know, in advance, that I'd be ducking, hiding, and running for cover.

"It's not about you, not really. It's about *me*. It's about being able to look myself in the mirror. I'm not five years old anymore. I need to do this—for me. Can you live with that?"

"I'm not exactly a disinterested observer," Emma finally manages to say. Nathan knows the tone; she's close to tears. Emma doesn't cry in public. Even the good tears, and these would be good.

He understands what Emma sees in Allison. He understands that Allison mostly doesn't. He knows that Allison wasn't happy to see him, and given Eric's reaction, he's terrified that she's right.

Nathan knows Emma. He knows that Emma's not nearly as certain as Allison; he knows that Allison's belief in Emma is way stronger than Emma's belief in herself. But he could turn it around: Emma's belief in Allison is stronger than Allison's belief in herself. They shore each other up when the insecurities bite them.

They could, if they were different people, break each other down instead.

"Don't hate Chase," Emma says instead. "I can't. I know you think he doesn't care about what you need—but Ally, he does care about you. He's a guy. He's just got a crappy way of expressing it."

Eric clears his throat, loudly, to remind them there's a captive guy behind the steering wheel of the car.

"I want to slap him, and I want to spend an hour screaming in his ear, but—I don't hate him. If I hated him, I wouldn't care. No, I'd care because I care for you—but I wouldn't be so *angry* with him. I don't know why, but I expect better."

Emma laughs. "Having spoken with Chase, I don't know why either."

CHAPTER
FOUR

THIS EVENING HAD CONTAINED NECROMANCERS, near death, and death; it contained Allison and her anger at Chase—Chase was almost always angry, so his anger in response didn't matter as much. It contained the difficult non-conversation about Nathan—a conversation Emma was no longer certain she wanted to have.

But another unexpected surprise was waiting in the driveway of Emma's house. It was a car. Technically, it was an SUV. The night was too dark for her to tell immediately what color it was, but Emma instantly knew three things: It wasn't a Hall car, she'd never seen the car before, and the driver wasn't sitting behind the wheel. Even if her mother had somehow been talked into buying a new car—which they couldn't really afford at the moment—there's no way she wouldn't have spoken to Emma about it first.

"New car?" Nathan asked, when she'd been staring at the license plate for a little bit too long.

"No. It's not ours." Her left hand was numb. She hadn't held on to Nathan for most of the evening, but she hadn't recovered from the early contact, and she rubbed the numb hand absently. She took two steps up the drive, turned, and said, "I'll see you again tomorrow?"

He nodded. "I'll hitch a ride to school in the morning, as long as you promise you won't make me speak to anyone—I think I still owe Brady some money."

She laughed, but the laughter lost ground as she looked at the strange car. "I have to go talk to my mom."

He nodded, leaned in closer, and then stopped himself. She wanted to kiss him. She didn't want to go into the house with blue lips.

The lights were on. It was dark because it was November, not because it was late, although it was closing in on nine o'clock. Petal bounded into the house, his stump wagging in a way that implied he'd been homesick for *so* long. He couldn't be hungry—scratch that. He was always hungry, but he couldn't need food yet; she'd fed him dinner before they left for their disaster of a walk.

The lights in the living room were on. The lights in the dining room were on—but Emma paused in the arch that led to the dining room because she could actually see the tabletop. The perpetual stacks of paperwork that defined half her mother's home life had been removed. There were flowers—real flowers—in a slender crystal vase atop a table runner.

"Okay, Petal," Emma told her dog. "This is really creeping me out."

She looked at this new incarnation of a dining room. It could have walked straight out of *Coraline*. Clearly this didn't bother Petal as much as it bothered Emma. Worse, though, was the sudden sound of her mother's laughter. It came from the kitchen.

Emma's mother did not love the kitchen. Some of her friends were foodies, and while Mercy Hall enjoyed eating as much as the next person, she didn't enjoy the cooking; she often forgot ingredients or petty things like timers. Emma was a better cook than her mother. Brendan Hall had done most of the Hall family's food preparation in the early years, and he had started teaching Emma.

But that was undeniably her mother's laughter, and unless the kitchen had suffered the same transformation as the dining room, she was in the Hall family's kitchen. Emma hesitated for a long minute and then headed toward the sound of her mother's voice.

Mercy Hall was laughing. She was wearing, of all things, a dress, and faint traces of makeup. She looked about ten years younger than she normally did, which wasn't the shock—although admittedly, it was a bit surprising. The shock was the person who was standing beside her—standing *way* too close, in Emma's opinion. She'd never laid eyes on him before, but he was clearly laying eyes on her mother.

He looked up first. It figured. He also took a step back from her mother, who noticed and looked up as well. "Emma, you're home late," she said, the happy, open smile on her face fading into a more familiar expression of concern.

"We ran into a couple of friends," Emma said automatically.

"I was hoping you'd be home a little earlier. I wanted to introduce you to someone." She turned to the strange man. "This is Jon Madding. Jon, this is my daughter, Emma."

Emma tried to dredge up a smile. She might as well have kissed Nathan; her lips felt frozen anyway. She extended a hand as Jon Madding—what kind of a name was Madding, anyway?—stepped forward. He took her hand, shook it; she thought his grip was a little on the weak side. He was taller than average, but sort of balding, and he had a beard. Emma wasn't all that fond of beards.

"I'm so pleased to finally meet you," he said, with a broad smile. "Mercy's told me a lot about you; you must be so proud of your mother."

Emma smiled and nodded. "Oh, I am. So, how did you meet my mom?"

"At work."

"You work in the same office?"

"No, I work for one of her firm's clients. But we've crossed paths a number of times." He smiled at Mercy and added, "She's got a sharp tongue when she's under a deadline, but she focuses and she gets things done."

"Oh, don't say that to Emma," Mercy told him, reddening. "She has to live with me; she knows what I'm really like." She smiled at her daughter. Her smile was more genuine than Emma's, but because Emma *did* know her mother, she could see anxiety start to surface.

Keeping her own Hall standard smile plastered to her face, Emma asked, "How long have you known my mother?"

"Three years? Four? Mercy?"

"Four and a half."

"Your mother's never mentioned me? I'm hurt," he said, laughing.

"No, my mother's never mentioned you. I guess she's been too busy. Speaking of which, I've got a ton of homework to do, and I won't get it done if I don't start an hour ago." She turned, stopped, and turned back. "Nice to meet you, Jon."

"Maybe we'll get a chance to talk on a night you don't have homework," he replied, turning back to her mother.

Emma couldn't force herself to say something equally pleasant. She headed straight to her room, pausing only to lift her schoolbag from its perch in the hall.

"Em, that was unkind."

Her back was against her bedroom door; her eyes were closed. She didn't want to open them because she knew damn well who was speaking. "What was unkind?"

Her father was silent, as he often was when disappointed. It had been one of his most effective weapons in the intermittent war that was childhood; she'd forgotten just how much she'd hated it. She forced herself to look at her dad, afraid that she would see pain in his expression. It wasn't there; there was plenty of disappointment to make up for it, though.

"You *knew*," she said, voice sharpening.

He said nothing.

"Dad—you knew she was seeing someone."

"Em—"

"How long has this been going on? How long as she been seeing *Jon*?"

"I think that's a question you'll have to ask your mother. If it helps, this is the first time she's brought him home."

It didn't. It didn't help at all. Petal interrupted the conversation from the other side of the door, mostly by scratching and whining. She managed to pry herself off the door and let him in. He padded pretty much through her father's ghost and headed straight for the bed.

"You're not supposed to let him do that," her father observed; Petal was rolling in the duvet, having pulled off the counterpane he detested.

"I have more important things to worry about at the moment. Why won't you answer the question?"

"Because," he replied, folding his arms across his chest, "it's none of my business."

"P-pardon?"

"It's none of my business, Em. It's been eight years. I didn't come back here to watch Mercy wallow in grief and misery; I came because I wanted to know that you were both okay."

A peal of laughter rose in the distance. Mercy's. If Jon was laughing, his register was too low to carry as far. Emma hated it anyway.

"Have they—"

Brendan lifted a hand. "Do not even think of asking me that question. Don't ask your mother either."

"Because it's none of *my* business? Dad, in case it escaped your notice, I live here too."

"Yes, Emma, but he doesn't. You didn't tell your mother everything about Nathan; she didn't ask. Do her the favor of extending her the same respect."

Emma was silent. She was cold. She hadn't lied; she did have some homework. She sat at her desk, opened her bag, and pulled out her laptop. Flipping it open, she stared at a white, white screen with a menu bar somewhere on top of it.

Petal whined. He knew she was unhappy because he could clearly hear her side of the argument. He couldn't hear her dad's, and that was just as well, since Petal had never been fond of the Disappointment, either.

"Emma."

"I have homework, Dad."

"And you're getting so much of it done."

She swiveled in her chair. "What do you want me to say?"

"Your mom's dating choices aren't the only thing in your life at the moment," he replied. "To my mind, they're not even the most important."

"Thanks." She bit her lip, staring moodily at her screen.

"Give him a chance."

"I thought you said there were other things to talk about."

His silence was heavy, but after a moment he abandoned it. "What happened tonight?"

"Allison nearly died." She looked down at her hands; they were shaking, and the left was still numb. Her father walked over to her, reached for her hand, and then pulled back with a grimace.

"Sorry," he said. "Sometimes I forget."

"That you're dead?"

He nodded. "If I were alive, I'd be able to help, somehow."

But Emma shook her head. "If you were alive, you wouldn't be in my room, and even if you were, I wouldn't be talking to you about—about Allison. Or Necromancers. I'd be talking about homework."

"Jon wouldn't be here either."

". . . I know. Dad—"

"Sorry, that was unfair of me."

It bloody well was, but Emma suspected she deserved it. "Two Necromancers came after Ally and me while we were out walking Petal. Dad—they were going to just kill her."

He closed his eyes. "I wasn't there."

"No—but you can't be."

"Actually, I pretty much can; I don't have a lot else on my plate. But Nathan—"

She swallowed. Looked back at the screen that was only a little less white. It was true. She did want—she did *need*—some privacy.

"What happened to the Necromancers?"

"Eric and Chase killed them."

He looked away again. "You were there, for that?"

She nodded. "I didn't even mind it at the time."

"Emma—"

"Maybe this is how it starts. I didn't mind that they'd killed the Necromancers, and the Necromancers are human too. But if they hadn't, Allison would have died. Chase was pissed. He wants Allison out."

"Out?"

"Of my life. Of danger. I can't blame him. But if she's not going to leave me—and she won't—then I have to be able to do something if it happens again."

"You mean you have to learn how to kill."

She felt the shock of his words as they settled around her. She wanted to deny it, but she couldn't. She had no idea how far she'd be willing to go to save the life of someone she loved. She could imagine herself killing someone. But even thinking it, she could hear the sound of a knife hitting flesh and bone, and she almost stopped breathing.

He watched her, his eyes that noncolor of dead eyes, his expression painfully familiar. After a long moment, he breathed in, like the inverse of a sigh, and the line of his shoulders softened. This time, when he reached for her, he didn't hesitate, didn't pull back; he caught both of her hands in his.

He was *so* cold.

And then, for a moment, she was warm.

She wanted to cry, to tell him she didn't want or need this, not from him. But the truth was, at this very moment, she felt she *did*. She wasn't a child anymore, and she'd been nothing but a child the last time he'd hugged her when she was—as he put it—down. She let him fold her in his arms while she drained something from the touch that went both ways.

"Remember," he said, into her hair. "Remember, Emma. What Eric or his friends ask of you, what they think they want—it's not the only way. It's their way, but you're not them."

"I don't understand," she said, into his chest. "I don't understand what the Necromancers get out of this. I don't understand why they do what they do."

"No. But you will." His voice was softer.

In the morning, Jon's car was not in the drive. Emma knew; it was the first thing she checked when she crawled out of bed. She was grateful for small mercies. Large ones seemed to be beyond her, at the moment.

Her mother's door was closed, but that wasn't a big surprise; her mother and mornings weren't the best of friends. She wondered if her mother would drag herself out of bed if Jon had stayed, and the thought soured the optimism that lack of his car had produced. She climbed into the shower, hoping to wash the uglier bits of her mood down the drain.

Getting dressed, making breakfast, and feeding the animal that was dogging her heels, helped. Making coffee for her mother helped as well, because it was normal.

Her mother came down the stairs straightening her blouse and holding a pair of nylons in one hand. She looked as bleary-eyed as she normally did, but there was a thinness to her lips that was new. Or rarer, at any rate.

"Emma," she said, as she entered the kitchen.

"Coffee," her daughter replied, handing her mother a large mug with a chipped handle. "Blueberries are on the table with the granola. There's milk as well, but we need more."

"I'll get it on the way home from work. Emma—"

The doorbell rang. Emma had timed breakfast and coffee with a merciless eye toward the very accurate clock because she knew Michael would show up at her door, the way he did every day on the way to school. It was precisely 8:10 in the morning. Emma kissed her mother on the cheek and said, "I've got to run, sorry breakfast was late."

"Emma—"

She answered the door; Michael was mobbed by Petal—if one dog didn't normally constitute a mob, Petal tried really hard to make up for it—and Emma grabbed her hat, her scarf, her gloves.

Mercy knew better than to start an argument—or a discussion—when Michael was on the clock, as it were. "Will you be in tonight?"

"Tonight? Did you forget I'm going to Ally's for dinner?"

Mercy grimaced. "Clearly."

"I won't be home too late after that. Have a great day at work," she added, shrugging her shoulders into her coat and heading out the door.

Allison's mother came to the door to see them off, and she had a very open, very obvious expression of parental worry etched into the corners of her eyes and mouth. Allison kept a cheerful smile more or less fixed to her face as she turned to wave, but to her friends it looked hideously forced; she only relaxed it once they'd turned the corner, which Emma did as quickly as possible.

"You can stop smiling now. If your face freezes like that, it's going to be scary."

Allison's grimace was far more natural. "I told her as much of nothing as I could get away with. But apparently *I* look worried. Or not cheerful enough. And she noticed the bruising."

Emma wilted as Allison's jaw snapped shut. Michael, however, said, "What bruising?" in exactly the wrong tone of voice.

Emma and Allison exchanged a look that Michael couldn't have missed had he been sleeping. And while Allison was a better liar than

Michael, it was only by chance; anyone over the age of three who was still breathing was, after all.

It was—it had always—been tempting to treat Michael like a child; it was also both unfair and a mistake. But it was Allison who made the executive decision as they walked the rest of the way to school.

"Emma and I took Petal for a walk last night," she told him quietly. "And we met two Necromancers just outside the cemetery."

Michael's eyes widened. After a moment, they narrowed. "They hurt you?"

"They tried."

"Bruises don't—"

"Yes, they hurt me—but not badly. I'm just bruised, and it's not a big bruise, either." The executive decision had clearly faltered.

Emma picked up the slack. "They tried to kill her."

It was Michael's turn to miss a step, but when he righted himself, he'd stopped walking.

"Talk while we walk, Michael; you'll be late if you don't."

For once, the panicky prospect of being late didn't move him, much. "What happened?"

"Eric and Chase showed up."

He took a deep breath and began to walk again. "They killed the Necromancers?"

"They did." Emma watched him out of the corner of an eye; Michael didn't like violence, much. To be fair, neither did Emma or Allison.

This particular violence, however, didn't shatter his equilibrium; he nodded as if he hadn't heard. "Emma will need to learn how to defend herself," he finally said.

The girls exchanged a glance; this one had higher eyebrows.

"But I guess she'll have to be careful not to—not to be like them."

"Emma could never—" Allison began, hotly.

"But, Allison, they couldn't have started out that way either, could they?"

"Why not?"

Michael looked confused. "When they were born—"

Allison lifted a hand. "I'm sorry," she said quickly. "You're probably right. They probably weren't like that to start, but it doesn't matter; they're like that *now*, and Emma's *not*."

"Of course she's not." His look of confusion deepened.

Poor Michael. Emma caught his arm. "Ally and Chase had a very loud fight about me last night. Pretty much about this."

"Oh." He turned to Allison. "I'm sorry."

Michael wasn't Chase; Allison couldn't be enraged at him if she spent all day trying. "It's fine. We're going to Eric's after school today, though." She paused. "Do you want to come with us?"

It wasn't clear that Michael had even heard the question until they reached the entrance of Emery. They were used to this. "I think I would like to go with you," he told them, "if Eric doesn't mind."

"I'm sure Eric won't mind," Emma replied.

"Are you *crazy*?"

The lunchtime cafeteria was, as usual, loud enough to deafen—but not apparently loud enough to completely blanket Eric's voice. People—a handful of whom knew Emma fairly well—swiveled in the lunch line to stare. Emma pretended he was shouting into someone else's ear and kept both hands on her tray as she headed to the cashier.

Eric recovered pretty quickly and followed, but he'd clearly lost all appetite for food. Since Michael was waiting at the emptiest table in the cafeteria, Emma slowed down to allow Eric to catch up with her.

"Michael is *not* Allison."

"If it weren't for Michael, I'd have disappeared at Amy's party. I know he seems like a child or a simpleton to you," she added, "but he's not. He's capable of very complex thought and action—just not complex *social* action. It's just going to bother him, and he'll have no outlet for it, otherwise."

"How, exactly, is it going to bother him? Never mind. Let me guess. You told him what happened."

"We didn't plan on telling him, but it came up while we were walking to school. Sorry."

"Emma—"

"He's been a part of this since it started."

"I get that—but this isn't a goddamn party. Allison almost died. Michael will be at risk in the same way. I don't want to be responsible for—"

"You're not. Tell him the risks—when we get to your place—and let him decide. He may decide to bow out; there's a lot of stuff he won't join in on because he doesn't like the possible consequences. But let him make that decision. He's not four; you don't have to make it for him."

Eric fell silent; it didn't last. "He's not four," he said, speaking through clenched teeth, "but he still needs to be walked to school every morning."

Eric had saved Emma's life not once, but twice—and at the moment she wanted to slap him anyway. She couldn't recall being so angry with him before, not even when he'd discovered the truth about Andrew Copis and hadn't cared enough to try to help the child. Her hands were full of tray, and she wasn't close enough to the table to set it down. She embedded the edges into both of her palms and kept walking instead, trying to keep the momentary expression of murderous rage off her face, because Michael was watching.

Eric didn't seem to notice; he was looking pretty angry himself. That much anger at a cafeteria table wasn't comfortable; Allison, watching them approach, fell silent, which was unfortunate because she'd been halfway through a sentence to Michael. Michael looked at Allison's less than familiar expression, then looked at Emma and Eric.

"Is something wrong?" he asked.

"No," Emma said curtly, as Eric said, "Yes."

They exchanged a glare, but Eric still waited until Emma was seated before he took a seat himself. This took about four minutes longer than usual and was followed by a tense silence, because the sound of chewing didn't carry far in the uncarpeted acoustics of the cafeteria.

"There's nothing wrong with you," Emma finally said. "It's our problem."

Eric said nothing, but he said it loudly. Allison started to push her food around her plate. When she wasn't angry herself, she was quite uncomfortable around angry people.

Rescue came from the outside. Two of Michael's D&D friends—Connell and Cody—saved them by descending on the table and taking seats on either side of Michael, which forced Allison to move over. While they didn't have Michael's autism spectrum diagnosis, they were frequently socially clueless; silent, uncomfortable anger didn't hit their radars at all. They were deep in the middle of a technical discussion about a game of some sort, which involved cards, numbers, and strategies that seemed far more like math and statistics than fun to Emma. Michael was drawn to the magnet of the game, though, and as he began to enter the state of animated compulsion that was most of his focused discussion, Emma felt her jaw relaxing.

She still couldn't have this conversation in front of Michael; she wasn't certain she could have it at all at the moment. She was angry enough that her food now tasted like sawdust—undercooked sawdust; it caught in her throat.

"He's wrong, you know," a familiar voice said. She looked up; standing just over Michael like a slightly ratty Angel stood Nathan. He was smiling down at the top of Michael's head, and that smile deepened around the edges as he met Emma's eyes. "Michael's not a child. In some ways, he's more responsible than most of us."

Emma felt part of her anger cool. "I know he's wrong. It's just that—what if something happens—" Allison nudged her under the table, and she realized that she was, to all intents and purposes, talking to thin air, which wasn't something she wanted to be seen doing. She grimaced as Nathan laughed.

Nathan had never treated Michael like a child. It was one of the first things she'd noticed about him and one of the first things she'd appreciated. She bent her head over her lunch as Nathan began to walk around the cafeteria, occasionally passing through people as he looked around, hands in pockets that looked physical but couldn't be.

She wanted to leave lunch behind and walk with him, to hear what he had to say because Nathan was perceptive, and he could afford to be blunt at the moment; no one else would hear him. No one but Eric.

She glanced at Eric and saw that he was watching not Nathan, but her. "I'm not wrong," he told her softly. "It's not his age. That's not what it's about."

"You didn't say that about Allison."

"No. I didn't." He looked at Allison and then offered Emma a pained, lopsided grin. "She'd've killed me."

"I would have, too," Ally said.

Emma accepted this gesture of partial surrender. She was still angry, but what had she expected? Eric didn't *know* Michael; he didn't know what Michael was capable of. He *did* know that the posse of girls who'd all drifted from the same school kept an eye out for Michael; he *did* know that the teachers made allowances for Michael's particular peculiarities.

He could learn the rest. She told herself that firmly. He could learn.

But she looked past him, through the crowds in the cafeteria that were slowly dwindling as the lunch hour passed, and she thought that Nathan had never had to learn; he'd just known. He'd just accepted.

AFTER SCHOOL, Allison and Michael met Emma at her locker. They walked to Eric's in silence; there was enough snow on the ground that Allison regretted her decision not to wear boots. Emma spoke very little, and Allison was too annoyed at Chase to try to carry a conversation without a lot of help.

Annoyance was better, by far, than worry. Worry was better than all-out fear. She held on to her anger as if it were a talisman, noting that Emma wasn't walking beside them; she was trailing behind. Michael, thinking, didn't notice. Allison knew that Emma wasn't alone.

Michael didn't. He accepted that the impossible had happened: Emma could see the dead. But he accepted it because he'd seen it himself, and he had no other reason to doubt his sanity. In that, he was practical. He was almost unswerving. If Michael believed something to be true, he had all the facts lined up, and it was nearly impossible to move him; social censure certainly couldn't do it, and that was the lever most people tried to use.

"Michael," Emma called.

Allison tapped his shoulder to get his attention, and he turned. So did she.

Standing beside Emma, left hand in her right, stood Nathan, conspicuously dressed for summer when all the rest of the gang was in heavy November clothing.

"Hey, Michael," Nathan said, when Michael failed to say anything.

Michael nodded. He glanced at Emma, who was watching him with an uncertain smile on her face. "I promised you you'd be the first to see Nathan when he came back."

Technically, she had broken that promise, but best friends didn't count.

"Did Emma find you?" Michael asked, after a long thinking moment had passed. The sun was heading to the horizon, and it wasn't getting any warmer.

"I found Emma," he replied.

Emma began to move, and Nathan came with her.

"Have you come to take her away?" Michael asked.

Emma's eyes widened in the silence that followed. Allison started to answer, but no words came out of her open mouth.

Nathan, however, shook his head. To Nathan, it was one of Michael's questions: the kind no one else would ask, even if they were thinking it. Some people found it off-putting; Nathan had always accepted it entirely at face value. It was one of the things that Allison had respected. Nathan wasn't Mr. Popularity; he was low key, but he got along with pretty much everyone.

"Emma's alive," Nathan said quietly. "Just like the two of you. I wouldn't wish being dead on anyone I loved."

Michael slowly relaxed. "What is it like?"

"Being dead?" Nathan asked.

Michael nodded.

Nathan frowned. "It's hard to explain," he finally said. It sounded lame to Allison, which surprised her. Nathan didn't generally try to protect Michael by simplifying or hiding facts. For one thing, it was condescending, and for another, it didn't work. Michael was young for his age in a lot of ways, but he had the base practicality of a much older person. He was certainly more practical than Allison on a bad day.

"Do you remember what it's like to be alive?" Case in point.

"Oh, yes."

"How is dead different, then?"

Nathan grimaced. From the expression on his face, he was trying to decide whether or not he wanted to answer the question; he wouldn't lie to Michael, but he had very few problems declining to answer Michael's questions if he felt they crossed a line. To Michael, the idea that a line could be crossed wasn't natural; but he accepted it, although a gentle reminder was often in order. To be fair, there were very, very few questions that could offend Michael and very few he wouldn't answer.

"Dead is a bit like sleeping," Nathan finally said.

"Sleeping's not bad," was Michael's hesitant almost-question.

"Not regular sleep. Have you ever had an operation? In a hospital?"

Michael shook his head. Hospitals were a source of morbid fascination, as long as there was no chance whatsoever that Michael himself would be the patient.

Nathan grimaced. "Wisdom teeth? Did you have yours pulled yet?"

"Not everyone needs to have theirs removed," Allison added quickly, just in case.

Michael, it appeared, was still in possession of those teeth.

"Well," Nathan continued, aware that as an example this was going to fall a little flat. "It's like that. You go under. You wake up confused. It takes a while to get your bearings, and the waking is cold—very cold—and unpleasant. Once you're awake, once you realize where you are and why you're here, it's fine."

"So you're fine, now?"

Silence.

Emma, who'd been watching Michael, turned to look at Nathan; had they not been walking side by side, Allison might have missed it.

"You don't stay awake, do you?" Emma asked, in the quiet Hall voice that was loud in every way but volume.

Nathan glanced at her, then away.

She squeezed his hand. "Nathan."

Without looking at her he said, "No." It was almost inaudible.

Michael started to speak again; this time, Ally ran interference, leaving the question in Emma's hands.

"Do you get any choice in when you—when you fall asleep again?"

"Em—"

"Answer me, Nathan. Please, answer me."

"You already know the answer."

"Only because you won't say it."

"Em, if I don't want to say it, and you know what it is I don't want to say, why is it important that I say it at all?"

Emma fell silent then.

But Michael said, "Why is it important that you don't?"

The conversation came to a halt not because it was finished—although as conversations went, Nathan's refusal to answer the question had kind of killed it—but because Eric's house was now in view. In the daylight, it looked like a perfectly normal house. Nothing about it hinted at the occupations of those who lived within, but then again, did it ever, really?

Nathan extracted his hand. Michael's frown indicated that Michael, at least, could no longer see him.

"Is Nathan still here?" he asked Emma, as they approached Eric's door.

Emma smiled stiffly and nodded. She pushed the doorbell and stepped back.

Before Michael could speak again, someone opened the door. It was, to her surprise, Ernest—called the old man by Eric and Chase when he wasn't actually present—looking much more modern than he usually did. The rustic and ancient jacket was gone; the button-down shirt had joined it. He was older than Emma's father would have been, had he lived, older than her mother. He wasn't as old as some of the teachers, nearing retirement, who taught classes at Emery.

Emma had met him a grand total of once. He'd been on the wrong end of a gun he'd been pointing at her; he'd have fired it, too, if Eric hadn't been standing stubbornly between them. She knew, however, that he was responsible for keeping information about both the Necromancers and their hunters from spreading; he could—and did—move corpses and somehow keep them out of sight of local authorities.

At the moment, he looked like a normal parent, not a man who dealt with bodies and owned at least one gun.

"Is something wrong?" His question was almost the definition of curmudgeonly.

It was Emma who said, "You look—you look very different."

He raised a brow. "Do *not* ask me. If you want to pester someone with trivial questions, you have my leave to grill Margaret."

Emma dared a glance past him into the empty hall. Margaret Henney was one of the dead; a woman who had died sometime in her fifties, and who had the distinct advantage of intimate understanding of Necromancers, because she'd once *been* one.

If she was giving Ernest fashion advice, she was doing it on her own time; the hall behind Ernest was empty.

Chase was in the living room, or what passed for the living room; he was arranging logs in the fireplace, but took a chair when they entered the room, slumping into the cushions as if he weighed about three times more than he should. He wasn't wearing a jacket, although studded black leather adorned the arms of the room's largest chair; he had nothing to do with his hands, so he fidgeted, in silence, with his keys.

Chase kept glancing at Ernest, as though he was either suspicious or expected a tongue-lashing at any minute; he wasn't entirely comfortable.

Eric, on the other hand, was doing something practical; he was lighting a fire in the fireplace. Allison was surprised; many homes had fake fireplaces or none at all. She preferred none; she couldn't see the point in a fireplace that didn't actually burn things.

"I suppose smoking is out of the question," Ernest said.

Michael's brows rose; Allison grimaced. Emma, however, said, "We'd really prefer if you didn't, but it's your house."

"Technically, it's Eric's house."

"He doesn't let *me* smoke here," Chase pointed out.

"You don't have to deal with the two of you," was Ernest's more acid reply.

Chase muttered something under his breath.

"We need to talk about self-defense." Eric, satisfied with the stability of the small fire burning between the new logs, rose. "The reason we wear these jackets," he said, lifting one of the uglier ones that lay over the arm of a chair, "are the studs." He hefted the black leather blob in both hands and tossed it to Allison.

Allison's eyes widened. "This is heavy."

"There's a chain of iron sewed into the hem in the lining. It's a bitch on the fabric; we replace a lot of linings. If you look at the collar—"

She was already turning it up.

"That would have effectively stopped the problem you had last night. You might have felt uncomfortable; there might have been a tightness about your throat, but the iron works to prevent the grip of Necromantic magic. Silver cuts it better, but in the case of silver, the contact has to be direct.

"It's not much in the way of armor," Eric continued. "It's not meant to be bulletproof—and bullets can be a problem. It'll slow down a small knife; it won't stop a sword."

"No one carries swords," Michael pointed out.

"Necromancers don't, no. They don't carry many knives, either. If you see a Necromancer pull a knife, you know he—or she—hasn't reached the height of their power yet. But the knives are still a danger if you don't know how to fight."

Chase snorted and said something rude under his breath, which caused Allison's hands to turn into white-knuckled fists. She didn't respond in any other way because she was practical: She *didn't* know how to fight, and knew it.

"So a getup like this," Eric continued, as if Chase didn't exist, "is meant for the heavy duty Necromancers who usually hunt us. They don't send out the scrubs when they're looking for us."

"We can't wear these in school," Allison said. She handed the jacket to Michael, who'd been staring at it with some fascination. He touched the interior fabric and relaxed. Michael was sensitive to weaves and cloth; he couldn't, for instance, stand real wool and never wore it.

"No. We're hoping we never face a Necromancer in the school."

Emma turned widening eyes on Allison, who looked grim. Just grim.

"They don't want to be discovered," Eric told her. "And we don't want them to *be* discovered either. If they know their cover is blown, they generally feel they only have one recourse."

"Kill all the witnesses?" Michael asked.

"Yes."

"Can they?"

"Yes. I don't think they could take out the entire city of Toronto. They can—and will—take out dozens of people if necessary."

"One school's worth of students?" Emma asked, voice tight.

Eric said nothing.

Chase opened his mouth, and Allison glared at him; he snapped it shut. It was audible.

"The Queen of the Dead isn't one of the dead," Eric finally said. "She's alive. Anything living can be killed. If she destroyed a city or a large town, a lot of people would suddenly be looking for her."

"So the City of the Dead is a physical place?"

Eric nodded.

"Where is it located?"

Eric and Chase exchanged a glance. "It doesn't have a fixed location."

This answer confused Michael, which was fair; it confused Emma and Allison as well. On the other hand, Michael was the only one to press the issue. "How can it be a physical city without a fixed location?"

"Look, Michael—" Eric caught Emma's pointed stare, and ran his hands through his hair. "All of you already know too much. If she thought you knew this, she *would* nuke your city just to make sure you couldn't share the information. I understand you need to know things. Understand that there are some things no one living should know. If you ever have the misfortune to visit the City of the Dead, you'll have all the answers you need."

"I doubt that," Allison said quietly.

Eric grimaced. "I didn't say you'd be able to do anything useful with them. Necromancers can travel to the City of the Dead. In very rare cases, they can travel elsewhere, but someone at the other end has to have a *lot* of power prepared as a terminus. The Queen could anchor that kind of transport, but I don't think many of the others could. They can open gates *to* the city—but even that requires a lot of power, and some preparation on the part of the Necromancers. It's also harder to do in the presence of iron; it's hard to do in a building with, say, steel-beam construction. If the gate is aligned properly, it will work, but modern construction makes it more challenging. Again, it's not trivial."

"Then the two men—"

"Yes. They didn't intend to fly home; they intended to grab you and run. The portal wouldn't have to be open for long. If they had to leave a functional door between here and their City, they'd have to find a lot of the dead on very short notice."

"They can see the dead."

"Yes—but the dead who have the most potential often don't want to be seen." He hesitated again, then looked at Emma. "The Queen of the Dead can find the dead if she needs them; she's extraordinarily sensitive."

"And powerful," Michael added.

"Yes." Eric lifted another jacket and tossed it to Allison; she'd passed the first jacket to Michael, who had let it pool in his lap as he focused on the conversation. "Try it on."

Before Allison could answer, he picked up a third jacket and tossed it to Emma. "You too. How does it feel?" Eric asked Emma.

"Heavy. Kinda ugly."

Chase snorted and corrected her. "It's hideously ugly, but we don't ask Eric for fashion advice unless we *want* to look like Goth clowns. That's not what he's asking."

Emma frowned. The frown deepened.

"Can you still see Nathan?" Eric asked, correctly divining the source of her surprise.

She nodded. "He's—he looks less solid."

Eric said, "There's almost nothing you could do that would make the dead invisible to you."

Emma recovered quickly, for Emma. "Could we get a less ugly jacket?"

"Sure," Chase said. "But by the time we finished with it—or *you* finished with it, because you're going to be doing some of the damn work—it'd be almost as ugly. I never buy decent jackets anymore— hurts too much to ruin them."

"Allison?"

She was less amused by his rationale than Emma, but she did try the jacket on. It was *heavy*. It was heavy and about two sizes too large. But she slid her arms into loose sleeves, and the very ugly jacket let gravity pull it more or less straight.

"Well?" she asked Emma.

"I think it looks better on you than it does on Chase."

Chase opened his mouth, looked at Allison, and frowned. After a pause of several seconds, he said, "Damn it, she's right."

Emma's brows rose. "You agreed with something I said?"

"You've got a better eye than Eric. For fashion."

"And friends. Don't forget the friends."

"I've never criticized your taste in friends—except for Eric."

Allison cleared her throat, loudly, before he could continue. "Better on me than on Chase isn't really saying much. How bad does it look?"

Emma winced. "We can try a better jacket once we can figure out—"

"You need some kind of leather," Chase said, voice flat. "Thicker is better. No kid glove leather, no Napa—you'll rip the coat to shreds trying to put it all together. You might be able to get away with trench coats. We don't use 'em."

"Why?"

"Too cumbersome. When we need to move, we need to move; we can't afford the hems getting caught on any protrusions. I think they'd work for you."

Allison removed the jacket. "Is this all?"

"Hell no. We're just getting started."

An hour later, they were wearing necklaces of silver, with weighted pendants that were some combination of silver and iron. The pendants themselves were simple but heavy, and hard to hide under anything other than a loose knit or blouse. Emma asked if they could use a longer chain; Eric shook his head. Chase snorted and pointed out that it was the *pendant* that was important, and if silver could be made into a comfortable choker, that was best.

"So that stupid dog collar you were wearing wasn't ancient, bad Goth?"

"No. Don't look at me like that; I make sacrifices like this all the time. We've got rings; the rings are easy. Wear 'em. They're not there to protect your hands; they're there in case something like last night happens again."

"If I'd been wearing these rings, I could have pulled the—the tentacle away?"

"It's not guaranteed but you'd have had a much better chance."

"Why do silver and iron work against Necromancy?" Michael asked. He accepted the weight of the jacket, accepted the necklace, but cast a dubious glance at the rings. Michael didn't like having things on his hands. Even gloves in the winter, although he'd wear them if it was cold enough.

Chase shrugged. "Does it matter? They work."

"It matters to Michael," Allison said quietly.

Chase opened his mouth and closed it before more words could fall out. "Eric," he said, "it's all yours."

Eric grimaced. "We don't know, Michael. We weren't given a lot of explanations. We were told that it disrupts Necromantic magic—but not why. It made no sense to me the first time, but it worked. It wasn't complete negation; I'm not sure that exists unless you're a Necromancer yourself.

"I'd explain it if I had the answer. I don't. Old Man?"

Ernest, who'd been silent throughout, shrugged. "It's something to do with earth, with the bones of the earth."

Which made about as much sense to Michael as it did to Allison. Emma turned to Michael. "They can't explain it themselves. But I think we need to trust them."

Michael *did* trust them. He didn't understand them, and lack of understanding always made following instructions vastly more difficult. If you could explain something to Michael, he had no trouble following orders. It's what made people so difficult for him. A smile did not mean the same thing to two different people; laughter didn't either.

He looked at the rings again. Emma looked at them as well; they were *not* subtle. They were large, thick, and on the ugly side.

"If these are mostly silver, is there any reason we can't find silver rings of our own to wear?"

Chase rolled his eyes. "Something is better than nothing," he conceded. "These have the advantage of being both free and heavy."

"Probably their only advantages. Did you make these?"

"The old man did."

Emma grimaced and offered Ernest an apology. Ernest was looking wintery and less than amused. "It hasn't escaped my attention," he said, although he was looking at Chase, "that some people find my work less than aesthetically pleasant."

Michael took two rings. Allison took two. Emma sighed and took two as well; there were dozens, after all.

"Is there anything else we can learn in an evening?"

"No. Not in a single evening. These are the most useful things we can give you at the moment. If you're amenable, we can begin to train you in basic self-defense. But as Eric has pointed out, the Necromancers don't generally resort to brawls and physical beatings to kill people. They will—and they have in the past—but it is not their preferred method." Ernest rose. "In other circumstances, we wouldn't remain here. Part of the ability to survive Necromancers who come hunting is not being present when they arrive. We move."

"A lot," Chase added.

Allison started to shrug the jacket off her shoulders, but Chase caught it before it could fall. "Promise to wear it home," he said, pulling it back into place by the collar. "Wear it to school. Wear it shopping. I know it's not what you'd normally wear—but wear it."

She met his gaze and let her arms fall to her sides.

"Give me your phone," he said.

She frowned. After a moment, she handed Chase her phone.

Chase turned it on and fiddled with it for a bit. "It's a speed dial," he said. He called his own phone from hers. "If something or someone looks suspicious, call. I don't care if nothing comes of it—*call*. Eric and I patrol most nights." He hesitated, exhaled, and finally said, "You're not a Necromancer-in-waiting; they won't have an easy way to find you if they don't know what they're looking for. But we killed two, and there was either one or two more on that plane with them."

Ernest surprised everyone by ordering pizza. It was really strange to be in a living room with paper plates, cups, and pizza, discussing the ways in which total strangers would try to kill them, but their lives had been strange since October.

They agreed to meet up at Eric's in three nights, provided no immediate emergencies prevented it. Emma and Allison walked Michael home; he was silent, although he was fidgeting with the rings on his fingers. Emma was almost surprised he'd chosen to wear them.

But Michael had seen the Necromancers in action. Michael knew they'd tried to kill Allison. He hadn't been there when Allison had almost died, but that didn't change the facts. Being utterly defenseless against a known danger was a greater threat than having things encircling his fingers.

Emma was tense; she was nervous. She couldn't help it. But they looked so *ridiculous* in these jackets, she had to laugh. Ally, seeing the direction of her gaze, started to chuckle as well. Michael didn't. He knew them well enough to know they weren't laughing *at* him, but he honestly didn't see anything worth laughing about.

"Does this make me look like Chase?" he asked, pointing at his own jacket.

Allison, by dint of will, didn't laugh louder. "No. Maybe a little more like Eric. No one else looks like Chase."

"It's his hair," Emma added. She glanced at Nathan, who was smiling in Michael's direction.

Nathan had hardly spoken a word for most of the evening. He'd stayed, as he'd promised, but he'd looked distinctly uncomfortable—and that wasn't Nathan. She wanted to talk to him, but it was cold enough tonight that she didn't want to hold his hand so Michael and Allison could also participate.

She waited, instead, walking Michael home and dropping Allison off next. Ally wasn't happy about the order.

"Eric and Chase are close," Michael told her before he entered his house.

Allison immediately swiveled to look over her shoulder; Emma, squinting into the darkness, couldn't see them. "They are?"

Michael nodded. "I think Chase is worried about you."

"Chase isn't worried about me," Allison said, with more than her usual heat.

Michael frowned. "He isn't?"

"He is," Emma said. "Allison doesn't like the *way* he's worried, that's all."

"Why?"

She bit back a sigh. It was Michael. "Chase doesn't think Allison should spend time with me anymore, because of what happened. He doesn't think it's safe."

"He doesn't want you to be friends?"

"No, he really doesn't. He thinks if I were a good friend, I would stop seeing Allison until this was all over."

"But . . . but when is it going to be over?"

That, of course, was the million-dollar question. Emma squared her shoulders. "Chase isn't completely wrong." Before Allison could interrupt, she continued. "It would be safest for Allison if she wasn't with me. The Necromancers don't want to kill *me* yet. My life's not in danger. But Ally—"

"Wants to help you."

"Yes, Michael. Yes, she does." Emma smiled at Allison.

"Then it's her choice."

"Exactly," Allison said. "If it makes you feel any better, he's not all that thrilled that you're involved, either."

"He doesn't want Emma to have any friends."

"No," Allison agreed uncharitably.

CHAPTER
SIX

EMERY'S CAFETERIA SOUNDED LIKE a human hive. Stray syllables and the sound of sharp laughter permeated the buzz of too many conversations, but as most of those conversations weren't directed Emma's way, they could be safely ignored. Connell and Cody bracketed an animated Michael. Allison, beside Emma, was absorbed with Chase, and given the color of her cheeks, their conversation wasn't one Emma wanted to join. Eric was eating—slowly and meticulously as he usually did.

She could now look at Allison without thinking about Necromantic murderers, but it was hard. Allison hated guilt when it wasn't her own, and Emma's guilt was a burden; she tried to keep it to herself. Tried not to think about what Chase had said so often. Tried even harder to believe he was wrong. Friendship with Emma wasn't a death sentence.

"Lunch not edible?" Eric asked.

"It's not likely to kill," she replied. She turned to smile at him. He wasn't smiling back.

"We think we've got a few weeks in the clear before things get really messy."

She wanted to quibble with his definition of not messy, because the past few days defined fear for her. She said nothing. "Emma—"

She waited, hearing the start of a question in the way he said her name. The rest of the question failed to emerge. It was clear why; Allison's sudden increase in volume would have swamped it.

"And *I* think Emma would find it useful *as well*." Allison had been two bites into lunch, and given the set of her lips, no more food was going to enter her mouth.

"Emma isn't the *target*. She doesn't need to know this shit. She's—" He stopped and glared across the table at Eric. Emma guessed Eric had just kicked him sharply in the shins.

"Not the *place*, idiot," Eric said, with a friendly, casual smile. Given his tone of voice, it was forced. It didn't *look* forced.

"Fine," Allison said. She stood, abandoning lunch.

Michael stood as well. He had, of course, been listening. He could listen to two streams of conversation without losing either if both were interesting, although people who weren't used to him were often surprised or offended when he inserted himself into the conversation with no warning.

Allison, however, turned to Michael before he could leave the table. "Chase and I are going to have a fight. It will not be pleasant. I don't mind if you come, but—it's going to be loud and we're both going to be angry."

Michael sat down.

"Smart," Eric said, as he moved to follow Allison. He was surprised when Emma caught his hand.

"Sit down," she told him, smiling exactly the way he had.

"You don't want to leave Allison alone with Chase. He has an ugly temper."

"Are you saying he's going to hurt her?" Emma demanded.

"He has an ugly temper."

"Ally has a temper. He is not going to steamroll her. Eric?"

He stared at her for a minute and then turned to see Allison and Chase leaving the cafeteria by the back doors. "I'm not sure about this."

"You don't have to be. She's not your best friend. She *is* mine, though, and I *am* certain. Look, she's embarrassed when she loses her temper. Something about your friend makes her lose her temper. I think, overall, she'd be happier if we weren't there to witness it."

Eric sat. "I don't understand women," he said.

"You and fifty percent of the species."

By the time they reached a spot in the schoolyard that could be considered private, Chase's mouth was a compressed line that was white around the edges. He'd folded his arms across his chest and drawn himself up to his full height. He did not look friendly. When they stopped walking, he planted his feet half a yard apart and stared down at her.

Allison was not nearly as still or self-contained when she was angry. Most of the things that made her angry were things that embarrassed her. No one liked to think of themselves as small-minded or jealous or petty; Allison was not an exception. Or maybe she was; her sense of self-respect and consideration ran roughshod over that temper on most days.

There was nothing to repress her anger now. She tried. She tried to tell herself that she didn't *know* what Chase's life was like. She didn't know what she'd be like if she had to live every day knowing that random strangers with bigger weapons would be trying to kill her. But looking at him now, the little voice that struggled for civility was swamped.

"Well?" he demanded, as she struggled to find the right words.

"I know you don't trust Emma," she said, keeping her voice even and quiet with difficulty. "But *I* do."

Chase didn't reply.

"Chase, she risked her life to save a child who was *already dead*. She gave his mother a chance to find a little bit of peace. She had no reason to do it—she had nothing to gain and everything to lose."

He said nothing, but he said it loudly.

"You're afraid she has power. Fine. She has power. What good does it do her? If she'd understood what she's capable of doing, saving Andrew Copis wouldn't have been so risky. Putting power in Emma's hands is never going to be a bad thing!"

"You don't understand," he said.

"Then *make* me understand. I'm not going to take it on faith that she's going to become something evil and heartless. I'll take some things on faith—but not this. Yes, you have experience with Necromancers. But never as friends. Never as *people*. I *don't* have your experience—but I know Emma Hall. She is never going to become someone who kills because it's convenient. She's never going to be someone who undervalues life because we all wind up dead in the end.

"And I'm always going to be her friend. I want to learn how to be—how to be less helpless. I don't want to walk to my *own* death."

"If you cared about that, you'd leave her alone. Your life wouldn't *be* in danger if she wasn't your friend. If she cared about you more, she'd acknowledge that."

Allison's hands were fists. "So you want us to abandon each other. Me because I'm a coward and Emma because she's afraid she'll lose me anyway, and it'll be her fault."

"That's not what I'm saying—"

"Damn it, Chase—it *is*. It is what you're saying." She knew she was flushed; she always flushed when she was emotional. She hated it more than ever today. Because the ugly truth was that she *was* afraid. She'd had nightmares for two nights, and she found herself thinking about Necromancers and the thin line between living and dying when she wasn't actively thinking about something else. She could still feel the vine tightening around her throat. She could still feel the bruises it had left.

And she knew—she *knew*—that Emma was *this* close to retreating. To shutting herself off. To walking away from her friends for *their own* sake. She wanted Emma to walk away from Michael, but she wouldn't—couldn't—say it. Michael wasn't a child; he could make his own decisions, just as Allison could.

She held her ground as he took a step forward. Held it, getting angrier, as he took another. She stood entirely in his shadow by the time he'd stopped moving; there was almost no space between them. It would serve him right if she punched him in the stomach.

"I didn't start out as a hunter. Unlike Necromancers, we're not born that way. We train. We train hard." He lowered his hands to his sides. "We all have stories. Some of them involve the deaths of entire communities. Most of us were lucky; we only lost our families." He swallowed. His Adam's apple bobbed. She stared at it; she couldn't lift her gaze to meet his eyes.

"Do you know why I survived?" His voice was a whisper.

"No."

"She wanted to send a message. She wanted to send a message to someone, and I was it. I wasn't a Necromancer. I wouldn't be killed on sight. I watched, Ally." His hands were fists; his shoulders drew in toward his body, robbing him of inches of height. His skin was always pale, but this was different. "I watched. I screamed. I begged. Not for myself. For them. For my parents, my sisters, my little brother. They killed the dogs," he added. "Even the dogs.

"The only person they didn't kill was me. You understand why I'm a hunter."

She nodded. She did.

"I don't care if I die. I spent two years caring very much. But I couldn't kill myself. I couldn't do it. If I die killing them, I'll be grateful." He grimaced. "I have no idea why I'm telling you this."

"You want me to understand what Necromancers mean to you."

"Is that why?"

"Yes."

"I wasn't that keen on the rest of humanity, either. I don't care for most of the hunters, but at least I understand them. I work with Eric because I want to see him kill her."

"Her?"

"The Queen of the Dead." He ran a hand through his hair; it was shaking. "I wanted to kill her myself, but I'm not that lucky. In the end, I'll settle for second best. I don't want to care about other people's lives. I'm done with it."

She felt awkward and self-conscious; her anger had deserted her, and she couldn't claw it back. In its absence, she was shaking as much as Chase, and for far less reason.

"Chase?"

"What?"

"Be done with it." She swallowed. "Stay done with it, if you have to. Leave Emma alone. I'm not a child. It's my decision. I understand the risks, now."

"You would have died if we hadn't been there."

"I *know* that." She exhaled. "You hate yourself because you couldn't do anything for the people you loved. But you want *me* to accept that *I* can't—without even letting me try."

He stared at her, arrested. "I'm not—I'm not saying that."

"How is it different?" She had to look away from his expression again.

He stared at her for a long, uncomfortable moment. "I'll try."

"You'll try?"

"I'll try. I can't promise anything. I don't hate Emma. I hate what she *is*. You can't even see it." He turned back toward the school. "Allison— it's been a while since I was forced to spend this much time with other people. I'm not used to it anymore. I can't see them as anything other than walking victims. And no, Eric doesn't count." He stopped, his back still toward her as she started to catch up.

"I will never, ever forgive you if you get yourself killed."

*　　*　　*

Emma was waiting for Allison by the back doors. She was trying not to look worried and mostly failing—but failure didn't matter if no one could see it. When Chase strode toward the door, she put on her game face. She was surprised when he yanked the door open and headed straight for her.

"I don't know what you did to deserve a friend like Allison," he said.

Emma braced herself for the rest.

"She says I don't understand what you give her. I'll try. But Emma? I'll kill you myself if anything happens to her." The last words were soft; they were all edge. She met his expression without flinching.

"Deal," she said.

He blinked. "What?"

"It's a deal. If anything happens to Allison, you can kill me." Her smile was shaky but genuine, and it grew as his eyebrows folded together in a broken, red line. "I'll probably be grateful, in the end."

For just a moment, she thought Chase would smile. He didn't. Instead, he headed past her and into the post-lunch school. Allison was only a few seconds behind.

"What did he say to you?" she demanded.

Emma laughed. "He made very clear that you're important to him, and I'm not."

"Emma, it's not funny."

"No, probably not. But if I don't laugh, I'll cry, and I can't cry. I'm not used to people hating my guts out, but—he's worried about you, and I can't fault him for that." She caught Allison's arm as Allison began to stride—there was no other word for that determined step—in the direction of Chase. "He said he'll try, Ally. He promised he'd try. I'm okay with that. Don't ask him for more."

Allison exhaled. "He doesn't even *like* people," she said. "I don't understand why he cares so much."

"About you?"

Allison didn't answer.

Emma slid an arm through hers and dragged her gently back to reality.

Reality these days had its own problems. Amy Snitman careened around a corner, walking in the militaristic fashion that made people of any age move out of her way as quickly as humanly possible. Emma had already stepped to the side, but Amy came up short in front of her, glancing once at Allison and nodding curtly.

"Have you heard the news?"

"No—who died?"

"No one, but only barely. Mr. Taylor is in the hospital, and he's unlikely to be out of traction in the next three months."

"Oh, my god—what happened?"

"He was apparently driving under the influence."

Emma frowned. "Mr. Taylor drinks?"

"I'd've bet against it," was the curt response. "We're sending flowers," she added. "Your share is twenty dollars."

Emma immediately fished a wallet out of her computer bag. "Are you going to visit him?"

"Mrs. Esslemont says he's not taking visitors at the moment."

Which wasn't a no. In general, Amy expected the natural world to conform to her sense of generosity. "What's happening with the yearbook committee?" Mr. Taylor was the supervising teacher; all school committees and clubs required one.

"It's up in the air. Mr. Goldstein has offered to step in."

Emma hoped she didn't look as horrified as she felt. Mr. Goldstein was *this* close to retirement, and most of the students privately felt it was on the wrong side. He was also condescending in a parental way, and it grated.

"You're right," Emma said.

"Of course I am. Which particular flavor of right?"

"It's an emergency." And in a peculiar way, Emma felt grateful for it. It didn't involve dead people. It didn't involve the near murder of her best friend. "Have you talked to Mr. Hutchinson?"

"Not yet. Heading that way."

"I'll come with you." She turned to Allison, who wasn't on the year-book committee but was well aware that Amy was in a foul mood. "I'll see you in class?"

Allison nodded.

Mr. Hutchinson was the principal. Amy believed in going straight to the top when she wasn't happy with a situation. Since it was impossible to teach at Emery—or to be breathing anywhere in its vicinity—and *not* know Amy Snitman, most of Amy's friends were assumed to be caught up in Amy's tide. Teachers might hope for and expect a certain amount of intellectual independence, but they weren't idiots; they knew that peer pressure counted for a lot. Emma had never been on Amy's bad side.

Then again, you didn't land on Amy's bad side unless you were extraordinarily stupid or thoughtless. If it weren't for the social pressure exerted by Amy Snitman, Michael's life might have been a lot harder at Emery. If you were the idiot who was stupid enough to bully Michael, that spelled the end of your social life for a few weeks.

And the petty pleasure of bullying Michael was not worth the price.

Mr. Hutchinson was in his office; he was eating lunch there. His desk was a fabulous clutter of slips. Emma caught sight of an application for transfer floating on top of them. The principal was almost as old as Mr. Goldstein, but on Hutchinson, the age didn't show. He met all of Emery's many inhabitants as if they were people, rather than excuses to draw a paycheck.

"What can I do for you, Amy?" he asked. He nodded at Emma, but he was busy, and he knew who was in charge. Emma didn't resent this. One couldn't and remain Amy's friend.

"I'm here on behalf of the yearbook committee."

His smile faded. "Yes?"

"I've heard rumors that Mr. Goldstein has volunteered to oversee it."

"He has."

"If I can find you another teacher, will you take him instead?"

"Amy, Mr. Goldstein—"

"Yes, I know. He's experienced and well-respected." She folded her arms across her chest.

"As it happens, I'll be interviewing the temporary replacement for Mr. Taylor. He's new to teaching, and he's been working as a substitute; he could start, without causing difficulty for another school, within the week. He's indicated a willingness to undertake Mr. Taylor's extracurricular activities within the school."

Amy's arms tightened. She couldn't exactly demand to be present for the interview. She could find adults who served as trustees, and they could bring pressure to bear where necessary—but it wouldn't be immediate.

"Give him a chance, Amy. If you have concerns after you meet him, we can talk about a suitable replacement."

"Fine."

By the time school dragged its way to a close, the entire student body had heard of Mr. Taylor's accident. Michael was concerned because he took a class with Mr. Taylor, and he was comfortable in that class. A new teacher often created a mess of subtle problems until he or she was accustomed to Michael.

It was Emma's job to speak with whoever the replacement was about Michael's current classroom needs—not that Mr. Hutchison wouldn't have most of them covered. Pippa had offered, but Amy turned her down; she felt that the replacement was likely to listen to Emma because it was already Emma's job to get Michael to school on time.

Not that he needed it anymore. But he clung to the familiar when things got strange—and given Necromancers and dead people, they were pretty damn strange at the moment.

Emma almost headed home but remembered at the last moment that her efforts to avoid talking about Jon Madding had her "eating dinner at Allison's." She walked Michael and Allison home and paused at the foot of Allison's drive, waving once to Mrs. Simner before she walked away.

What she wanted, even though it was November and it was cold, was to see Nathan.

And Nathan, as always, knew.

NATHAN

EMMA LOOKS LOST AND A LITTLE FORLORN. It's an expression that's not at home on her face, but it's also a gift: it gives Nathan something to do. He slides an arm around her shoulder, but it passes through her jacket, stopping at nothing solid in between.

But she can see him; she can hear him. She was never big on public displays of affection. He can pretend—if he tries hard, and he does—that things are almost normal.

"What happened?" he asks, falling in to her left, on the road side of the walk.

"Mr. Taylor was in a car accident. They say it's lucky he survived."

He steers by walking ever so slightly ahead; he can tell by the flush in her cheeks that she's cold. They used to spend time at the local Starbucks, and it's close enough to dinner that it won't be crowded. He doesn't ask her why she's not at home; he knows.

He doesn't go home either. The reasons are different, but the end result is the same.

He passes through the door; he tries to open it and fails. It's frustrating. On a normal day—for a dead person—he's now used to the idea that everything is permeable. When he's with Emma, he regresses. He hates being dead.

Emma doesn't seem to mind that he can't open doors anymore. He can't buy her coffee. He can't do anything but pretend to sit in the seat across from hers and watch her while she drinks. The latte cupped between her palms steams, curls of white between their faces.

She starts to talk, but she realizes that while he's listening, so is half the cafe. Nothing about their conversation would be forbidden or embarrassing in public—but having one half of a conversation, no matter how innocuous, would be. She drinks her latte while it's still on the edge of too hot and then smiles at him. The smile is shadowed by death—his.

He often wanted to be alone with Emma, but he's sharply aware that there's a difference. The only time she can respond to him without causing concerns for her sanity is when they're alone. But most of her life isn't spent in isolation. She's isolating herself now.

She's doing it because of him.

If he were a stronger person, he'd leave. He knows Eric's right. He's seen enough of the Queen of the Dead to know his presence here can't be a good thing, not for Emma. But she's his entire world right now. There's no school. There's no worrying about college. There's no parental disapproval. There aren't even other friends. The friends he did have, he can't reach without Emma. She's the gate that stands between Nathan and the pain of eternity, and she is incandescent.

Even in her pain or her fear.

He wants to touch her. He wants to take her in his arms. He wants to kiss her. You'd think being dead would get rid of all that; it doesn't. It hones it, makes it sharper. When he was alive, Nathan thought Emma was the most important person in the world. Now he *knows* it.

But he also knows that if her touch warms him and makes him feel alive, it has the opposite effect on her; it chills her. It's like he's frostbite. What Eric said bothers Nathan, and it's hard not to drown in the worry; there's not much he can do to distract himself.

He can read over someone's shoulder. He can slide into a movie theater and watch. He can't talk while he's watching it, which is probably a good thing—but he can't talk to anyone about it afterward. He can't drink, not that he did that much drinking while alive; he can't drive. Driving was one of his refuges.

But mostly he drove to get Emma or to take her home. Now he can only walk beside her as she leaves Starbucks.

"Em," Nathan says. "It's cold. You should go home."

She's silent for half a block, but she doesn't change direction.

"Em—"

"Do you want me to go?" she asks.

The truth is he never wants her to leave. He never did. But he had homework and parents, and so did she.

"I don't want you to freeze to death," is his compromise.

"Then I'm staying. I don't mind the cold." Her teeth are chattering. "I know I'm being unfair. But I don't want to see a stranger's car in the driveway. I just need a couple of days to get used to the idea. Is that too much to ask?"

"No." He watches the wind shuffle strands of her hair. He sees her breath in the white mist that dissipates. He's wearing a T-shirt and jeans. "No, it's not. But—"

"But not more than a couple of days?" Her smile is rueful.

"Not many more. Your mom's not an idiot. If you give Jon a chance, he might surprise you."

"He's like olives?"

Nathan laughs. He hates olives.

Emma returns home sooner than she'd planned, but it's not an act of kindness, not that way. She doesn't want to go home, and starts walking in that aimless way they often had. Nathan follows. He knows he should tell her to go home, but he doesn't want her to leave, not yet. Instead, they walk down roads where houses and lots get larger, and from there, they walk down sloped streets toward the ravine that occupies a large chunk of city real estate.

Emma's breath comes out in mist, adding visual weight to the sound of her breathing. Even though they're alone on the stretch of street that girds the ravine, it's not the only sound they can hear.

"Nathan?"

He frowns. "You're not imagining things. Someone's crying. I think whoever it is isn't very old."

"I don't suppose you have a flashlight?" she asks, with a grimace.

He smiles and shoves his hands into his pockets. "Next time, I'll try to die prepared."

She is silent for one frozen moment, and then she spins around to punch his shoulder. "That's not funny!"

"You're laughing." So is he.

"Because I have to laugh or I'll cry."

"Laughter's better. Do you want me to go down there and take a look?"

"You can come down with me."

"*I'm* not likely to slip, fall, and break anything on a tree I can't see. You might have noticed the snow in the ravine." Most of the snow on the roads has turned to salty slush, but in the ravine there's a thin blanket of white. It's the type of snow that often covers patches of ice.

"Neither am I." She laughs at his expression. He loves the sound of her laughter; he doesn't hear it so much anymore. "Okay, maybe. But you can't talk to the child if you do find him—or her; you can't help if he's lost or stuck."

"I could at least tell you whether or not he's *there.*"

She shakes her head. "Come with me," she tells him, in a final-offer tone of voice.

"Em," he says, shaking his head in a way that once made his hair fly, "Don't change, okay? And be careful—I don't want to be with you so badly I want you to—"

She touches his lips. It sends a shock through his body, and he leans into the tip of her finger.

*   *   *

It's the dark gray that means night, but the moon is still silver. Emma begins to navigate her way through the snow, heading in the direction of the voice.

She freezes when the crying stops. She fumbles in her pocket for her phone. "I don't know where he is, but he can't stay out here. Not at this time of night."

"He might be with his parents—"

She gives him a look and turns back to the phone. The crying starts again, and she snaps the phone shut. "That way," she tells Nathan.

The trees don't so much open up as follow the line of a small stream that sometimes floods in the spring; Emma finds it easiest to follow the twisting line of the buried brook.

Cupping her hands over her mouth, she takes the risk of shouting. "Hello!"

Silence. The crying stops.

"I'm here to help you. Stay where you are, and I should be able to find you. I'm Emma," she adds. "Emma Hall."

Silence again. Emma bites her lip. "I know you're not supposed to talk to strangers," she says, in her loud, clear voice. "But it's very, *very* cold outside, and I think tonight, just this once, it would be okay."

It's a good guess. It's not a guess Nathan would have made.

More silence. Emma swears under her breath. "I should have gone home for Petal," she says, forgetting Jon Madding and her mother. "He could have found the child." She inhales and exhales a cloud, squaring her shoulders as she tries again.

Emma never gives up. Not when it's important.

"I was walking home from a friend's house when I heard you," she tells the invisible child. "I can just go home, if you want." She's lying. She isn't leaving until she finds this child, one way or the other. "I have a phone if you want to call your mom. You don't have to talk to me at all if you don't want."

Silence.

"But I'm freezing out here. It's *really* cold. I need to go home."

More silence.

"My mom won't let me talk to strangers either. I got lost on the subway once, and I was really afraid. I thought I'd never, ever get home again. I started to cry. But a woman noticed I was crying, and she stopped and asked me if I was lost. I answered her, even though she was a stranger and my mom had told me not to speak to strangers, because my mom had *also* taught me I should be polite to strangers.

"I never understood how you could be polite if you weren't allowed to talk at all. But that woman? She helped me get home. She was going home, too, and she was going to the same station I was supposed to go to.

"When I got home, I was very late, and I thought I'd be in a lot of trouble when I told my mom what happened. But my mom wasn't mad at me. My mom was grateful that someone was there who could help me.

"Your mom would be grateful, too. I'm sure she would."

Silence.

"Emma," Nathan says softly, nodding toward the trees on the far, far left. "Keep talking. I think I saw movement. I think he's following your voice."

Which is technically not breaking any rules about strangers. Children have the oddest notions; they take things so literally. Emma is sort of used to that, because Michael does it as well.

"My mom told me, afterward, that not all strangers are dangerous. In fact, she told me that *most* strangers are just like me—they want to help. They're nice people. The lady who helped me was a very kind person." Emma looks helplessly at the trees that Nathan indicated; she can't see what he saw. There is no movement of branches, no definitive crunch of icy snow—just the silence. The silence has become almost unbearable. She's stopped talking.

She picks it up, kneeling in the snow, trying instinctively to make herself seem smaller and less threatening. Her coat is long enough to cover her knees as she does.

"Because I remember that lady and how much she helped me, I try to help other children if I see them crying. I try to help them if I think they're lost. I think you're lost," she adds. "And I want to help."

She holds her breath as she finally sees what Nathan has seen: a flash of movement, a small change in the darkness to the left. She still can't hear much—the child must be really light or really small—but the glimpse gives her hope. She holds out both of her arms, and as she does, the child begins to cry again. The crying is different this time; the child is still frightened, but the fear has shifted from hopeless despair to something less heartbreaking.

"I'm lost," the small voice finally says. "You can take me home?"

But Emma, arms out, freezes completely as the child finally peers out from behind the trunk of a leafless tree. She finally understands why she'd heard the child so clearly from so far away: It is far too late to take him home. He is already dead.

CHAPTER
SEVEN

"THIS IS WHERE I LIVE," Emma said quietly. There was no strange car in the drive, which meant no stranger in the house. It should have been more of a relief than it was.

The dead child was a young boy. Emma thought him six at most, but he calmly told her he was eight years old. He was skinny and short for his age, and he had the same kind of calm vulnerability of—of Michael at that age. His hand was firmly in hers; if she could have, she would have carried him. Her hand had passed beyond pain three blocks ago; it was numb. Her upper arm was tingling from the cold of both winter and a dead child's hand.

The boy nodded as he looked at Emma's house. His name was Mark Rayner. He had one brother and one sister. He lived with his mother; his father mostly lived somewhere in America.

"Will we go to my house after this?" he asked.

Emma's careful smile faltered. She had asked Mark where he lived, and with whom. She had explained that her own mother might be worried if she was out so late in the cold. And she hoped that Mark knew he was dead. If he did, he wasn't sharing.

She managed to get the front door open with one hand, which took effort; she was afraid to let Mark go. Why, she didn't know; she didn't cling to Nathan in the same way, and she certainly didn't need to touch her father. But the boy seemed to take some comfort from the contact— and it might be the *only* comfort she could offer him. For her troubles, she got a face full of Petal as he ran full tilt at the door, his tongue wagging almost as much as his stubby little tail.

Mark's eyes widened, and he tried—still holding Emma's hand—to hide behind her.

"It's okay, he doesn't bite. He's a really friendly old dog. You can—" pat him? She was irritated at herself for speaking without thinking. "He won't hurt you. I don't think he's ever hurt anyone but himself; he's a bit of a klutz."

"Emma?"

This was *so* not what Emma needed. Mercy Hall walked out of the kitchen and into the front hall as Emma tried, very hard, to disentangle her hand. She didn't quite manage in time. Her mother blinked. Emma could still see Mark; Mercy Hall couldn't. But she'd probably seen something.

"Who were you talking to?" she asked, in exactly the wrong tone of voice.

Emma was too tired to lie; lying was a lot of work. She said nothing instead, removing her coat and her boots and putting them in the closet, her back—and her face—turned away from her mother. Composing her expression, she finished and turned around. "No visitors tonight?"

"No. I have a lot of work. You're alone?"

"I'm alone."

Nathan had left her, not at her house but in the ravine. *I don't want to scare him,* he'd said. *And he's already taken the risk of talking to one stranger. I think there's a chance he'll run if there are two of us.*

Mark was watching both Emma and her mother with a faint air of confusion.

"Emma, I wanted to speak with you about Jon."

So not the conversation she needed to be having right now. "You said you have a lot of work?"

"It doesn't have to be a long conversation."

"I have a lot of homework. Unless you're going to tell me you want him to move in, can we try this tomorrow when we both have more time?"

Mercy opened her mouth, shut it, and stood very still, as if she were counting. Then she nodded. "You'd like him if you gave him half a chance."

"I didn't hate him," Emma replied. "He seemed like a perfectly nice guy."

"He is."

The silence was awkward. The smiles that filled it were brittle, and not much better. Emma kept hers on her face until her mother slid back into the dining room. The dining table was once again a mess of scattered paper piles, which was all Emma saw of it before she turned to Mark.

"I'm sorry," she said quietly.

"That was your mom?"

She nodded. "She has a lot of work to do, and when she brings it home, I'm always careful not to disturb her too much."

"Mine, too."

"Come upstairs? My dad's not busy right now; I'll introduce you."

He clearly had no desire to meet strange men. Emma wondered how he had died. She couldn't ask, not yet. But she held out a hand, braced herself for the rush of cold as he took it, and led him upstairs to her room. Petal followed, whining.

Her dad was, in fact, in her room. He had a pipe in his hands and appeared to be inspecting the bowl. It wasn't lit, or if it was, ghost smoke had no scent. But he turned to face her as she entered the room with her visitor and set the pipe on the windowsill, where it vanished instantly without, oh, setting the curtains on fire.

"Emma," he said, smiling, his gaze on the stranger.

"Dad."

"You're late, tonight."

"I'm sorry. I—I heard someone crying in the ravine, and I climbed down to find him. This is Mark; he got lost there."

Mark was, once again, peering out from behind Emma. "Mark, this is my dad, Brendan Hall."

Mark said nothing, which wasn't a big surprise.

"This is my room. That's my computer—"

"You have your own computer?"

She nodded. "Do you want to see it?" Crouching, she hit the power button. She knew her dad could do something to make the computer respond and hoped it was a natural ability of ghosts, because Mark was going to be pretty disappointed, otherwise.

As it powered up, she glanced at her father and mouthed the word "help." Mark slid into Emma's chair, his hands hovering above the keyboard, his gaze riveted to the monitor. Brendan Hall gestured, and she quietly stepped away.

"What happened?" her father asked, his voice very soft.

She told him exactly what had happened, because at the moment, that wasn't her concern. "I don't think he knows he's dead, Dad. And I'm not sure what to tell him."

"How long has it been?"

"I don't know—I can't exactly start Googling for details about his death while he's on the computer."

"Go ask your mother if you can use hers."

"No way."

"Em—"

"I'm not explaining why. She doesn't want to know, but she'll ask. I'm too tired to come up with a decent lie."

"Emma—"

"She wants the dead to be dead," Emma continued bitterly.

"The dead *are* dead."

"Well, she wants them to be *safely* dead. And quiet. She doesn't want to know that her only daughter is touching their ghosts."

"Emma, I'll only say this once. What happens—or does not happen—between Mercy and me is none of your business. You are our child, but we're not one person. I'm dead, and I accept it. So, finally, does she."

"But you're *here*."

"Yes. And I shouldn't be. You know that." He nodded at Mark's back. "I think your young guest has some suspicions."

Emma frowned and looked over her shoulder to see a familiar Google logo on the screen; the rest of the type was too small, at this distance, to read. She walked, quickly, to the desk and did something she hated: She stood over Mark's shoulder, reading what his search had pulled up.

Mark Rayner.

She fished around in her pocket for her phone, pulled it out, and hit the first speed-dial button. Allison answered on the third ring.

"Emma?"

"Can you come here—with Michael—right now?"

There was a small pause, and Emma glanced at the clock; it was 9:45. "Never mind," she said. "I didn't notice the time. Don't come. Your mother will just worry at you."

"At me? I'm going to tell her it's your fault." She could almost see Allison's grin.

"No, Ally, I'm fine—"

"You're always fine. I'll call Michael's mother as well. We'll be there soon."

They arrived ten minutes later, which was fast enough Emma was instantly suspicious. Her suspicions were confirmed when she answered her mother's up-the-stairs summons: Allison and Michael stood in the hall, which she'd expected; Eric stood behind them, his back to the door. He looked over their heads and up the stairs at Emma.

Aware of her mother, Emma smiled a full-on Hall smile. "I'm sorry," she said, heading down the stairs, her father and a young boy safely ensconced in her room. "I didn't mean to drag you guys out so late."

"Eric drove," Michael replied.

Mercy Hall, like Eric, was looking at her daughter with question marks in her eyes. But she was a Hall as well; she kept them to herself while they had guests. Emma waited until shoes, boots, assorted mittens, scarves, and hats had been more or less closeted, and then led them all upstairs. "It's a bit of a mess," she told them before she opened her door. Petal joined the entourage, which guaranteed it would be even more of a mess in a handful of minutes.

He was the first one through the door, because he didn't wait for it to be fully open; he was also the first one on the bed, where he was technically not allowed to go. The duvet engulfed him, mostly because he was rolling in it. Allison and Michael walked in; Michael sat on the edge of the bed, nearest Petal; Allison sat on the ancient beanbag chair in the corner. Eric, however, stood in the center of the room, somewhere between Emma's dad and her visitor.

Emma took a deep breath, closed the door firmly behind her and glanced at Eric.

"I have a visitor," she said. She walked over to her computer; Mark was still seated in the chair, staring at a screen full of Google.

"Would his name be Mark Rayner?" was Eric's soft question.

The child turned at the sound of his name, his eyes widening as he saw Emma's friends. He had apparently failed to hear the door or see Petal, Allison, Michael, or Eric when they'd entered the room. It was almost as if he were a younger version of Michael. This impression was strengthened when he said, "Yes, I'm Mark Rayner," before turning back to the computer screen.

Eric raised a brow at his back. "Where did you find him?"

"In the ravine," Emma replied. She struggled with tone of voice, and lost. "I heard someone crying when we—when I was walking home."

"And you went into the ravine on your own in the dark to find him." Said like that, it sounded like an accusation.

The beanbag made its usual squeaking noises as Allison pushed herself out of it; Eric immediately fell silent.

"I did. It took me a while to find him. He's not supposed to speak to strangers, and I'm a stranger."

Michael stood as well. When Michael stood, it was generally a signal. "Emma, can I meet him?"

She nodded. She approached the chair in which Mark sat, and knelt beside it, bringing her eyes in line with his. He didn't look at her; he looked at the screen. His fingers hovered above the keyboard—or the mouse. Emma wasn't certain how he could use either, and now didn't seem like the right time to ask.

"I want to go home," Mark told her, without looking down to where she now crouched.

Emma closed her eyes. "Can I introduce you to my friends, first?"

"Yes."

"You'll have to get down from the chair."

"Why?"

She almost laughed. "It's important, when meeting people who don't know you and don't understand you."

"Why?"

"If you don't, they'll feel like you're ignoring them."

"Oh."

Since it appeared that he was ignoring them, and since Eric clearly felt he was, Emma gently forced the chair around. He came with it; she hadn't been certain he would. He frowned as she held out her hand. But after a long, silent minute, he placed his hand in reach of hers. "It feels different," he told her, sliding off the chair, looking for all the world like a living boy.

Her hand should have been numb at this point, but it wasn't, and the cold of his small palm burned.

"Mark, this is Allison, my best friend."

Mark nodded.

"This is Michael. I think Michael and you might have a lot in common. That's Eric."

Mark frowned as he looked at Michael. "Are you normal?" he asked.

It wasn't the question that anyone expected, but Michael was seldom floored by questions that weren't laced with anger or pain. "I'm normal for me."

"I'm not," Mark said quietly, staring at a fixed point on the floor. "I'm not normal."

A long silence followed. Emma had to resist the urge to put her arms around the child; she *also* had to resist the urge to ask him who'd told him this and, more important, why they'd said it. "No one is normal," she told him instead.

"Other people are normal."

"But you're not other people," Michael said, which was good; Emma was silent for a moment, struggling with a sudden surge of protective anger. Michael spoke calmly because he was stating simple, irrefutable fact.

Mark nodded, but he added, "If I were other people, if I were like other people, people would like me."

Allison's expression mirrored Emma's feelings; Ally had never been as good at the Hall face.

"Do you like dogs?" Mark asked.

Michael nodded.

"I don't like the smell. And their breath. I don't like the sound the lights make." These two statements were not connected. Mark really did remind Emma of Michael as a child.

"He doesn't smell bad, to me. He smells like dogs smell." Michael thought for a minute and then asked, "Do cats smell bad to you?"

"Not all cats. Some cats."

"Do these lights make bad noises?"

Mark frowned. He looked at Emma's hand, still entangled with his, and then tilted his head to one side. "No." He looked confused. "Emma's hand doesn't hurt. The lights here are quiet."

"Maybe it's different," Michael said, as Emma opened her mouth to speak, "because you're dead now."

Silence.

Mark proved that he was not like Emma, not like Allison, and not like other children. He blinked, then frowned. "Am I dead?" he asked Michael.

Michael nodded.

"Oh." He looked down at his hands, one of which was still wrapped in Emma's. "It doesn't hurt," he said. He sounded surprised. "Am I a ghost?"

Michael nodded again. "We can't see you if Emma's not holding your hand."

"Oh." Pause. "Why?"

"I don't know. Emma," he added, "can see dead people. But most of us can't."

"Why can Emma see dead people?"

"I don't know."

He turned to Emma. "Why can you see dead people?"

"I'm sorry, Mark, but I don't know, either. I can't—I can't always tell they're dead. They don't really *look* like ghosts look in stories or on television. I didn't know you were—"

"Dead?"

She nodded. "I could hear you—but I couldn't tell until I saw you."

"But you said—"

"When I could see your eyes, I knew."

"My eyes look dead?"

She shook her head. "It's their color." She paused, and then said, "My dad's dead, as well."

"Did you find him, too?"

"No." She hesitated, then looked at her father, who had been standing in the room the whole time. "No, he found me."

Mark's blank expression probably meant confusion; it's what it often meant on Michael's face.

"My father wasn't lost. He was dead, but he knew where he was."

"Oh. How did he know?"

"You'll have to ask him. You can see him, right?"

Mark nodded.

"Michael and Allison can't. They know he's there because I've told them, but they won't be able to speak with him until I hold his hand. I'm like a—like a window."

Allison shook her head. "Emma is alive, but Emma can see the dead, and when she touches the dead, she makes them visible for the rest of us."

Mark was silent for a full minute. Emma's father was watching him, hands in his pockets, his brow creased in concern.

"I want," Mark finally said, "to go home."

The silence was awkward, but there was no way to avoid that. Allison didn't exactly break it, but she did move toward Emma's computer. "Mark, what is the last date you remember?"

He frowned.

She tried again. "What was the date yesterday?" When he failed to answer, she said, "The day before yesterday?" She waited for another minute before she sat in the chair.

Ally moved to occupy the space in front of Emma's computer. The resultant sound of keys and mouse-clicks were audible.

Emma's hand was numb. Her lower arm was heading that way as well, but at the moment, the cold was painful. Eric was painful in a different way. Throughout the entire discussion he'd said nothing; he'd watched Mark and Michael in a stiff silence. Petal was agitating for Milk-Bones, and slathering Michael's hand in dog germs; Michael didn't appear to notice—hard, when a rottweiler was sitting *on* your feet.

"Three years ago," Allison finally said, into a lot of silence.

Emma, hand in Mark's, looked over her shoulder. She wasn't certain how much she could or should ask, given that Mark was in the room. But if Mark was like Michael, it wouldn't matter. "Exactly three years?"

"Three years in two months. He was eight years old, but on the small side for his age. He went out for a walk during the day and failed to come home. They mobilized most of a police division searching for him, but they didn't find him for two and a half weeks."

"Hypothermia?"

"Yes."

And he'd been there ever since.

"Are you cold?" Emma asked.

Mark frowned. He was wearing a simple ski jacket and equally simple shoes, neither of which he'd tried to remove on arrival. The shoes were in no way appropriate for tonight's weather—and it wasn't January yet, which was usually colder. "I'm not cold," he finally said. "But I'm not warm, either. My hand doesn't hurt," he added, looking at hers. "And the lights are quiet." He let go of Emma's hand, or tried; when he pulled her hand followed.

"I'm sorry," she told him. "My hands—they get really, really cold when I'm touching a ghost, and my fingers get numb enough I can't really feel them."

"That's not good," he replied, as she pried her fingers free. He walked toward where Allison was still reading the computer screen, and stood to the left of her, reading as well. "I wasn't alone," he told them. Only Emma could hear.

Emma stiffened. "When, Mark?"

"I didn't go out alone. That part's wrong."

Emma turned; so did her father and Eric. She reached out and caught Mark's hand, and he allowed it, now that he was beside the computer.

"Mark didn't—didn't go out alone," Emma told Allison.

Allison's hands froze for a second. She turned to look at Mark, who was standing beside her. "You went to the ravine with friends?"

Mark seemed to shrink at that. ". . . I don't have any friends."

Allison's lips compressed. Emma started to say *everyone has friends*, but managed to stop those words as well. It didn't matter what she thought, after all; it was the truth as Mark saw it. It was just *so* hard to hear from the mouth of a child, especially a dead one; the urge to comfort him was visceral. But . . . when had meaningless, hopeful words been much of a comfort in her own life? Even with the best of intentions behind them?

Michael said, in all the wrong tone of voice for Michael, "Who took you to the ravine?"

Mark hesitated, and then said, "My mom."

CHAPTER
EIGHT

EMMA HAD SUFFERED AWKWARD SILENCES BEFORE; this one was charged. She took refuge, for a moment, in confusion. She wanted to cling to it. She might have even managed, but Michael was there, and Michael now walked to the computer. He was almost twitching, which was never a good sign. He looked over Allison's shoulder as if she weren't there, and didn't appear to notice when she moved, surrendering both mouse and keyboard.

He knew—they all knew—that not everything reported in the papers was exact; editors changed little things—like, for instance, dialogue—in the name of saving space. Why they did this for articles that were on the web, no one understood. Space wasn't an issue—maybe attention span was. But almost every article Allison had managed to find contained a quote from the grieving mother, and in each, she clearly stated that she had come home to find Mark had gone out.

Emma wanted to speak with her father, but she had Mark by the hand, and she couldn't think of a way to detach herself. She sent her father an imploring look and froze at his expression; he wasn't looking at her. He was, like the rest of the people in the room, looking at the computer.

"Mark," Emma finally said, "I don't think going home is a good idea."

He looked up at her. "You promised."

"I—" She swallowed. What was she going to say? She hadn't known he was dead? Her father approached Mark as she struggled to find useful words, and crouched—in much the same way Emma had when she'd coaxed Mark out of the ravine.

"Mark, why don't you come for a walk with me? You can show me where your house is."

Mark hesitated.

"He won't hurt you," Emma told the young boy.

"He can't," Michael added.

"My father lives in America," Mark told them. "Because of me."

Emma wanted to scream. "Sometimes my dad thought I was frustrating. We used to argue about Petal—that's my dog's name."

Brendan Hall chuckled. He didn't hold out a hand; he did rise. "I haven't been outside in a while. Let's take a walk." Glancing at Emma, he added, "Emma's not very good at reading maps. If she tried to find your house without help, she'd probably get lost for hours."

It was true. Emma didn't even mind that he'd said it. She wanted Mark to go with her father because she didn't want him to hear anything she had to say. *What will you be protecting him* from? she thought. *He's already dead.*

But dead, he was an eight-year-old boy who looked like he was six and spoke as if he were four. Dead, he'd been crying in the ravine for— for how long? He didn't have a body; he couldn't be murdered. He could no longer freeze to death, because according to Google, he'd already done that. But he could be afraid. He could be lonely.

He could definitely be hurt in all the ways that didn't actually kill you. Some of those, Emma thought, death was *supposed* to end. Clearly, it hadn't.

Mark still hesitated, and her father said, "I need to be able to find your house so I can tell Emma exactly how to get there from here. You don't want to be lost for hours, do you?"

Mark shook his head. "I want to go home," he whispered.

Emma knew her father would have picked Mark up if he could; he would have hugged him, or put him on his shoulders, or any of the things he used to do with Emma's friends when he was alive. He didn't try that with this one; she wasn't even certain he could. He couldn't touch the living—were there rules that governed the way the dead interacted?

Probably, she thought grimly. She had a good idea of who'd made those rules. She headed to the door and opened it, although it wasn't, strictly speaking, necessary. "He'll bring you back," she told Mark, "if you want to come back. He won't leave you, and he won't lose you."

Mark nodded. Brendan Hall walked through the open door. Staring at the floor—or at his feet, Emma wasn't certain which—Mark followed him out. She closed the door behind them and leaned back against it, thinking that bashing it a few times with the back of her head would actually feel *good* at this point.

Eric said, "You don't want to do this."

Emma and Allison both swiveled heads to look at him; Michael was in Michael-land. Allison gently pushed him into the chair she'd vacated. He sat without really paying attention, adjusting his posture in the same way.

They then moved toward the wall farthest away from Michael. Petal joined them for a bit, sniffing at their hands and whining like loud background noise. Emma scratched behind his ears because she could do that in her sleep; it didn't require a lot of attention.

She wasn't sleeping now.

"I told him I would," she said, keeping her voice low. "He's not wrong about that. I didn't—I didn't realize he was dead when I heard him the first time. He was crying; he sounded—" she bit her lip. "I didn't want to leave him in the damn ravine in this weather at this time of night. I almost called 911—" She stopped, aware of how badly *that* would have ended. "But I told him I would take him home."

Eric folded arms across his chest in silence.

"Don't even think of telling me it's not my business."

"I won't. I understand how you've made it your problem—" He held up a hand as Allison opened her mouth. "—And I sympathize. I don't fault you for trying to rescue a lost child. You didn't know he was dead, but Emma? Even if you'd known, you wouldn't have done things differently."

"I wouldn't have promised to take him home."

One dark brow rose. "Chase tells me I look stupid at least three times a day—but not even Chase would accuse me of being *that* stupid. If there was no other way to get him to come to you, you'd've done exactly what you did."

"Not if I knew—"

"Knew what?"

Her hands were shaking. This time it wasn't because of the cold, although the fact they weren't both bunched in fists was. She didn't want to say the words that were stuck in her throat.

Eric once again folded his arms across his chest.

Allison came to her rescue. "She wouldn't have promised to take him home to a mother who'd left him there in the first place." She now dropped her hands to her hips, the Allison equivalent of Eric's crossed arms. "No child needs to know—" she stopped speaking.

"If you can't even say it, how are you going to handle him while you're there?" He let his arms drop. "Emma—this is not a good idea."

"I *know* that. But I told him—"

"I know what you told him. I understand that you don't want to be the person who breaks her word—I don't usually consider that a bad thing. But in this case, what good will it do? This isn't about Mark—or not only about him. It's also about Emma Hall."

"He knows what we know. Or suspects what we suspect. It's already hard for him—if he *wants* to go home, how can I say no?"

"It's a single syllable. I think you can manage it."

"I don't think—"

"Tell him that you didn't know he was dead. He can't live at home, anymore. He can't live anywhere, period."

The breadth and depth of Eric's callousness robbed Emma of words for a long, long moment. The words that did come rushing in were words she was pretty sure she'd regret—sometime. At the moment, she was having a hard time seeing it. "Why do you think it's a bad idea?" she managed to get out.

"He's dead."

"My dad is dead—but he's here."

"Yes. But your mother can't see him. Only you can. He's had to come to terms with his near invisibility and his death, and he's had time to do that. Mark—from what I can tell—hasn't. He's had enough time to figure it out, but he didn't *take* that time; I don't think he was aware of the passage of time at all. What will home give him?"

"I don't know—what does it give my dad?"

Eric closed his eyes. When he opened them, he'd smoothed the edges off his jaw and out of his voice. "Comfort. He wanted to know you—and your mother—were doing all right. You both are."

"Maybe Mark—" But she couldn't say it. "We don't know what she said to him. We don't know how it happened. We know nothing, Eric. All we really know is we have a very young eight year old who's only just discovering he's dead. He wants to see the world he knew. And I—I promised I would take him home."

Eric slowly lowered his arms. "Emma—he's not alive."

"I *know* that—if he were, we wouldn't be having this problem."

"You'd have an entirely different problem."

It was true, but Emma was too tired for what-ifs and theory. She was too tired to argue with Eric. "Maybe my dad will have some luck talking to Mark. Maybe Mark will decide he can't—can't go home."

Silence. It wasn't Nathan's silence; it was built on accusation, anger, even guilt. Emma didn't want it; she wanted—briefly, ferociously—to see Nathan.

"Where will he stay, if he doesn't go home?" Allison finally asked.

Eric just shook his head. "Emma—I know you see the dead as people; you see them as more than dead. I understand that. But there's no orphanage for dead children. There's no place they gather—" he stopped.

Emma said, in a very soft voice, "The City of the Dead."

"They don't gather there by choice," was his cold reply. "They don't need food, clothing or shelter; they don't need school. They don't even need to take up space. Yes, they're part of the world you now see—but you're not trying to find a home for wind or rain."

"They're not forces of nature, Eric. They're *people*. They have feelings, and they're the same feelings *we* have. I don't know where he's going to stay," she added, looking around her room. "But there are worse places than this one."

Eric said nothing.

"My dad's here. My dad's great with kids. If Mark's parents are alive, why can't he stay with my dad?"

"You don't even know where your dad is, most of the time."

"I don't need to know—Mark does. But my dad would do that, for him."

"Or for you?"

It was her turn to cross her arms. "For him."

"Fine. Maybe it's genetic. I hope your dad can talk him into staying here, for your sake."

Michael rose, leaving the computer and the keyboard behind.

Emma glanced at the time; it was already past late. "Michael and Allison have to get home."

"I'll drive them. But Emma? Don't take him tonight. You're exhausted. It's late. If you have to go, go during the day, and take me with you."

Given his attitude tonight, she was absolutely certain she didn't want him there.

". . . Or take Allison and Michael if you won't have me."

"I highly doubt his mother is a Necromancer."

"So do I. If I thought she was, I'd approach it differently. Michael?"

Michael stood in the open door, one foot over the threshold, as if stuck there. He swiveled. "Emma promised," he said quietly.

"You heard that?"

Michael looked confused, but he nodded. "It's important. To keep your promises." But he looked at Emma and Allison and said, "I don't understand what happened."

They exchanged a glance. "Neither do we," Emma told him.

"Why did she take him to the ravine? Why did she lie to the police?"

"Michael—we don't know. We don't know what happened."

"We can ask Mark."

Emma felt a little like the floor had suddenly dropped out from under her. She swallowed. "Sometimes it's upsetting to be asked—"

"It's not more upsetting than being left in the ravine in January," he pointed out. His eyes were starting to rapid-blink. Allison walked over to him, put an arm around his shoulders. He leaned back into it.

"Tomorrow. Tomorrow, we can ask him. But, Michael—if he doesn't want to talk about it, we can't force him."

Since this seemed self-evident to Michael, he ignored it. Allison pulled him out the door. Eric watched them leave, and then turned to Emma with an expression she couldn't interpret on his face. "I'm sorry, Emma," he said. It didn't sound like he was apologizing for their argument.

"Send Chase to Siberia and we'll talk," she replied.

He laughed. Laughter, as Nathan had said, was better than pain.

* * *

"I went home."

Emma turned as Nathan appeared in her room. He was leaning against the back wall, his hands in his pockets, his head tilted up in a way that exposed his neck. She wanted to hold him. Or to be held by him.

"I went home," he repeated, "and I saw my mom. My dad. It was a totally different house. Do you know what she's done to my room?"

"She hasn't turned it into a guest room."

"No—it's like a small shrine. There's a picture of me on my pillow. The bed is made. All of my stuff is still on my shelves—but it's really, really tidy, now." He laughed. It wasn't a happy laugh. "She goes to my grave every day. She gets up in the morning before work. She stops by after work. If work was closer, she'd be there at lunch." He took his hands out of his pockets, lifting them in something that was like a shrug, but heavier. "She marks my *calendar*, Em.

"I can't talk to her. I can't touch her. I can't tell her I'm not in pain, I'm all right. She cries," he added, looking at the ceiling again. "I think she's driving Dad nuts."

"She did that anyway," Emma pointed out, and Nathan did laugh.

"True." The laughter faded. "It's not home. It's not home the way it is—everything in it is a reminder that I'm dead."

"That's not what she's trying to do—"

"I know. I know she wants to remember that I did live, I was there. But—I can't make her laugh, anymore. I can't stop the tears." He shoved his hands back into his pockets and looked directly at Emma. "But I don't know how I'd feel if there was no sign of her grief. I don't know how I'd feel if she was happy all the time. I don't know what I'd want if I—"

"If you were Mark."

He nodded. "It's different, for your dad. I think, right now, I want what he wants—I want my mom to be happy. I *know* that she loved me. I know that she misses me. I know that if her death could bring me back, she'd kill herself in a heartbeat. But it won't—and if it could, and she did, I would hate being alive.

"But I can think this and feel this because, right now, it's so clear that I was the center of her universe."

"You were the center of mine."

He actually winced. "I was only one of the foundations. You had Allison, you had Michael, and they both needed you at least as much as I thought I did. My mother—"

"Lived for you."

"Lived for me. I've gutted her life, and I hate it. But—"

"If she hadn't cared at all, you'd have hated that as well?"

"People are contrary. Yeah, I'd've hated it—if no one missed me at all, what would the point of my life have been?" A pained, quiet smile rippled across the stillness of his expression. "I don't want her to suffer," he said.

"But love causes suffering?"

He laughed. "Only when it ends."

"It never ends, Nathan. You're dead, but I still love you."

"You can talk to me."

"How do you think I know what your mother does? How do you think I know what she does for your grave? I was *there*. Not at the same time as your mother—but after. I saw the flowers she left, and the notes, and the Game Boy. Maybe she thought it would reach you somehow. She still loves you, Nathan—we both do. The fact that you died doesn't change that. It only changes—" she stopped. "She's never going to stop. I'm never going to stop."

"I don't want her to stop. I want her to move on."

"That's not your decision to make." She turned away.

"Emma."

"Yes?" She began to straighten her duvet, which was hard because Petal was flopped out in the middle of it and didn't want to move.

"Could you—could you let her—"

"Talk to you?"

"Yes."

"I could. If you want, I will." But she hesitated, and he caught it—he'd always noticed everything.

"You don't want to do it."

"I *do* want to do it," was her low, low reply. She bent a moment over the bed as the world became blurry. "I want to do it for her because it's what *I* would want. I'd want that last chance to say good-bye. I'd want to tell you all the things I didn't tell you because I didn't *know* it would be the last day. I'd *want it*, Nathan, because it would be peace."

"You don't think it would be peace for my mother."

"I do—but . . ." She looked down at her hands; they were shaking. "But if I knew that you could be called when I needed to—wanted to—see you, I don't think I'd ever let go. If she knows it's because of me, she'll be here. Maybe not the day after, but the week after, and every week after. She'll ask questions I can't answer—and she'll ask questions I *can* answer, but they'll put her life in danger.

"And I'll hate it—but I'll do it because I'll understand what she needs. I'm—I'm lucky. I *can* talk to you. I *can* touch you."

"Not without cost."

She laughed. It sounded like crying. "I don't want to deny her anything because what she feels—it's the closest to what I feel. My friends worry for me; Michael misses you. But they don't feel the loss the same way because they didn't—"

"Love me."

"Not like I did."

His smile was hesitant. If you didn't know him, it would have looked shy. Emma knew him. "Am I wrong?"

He shook his head. "No."

"But?"

He laughed. "But you were so angry at Allison for saying almost the same thing about *your* mom."

"I wasn't. She didn't say the same thing—"

"You were, Emma. It just didn't sound the same to you because you were talking about your mother, not mine. You don't want to give my mother hope when you can't guarantee you can carry it—but you want it for yours, anyway."

"It's not the same," she finally said, voice heavier. "Your mom wants to see you. I'm certain it's the only things she wants. My mom—"

He lifted a hand and touched her lips with his cold, cold fingers. "Don't. Don't say it."

"Why not? It's true."

"Not everything true deserves to be said."

"I'll do it, though. If you think it'll help her."

"It's not just what I think that counts here."

An argument was hovering in the air between them, growing denser and thicker as the silence stretched. Emma wanted to avoid it, but it loomed so large it was almost impossible to speak around it. It would have helped if she'd understood why; the last thing she wanted—the last thing she'd've said she wanted—was to fight with Nathan.

It was with some relief that she saw her father flow through the closed door and come to rest with his back against it. Her father looked aged and tired, even if the dead didn't change.

"Dad? Where's Mark?"

"He's outside."

"Outside the house?"

"Yes." The way he answered made it clear that it wasn't outside *this* one.

"What happened?"

Nathan had fallen silent, but he remained in the room; his hands were in his pockets, in fists.

"We went to his house," Brendan Hall replied. He left the door and walked toward the curtained windows, staring in the direction of the veiled sky. Back turned to Emma, he said, "If at all possible, Em, I think you should avoid this."

"How?"

"It's not—it's not like the last time. I don't think there's anything you can do at that house that will help Mark."

"Dad—" She knew it was bad; he kept his back toward her as she approached. She had to touch him before he would turn, and his elbow—the closest thing to her hand—was cold. To her surprise, he reached out and hugged her tightly; if his elbow had been cold, his hug wasn't. "I'm not telling you not to care," he told her. "I don't think you'll get rid of Mark any time soon; he's just come in from the—the cold; he needs company.

"But that part of his life is over. Maybe he can come back to it later—but not now."

"Then why is he there, Dad? Why didn't he come home with you?"

Her father's grip tightened for a moment; it was his only answer.

In the dark, Petal snoring on the foot of the bed—where foot, in this case, meant the entire lower half—Emma could hear the dead. She could hear them the way haunted people in movies did: they wailed, they cried, their words were stretched and attenuated. There was a hunger in their voices that distorted them so much they were barely recognizable as human. Emma knew; she tried.

One glance at the clock told her it was 2:30 in the morning, East Coast time. Sitting up, Emma slid her foot out from under Petal and swiveled on the bed. She had two tests tomorrow—tonight was *not* the night to listen to the wailing dead if she wanted better than a bare pass in either.

Explaining this to the distant voices, on the other hand, was a lost cause; all it did was wake up her dog, who assumed she wanted to take him for a walk. Loudly.

"Petal," she said, catching his face in her hands, which was always dangerous unless you *wanted* a whiff of dog breath, "we're *not* going for a walk, and if you wake Mom up, she'll bite *my* head off."

He not only breathed in her face, but licked her chin as well. She hugged him tightly, and only in part to avoid his tongue. The dead didn't bother him, he hadn't brought home a stray boyfriend, and he wasn't giving her advice she couldn't bear to follow.

The temperature in the room took a sudden dive; she tightened her grip around the rottweiler's neck before letting him go. He, on the other hand, had both large paws in her lap; he was whining. The room was dark enough that the sudden blink of the computer monitor made her shut her eyes. When she opened them again—slowly—she saw Mark's back. He was standing in front of the monitor, his hands by his sides. There were no key clicks, no mouse clicks, but the images on the screen were changing as she watched.

She remembered her dad reading a letter she'd written and posted; she couldn't remember whether or not he'd gone through the motions of touching the keys in order to make her more comfortable. It was something her dad would do—but Mark was not a child who would understand the need for that kind of make-believe. Neither, she thought, as she approached him, would Michael.

The light of the computer screen turned most of the nearby room a pale shade of gray and blue; it didn't touch Mark. The dead seemed to radiate their own light; regular light didn't change their appearance at all.

"Mark?"

His profile, silent and almost graven, didn't change. She wondered if he'd heard her. She almost reached out to touch him, but remembered that he didn't like to be touched. With Michael, it was the only certain way to get his attention when his focus was buried inside his own head. Mark wasn't Michael—but he reminded Emma of Michael in his childhood. Michael, however, was alive.

"Mark, shut it off. Come away. There's nothing there you haven't seen."

He didn't move at all.

She came to stand behind him, her palms hovering over his shoulders. His search terms—he was Googling—made her flinch. Mother. Kills. Child. Before she could find words, "Murders" was substituted for "Kills." On her best and brightest day, headlines like this were a horror she didn't visit.

She wished that Allison were here. Or Michael. Or her father. Anyone but her. At this time of night the only person who might wander by was her dad, and only because he no longer had to work in the morning. Brendan Hall remained conspicuously absent; Emma was alone with her slobbering dog and a boy who stood like a statue and read, and read, and read.

CHAPTER
NINE

AT 8:10, Emma managed to be in the front hall, decently dressed but distinctly underfed. She hadn't made her mother's coffee but had managed to fill Petal's food and water bowls; her mother could buy a coffee at a dozen places on the drive in to work; her dog, however, couldn't open a can by himself. He *could* navigate the dry food bags and had in the past, but no one in the Hall house really *wanted* the contents of the bag spread across the kitchen floor.

Michael was on time, no surprise there. But he was tense, his eyes slightly wider than usual, his lips compressed. His hands were rigid by his sides—which didn't stop Petal from nuzzling them. It also didn't stop Michael from feeding the dog, but it took him a minute to zone back in.

"Emma," Mercy called from the top of the stairs, as they were just about to leave.

Emma turned.

"Jon is coming over for dinner tonight. You'll be home?"

"I'd love to, Mom, but I promised Allison I'd—I'd do some work with her at the library."

Her mother said nothing for a long minute. "Well. Don't be home too late."

"I won't." Emma escaped the house; she couldn't escape the tone of her mother's weary voice.

"Who is Jon?" Michael asked as they headed down the walk.

"My mother's new boyfriend."

"Oh."

"You can say that again."

Michael, who was watching the ground as if he expected it to break beneath his feet at any minute, said, "You don't like him?"

"I—" She held her breath for ten seconds. "I don't know him well enough to dislike him."

"But you don't like him."

She grimaced. No one else would have asked the question, because the answer was so clear. "It's not him, not exactly. I don't like the fact that he's my mother's boyfriend. I don't know him at all—I just don't want to *get* to know him. Not like that."

"But your mother likes him."

"Yes, clearly. And she doesn't care if I don't."

"She doesn't? Have you asked her?"

"No. We don't often ask questions in the Hall household," she added, speeding up slightly and hoping for rescue by Allison if she could just reach her house under the barrage of questions.

Allison was two minutes late and came careening around the Simner door, clutching the backpack she hadn't taken the time to loop over her shoulders, but Michael was so absorbed that he didn't notice. This should have told Emma something. Allison hit the sidewalk taking longer than usual strides—mostly to match Emma's.

"Michael," Allison said, before any of the usual morning greetings could be exchanged, "what exactly did you say to your mother last night?"

Emma froze in midstep, which, given the temperature of the morning wasn't as hard as it should have been. The shadows she cast in snow made brown by dirt, salt, and many feet had become desperately interesting. She turned to look at Michael, who was still concentrating on the ground. "I told her that we were late coming home from Emma's."

"That's all you said?"

"No. I told her about history and Mr. Taylor's accident."

Allison exhaled. "What did you tell her about—about Mark?"

This did get his attention, possibly because Allison's intensity was ratcheted up to a much higher level than usual. Attention, on the other hand, didn't mean that he shifted his gaze much. "I didn't tell her anything about Mark," he said. "You said it wasn't a good idea to talk about the dead."

Allison didn't relax much; Emma, who had started to, thought better of it when she looked at Ally's compressed lips. "Your mother called my mother this morning. That's why I'm late."

Michael did look at Allison then, possibly to see what her expression actually was. "My mother phoned your mother?"

Allison nodded.

"Why?"

"That's what I'm trying to find out," Allison replied. She now glanced at Emma, who shook her head. "Was your mother upset last night, Michael?"

"No."

"Did you—did you talk to her this morning at breakfast? I mean, this morning *at all*?"

"I always talk to her in the morning."

Allison, by dint of will and familiarity with Michael, did not pull her hair or shriek. "Did you talk about anything related to what happened last night at all?"

He was silent while he considered the question. "Yes," he finally replied.

Emma now stepped in. "Allison, what did she say to your mom?"

"She was worried about Michael. She asked if we knew of anything that had happened at school—at all—that might cause him to ask her about parents killing their children because their children weren't *normal enough*."

"Michael, we don't know that that's what happened," Emma said, voice low, glance sweeping the sidewalk for possible eavesdroppers.

Michael said, "We do. We do know that's what happened."

"No, we don't. We know that—that Mark's mother took him for a walk. We know that he—" she took a deep breath. "We know that he died. But we don't know why she left him there. It might be—"

"Emma, I'm not stupid."

Allison briefly raised her hands and covered her face with them. Michael, who was genuinely sweet most of the time, was not without a temper.

"I heard what he said," Michael continued. He'd stopped walking. "I understood what it meant. Were you listening to him?"

"I . . . I was."

"Why do you *think* his mother left him there?"

She had to look away from what she saw in his face. "I don't know, Michael. I can't ever imagine doing that to *anyone's* child—and I've babysat monsters." She tried to smile at the joke, but it was pathetic, even by Hall standards.

"I know I'm not normal—"

"Michael, *no one* is completely normal."

"I know that. But—"

"I'm a Necromancer," she said, digging hands into her hips. "How much *less* normal could a person be?"

That stopped him for a few seconds; it didn't, however, start him walking again. Allison glanced at her watch, but she didn't start walking either.

"People have already tried to kill Allison because I'm a Necromancer."

"Yes, but none of those people were her mother. Or yours. Do you think your mother would—"

"No!"

"Why?"

"She's my *mother*—" Emma lifted a hand because she couldn't stop the words that had just left her mouth, and she had no way to claw them back; not with Michael. "She knows *me*. She loves me, even when she brings strangers into *my* house that I don't want there."

"It's her house, too," Michael replied—as automatic in his response as Emma had been in hers.

"Yes. Technically it's entirely her house. But I live there, and she never asked me for permission. But even if she's disappointed at my reaction to her—her friend—she would never just lock me out to freeze to death."

"If she did," Michael replied, "You could come and stay at my house."

Emma smiled, and the smile was genuine, if pained. "Michael—your mother loves you. She always has. Yes, you're different. You've always been different—but different's not bad. You're normal for *you*. I'm normal for me. Allison is normal for Allison. None of the three of us are the same—but we're still friends, we still care about each other."

His shoulders slumped, half-inch by half-inch, as some of the tension left him. In the wake of tension, however, confusion opened up his expression. "Why did she do it, Emma?" His eyes were round; Emma thought he was close to tears. Michael had never been particularly self-conscious about them.

"I don't know, Michael."

"She couldn't have loved him."

"No."

"But he was her child!"

"Yes. If I could explain it, I would." She swallowed, and added, "I've been thinking of nothing else all night—because Mark wants to know as well. He wants to know more than any of the three of us do. It happened to him. I don't know what to say to him," she added, as she began—slowly—to walk. Michael was upset, yes—but being late wouldn't help that at all. "If you can think of anything—anything at all—"

"I have to understand it," Michael replied.

"There's not much to understand," Allison told them both. "His mother is a monster."

Michael was silent for a long moment before he turned and began to follow Emma. "She isn't," he said, his voice soft. "She's a person. If she were a monster, it would be easier."

"Mom?" Emma cupped her phone to muffle the pre-class noise in the hall and hoped she was audible.

"Em? Is something wrong?"

"I—I got my library date confused. I'll be coming home for dinner tonight. Do you want me to pick up anything on the way home from school?"

"Milk. And eggs. Not for dinner," she added. "But I think we're out." There was a pause, and then her mother said, "Thank you, Emma."

Emma felt a rush of something, a mix of guilt, affection, worry—and, ultimately, trust. Michael wasn't the only person affected by the morning's discussion. "I'll try, Mom. I don't always handle surprise well."

Allison waved her over as she ended the call. "Amy wanted me to tell you the yearbook committee is meeting after lunch."

"Is she still on the warpath?"

"It's Amy." Allison readjusted the necklace Ernest had given her. She didn't generally like things hanging around her neck. Her eyes widened in a particular way, and Emma turned; Michael was standing in front of his open locker staring vacantly at its interior. He hadn't removed his coat or his backpack.

Allison and Emma exchanged a single glance.

Michael had seen Necromancers. He had seen the dead. He'd even kept two dead children amused until Emma's arms were numb with the cold of making them visible. He'd seen men with guns, and he'd seen their corpses. But it was Mark that had caused the internal meltdown, because Mark's situation seemed so similar to his own, and Mark was dead.

"Michael," Emma said quietly, putting a hand on either shoulder.

He startled and turned.

"We're at school now. You need to take your coat off or you'll miss math."

Allison took his computer out of his pack, and waited until he'd removed his coat. She handed the computer to Michael, who stared at it as if it were a new and unknown object. No wonder his mother had been upset; Emma hadn't seen him this stressed since elementary school.

"Will you take Mark home?" Michael asked.

Emma couldn't even tell him that it wasn't safe to talk about Mark at school. "I don't know."

"You promised."

"I did. But I don't think his mother is going to be happy to see him, and I don't think that's going to help. What would you want, if you were in Mark's position?"

"I'd want to know *why*," was the low, intense reply.

"Math," she said quietly. "Whatever happens, it won't happen until after school."

"Can I come with you?"

Emma closed her eyes. She hadn't lied—one didn't, to Michael. She was afraid of what such a confrontation would do to Mark. He was eight, but a *very* young eight. His mother had taken him out for a walk on a literally freezing January day, and she'd left him in the ravine, returning to "normal" life without him.

What could she possibly say to Mark that would explain that? What could she do that would give him any peace?

"Yes," she said, after a long pause. Her voice was thick. "If I can't talk Mark out of it, you can come with me."

"Allison too?"

"And Nathan," Emma said, surrendering.

Michael inhaled and exhaled deeply. Then he straightened his shoulders and looked around the school halls as if they'd unexpectedly coalesced when he hadn't been paying attention. Emma steered him toward his class, just in case.

Lunch might have been awkward, but Emma only had to endure fifteen minutes of it. Given Eric and Chase, she wasn't certain she'd survive five; they were in a foul mood. They spoke normal sentences as if each word were a bullet, no matter who their target was. Michael, who brought his own lunch, had held the table. Nothing said in the cafeteria line—and admittedly, on committee meeting days, Emma got to jump to the head of the line—had indicated rage or fury.

But Michael was silent throughout most of lunch; not even Connell's question about mana decks could fully engage him.

Emma was hugely relieved when she had to leave the table to attend the yearbook committee meeting; she threw Allison one guilty look. Allison grimaced. Emma wasn't likely to be able to budge Chase, Eric, *or* Michael today. If she missed the yearbook committee meeting, she'd be adding angry Amy to the mix for no reason.

"I can't understand," Chase said, as Emma all but fled the cafeteria, "why everyone's so terrified of Amy."

"Given the caliber of your enemies, that's understandable," Allison replied. "But think about it on the inside of our lives for a minute. Amy is the reigning queen of the graduating year. She is gorgeous, she's on the Head's honor roll, she's talented, and she knows everyone. If she wants to make your life miserable, you will—while in school—be miserable."

"Amy can be nice," Michael interjected. "She's not a bully."

"I wouldn't call her a bully," Allison replied, realizing that she was skirting the edge of exactly that. "It's not that she makes people suffer because she enjoys random suffering. If she makes you suffer, she's absolutely certain there's a good reason for it. It just happens to be Amy's version of a good reason. But she's a steamroller. She's driving heavy machinery while the rest of us are digging ditches with our hands."

"Have you ever been on her bad side?" Chase asked.

Allison shook her head. "She mostly doesn't notice me. She's not looking for victims, but she has her friends."

"I would have guessed you were one of them."

"I like Amy the same way I like thunderstorms; she's a force of a nature. But . . . I'm not really Emery mafia material." She didn't generally talk about things like this, and she found herself almost embarrassed to say it so clearly to Chase. The embarrassment rattled her, but not enough that she wanted to hide the truth or, worse, lie.

"And Emma is."

Allison held up a hand. "I'm now instituting a rule."

"A rule?"

"You and I—that being Chase Loern and Allison Simner—are not going to discuss Emma Hall unless her life is in immediate danger and discussion will save it."

Chase blinked. So did Michael. With an air of someone who'd just remembered a question he'd forgotten to ask, Michael said to Chase, "Why don't you like Emma?"

Chase laughed at Allison's expression; when the laughter faded, some hint of it lurked at the corners of his lips and eyes.

"You're impossible," Allison told him.

"It's my middle name. One of my middle names. I have several."

"I'm not sure I want to hear the rest."

Eric said, "You really don't. Some of them aren't meant for polite company." Eric wasn't Chase; his smile didn't light up a room. He smiled now, and Allison realized, watching him, that he was tense. She almost asked him why, but she wasn't certain Michael needed more stress. She was fairly certain that she didn't.

"But why don't you like Emma?" Michael said again.

"I don't think I'm allowed to talk about Emma while Allison is in the room. Everyone else can be scared of Amy, but I personally think Allison is more terrifying."

Michael made the face he made when he was almost certain someone was joking. Sarcasm and humor had been hard for Michael when he was in elementary school; he was famously literal. But he'd become more comfortable with both as he'd marched through high school.

"Amy," Chase said, in a mock-sober tone, "has never hit me."

"I've never hit you either!"

"Not yet," he said, grinning. "I don't imagine it'll be long before—"

"Chase," Eric said, in the tone of voice reserved for emergencies that would inevitably lead to death.

The smile dropped instantly off Chase's face. Emma had just entered the cafeteria; Amy was by her side. Both of them were the color of chalk. Allison rose without thinking. When Amy looked frightened—when Amy looked even a tiny bit uncertain—it was big.

"Short committee meeting," Eric said, in the wrong tone, as they approached the table.

"We didn't go," Emma whispered. "We're heading out to find coffee."

Michael frowned; he rose as well.

"Em?" Allison said.

Emma shook her head and smiled brightly. It was, Allison realized, the same smile that Eric had been using throughout lunch—when he'd bothered to smile, that is. Allison nodded and headed toward the cafeteria doors.

"We're going to miss a period," she told Michael.

Michael hesitated. It didn't last. He accepted the disruption to his daily schedule as if it were the natural outcome of finding a boy who had in all probability been left to die on a winter hillside by his own mother.

*   *   *

There was no way to break this tension. Both Amy and Eric drove; Amy chose the venue. She wanted something a little farther away than normal lunch-hour traffic. The one thing about Amy that even Allison had to admire was that she never dithered. If given a choice, she made it quickly.

Sadly, this meant her patience for other people's indecision was practically zero. Had Amy been the type of person to rule by consensus rather than by fiat, it would have been a disaster. No one spoke in Amy's car; the silence was thick and uncomfortable.

No one spoke—aside from giving a waitress their order—until lattes and hot chocolate had hit the table.

For people who needed to find coffee, they didn't drink a lot of it; Allison didn't touch her hot chocolate either, although she made signs of finding it hot enough it needed time to cool. Amy didn't bother. She lifted her latte and set it down with an authoritative clunk, as if it were a gavel and she was calling Court to order.

"We know who the temporary replacement for Mr. Taylor is," she said, voice flat.

Emma glanced at her. She hadn't picked up her own drink; Allison guessed it was because her hands were shaking too much. She was willing to cede the floor to Amy; she looked almost grateful to be able to do so.

Eric waited. He'd taken his phone out of his pocket and placed it on the table; Allison wondered if he were recording the conversation. Amy didn't have any issues with being recorded.

"You'd recognize him." Even stressed, Amy knew how to draw things out. "All of you would."

"Emma?"

She shook her head.

"The last time we saw him," Amy continued, when Emma failed to interrupt, "he was a bloody, messy corpse."

Eric and Chase froze. It was clear from their reaction that this wasn't somehow impossible—to them.

"Merrick Longland. He's apparently just out of the faculty of education; he has a teaching certificate; he doesn't have a full-time job. He's been doing piecework and temporary work as it comes in, and this job is a godsend. He's grateful to have it and eager to work with new students."

Emma was white and silent while Amy continued to rattle off the talking points she'd pried out of the principal.

"On the off chance that Merrick Longland didn't have a twin, we decided to skip the yearbook committee meeting. So. What are the chances that our teaching replacement is the same Merrick Longland who took several wounds to various body parts and died? Judging by your reactions," she added, jabbing the air in front of Eric and Chase for emphasis, "the odds are damn high. What are these Necromancers? Vampires?"

"It's the middle of the day," Michael pointed out.

"So? He's not standing in direct sunlight."

"He'd have to walk in direct sunlight from his car."

Amy snorted. She understood Michael as well as Allison or Emma did, but didn't see any pressing need to treat him differently than she treated anyone else. It was one of the things Allison admired about her. She might expect everyone else to make allowances, but Amy's version of allowance involved very little condescension.

"We want to speak to your Ernest," Amy concluded, folding her arms across her chest.

Eric and Chase exchanged a glance.

"I *mean it*," she added. "He was supposed to be responsible for the cleanup, if I recall correctly. Cleanup doesn't generally involve hospitals and healing. Even if it *did*, that kind of knife work leaves scars. Our Merrick Longland would look like a more attractive Frankenstein monster; this one doesn't. I'm not sure he'd've recovered from extensive plastic surgery by now, either."

"Our Ernest, as you call him, works on his own schedule," Eric began.

Amy reached out and plucked Eric's phone off the table. Eric's eyes widened; he was the only person at the table who looked remotely surprised. She turned the phone on, while Eric's eyes rounded further, and after a few seconds, shoved it up beside her ear.

Even Chase now looked dumbfounded.

"Hi. Ernest? We met recently. My name is Amy Snitman. No, Snitman. Yes, that's right. I'm one of Eric's classmates. Eric and Chase are with me, and we are coming to your house to visit. We've got a few questions about your work and a possible emergency; we should be there in half an hour." She hung up.

"I take it back," Chase murmured.

Allison would have laughed, but Emma's expression killed all mirth.

CHAPTER
TEN

CHASE JOINED EMMA AND ALLISON in Amy's car; he provided directions. Amy was annoyed, and let it show—she had GPS installed. All she needed was the address. Chase told her he didn't remember the exact address.

No one, not even Allison, believed him.

Michael went with Eric. Amy's driving was always exciting and Michael had had enough excitement for a month. He believed that Emma and Amy thought they'd seen Merrick Longland—but he also believed that Merrick Longland was dead. As this was more or less giving Allison whiplash, she didn't expect anyone else to take it in stride; the only person who did was Amy.

Allison privately thought that Amy would prefer to be given a rational, logical, and above all believable explanation, which was why she was driving directly to Eric's. Chase's verbal directions guaranteed two things. The first, that Amy would be in a fouler mood, and the second, that Eric—with Michael in tow—would arrive first.

This wouldn't have been necessary if Amy had returned Eric's phone, but Allison kept that firmly to herself. She felt as if she were only barely treading water, now. Because she, like the rest, had seen Merrick

Longland's death. She had nightmares about it. She kept them to herself.

Amy kept none of her thoughts to herself, which meant the ride wasn't silent. It was awkward, but given Amy was upset, awkward was as much as they could hope for.

She parked about three feet away from the curb, opened the door, and stormed out. Michael, had he been in the car, would have pointed out that she was too far out. No one else dared, but Allison suspected that no one else noticed. And if she were any kind of a decent best friend, she thought with guilt, she wouldn't have either.

She hurried to catch up with Emma; Emma was staring pointedly at a spot to her right. Allison guessed that Nathan was here. Or that he wasn't, and she wanted him. It didn't matter; she took up the position to Emma's left.

"Em?"

Emma smiled wanly. "I'm fine." It was the Hall version of fine: it meant, in more accurate English, shattered. She exhaled, and headed toward the door, which was already opening to allow Chase and Amy entry.

Allison hung back. She was afraid of leaving Emma on the front steps, because Emma looked at the door with an understated dread. "We don't have to stay," she offered. "It's not like we're going to be able to get a word in edgewise."

That made Emma smile a real smile. "Amy's something," she said, shaking her head. "I'm so glad she was there. I don't know what I would have done."

"You wouldn't have gone to the meeting."

"I don't know if I would have noticed in time to back out. Longland didn't *see* us; she saw him first. Amy notices everything."

"And usually points it out loudly, just in case anyone missed it."

Emma laughed. She straightened her shoulders and added, "Should we go rescue Ernest? He won't know what hit him."

"He's got Eric and Chase."

Emma winced. "Exactly."

The living room was like a parent-teacher interview gone insanely wrong. Ernest was seated in the large armchair. His posture was stiff and his expression caught between bemusement and serious annoyance.

Eric was on the far end of the couch—as far from Ernest as the seating allowed. Michael, conversely, had taken the seat closest to Ernest and had left room for Allison and Emma. Chase hadn't bothered with a chair of any kind; he'd plunked himself down on the stone of the fireplace, crossing his legs.

Amy, on the other hand, was prowling the room like a tiger. Since she'd introduced herself on Eric's phone, she probably hadn't bothered with introductions either—she'd gotten straight to the point, which Allison and Emma, slower to enter the house and remove all the winter clothing, had missed.

"So let me get this straight," Amy said, her voice growing louder as Emma and Allison joined the awkwardness. "Merrick Longland was dead. You checked. You didn't convey him to an emergency ward anywhere in this city; you did not buy him plastic surgery, and you disposed of his body."

"I believe I've already answered all of these questions," Ernest said, in a clipped voice that clearly implied he was not the one who was usually on the receiving end of pointed, icy questions. "I fail to see why they're relevant."

"Leaving aside the fact that murder is illegal—"

"Self-defense is not illegal in Canada."

"Which the courts, not tweedy old men, decide—leaving aside that fact, it's relevant because the selfsame Merrick Longland has apparently taken a job at *my* school as a replacement for a teacher who's going to be in traction for a couple of months. He's taken over the supervisory role of *my* yearbook committee.

"Can we assume that he *is* the same Merrick Longland?" She folded her arms and came to a stop inches away from Ernest's feet.

Ernest was silent.

"Can we further assume that he retains memories of his death and all the stuff that led up to it, including our presence at the former Copis household?"

More silence.

It was hard to take eyes off Amy when she wanted attention, even if the attention she wanted wasn't yours. Tonight was no exception; she was *angry*. She wasn't angry with Emma, Michael, or Allison, but the full storm of her rage could easily encompass Chase and Eric, neither of whom wanted to meet her gaze. Allison knew. She was one of the few people present who could look at something else when Amy was on fire.

"If he's a teacher, he'll have access to our records. He already knows where *I* live," she added, each word a figurative bullet, "but he'll now know where everyone *else* lives. This would include Emma. And Eric and Chase."

Ernest failed to answer. He had at least thirty years on Amy, possibly forty. He clearly had experience in a variety of deadly situations; he could clean up savaged bodies without raising a brow. He owned at least one gun, and he'd shown no hesitance whatsoever in using it. But even Ernest looked distinctly uncomfortable.

"What are the chances we survive that knowledge?"

Ernest rose. "These are all very good questions," he finally said, in a voice that made November wind seem warm. "Or they would be, if you didn't already know the answers."

"I didn't, until now," Amy snapped. "Believe it or not, where *we* live, dead people don't come back to life. Among other things." She drew, and held, her breath, exhaling it in a burst of nonverbal anger. "If we kill Merrick Longland—no, if *you* kill Merrick Longland—will he stay dead this time?"

"He is already dead," Ernest replied, his jaws clenching.

"We want a definition of dead that only Emma can see," Amy shot back.

"If we, as you put it, kill Merrick Longland, he is likely to remain just as dead as he is now."

Someone cleared her throat. Allison, breath held, turned to look at Emma.

Emma had been beside Amy in a crowded school hall, and she'd watched as Amy froze in midsentence, all of the words she'd been about to say lost. Amy had said two words: Merrick Longland. She'd grabbed Emma's arm as Emma turned to stare, realization and recognition freezing her in place.

The dead looked alive to Emma. They wore the clothing they'd worn at the moment of their death, but they didn't sport the wounds or the other clear signs that their physical bodies were corpses. She'd seen enough of the dead to know that she couldn't easily differentiate between the dead and the living—but one of the dead she hadn't expected to see was Merrick Longland.

Amy wasn't an idiot; she'd seen the same thing.

This Merrick Longland, extraordinarily well-groomed and handsome, was *not* dead. Not in the way that Emma understood death.

Nathan had been standing in the hall; he saw what Emma saw. His eyes widened, and he turned immediately to Emma. "Leave," he said, voice low, urgency stripping it of the usual social graces. "Leave now."

Emma nodded. She didn't answer, not because she was afraid that talking to thin air would make her look crazy, but because she was afraid to speak a single word that might draw Longland's attention. She caught Amy's elbow and gave it an urgent tug, and Amy turned immediately, her face drained of color.

They'd retreated to the cafeteria, by which time Amy at least had found her voice.

And now they were here. They were at Eric's, Amy going toe-to-toe with the old man, Eric and Chase looking distinctly uncomfortable—or worse.

Amy was right: Longland would have access to all of their school records. He could, if he knew their last names, find their home addresses with pathetic ease. And at those homes were parents and siblings and half-deaf rottweilers.

Emma knew what would happen to their families if the Necromancers came to visit: They would die. Maybe they would die quickly and painlessly; maybe they would die horribly and slowly. But Necromancers didn't care about the living. Life was a cocoon state, as far as Necromancers were concerned; death was the eternity.

Death as a power source, with no voice and no choice in the matter.

She was nauseated. She wanted to throw up or cry, which was a first. Emma had cried tears of loss and grief; she had cried tears of humiliation, although she could be forgiven that act at the age of four or five; she had cried tears of joy. She had never cried because she was so terrified all other options were lost to her.

And she was *not* about to start now.

"How is Longland alive?"

Ernest glanced at her. It was the only sign he gave that he'd heard the faint question at all.

"I won't argue with you. If you say he's dead, I'll accept it. But—he's walking around in a way that the living can see. Clearly."

Ernest glanced once at the open arch. "We'll take care of Merrick Longland."

"Because it worked so well the last time," Amy cut in. Acid would be less corrosive.

"We would be pleased if you demonstrated how we could do better," Ernest snapped.

Emma was terrified that Amy would take him up on the challenge. She'd watched Chase finish Longland off. It still gave her nightmares.

"Ernest, that was uncalled for." From the direction of the kitchen, clothed in a way that suggested the fifties and coiffed the same way, walked Margaret Henney. Unlike Merrick Longland, she was a dead that no one could see.

No one but Ernest, Eric, and Emma.

Ernest didn't particularly care if the young people caged in his living room considered him sane or not. "It was not uncalled for," he said, an edge in his voice. "You've clearly chosen your usual brand of selective eavesdropping."

Margaret was not Amy, but in her own way, she was intimidating. She was also, judging by the tightening of an already unimpressed expression, ill pleased.

"Ernest," Emma said, her voice much softer than either the living Amy's or the dead Margaret's, "stop digging."

Chase laughed. He was the only person in the room who did.

"More dead people?" Amy all but demanded.

"Margaret Henney," Emma replied. "She was there when we rescued Andrew Copis, but I don't know if you saw her directly. She's less than impressed with Ernest's response."

"That makes two of us."

"At least three," Allison said.

Emma said, quietly, "Margaret?" She held out a hand.

Margaret shook her head. "I don't need to hold hands to make myself visible. I need your permission, Emma. You hold me." Before Emma could reply, Margaret added, "and I won't ask that permission, now. I've told you before: It takes power. You won't use ours. You might not even understand how. But if you won't, you're using your own life to sustain our appearance, and you can't afford that at the moment."

"Margaret—how is Longland alive?"

"He isn't. Not in the sense that you or your friends are."

"But he's—"

"Yes. He is walking among the living as if he were actually alive. There are differences, but they'll be noted only as time passes. For one, he will not age."

"Will he bleed?"

"Yes. He will also feel pain. He is a threat to you for precisely the reasons your Amy states: He can interact with the real world. He can find information that would not otherwise be immediately found. He can kill you—but he will have to do it the old-fashioned way."

"Meaning the way Chase killed him the first time."

"Meaning exactly that, yes."

"That means he's not a Necromancer anymore?"

"It means, more precisely, that he doesn't have Necromantic powers or abilities any more. He's dead. The dead don't."

"How can he be—"

"He is not alive, Emma," was her much gentler reply.

"Is the Queen of the Dead alive?"

Silence.

Allison was holding her breath. She exhaled slowly and quietly; unlike Amy, she didn't use breathing as an act of aggression. She glanced at Chase and was surprised to see that he was watching her.

She could only hear Emma's half of the conversation. But ever since Emma had asked the question, it hung in the air like a nuclear cloud. *How is Longland alive?* Allison had no idea if Nathan was in the room; she had no idea if Nathan had followed them to Eric's. She guessed that he hadn't, because Emma's glance hadn't strayed to him.

But her thoughts had, even if she wasn't immediately aware of it.

Because if Merrick Longland had died a horrible death—and he had—so had Nathan. If Merrick Longland was, to all intents and purposes, alive, it didn't matter that Ernest said he was dead. What had happened to Merrick Longland *could* happen to Nathan.

* * *

It was Ernest, not Margaret, who chose to answer the question. "Yes. The Queen of the Dead is demonstrably among the living: she is a Necromancer."

"But—but—"

"Yes?"

"How old is she? You've been fighting Necromancers your whole life!"

"Not my whole life; I did, in the age of the dinosaurs, have a childhood."

Emma frowned. "I saw her. I don't—I don't mean to be offensive, but . . . she looked a lot younger than you do."

His smile was dry enough to catch fire. "She is much older than I am."

Amy, lips pursed, forehead momentarily lined, said, "So you're saying Necromancers are effectively immortal? Merrick Longland could be my grandfather's age?"

"Merrick Longland, as you've so bluntly pointed out, is dead. Before his death, yes, it's possible that he could have been as old as your grandfather. Or great-grandfather. It may come as a surprise to you, but we do not have an FBI style of dossier collection. Age is not necessarily an indicator of power."

Folding her arms across her chest, Amy said, "You're lying."

Margaret turned to Emma, "Dear," she said, which Emma was willing to tolerate given Margaret's age, "your friend—"

"Yes, she is my friend, and yes, she's very blunt."

Ernest met—and held—Amy's glare. Chase and Eric, who'd killed at least four people that Emma knew about, were looking anywhere else. "I am not lying; we do not have the resources to track every known Necromancer. But," he added, lifting a hand before Amy could break in, "Necromancers with Emma's knowledge—not her innate natural ability, but her actual, practical knowledge—will age at the expected rate. Lack of visible age is not a natural occurrence for Necromancers;

it is a skill that can be learned with time. It requires an ability to harness the power of the dead on a continuous, low-level basis.

"It is a gift of knowledge that the Queen grants those in her Court who have done her service."

"You know this how?" Amy demanded.

Emma swallowed. "Some of the dead are Necromancers," she replied, aware that Margaret couldn't speak for herself. "When you're dead, it doesn't matter."

"That is not entirely true," Margaret replied softly. "If you have died in the line of duty—where by duty one refers to the demands of the Queen—you are elevated in her eyes. Should that be the case, you are declared off-limits for harvesting."

"Would most Necromancers care?"

Margaret's smile was all edge. "There have been breaches of the Queen's law in the past. There have also been challengers. Unless one wishes to join the dead, one does not break the Queen's law; it is absolute. In the mildest cases, she can refuse to teach you the arts of self-preservation—what you would call immortality. In the more extreme cases, she makes you an example—both at the end of your life and the eternity that follows."

"You betrayed her."

Margaret glanced at Ernest. "Yes."

"Did you attempt to kill her?"

"That's a rather personal question, but I'll answer you. No. I was not—I was never—a Necromancer with the raw power the Queen of the Dead possesses. I have only met one other who might rival her, in time. My treachery, such as it was, was simply to choose life.

"But it was a crime, and it was met with the inevitable penalty. I was caught, trapped, and given in service to Merrick Longland—a knight of the Queen's Court." When Margaret used the word "knight" it didn't sound inherently ridiculous. "I was rescued by you. I want to say unintentionally, but—on a visceral level, you knew what you were doing.

"Merrick Longland must have risen high in the Queen's esteem. She has cloaked him in flesh and form and sent him, once again, into the world. He serves her, and he will now do so until her death."

"He knows what I did."

"Yes. And if he knows, the Queen will know. It cannot be a coincidence that he has been sent here; this is the place where failure cost him his life. He lives, now, at the whim of the Queen—and if she so chooses, he will return to the ranks of the truly dead."

Amy said, "Em, you're talking to air here. Enlighten the rest of us." It wasn't a request, but Amy didn't do requests.

Emma obliged, haltingly repeating Margaret's words as if by doing so, she could understand them better.

"I think it best, until Longland is effectively neutralized, that alternate living arrangements be made," Ernest said quietly.

Emma stiffened.

"You said he's not a Necromancer now, right? He can't use his power to talk idiots into flying home on a whim without warning?" Amy demanded.

"Correct. But he is unlikely to be here alone. There is almost certainly at least one Necromancer in the field."

"Longland will report to him?"

"Longland will report directly to the Queen of the Dead," Eric said, speaking for the first time. "The dead communicate in ways the living can't trace. He'll need to use phones or computers to communicate with the Necromancer in the field—but we haven't found him yet. Or her."

"While the Necromancer's at large, any information Longland feeds him is possibly deadly—for the three of you."

"For two of you," Chase cut in. "Allison and Michael."

"And I'm chopped liver?" Amy demanded.

"You're a force of nature," Chase replied. "I wouldn't bet money on a Necromancer faced with you."

Emma smiled.

"You realize making your 'alternate arrangements' is going to be a huge problem if we can't tell our parents what's happening, right?" Amy said.

"If you tell your parents, they will in all likelihood die," Ernest replied. He fished about in his jacket pocket for a pipe. Amy gave it the dirtiest look in her arsenal, but didn't come out and forbid it; it wasn't her house after all. In Amy's house you were allowed to smoke only if you were actually on fire—and even then, it was dicey.

"And the Necromancers won't assume they already know?"

"Unclear. In their position, I wouldn't make that assumption. Understand that they are accustomed to secrecy and isolation. They believe, on a visceral level, that they are the misunderstood and the despised; they believe they'll be hunted with figurative pitchforks by angry mobs that will then burn them at the figurative stake. They trust the Queen if they trust at all—but in general, they don't. They trust their power. They work to amass a power base, and it's a power that's built on the dead.

"Not all of the dead have significant amounts of that power. Young lady, I am trying to explain, as quickly and clearly as possible, to those of you who have short attention spans. I would appreciate a little consideration."

Since Amy had not interrupted him, Emma felt Ernest was getting what he said he'd appreciate. Amy was, however, tapping her left foot, and her lips were one thin, white line. She said nothing, and after a pause, he exhaled and continued.

"Your young Andrew Copis had a *considerable* amount of power. If Emma understood how to bind him, she would have access to power that would immediately place her in the upper echelons of the Necromantic society, such as it is. But very few of the dead are Andrew Copis."

"Do Necromancers have more potential—as dead people—than the rest of us?"

"Not to my knowledge. There is a large line that divides the living from the dead. In the ideal universe, the dead would be free to leave the world the living inhabit. I am not a particularly religious man," he added, in case this was relevant, "so I have no opinion whatsoever on where they might ultimately arrive.

"Even absent Necromancers, the world would not be ideal. Your young ghost would have been trapped in the remnants of his burned-out building long after the building itself had been demolished and new homes built on the lots. Some of the dead get stuck this way.

"Only those who are Necromancers notice."

"And most don't care," was Amy's flat reply.

"I would not say that; most, however, are aware that there's a risk in such an approach. No one would have tried to harvest Andrew Copis in his current state; I am not even certain the Queen of the Dead would have taken that risk."

"But she could?"

Ernest glanced at Margaret.

Margaret, however, was watching Emma. "Emma could," she finally said.

"He almost killed Emma," Amy pointed out, although she hadn't heard Margaret's words.

"Not intentionally. But, yes, the fire was strong, and Emma is alive. There is a reason the divide between the living and the dead is so extreme. It was never meant to be crossed."

"Emma didn't bind him," Allison said, a slow heat in the words. "That's not why she—"

"We're aware that she didn't approach the child with the aim of adding to her power. It's almost a certainty that Longland *did*. Emma had effectively stripped him of his power; he had nothing to lose. I don't believe he expected Emma to be present; I do believe that when he discovered that she was, he chose to act. If she succeeded in binding Andrew Copis, she would have been a significant power—and he would have been much diminished. He knew that she had taken five of the dead from his grasp."

"That doesn't happen often?"

"No," Ernest replied. He eyed Amy as if she were a feral dog. Or a rabid one. Amy didn't particularly care, and if Amy wasn't going to take offense, it was never smart to take offense on her behalf.

"It shouldn't happen at all," Margaret said quietly.

Emma frowned. "Why?"

"It takes power to bind the dead. I know I've mentioned this before," she added, in a more severe tone.

"In theory, I *have* power," Emma said. "If it takes power to make the binding, it makes sense it would take power to break it."

Margaret was silent for a long moment. "Understand that I was rescued by the Queen of the Dead. I would have died—just as you should have—otherwise. Everything I know about my former power, I know through her teaching. She was not a particularly kind woman, as you might suspect. But in her fashion, she considers the Necromancers her only family.

"I don't know how she sees the dead. I know how I saw them, before Ernest. I didn't speak with them, Emma. I certainly did not stoop to rescue them. Had I known of Andrew Copis, I might have waited, watching the situation over the passage of a few decades. He would have been a coup. You couldn't—or wouldn't—see the power inherent in his condition, and even if you had, you wouldn't have kept him here.

"You set him free. You set all possible sources of power within the area free, as well. It is the one saving grace you will have should you choose to remain in your home—very, very few dead remain here. If you can break the bindings that give the Necromancers their power over the dead, they will be forced to retreat. They will, in all likelihood, be forced to flee using the normal methods of transportation available to the living."

"Merrick Longland—"

"Is no longer concerned with sources of power. He serves the Queen directly."

"Why did she send him?"

Margaret frowned. "I don't know. What will you do now?"

Emma exhaled. "Amy."

Amy nodded, although her glare didn't falter.

"If we can find the Necromancer, and we can free the sources of his power, Margaret thinks we'll be safe. She considers Toronto—or at least our parts of it—a wasteland as far as Necromancers and power are concerned."

"Allison?" Amy asked, still glaring at Ernest.

"I don't want my family hurt," Allison replied, after a long pause. "But I don't want to have to explain this to them. They'll think we're crazy. At best. If we prove we're not, they'll be terrified, and they'll call the police at the very least."

"Michael?"

Michael was silent for longer. "Emma," he finally said, "can you do it?"

She swallowed. Like Allison, she was afraid of the truth. Using it had costs. Hiding it had costs. "If Chase and Eric can tell us where—and who—the Necromancers are, I can break their power." But she turned once again to Margaret, who was silent and watchful.

"You're dead," she said, voice low. "And you were part of Merrick Longland's power base. If you didn't know—as a Necromancer—what it was like for the dead, you *do* know, now. What I did—what I shouldn't have been able to do, according to your teaching—why did it work?"

"You saw us as people," Margaret replied.

Eric rose. He was silent as he headed out of the room.

"What did she say?" Amy demanded.

"She said—she said I saw them as people."

"Well, duh."

"I'm not entirely certain your Amy is not like our Chase," Margaret said.

"She's scarier. Margaret—what do you mean?"

"You knew we needed help. You never doubted you *could*. Do you understand that most people would not be in a desperate rush to risk their lives just to save a child who was already dead?"

"He didn't know he was dead."

"No, but, Emma—you did. You knew that nothing you could do could change that."

Emma said nothing.

"What I did not realize as a Necromancer is that the dead still have some choice. It is slender, and against the brute force of Necromantic bindings, it is insignificant. But it was not absent. I was not aware of you until you touched what you describe as golden chains. When you did, Emma, I saw you. I understood in that moment that you saw me. I knew where I was; I knew that I was dead. But I felt as if you had finally found me."

Emma blinked; Margaret looked slightly embarrassed. "I know that sounds odd, dear. I didn't have a sense of who you actually were; I felt relief and warmth. The dead seldom feel warmth. I felt as if I had been offered a hand out of a very dark hole, and I took that hand and emerged.

"It's not a perfect analogy; there are some things you would have to be dead to experience. I could not have escaped Merrick Longland without your intervention, but you gave me the choice. I believe you did the same when you met Merrick Longland a second time.

"Even then, you would not take the power available in order to fight him."

"But I *did*."

"No, Emma. We gave. There is a difference. Even when you showed us the way by lighting the lamp, you *asked* and we *gave*. I believe, were you to hold that lamp, that any of the dead—no matter how weak or unaware—would see you and know you."

"Margaret," Ernest began.

Her look, in theory much milder than Amy's glare of death, did what Amy's couldn't: It silenced him.

"Longland is, of course, capable of killing without the power he defined himself by in life. But he is not of the living the way you now are. You must decide what you're willing to risk." She glanced at the rest of Emma's friends and added. "All of you. I'm sorry."

CHAPTER
ELEVEN

EMMA DISCOVERED SOMETHING over the next uncomfort-able half an hour: She was the only person present who was com-fortable talking about a parent's death as if it were a reality. Amy was practical enough to consider it a serious risk, but she was arrogant enough to assume it happened to other people. Allison was subdued, probably because Chase was a whole lot of angry, even if he kept actual words to himself.

Michael was pale.

Eric offered strategies for essentially lying to their parents; he offered help if they wanted to disappear for the foreseeable future. He didn't offer advice, for which Emma was grateful.

Forty-five minutes later, there was still no solution that somehow made everything normal and safe again, and Amy decided she'd had enough for the day, which meant the discussion—and the visit—was officially over. School, however, was not. She left Eric and Chase to Eric's car, and gathered Michael, Emma, and Allison in her own.

"Do you want to keep having this discussion without Ernest?" Amy asked, as she pulled into the school lot.

"Any night but tonight," Emma replied.

"What's tonight?"

"I'm having dinner with my mother and her new boyfriend. I can't miss it. I can't be late for it. If something happens during dinner, my dad will be there to help me."

"With your mother's new boyfriend?"

"I know. It's awkward." But it felt less awkward, now. Emma and her mother had their differences—but Emma knew her mother was there for her. She was loved, had been loved, for as much of her life as she could remember. She didn't want to repay that with secrecy, lies, and death.

But she didn't want to leave home, either. Her mother would be beyond terrified—and she'd probably blame herself. The timing couldn't be worse. Maybe she'd assume Emma was running away from home because of the boyfriend. Her mother didn't deserve that. She didn't deserve that fear.

But she didn't deserve the fear the truth would give her either.

"Sometimes you get what you don't deserve," Amy said sharply.

"Did I say that out loud?"

"No. But it's all over your face."

Emma grimaced and got out of the car, wondering if this kind of worry plagued her mother. Probably, given the Halls.

"Let's see how long we can avoid Merrick Longland," Allison said quietly.

Emma didn't answer.

There were two ghosts in the parking lot, and both of them were familiar. Her father was standing beside Mark, who stood slightly behind and to one side, his shoulders hunched and stiff. Emma exhaled. "You guys go in; I'll catch up later."

She waited until they started to move; Allison lingered, and Emma mouthed a silent "it's my dad," which was as much comfort as she could offer.

"Mark," she said, defaulting to the Hall smile.

Mark looked up—he had to. "I went home," he said, in a quiet voice. She swallowed.

"I tried to talk to my mom. She couldn't see me. My brother and my sister couldn't see me either. You can see me."

Emma nodded.

"Your friends could see me because you wanted them to see me."

She knew where this was going; she could see it yawning, like a sudden chasm, inches from her feet. She looked over Mark's head to her father's drawn face.

"I want you to take me home."

"My father took you home and—"

"I want to ask her if she forgot about me."

Her father closed his eyes; Emma, however, slid her hands behind her back; they were bunched in fists. Did she pity him? Yes.

It was a tricky thing, to pity someone. There was a difference between sympathy, empathy, and pity. Pity was what you gave to injured animals, not people. Not even dead boys who looked like they were six years old.

"You already know the answer," she said, her voice calm and matter-of-fact.

Mark's gaze slid off Emma's left cheek. He wouldn't meet her eyes for a long, awkward moment.

"Mark."

He swiveled. "I want to go home," he whispered. She heard anger in the softly spoken words—and behind that wall of anger, nothing but pain and loss. Emma seldom hated anyone as much as she hated Mark's mother at the moment. And she knew it wouldn't help Mark now—but she couldn't think of a single thing that would.

Had she never known Michael, she might have tried lying. Lies—lies a person wanted to believe—could be comforting; they could be an act of kindness. But they could also be an act of weakness. There was no way to minimize the wrong, no way to minimize the pain. Telling him that his mother wasn't worth this pain was the truth, but sometimes truth didn't change things, either. Not quickly.

Not at all.

The worst truth Emma had ever faced in her life was Nathan's death. For the first time that she could remember, she felt, viscerally, that Mark's truth was worse. There had been whole days when Emma had raged—in perfect Hall silence—against the pain of loss; hours when she had wished—and, oh, the guilt she felt—that she had *never* loved at all if all it amounted to was emptiness and endless pain.

But Nathan had loved her. She had been loved.

Mark's mother couldn't have loved him and done what she did. What kind of life had Mark known? What kind of death?

"Em," her father said softly. She looked up. "It's not that simple. Nothing ever is."

She wanted to argue; she would have. But Mark was standing between them, and she couldn't. The urge to somehow protect this child was so strong, he might have been alive.

"Pain and fear make us do hideous, ugly things. Love and joy make us do beautiful things. At base, we're all human."

"Dad, don't. Just don't." Mark was watching her intently. It didn't mean that he couldn't hear every word her father was saying.

"I know it's difficult, but it never helps in the end to make monsters out of people; it prevents you from seeing them as they are."

"I'm not making a monster out of her. She—"

"Em."

"You would never have done this!"

"No." He was silent for a moment. Had he been alive, he would have gone for his pipe; he had that expression. "Do you remember, when you were five, a friend of your mother's died?"

Emma frowned. Five was so far in the past it existed in fragmented memories. "Aunt Carol?" she finally asked.

"Yes. She wasn't an aunt; you called her that because you saw her so often. She died eight months after the birth of her first child."

"A boy. I remember."

"Do you remember that her son died as well?"

Emma nodded. "There was an accident," she began. She stopped, considering her father's expression. "It wasn't an accident."

"No."

"Her husband?" she asked.

"No, Em. She shut herself in her car in the garage with her baby. She turned on the engine. Paul was at work. She didn't call him. She didn't leave a note. When he came home, the garage door was locked; the remote didn't work."

Emma froze, arrested.

"He went into the house to find the key. His wife wasn't home. He assumed she'd taken the baby and gone out somewhere. He didn't understand why the garage door was locked. He found the key when he found her; he had to enter the garage through the house. He was too late for either of them. Too late for himself. He didn't kill them, but he did blame himself for what happened.

"Carol committed suicide. The doctor—after the fact—thought she must have been suffering from severe post-partum depression. It happens. You don't consider Aunt Carol a monster."

". . . No."

"But she killed her son."

"She killed *herself*, Dad."

"Yes. She was probably afraid of the pain her son would feel in future if she abandoned him by dying. She took him with her. But he was an infant, he was helpless, he had no choice, and he died." Her father slid his hands into his pockets.

Emma watched him.

"You don't think of Carol as a monster. In the worst case, you pity her. You don't think of what she did to her own son as murder. But her son could have had a life, much like yours, with his father."

"You can't possibly be defending someone who could do something like this!"

"No. I'm not. But I am profoundly *grateful* that I was never compelled to make such an ugly choice. I tried for most of my adult life to be what passes for a good man. But there were days when it was nothing but struggle. It's not something we talk to our children about—we want our children to live as happily and worry-free as they can. We don't talk about money. We don't talk about marital difficulties. We don't talk about struggles on the job front.

"And I wonder, sometimes, if the choice to remain silent serves anyone well. We want you to grow up in a safe space. We make it as safe as possible. But—if something breaks, it's one more thing to lose."

"What is?"

"The faith and belief your children have in you. There's a fair bit of ego in being a superhero in the eyes of your children," he added, with a wry grin. "Because god knows we're no superheroes in anyone else's. I'm not trying to excuse what Mark's mother did. But it's the act that was monstrous—and it was the act of a moment, a day. Pity her."

"Pity *her*?" Emma tried to remember that Mark was watching her. "What does she need pity for? She got away with—"

"It will haunt her for the rest of her life. Life is a test, Emma. A constant test. We want to believe certain things about ourselves, but as we see more and more of the world, we realize how small we are and how short our reach actually is. Things we swore we would never do, we find ourselves doing. It's easy to judge from the outside."

"Mom wouldn't agree with you."

He grimaced. "No. Had she been faced with the same choice Mark's mother faced, she would have killed herself, first." He turned to Mark, as if he'd never forgotten that Mark was part of the conversation. And maybe he hadn't. "Would that have been better?"

Mark stared, unblinking, at her father's face. When he finally answered, his voice sounded even younger. "I don't want my mother to die," he whispered.

No, of course not. What he wanted—even now, dead at her hands—was his mother's love and acceptance. He didn't even want to be alive again—he just wanted something he'd never had.

"Do you love your mother, Mark?" Her father asked. Emma felt her lower jaw drop in outrage and shock.

Mark looked down at his feet. "Yes," he said, voice very small. "I try to be what she wants. I always try. But I forget, and it hurts her."

"Dad—stop it. Stop it now."

"We all love our parents," he told his angry daughter. "Even when they don't deserve it. Sometimes especially then."

"She has other children," Emma said, voice low. "If she did this once, she could do it again."

"She won't hurt them," Mark told her. "They're normal."

Emma didn't swear in front of her parents. Her mother hated it—although she wasn't above dropping a few choice words herself when she was angry. She was fairly certain her father would have disapproved as well—but at eight years of age, she hadn't developed the habit. It saved her from saying exactly what she was thinking.

"She told me to wait for her," Mark continued, oblivious to the anger that rested beneath Emma's silence. "And I waited. It was cold. I was cold. I'm still cold."

"Does it hurt?" her father asked quietly.

Mark shook his head. "Not any more. But I want to talk to my mom."

"I have to finish school," Emma told Mark quietly. "I've already had to miss two classes." She hesitated, then added, "I have to be home for dinner as well. My mom's invited someone over, and I promised I'd be there."

"After dinner?"

She had homework. She meant to say she had homework. But excuses like homework seemed so pathetic and minor in comparison that she couldn't force them out of her mouth. She didn't want to take Mark to his mother's house. She couldn't see how it could bring anything but more pain to a child who had had enough of it. She didn't trust herself near Mark's mother.

And what could she do to Mark's mother? Call the police? Accuse the mother of murder—of abandonment—when the only evidence she had was the ghost of the dead child himself?

It wouldn't be the first time she'd proved her words with the help of dead children. But that had been different, and she knew it. Andrew Copis' mother had been forced to leave her oldest son in a house on fire because she'd been carrying an infant and a barely mobile toddler and Andrew *could* walk. His death haunted her; it had almost destroyed her.

But Mark's mother?

"Emma?"

She exhaled. "After dinner. We have a guest. It might be late."

Mark said, in an uncomfortably familiar tone, "I don't need to sleep, now."

The Halls of Emery Collegiate hadn't changed. They were the same paint-over-concrete; the floors were the same faux marble. The lockers, some dented by the boisterous set over the past decade, framed the occasional door and glass display cabinet; the teachers served as informal patrol as they headed between classes. Since the halls weren't carpeted, noise bounced; no conversation was muted—you had to raise your voice just to be heard.

The noise was a comfort today. It was normal. It didn't matter that snatches of unavoidable conversation were about television, boyfriends, and unreasonable parents. Emma wanted to hear them, even if she could no longer join them. She wanted a world in which her mother was annoying, motherly, and *safe*. Even if that mother brought a new—

and unwanted—boyfriend into the house. There was nothing Mercy Hall could do that deserved death by Necromancer. Or death by anything, really.

But she didn't deserve to have her daughter disappear without warning—or forwarding address—either. She watched the doors to offices and classes closely, approaching them with caution; she didn't want to run into Merrick Longland. She caught up with Allison in social studies, just in time to avoid the late slip that should have been coming her way.

Allison's single glance held a question; Emma smiled in response. It was the silent version of "I'm fine," and caused Ally to frown. More than that wasn't possible. Michael sat at the front of this class, in part to avoid the chatting that often went on in the back. Emma wondered if he was absorbing anything the teacher said. She was having a hard time concentrating herself.

Boredom was highly underrated. She couldn't get Mark's expression out of her head, and when she tried, she was left with dinner, her mother, and her mother's new boyfriend. There was no resentment left in her, just a mouth-drying fear.

She'd accept the new boyfriend. She'd work hard to accept him. Just let everything else be okay. Let the Necromancers ignore her mother. Let Mark change his mind. Let her friends' families be safe.

This is why Chase hates me, Emma thought. She thought it without the usual sting. If it weren't for her, no one would be in any danger. She shook herself, took notes, and tried to find the discussion about willpower and its finite qualities interesting.

"Mark?" Allison asked Emma as quietly as she could in a very crowded stretch of hallway after the last class had ended.

Emma nodded. She headed straight for the front doors, without the usual social lingering. Allison was right behind her, and Michael was already outside. He'd chosen to wait in the usual place, but he watched the doors open and close with a twitchy nervousness. No one wanted to accidentally bump into Merrick Longland, and the minute Allison and Emma reached Michael, they began a hurried walk to put as much distance between Emery Collegiate and themselves as they could without breaking into an out and out run.

"Amy wants to meet at her house tomorrow after school," Allison said.

This surprised Emma. As a general rule, Allison and Amy didn't talk much.

Michael nodded, but Emma touched his shoulder anyway. When Michael was stressed out—and they were *all* stressed out at the moment—nodding came naturally; it didn't mean he agreed or even understood what had been said.

"I have track practice tomorrow," Michael told them.

"I'll talk to Amy. If it's okay with you, we can pick you up when you're finished." She steered him in the direction of his house. He was thinking, and sometimes Michael's thoughts became the whole of his geography; he could literally look up blocks from now in confusion, because he had no memory of walking them.

Today, Emma understood why. Walking down streets she'd seen all her life felt unreal. So much had changed in the past few months. She felt, on a visceral level, that the rest of the world should reflect those changes. It didn't.

And it made her question the life she'd lived up to now. It made every mundane street and every mundane corner sharper and harsher. Necromancers and their Queen had existed for longer than Emma had been alive, and until she herself had begun to see the dead, she'd never heard a word about them. Necromancers in the various games Michael and his friends played didn't have a Queen, and the dead were usually confined to the role of brain-eating, shuffling zombies.

The sun was low, but it wouldn't be dark for a couple of hours, and the lawns were, for the most part, buried under a pristine blanket of snow. Someone across the street was walking a black Labrador that didn't seem to be as deaf as Emma's rottweiler. Once, Petal had been that young.

She exhaled a cloud, shoving her hands deeper into her pockets. Maybe all of life was a little like this: You saw the parts of it you knew, and if no one pointed you in a different direction, that was the entire truth of your world. The different direction she'd been turned to face hadn't actually changed the world; it had just changed Emma's perception.

Her father had never been keen on ignorance; he felt that lack of knowledge was something to be alleviated, as if it were the common cold. She paused at the foot of Michael's driveway. "Don't forget to ask your mother about visiting Amy tomorrow," she told him, as she gave him a little nudge in the direction of his house.

"He wants to go home," Allison said, when Michael's front door had opened and closed behind him.

"Mark?"

Allison nodded.

"Yes. I don't want to take him," she added, although it was obvious. "And I waffled. I told him I couldn't do it tonight because I had important guests, more or less."

Allison winced on Emma's behalf, and Emma felt guilty. "I know my mother. I do. If Jon were a jerk, she wouldn't like him. But no, I'm not really looking forward to making nice at dinner. I don't know if I'm expected to impress him; I certainly haven't managed that so far."

"I think," Allison said quietly, "it's probably more important to your mom that Jon impress you."

"That's what I'm afraid of. I don't want my mom's new boyfriend sucking up to me. I don't know him. I don't have much to say to him." She held out a hand before Allison could speak. "I'll find something. I've always managed the small talk. I'm not even angry about him anymore. If things go wrong, a new boyfriend doesn't even register on the possible disaster scales.

"But I swear, if I walk into the house and there are any PDAs, I'm going to be ill."

The front hall was full of deaf rottweiler when Emma opened the door. Petal was happy to see her, although she suspected at the moment she looked like a walking food dish. Honestly, people who didn't know better would assume the Hall household regularly starved their poor, pathetic dog.

She wasn't immune to puppy-induced guilt and headed to the kitchen to remedy it. Unlike other forms of guilt in this house, food-related guilt was easily dealt with. When Petal had eaten enough—a rare occurrence—he left the kitchen and returned with a scratched, retractable leash in his mouth.

Emma shook her head. "Not tonight," she said quietly. This produced predictable whining. "I need to clean the kitchen and the dining room; we have guests coming for dinner."

She wasn't exactly lying; the kitchen and the dining room were in need of cleaning. But she needed the space of a few hours in which to think and make decisions—and if she took Petal out of the house, she was almost certain Nathan would appear.

Nathan.

She wasn't ready to talk to him again. Her mind was full of Merrick Longland, her mother, and the parents and siblings of her friends. It felt almost like betrayal, but she knew that Nathan—if he could hear her thoughts—would understand. The dead had time. Nathan had time.

And Emma had barely enough time to putter around the kitchen and the dining room in a silence broken only by dog whining. She didn't talk to herself as she worked because she had Petal, and Petal knew she was worried about something. He had stayed by her side during the long first month after Nathan's death, often with the leash in his mouth and his head in her lap.

He shuffled around her feet as she worked, and she let the work soothe her. It was normal. Meeting her mother's boyfriend, not so much. When the dining room was up to Hall guest standards—occupants having much lower ones—she headed up to her room to fix her hair and try to dress like a respectable daughter.

Her father did not show up, and given she was changing, that was a blessing.

When her mother arrived, Emma was in the television room, channel surfing in the hope that something would catch her attention. She set the remote aside when she heard her mother's car hit the driveway and caught Petal's collar before he charged up the stairs.

"Guests, remember?" she said, without much hope. She opened the door to see her mother fumbling with keys, a bag of groceries precariously cradled in her left arm. Jon was standing to one side, two bags of groceries in similar positions. Emma offered him her politest Hall smile, took the bag from her mother's arm, and headed toward the kitchen.

Jon followed, which wouldn't have been her first choice. But he didn't make himself at home in Emma's kitchen.

"Where did you want me to put these?"

"On the breakfast table," Emma told him, pointing. "I'll put them away." She hesitated, then added, "Can you reach the plates on the third shelf here?"

"With or without a chair?"

She smiled; it was less forced. She waited for him to say something stupid or awkward, because her mother had not yet entered the kitchen. He didn't. Instead, he got the plates and set them on the counter just in front of Emma. Emma tried to guess what exactly her mother intended to cook from the contents of the bags and came up with four possibilities. "I don't suppose she mentioned what was for dinner?"

"No. She bought desert, though." He looked at his feet and then up; he smiled. "She was nervous."

"It's a defining Hall trait," Emma replied. "That and guilt." She took a deep breath, held out her right hand, and added, "I'm Emma."

He took her hand as if he had never been introduced and said, "I'm Jon. Is your mother trying to give us time alone?"

Since it was the same thought Emma had, but with less annoyance and more genuine curiosity, Emma said, "Probably not. I know she's an ace at work, but she spends all her organization points in the office."

"Leaving the organization of the house to you?"

"More or less. If it helps, my locker at school is a class-A disaster."

"It helps a little. Look, I'm not great with small talk."

"Not great?"

"I suck at it."

Emma laughed.

Jon didn't. "I mean it. I'm seriously bad at making small talk. If I ask about someone's husband, they're in the middle of a divorce. If I ask about their family, their parents have cancer. If I compliment their clothing, they're wearing something their mother bought and they hate it." He held out both of his empty hands, palms up. "So mostly, I don't try."

"My mother's not bad at it."

"She's almost as bad at it as I am," he replied. He glanced toward the hall, which still contained Mercy, her coat, and, apparently, the family dog. "I'm not here to be your best friend. I'm not here to be your friend—that's presumptuous and probably unwanted." He ran his hands through his hair. "I care about your mother."

"Was this your idea or hers?"

"Pass."

"What?"

"I pass. I'll take question number two."

"Fine. Have you ever been married before?"

"How many passes do I get?"

She laughed. She couldn't help it. "As many as you need. This isn't an interrogation."

"You're sure?"

"Well, no, not really."

His smile deepened. The lines around the corners of his mouth were etched there; it made Emma realize that Jon smiled a lot. He wasn't a handsome man. He wasn't anywhere near as good-looking as her father had been. But she liked his smile. There were no edges in it.

"Teenage girls always make me nervous."

"You don't look particularly nervous."

"No. I'm better at hiding it. When I was a teenager, I kept my mouth shut. It mostly stopped the stupid from pouring out."

"Mostly?"

"I fidgeted more." He slid his hands into his pockets and leaned back against the edge of the counter. "I also suck under stress."

"You're under stress? Try meeting your mother's first boyfriend." She reddened. "I mean, first since . . ."

"You're always going to be your mother's daughter. If I screw up, I'm not guaranteed to hold the same position."

"You'd make a terrible daughter."

"If she's used to your caliber, probably. And I'm not willing to try—she's already got the only daughter she wants. So . . . what are our chances of eating dinner before ten?"

Emma pretended to consider the question. "Depends."

"On what?"

"If you want her in the kitchen right now, we could start shouting at each other."

He laughed. "I'll take dinner at ten, thanks."

*   *   *

To Emma's surprise, she wasn't in need of rescue. Jon looked just as surprised, because as it turned out, neither was he. When her mother entered the kitchen, she had the wary smile of a worried Hall attached to her face. It was brittle, and it was mildly annoying.

"I'm not bleeding," Jon told her.

Her mother had the grace to redden.

"He's not cowering in the corner either," Emma pointed out, with a little less humor than Jon.

Her mother winced. She didn't apologize, which would have been awkward, not that it wasn't already awkward. But Jon grinned. "She's your daughter. She's not going to wilt in the corner like a drama queen."

"Which proves," her mother said, in a more acerbic tone, "that you don't know the Halls well enough." To Emma she added, "I've given him plenty of opportunity to back out."

"And he's not bright enough to take any of them?"

"Apparently not." Her mother's smile was worn around the edges, but it was natural. "Jon, don't take this personally, but I need my kitchen."

"And your daughter?"

"Every chef needs a sous chef."

CHAPTER
TWELVE

THE KITCHEN WITH HER MOTHER IN IT was more awkward than the kitchen without her, an irony not lost on either of the Halls. "You don't have to love him," her mother began.

Emma, struggling with the theoretical sharp edge of a knife that clearly hadn't been sharpened in a decade, grimaced. "Good to know."

"You just have to understand that I might."

"Might? It's not decided?"

"I'm a little too old to fall head over heels in love," her mother replied. "It's been so long since I even considered being involved with anyone else at all." She set her knife down to one side of the cutting board and turned. "I didn't plan this. I wasn't even aware that he was interested in me."

Of all the conversations Emma could be having with her mother, this was the obvious one—but obvious or not, it was completely unexpected. Emma, who could cut and listen at the same time, nudged her mother away from the counter, but not before looking at her.

Objectively, her mother wasn't *old*. She wasn't young but then again, she had a teenage daughter. She dressed—and looked—like a middle-aged mother, to Emma. "You know," she said, half to Mercy and half to herself, "when I was four years old, I thought you were the most beautiful person alive."

"Were?" her mother asked. "Have I changed so much?"

Had she? "Well, after that I met Amy."

Her mother laughed. Hearing it, Emma wondered how long it had been since she'd heard that laugh. Her mother had laughed a lot more when her father had been alive. Emma finished slicing chicken and looked at her mother again. Her mother stood by the back screen door, her hands behind her. She thought about what her dad had said—the parts that didn't make her angry. Parents didn't *talk* to their kids; they wanted to give them a safe haven.

And safety was a myth.

"I know what I felt when I first got to know your father," her mother said quietly, looking out into the yard, her face reflected in the glass. She straightened her shoulders and headed back to the counter and their neglected dinner preparations. "I know this isn't the same. I'm not sure what I feel, but I don't want to overthink it."

"Mom—that's not the salt."

"What?" Mercy Hall looked at the glass jar in her hand. "Right. Sugar would be more interesting."

"Interesting food probably isn't the best choice for a first meal."

"I don't think Jon would mind too much. He's the better cook." That said, she put the sugar down and picked up the salt. "But Jon makes me laugh. He makes me laugh even when there's nothing remotely funny. Sometimes when I'm with him, I don't have to think." She turned to her daughter, who was silent.

"I know you miss your father. I miss him, too. I thought I'd spend the rest of my life in mourning. I don't know what I would have done if I hadn't had you."

"You'd've had an easier life."

"Easy and happy aren't the same—they only look the same when things are both hard and unhappy. I always thought your father was the better parent. He was more patient and more consistent. But I tried. I tried to live up to him."

"Tell her she did."

Emma closed her eyes as a familiar chill descended on the kitchen. She couldn't tell if her mother felt it or not; her mother was focused on dinner. And on the strange flow of words that Emma had never heard before. She turned to her father; her father was watching his wife making dinner for another man. His expression made Emma want to cry, but she was a Hall; she didn't.

She also didn't pass the words on.

"Tell her," her father continued when Emma failed to speak, "that she did better. I love her. I always have. And she's been lonely for long enough. She's not lying, Em. This *is* the first time she's ever been willing to risk opening up. To you," he said, in case this wasn't clear. "And to the possibility of life with someone else."

"I was too busy with you to be lonely," her mother said. She couldn't hear her husband's words, of course, but some instinct stopped their words from overlapping. "That's the truth. I knew we had to be a family, even if we were without a husband and a father. We still needed to keep a roof over our heads. Your grandmother offered to let us move in with her."

Emma grimaced but politely said nothing.

"But I had to know that we could make it on our own. And we have." She turned to the stove, wiping up invisible dirt from around the stovetop elements. "I don't know what happened the night we took you to the hospital."

Emma froze.

"I don't know if I was so frenzied with worry that I—" She shook her head. "No. That's not it. You saw—what I saw. Michael saw him. Allison did. I don't know if they remember. I don't know if they talk about it."

Emma started to speak, but her mother held up one imploring hand.

"I need to say this, and if I don't get it all out now, I never will. Can you—can you let me do that? I'm asking for a lot, I know."

"Mom—" Emma swallowed. "You're not asking for much. You're just asking for me to listen." Who listened to her mother? She had a few friends she saw maybe twice a year—old university friends who now lived across the continent in different cities. Emma had Allison. Who did her mother have?

Not Emma, not really. Parents didn't talk to their children about anything important. No, that wasn't true. They listened and talked about things that were important to their *children*. But they didn't talk about their own lives. And it had never really occurred to Emma to ask. Why not?

"I saw Brendan. I saw him. I heard him." Her eyes were red, but—Hall. She didn't shed tears. They changed the timbre of her voice anyway. "He hadn't aged a day. He didn't look—he didn't look dead. But he looked the way he looked when you were a child and Petal was a puppy. And his expression—" She swallowed. "He looked so worried. For *me*. He looked—"

"You are *not* a disappointment to Dad," Emma said, with more force than she'd intended. She crossed the small space that divided them, forgetting for a moment that they had roles they were meant to inhabit. She slid her arms around her mother's shoulders and felt a shock as she realized how *small* her mother actually was.

"I'd just taken you to the hospital. I was terrified. If Dad were here—"

"Dad was alive when I broke my arm."

"A broken arm can't kill you."

"I'm sure Michael could come up with exceptions."

Mercy laughed. It was shaky. "When I came home that night, I felt so lonely. I haven't felt that way for so long. I felt as if the eight years and the work and the keeping things going—it was empty."

"Mercy," her father whispered. He was standing so close to them, all

Emma had to do was reach out and touch him, and he'd be here too. But she didn't.

"And you hated yourself for feeling that way," Emma said softly.

Her mother blinked.

"I'm a Hall, remember? I know how this goes. You were *fine*. I was *fine*. There were probably days when you hated Dad for dying."

"Did you hate Nathan for dying?" her mother asked softly.

"Some days, I still do. Or I hate that I fell in love with him, because if I hadn't, life without him wouldn't be so bad."

Her mother nodded. "He cared for you."

"And Dad loved you."

Her mother put her arms around Emma. They stood together for a long, silent moment. "I don't regret a minute of the last eight years."

"The Candlewick project?" It had been one of Mercy's few—but significant—failures.

"Funny girl," her mother's voice was soft and fond. "But after I saw your father in the hospital, I couldn't shake that loneliness. I don't know if I love Jon, but when I'm with him, the world seems a little brighter and little more vibrant. He's so good at being who he is. It doesn't seem to matter if he's talking to an eighty year old or a toddler. He doesn't ask for anything, and he doesn't want a lot from me. He knows about your father, of course. He knows how important you are. He was nervous," she added.

"I know. I was nervous, too."

"I thought you were angry."

"I was." Emma tightened her arms. "I don't know Jon. But sometimes," she added, thinking about the conversation with her father earlier in the day, "I think I didn't really know Dad, either. I'll try, Mom. I will honestly try."

"I couldn't replace Nathan," her mother said. It sounded like an odd thing to say, but it mirrored what Emma couldn't put into words herself. "But I never doubted that you loved me."

"And I couldn't replace Dad."

"No one could. Jon isn't trying to be Brendan. He knows he's not your father. You only—and ever—have one." Her mother exhaled. "I'm not trying to replace my husband, either. He was my best friend and my pillar of support, and nothing Jon says or does will change that. But nothing anyone says or does can change the past. If I can't open up a bit, if I can't let go, the past is the only future I have.

"And you're almost an adult now. You don't need me anymore."

"I do, Mom."

"Not the way you used to. I miss it," she added, since this was a night for unexpected truth. "But no one gets to be a child forever—and no one should want to. You've grown. You've become so much stronger. I want you to keep growing up. I want you to go out into a world that doesn't include me. I want you to meet—" she stopped, stiffening at the words that had almost fallen out of her mouth, and the implication behind them.

At any other time, Emma would have been angry. But the anger wouldn't come. In a quieter voice she said, "I'm not ready to meet anyone new."

"No, of course not—I'm sorry, Em, I was just—"

"You took eight years, Mom. Eight years. Give me at least that long."

Her mother nodded and slowly disentangled herself. "We're going to have dinner at midnight at this rate," she said, running her sleeve across her eyes. Emma couldn't remember the last time she'd seen her mother cry.

"Jon won't care," she said.

"No, he really won't," her mother replied, smiling.

Dinner was late, even for the Hall household, but it wasn't midnight. It wasn't—quite—nine in the evening, although it only missed that mark by a few minutes. Allison texted before they'd even sat down, and Emma texted back a brief "I don't hate him." She avoided using the words "it's fine" because they always made Ally worry.

And the truth was, she didn't. She wasn't certain she *liked* him, but she was certain her like or dislike was irrelevant. Or it should be. But she lingered in the kitchen while her mother took the food out.

"Is this really okay?" she asked her father, who hadn't left the kitchen once.

"It's better than okay," he replied. "Nathan's death is too new to you. You can't see past it. You can't see a world that doesn't have him in it."

She almost said, *And I don't have to*. But she held her peace. She was in a strange state of mind; there was almost no fight in her.

"Your mother has had eight years of a life without me," he continued. "Sometimes she'd tell you that she missed me. But, Em—the life the two of you have now doesn't have a place for me in it. She's held that space empty, as if I might somehow return to fill it.

"It's not what I want for her. Maybe if I could come back—in the flesh, alive—I'd hate everything about this evening. But I think she's been in pain and been alone for long enough. I don't want you to compare Jon to me, because there's no point. Jon isn't me. Your mother is right—nothing will change our past. But it *is* past.

"If you can do one thing for me, help her."

"I've always tried—"

"Help her with Jon. He's a decent guy. He does care for Mercy. Maybe he can give her what I can't." He turned to his daughter, hands in ghostly pockets. "You were angry that she didn't ask about me. You were upset that she didn't want to speak with me. For you, speaking with Nathan is so much better than the silence and the absence.

"It's different for your mother. What she's seen of death is final; that door is closed. If she *did* speak to me, if she asked, it wouldn't make her life any easier because I can't be part of it." He closed his eyes. "What will you do?"

"I'll try to like Jon."

"No, Em, what will you do about the Necromancers?"

"I don't want to tell Mom. I think the worry would about kill her, if the Necromancers didn't do it first. But I don't want to run away without telling her anything—I'm afraid she'd blame Jon. Or worse, herself. This is the first boyfriend, and if I suddenly disappear, it'll probably be the last one. And . . . I don't want to leave home. I know she's not perfect, but I'm not perfect either." Exhaling, she said, "Tell me I'm wrong. Tell me she won't blame Jon or herself."

"You know your mother as well as I do. You probably know her better, by this point."

"Great. Sometimes I think life is just a way of accumulating guilt."

He chuckled. "For the Halls, it probably is. You should head out. Your mother's going to worry if she walks in and finds you talking to yourself."

Halfway through dinner, the doorbell rang.

Emma looked across the table at Jon. "Did you order pizza?"

He laughed as Emma rose. "I would never insult the collective cooking of the Halls; I like my teeth where they are." The smile faded slowly from his lips. "It's a little late for door to door salesmen."

"And we're not in the middle of election season. On the other hand, most people have probably finished dinner by now. Sit down, Mom. You have a guest. I'll get it." The last three words were said in a much louder voice, as Petal had set up barking.

She caught her dog by the collar and pulled him away from the front door, but she resented having to do it; at this time of night, random strangers who interrupted people at dinner deserved to have a face full of loud, suspicious rottweiler.

"Petal, sit. *Sit*."

One hand on dog and the other on doorknob, she opened the door and froze in its frame as she met the eyes of Merrick Longland.

CHAPTER
THIRTEEN

HIS SMILE WAS FULL-ON TEACHER. "Just the young woman I wanted to see."

"Emma? Who is it?" Her mother's voice approached from the dining room. Emma swallowed and met Merrick Longland's eyes; under the light at the side of the door, they were faintly luminescent, but she couldn't describe their color. They were, in every way, the eyes of the dead.

But he wasn't dead. She knew. Her mother came out of the dining room and headed straight toward him, wearing her best, distancing business smile.

"Mrs. Hall?" he said, extending his right hand. "Have I caught you at a bad time?"

"We're in the middle of a late dinner," her mother replied, thawing slightly. "What can I do for you?"

"I'm actually here to speak with Emma. My name is Merrick Longland, and I have the privilege of being her supervisor on the yearbook committee." He held out a hand.

For one immobile moment, Emma wanted to slam the door in his face. But it was too late for that; her mother's expression had relaxed, and she was already shaking the hand Merrick Longland had offered.

If being dead made any difference to the physical body, it was too subtle for her mother. "I'm Emma's mother, Mercy Hall. We don't usually get teachers visiting at this time of night."

"It's eight o'clock," he said.

Her mother lifted a brow. "It's past nine."

He looked surprised, checked his watch and then looked sheepish. As acts went, it was beyond excellent.

"Mr. Longland is replacing Mr. Taylor for the rest of the year."

Her mother's expression became instantly more drawn. "That was a terrible accident. Mr. Taylor was quite popular at the school," she added.

"So I've discovered," he replied, still with the sheepish. "Look, I'm sorry. I lost track of time. I didn't mean to come here this late." He paused and then added, "You said I was interrupting dinner?"

"Dinner was a touch on the late side." She turned toward the dining room as Jon came into the hall. "Sorry," she said. "This is Mr. Longland; he's a new teacher at Emery."

"And he makes house calls at this time of night?"

"Not deliberately," Longland said. "I lost track of time. I'd hoped to have a word with Emma before the yearbook committee meeting next week."

"So you hunted her down at home?" Jon's smile matched Longland's, and in spite of herself, Emma was impressed.

"I live not far from here."

Impressed and terrified. She put on her best Hall smile. "Why don't the two of you go back to dinner? I'm sure this won't take long, and I'll join you when we're done." She did *not* want Merrick Longland in her house.

But she didn't want to leave her house with him, either. She accepted the obvious: Ernest had been right. Longland now knew where she lived. He probably knew where they all lived. And if she behaved in a way that worried her mother, he probably had ways of dealing with that.

Jon held out a hand. "I'm Jon Madding," he said. "I'm what passes for a dinner guest in these parts."

"Not her father, then?"

"No, as you well know," her father said.

"Mom, Jon—please go eat before the food gets cold." Emma nudged her mother back into the dining room, which was easy. Jon seemed reluctant.

"Not your daughter, remember?"

"Right. Not." He glanced at Mercy and then followed her as she left Emma, her teacher, and the ghost of the man whose seat he now occupied, in the hall.

Emma then turned to Merrick Longland. "Living room," she said, her voice even, her expression neutral.

Longland kept his game face on until there was no possibility of line of sight from the dining room. He then walked over to the couch and made himself more or less at home. His expression chilled instantly, which perversely made Emma far more comfortable.

"Yes, I do know," Longland then said—to Emma's father. "But she didn't strike me as the type of person who would use her own father as a focus."

"Meaning she's not you."

Longland darkened. "No. She's still alive." As he said it, he turned to face her, his eyes very like her father's but with more anger in them. "I came here the first time to *rescue* you. I came because I knew the hunters would kill you. I never threatened you.

"You're responsible for my death."

Emma stiffened. Words crumbled. Merrick Longland had defined monstrous to Emma—but it was true. He'd come to save her life.

"What, then, do you owe *me*, Emma Hall? Your life? The lives of your family?"

✳   ✳   ✳

"Emma," her father said. "You are not responsible for this man's death. If he came to save your life, he didn't intend to give you a choice about where the rest of that life was to take place. He's responsible for the choices he made and the consequences of those choices."

"Thank you for the parental moralizing," Longland replied. "I don't believe this conversation is relevant to you. If you are truly free to go as you please, don't let us keep you."

"I'm also free to remain. This is more my home than yours." Her father folded his arms across his chest and looked down on Longland in, oh, so many ways.

Longland stared at her father, frowning. "Are you truly not hers?"

"I'm her father, but if you're asking if I'm bound to her, the answer is pretty obvious."

"If you're not bound to her, why are you still here?"

"It's his house," Emma said, more sharply than she'd intended. "He has every right to be here."

"That's not what I meant," Longland said, voice low. "And he knows it, even if you're too ignorant to understand."

She turned to her father because something in Longland's voice sounded like the truth. "Dad?"

"You're still here," Longland repeated. "There's no way you would be here if you weren't bound."

Her father was silent for a long moment, and then, of all things, he smiled. It was a sad smile, and it added lines to his face. "There are many, many bindings, Longland. I don't expect you to understand them all. Emma is my daughter, and I love her. No parent willingly turns his back—and walks away—from his child. Not when that child is in danger."

"My parents did," was the bitter—and unexpected—reply.

"And I'm not your father," Brendan Hall replied. "Nor is Emma you. The choices you've made might have been the only choices you saw, but there were always others."

"I would have died."

Emma had no desire to offer support to Longland in any way, but she remembered, in the silence that followed, the reason Eric had come to Toronto and the reason Chase had followed him.

Her father nodded. "Yes, in all likelihood." He knew what Emma knew. "But there's a world between dying and killing. A handful of people willing to end your life doesn't justify killing everyone else."

Longland closed his eyes. Emma wondered if closed eyes had the same effect for the dead that they would for the living. "You don't understand," he finally said, his shoulders sagging. "Death is forever. Life is so brief."

"Yet you valued yours enough to make the choices you did."

"There *are no choices*." His voice was low, intent. "One way or the other, we serve the Queen for eternity. We can do it while we live, or we can do it afterward. But if we serve her *well*, we don't have to die. We don't have to age. The only people who are spared an eternity of *this*," he added, with loathing, "are the Necromancers."

"You don't look particularly dead," Emma pointed out.

"Not even to you?"

"The dead don't generally teach classes and supervise yearbook committees. Trust me on this. How are you alive?"

His answering laughter was quiet and bitter. "I'm not alive. I'm as dead as your father."

"But you've got—"

"A body? Yes. I thought it was a privilege when I was alive. I thought it was something the dead might—just might—aspire to." He shook his head. "It's the same as being dead except that the living can see it. Food has no taste. The cold is stronger; nothing is warm. Every minute I'm here, I can see the way to the other side." He lifted his hands to his face. "The only difference is this: I can't be bound tightly to the Queen's side. If I'm to play at being alive, I have to travel. I can hear her," he added, his voice dropping, "but she can't command me to return; I'm willing to obey, but the constructs can't travel the way the disembodied can."

It took Emma a minute to realize that the construct he spoke of was his physical form.

"You can't be a—a power source for a Necromancer."

"No. I'm spared that. But that's all I'm spared." He rose. "People have always judged me. People have always misunderstood." It didn't sound like whining, but Emma had to bite back words. How did one misjudge the willingness to murder an infant? "But what I wanted, in the end, wasn't so different from what you want."

Emma was speechless.

Her father was not. "You wanted a place to belong."

"A safe place," Merrick Longland agreed. "Where love, not pain, is waiting around every corner. A place where I don't have to watch my back at all times and where power isn't the only hope of safety I have." He closed his eyes. "Someplace that wants *me*." When he opened his eyes again, they were almost blue in the living room light, but they retained their subtle shimmering transparency. "I see it every day. I *know* I don't deserve it—but whatever is waiting on the other side doesn't *care*."

Longland glanced at her father. "You *saw* the place we were meant to be. Your daughter opened the door the Queen has kept locked and barred."

"I didn't see her open the door," her father replied. "But, yes, I suspected she would. I wasn't certain that I would be as strong as I wanted to be; I left before she tried."

"But you know what waits—you could be there now!"

"Yes. But, Longland, if my home wasn't perfect, if my family wasn't flawless, it *was* a family. I'm human. Sometimes I was frustrated. Sometimes I was lonely. Sometimes I felt like a failure. All of these things are true."

"Dad, you weren't—"

He give a slight shake of head that meant he wanted to be uninterrupted.

"But I also felt loved, by my wife and my child. Even when I was failure. Maybe especially then." He smiled at his daughter, in almost embarrassing gratitude. "I can't—and won't—judge you. What I had, you didn't have. And, yes, I know what you see."

"Is it—is it the same? Isn't it better than what you had?"

"It's different."

Longland swallowed. In a voice that was painful and at odds with everything she knew about his life, he asked, "Will I be allowed to go anyway?"

"Yes," her father said. There was no doubt in his voice.

Longland turned to Emma. "Could you do it again?"

For the first time, Emma accepted the fact that Merrick Longland was dead. She'd been told, but the knowledge had been entirely intellectual. Now, it wasn't. Like her father, like Nathan, he was trapped here. What he wanted was out of reach.

And it shouldn't be.

"I don't know," she said, after a long pause.

When he flinched—which surprised her—she added, "I don't hate you enough to keep you here." But she had. She knew she had. If she tried, she could still see the gun pointed at the baby. And at Allison, in whose arms the baby was held.

"It wasn't personal," he told her. "I came here the first time to save your life."

She believed him. "Why have you come here a second time?"

"I don't know." When he saw the change in Emma's expression, he added, "It's the truth. I was sent here in the company of the Queen's Knights. I was given no orders beyond that. I was to accompany the Necromancers, and I was to find a way to meet you that wouldn't be suspicious."

"What orders were the Necromancers given?"

"They're not to kill you, except at need. They're here to make certain you arrive in the City of the Dead. The Queen is waiting."

"And you—you're just supposed to *talk* to me? This isn't about revenge for what happened to you?"

"There are whole hours when I forget whose fault my current condition is. I can't hold on to it when I look toward the light. Revenge doesn't matter—there's no way for me to come back." He hesitated and then said, "And if I could leave this place, I wouldn't want to come back. Your father's right. What he had—what he built—I didn't have. I couldn't build it. I couldn't even *see* it. Maybe that's why he's still here.

"When I first saw you, I saw a pretty, popular girl who had it easy. You had friends. You had potential. You even had a hunter on your side. Until I was found, I had no one. I was nothing. Being dead hasn't changed that. I was invisible until the Queen's Knights found me, and I'm invisible now.

"There's nothing for me here. Even if the Queen of the Dead were gone and I were free, there's nothing. You can speak with your father. Short of interrogation, there's no one who would spend the time—or the power—talking to me.

"You have everything," he added. It wasn't an accusation, but she knew that had he been alive, it would have been. Death changed things. "Everything I wanted was just handed to you." His voice dropped to a whisper.

And he could never have it, Emma though dispassionately. For a moment, Merrick Longland was painfully young in her eyes. She knew what he'd been willing to do, while alive. She hated it. At the moment, all she could see was pain. Pain, isolation, and a terrible loneliness. She glanced at her father, who nodded but said nothing.

"If I could—if I was certain I could—I would open that door again. But the last time—" she shook her head.

"What? What about the last time?"

Emma did not want to feel sympathy—or even pity—for Merrick

Longland. He was the type of person who justified the concept of Hell. He thought about his own pain but never considered the pain he left in the lives of others.

But if she had been without a father for over half her life now, the father she'd had had loved her. She'd never doubted it. Who would she be if her father were a different man? What would she be like if she'd had Mark's mother?

Dead, probably.

"Necromantic power requires the dead. It doesn't necessarily require binding them."

He frowned. "That's not how it works—"

"It's not how you've been taught," she replied. "But it *is* how it works, or can work. My father is free to come and go as he pleases. I don't know where he is when he's not with me. I don't *own* him. He chooses to stay. But he can give me power if he chooses to.

"The dead have a choice. That's the thing you don't understand—and you're dead. The dead are people. They're people trapped inside a giant, icy waiting room, but they're still people. When I opened the door, I did it for Andrew Copis. And for his mother. She would never have known a moment's peace if he'd remained trapped here. But it took—it took so *many* of the dead, and they gave me everything they had." She exhaled. "The Queen of the Dead has closed the way. I don't know how. I just know that the power it takes to open the door requires hundreds or thousands of the dead. Maybe more. I stopped counting."

He closed his eyes. His lashes were dark and long as they rested against pale skin. He *looked* alive, to Emma. But then again, so did her father. She felt a peculiar tightness in her throat as she watched him, because she knew that she could touch him and her hands wouldn't freeze or go numb.

"If the dead knew," he whispered, "they would come. You had thousands, but Emma—every person who's died in the last several centuries would come if you called them."

"I don't know how. How did you find the dead? Did you find them in the hundreds?"

He shook his head.

"The Necromancers who are in Toronto—"

"Two are already dead."

"There's a third?"

"And a fourth."

"Are they also at Emery?"

"No." He lifted his chin, straightening his shoulders. "I can teach you."

Her father stiffened. Neither he nor Emma misunderstood Longland's offer. "To bind the dead?" she asked softly.

"You don't understand what you can do with that power."

"I understand what's been done with it in the past," she countered.

"If you had enough power, you wouldn't age. You could be immortal. You're young, now. But in ten years, twenty, you'll be older. You'll understand why the gift is valuable, then."

She shook her head.

"I can teach you how to gather," he said, bending forward, his hands cupped before him as if he were waiting for them to be filled. "You said you need power to free us. I can show you how to gain it."

It hadn't done Longland a lot of good. Emma didn't point this out. Instead, she said, "If I don't get back to dinner, my mother's going to be suspicious. Or worried."

"Promise me you'll try," he said, catching her by the hand as she turned. She was right. His hand was warm. It felt like a living hand.

"I promise I'll try. I want something in return."

He stiffened.

"I want the other two Necromancers."

"What will you do with them?"

Emma looked down at the floor. "You already know," she said. "I'm not going to the City of the Dead. I'm not going to the Queen's Court."

"She says you have power," Longland whispered. "If you trained hard, you could become the Queen of the Dead."

"I'm going back to dinner." She turned, then turned back. "Will she summon you home?"

"She can order me home," Longland replied. "But without a Necromancer to create a path, it won't be instant; I have to travel the way the rest of you do." He rose. His expression shuttered, becoming smooth and almost lifeless. "Even at the height of my power, I couldn't have budged that door an inch. Untrained, you did what I couldn't." He headed out of the living room and into the hall, where he retrieved his boots and his winter gear.

"Does the cold affect you?"

His smile was strange. "I'm always cold. If you mean the weather, the winter, no. I imagine this body feels pain; that the flesh can freeze or burn." He spoke of it as if it were entirely separate from him.

"But—isn't it better than being dead?" She hated the hope in her voice, because she knew it was foolish. It was *wrong*. But it hovered there anyway. If Nathan were like Longland, she could touch him. Nathan could touch her. There wouldn't be pain and numbness.

"Emma, I *am* dead. Clothed in flesh or no, there's nothing that can change that." He turned and left the living room; Emma followed after taking one deep breath. She thanked him for coming, apologized in advance for Amy, and otherwise spoke as if he were the teacher he'd claimed to be.

She wasn't certain her mother was listening. But she wasn't certain she wasn't, either; the dining room had fallen momentarily silent.

After she'd shut the door, she leaned against the wall, her head tilted toward the ceiling.

"Em."

For a long moment, she couldn't speak. Her throat was too tight. "I'm fine," she told him softly. It was a Hall variant on fine. To stop her father from worrying about her, she said, "Do you think we can trust him?"

"He strikes me as a boy who's always focused on what he wants, to the exclusion of everything else."

"And he wants to escape?"

Her father shook his head. "It's not escape. He is standing outside his home in a snowstorm. He doesn't have the key, and the door is locked. He can peer in through the window; he can knock at the door. He can scream. He can't enter. But he has the right to be there. I think it's the only thing he wants, now. I think, as long as you're working toward that, he will do everything he can to help you."

"But he was sent here by the Queen of the Dead."

"Yes, Em. Do you understand why?"

She swallowed. Shook her head.

Halls did not accuse each other of lying. They respected each other's privacy. Her father was concerned enough to ask; he wasn't concerned enough to break Hall family rules. Not when he'd worked so hard in the early years to establish them.

"I have to get back to dinner."

"Jon is worried."

"Jon? I was thinking about Mom."

Her father's smile was brief. "She's not naturally as suspicious as Jon appears to be."

Emma turned, and then turned again. "Dad, you're really okay with this?"

"I am far less worried about your mother and Jon than I am about you," he replied. It was a very Hall answer.

She thought a lot about death at dinner, where the dead weren't. And she thought a lot about life, as well, watching her mother, watching Jon tease her mother. He never excluded Emma; she chose to step back, and he acknowledged it. It was subtle. Emma wasn't used to subtle adults.

Most of the adults in her daily life were teachers, and subtlety was generally a lost cause on the student body.

But she thought her father was right: Jon was suspicious of Longland. He was suspicious, but he mostly kept it to himself because in the end, it wasn't his house, and she wasn't his daughter. He was willing to follow her mother's lead. Emma was polite, because she could be and still be preoccupied. If her mother noticed, she left it alone, and when dinner was done and cleanup started, Jon actually helped. He was better at washing dishes than her mom, which was a disloyal thought, but also true.

But even helping, he didn't seem particularly eager to please; the dishes were dirty, he'd eaten, and he therefore helped clean up. It seemed natural, although her mother tried to shoo him out of the kitchen three times on the grounds that he was a guest. He pointed out that a decent guest helped out.

Given that Emma had been told exactly this for most of her life, she found the disagreement amusing. She held on to that because there were now two things she had to face that she desperately wanted to avoid.

One of them was waiting in her bedroom when the dishes were done and she could retreat to give her mother some privacy.

Mark was sitting at her desk in front of her computer. "How is it," she asked, as her father also materialized to one side of that desk, "that he can use the computer?"

Her father shrugged. "I don't know. Before you ask, I don't know how I can, either."

"That's not like you."

"Not knowing?"

"Not caring enough *to* know."

"When I was alive, knowledge made a difference. Knowing how things work now doesn't give me the ability to fix any of them."

"Dad—"

Mark turned in the chair. The chair didn't turn with him. "Are you finished dinner, now?"

Emma surrendered. "Yes. And the cleanup. You'll have to give me a few minutes to get my dog ready for a walk." She fished her phone out of a pocket and hit the speed dial. "Eric?"

"Emma?"

"I'm about to go take my dog for a walk."

"Where?"

She glanced at her father. "Where does Mark live? Can I walk there?"

"We can walk," Mark began.

"Dead people don't take as long to walk between places as living ones," her father told him. To his daughter, he added, "But it's not that far."

It couldn't be. Not and be close to the ravine. Mark had said his mother had taken him for a walk, not a drive. "My dad says it's within easy walking distance."

"You're taking Mark home."

"I'm going home with him, yes."

"To do what, Emma?"

"I honestly don't know." She hesitated and then added, "Merrick Longland paid me a visit during dinner."

There was a long, silent beat. "Tonight?"

"Yes. He left about an hour ago."

"What did he want?"

She exhaled. "He wanted me to force the door open again, the way I did for Andrew Copis."

Silence. "That's it?"

"He was sent here to talk to me. He wasn't told what he should talk about. He wasn't sent to aid the Necromancers, but said he arrived with four. Two of them are dead."

"The other two?"

"Not dead but not at the school."

"Do you trust him?"

Did she? "It would be stupid to trust him," she replied, hedging.

"But you do."

"I trust what he said tonight. If you know of a way to bring the dead back to life, tell me now—because if there is, and that's what he's angling for, he'll lie."

"There isn't."

She swallowed. It took her a little longer to dredge up a reply. "He looks alive to me."

"He looks alive to anyone living. The dead know the difference. Did he try to tell you—"

"No. He told me, flat out, that he's dead. He's wrapped in a—a construct. It's like a cage of flesh."

Eric exhaled. "He was at least that honest. What did you tell him?"

"The truth. If I could open that door for him, I'd do it tomorrow. I'd do it now."

"You can't."

"I don't think I can, no. Every person gathered at the door—every dead person," she amended, "was willing to give me everything they had on blind faith, and I still only barely managed to pry it open a crack. I'm not sure I could gather that many of the dead together again. And if I did, I think she'd know."

"She?"

"The Queen of the Dead."

"Did you tell him how you gathered the dead?"

"The lantern? No."

"Good. Don't mention it if he doesn't. Don't talk about it even if he brings it up." He exhaled. "Tell me the route you'll be taking with your dog. I'll meet you on the way."

"I don't—I'm not sure that's a good idea."

"Fine. If you're not sure, I am. Do the other Necromancers know where you, Allison, or Michael live?"

Emma hadn't asked. She'd been so surprised by Longland—and by the rest of the evening—that what should have been the first question out of her mouth had never left it. "I don't know. I'm sorry—"

"It's fine. We're spread a little thin at the moment, but the old man is out making the rounds, and Margaret's with him." He hesitated, then added, "I've spoken with Allison. Chase has her back."

"Is she okay with that?"

"She's not happy about it, no. But she understands what's at stake. Give me five, and I'll meet you."

CHAPTER FOURTEEN

IT WAS COLD, even for November. Petal was heavy enough to break the thin layer of ice that had formed on the snow on the boulevard. Emma, wearing gloves and holding a scuffed lead, could barely feel her hands; her cheeks were numb. Mark walked to her left, her father, on the street side. Her father made a show of taking steps. Mark trailed in the air, his legs unmoving. The appearance of walking wasn't necessary in order to move, and he'd discarded it. He was dressed for winter, on the other hand; her father wasn't.

Petal's breath was a constant white mist. It was a wonder his tongue wasn't frozen. He didn't look up from his hopeful inspection of the frozen ground until Eric joined them. Eric patted Petal while he nodded to her father and Mark.

Mark said, "You can see me."

Eric nodded again.

"Are you dead?"

"Do I look dead to you?"

"How am I supposed to tell?" Mark asked. "The dead don't look dead to me. *I* don't look dead. To me. But you can see me."

"Emma's not dead," Eric said quietly. "And she can see you." Months of talking to Michael had given him some of the tools necessary to talk to Mark, but he wasn't comfortable. Then again, at the moment neither was Emma. She would have been in other circumstances, even given two dead companions and a half-deaf rottweiler. But with the dead came the living: the Necromancers and their Queen.

"Are you like Emma?"

Eric didn't hesitate. "No. No one's like Emma."

"Emma is a Necromancer."

Eric winced. "Emma has the latent ability of the Necromancers—but she's not one of them."

"Why not?"

"Fair question," Eric replied. "But I can't answer it."

Emma glared as Eric grinned. "Chase would love this conversation."

"He'd only get half of it."

"My half, which means he probably wouldn't be listening to any of it." She turned to Mark. "Having power is like—like having a knife. You can't cook without one, but not everyone who owns one uses it to stab someone else. I have the equivalent of a knife. But I want to use it in the kitchen; I don't want to use it to hurt people."

"People hurt people," he said.

"Yes. But mostly by accident." Mark fell silent, and she mentally kicked herself. She glanced at Eric, who was watching Petal as if the dog were fascinating. Things could have been more awkward, but only with the inclusion of, say, her mother's new boyfriend.

She followed her father's subtle lead, but asked Mark if he knew the way home. He frowned and thought about this. "I know," he finally said, "that I can go there."

"But not how?"

"The streets look different when you're dead. They change a bit. They didn't do that when I was alive. I can't tell you how to get there because you're not dead."

"Could you tell my father?" It didn't matter, but she found herself asking questions that had nothing to do with the mother waiting at the end of this walk. Partly for his sake and partly for her own.

"He already knows."

"Can he get there the same way you can?"

Mark considered this. Turning to her father, he asked, "Can you?"

"Yes," her father replied. "But Emma and Eric can't. Neither can Petal."

"Petal is a strange name for a dog."

"I thought so, but I didn't choose it."

Emma, remembering the reason she'd chosen the name, shrugged. It wasn't the name she would choose now, but he'd grown into the name, or she'd grown attached to it. "I was eight," she told Mark. "My dad always called me Sprout. I thought Petal was a good name."

"For a dog?"

"Well, for this one. He doesn't seem to mind it." He did perk up, the way he often did when people were talking about him. Mostly because he assumed his name was synonymous with food.

"Is Michael like me?"

"Michael is Michael," she replied. "You're Mark. You have some things in common, but you're not the same person."

"Michael isn't happy."

She closed her eyes briefly. "Michael doesn't understand what happened to you. I mean, he knows what happened but not why."

"Me either."

"When things upset him, he needs to understand why they happened—usually in a lot of detail—or he stays upset. Sometimes we can explain things, but sometimes we can't. I can't explain this." She stopped walking, and remembered: she had promised to take Michael with her when she took Mark home.

But it was late. It was late, and she did not want an upset Michael at the door of the woman who had killed Mark. She hesitated, torn. Eric marked it.

"I told Michael he could come with me." She considered appearing on Michael's doorstep at almost ten in the evening, dog in hand. His mother would be worried—and with cause, even if they couldn't explain it all.

Sometimes, dealing with Michael was hard. If she'd promised Allison and she reneged, Allison would understand why. She might not be *happy* with the explanation, but she'd understand it. Michael tended to see things as black or white. But he was generally forgiving if there was a reasonable explanation. Or rather, an explanation that seemed reasonable to him.

Emma hesitated again and then said, "We need to take a slight detour."

Michael's mother answered the door, which was about what Emma expected; Michael often failed to register the doorbell when it rang. "I'm really sorry, Mrs. Howe," Emma said. "But I promised Michael I'd show him something the next time I went, and I'm going now."

Michael's mother nodded. She was a mostly practical woman, rounded with years but pragmatic about it; her hair was shot through with gray. Mercy Hall dyed her hair. Emma was certain that when she reached that age, she'd dye her hair as well, but Mrs. Howe's hair was dark enough that the gray seemed to add shine to it.

"I wouldn't be here," Emma continued, "but Michael's been a little stressed lately, and I didn't think a broken promise would help him much."

Michael's mother knew her son. "Let me get him. Are you—are you going to be long?"

"I hope not. In part, it'll depend on Michael."

"And the other part?"

"How long it takes for my hands to freeze off."

"Well, come in and wait. With luck, he'll decide to stay in."

Emma thought it would take more than luck, but agreed. The important part at the moment was that she was in his front hall, having remembered her promise. What he then chose to do with it was out of her hands; if he decided not to accompany her, no guilt accrued on her part.

Michael came thundering down the stairs. He'd never learned the art of walking quietly, and he generally took stairs two at a time in either direction. He wasn't carrying his computer, but headed for the closet to unearth his coat, his mittens—he disliked gloves—and his scarf. His mother found his misplaced hat and murmured something about stapling it to his forehead.

During this, he spoke very little; he kept peering out the door, as if he might catch a glimpse of Mark, although he knew that without Emma's intervention—Emma, who was standing alone in his hall—that was impossible.

And Emma knew, from one glance at Michael's mother, that she was worried. "Eric's with us," she said, "and he has a car. If we're going to be late—I mean, later—I'll call you."

"I don't think I've met Eric," his mother said.

"He's keeping the car running. He just started Emery this year, but he eats lunch at Michael's table."

"And the gaming discussions haven't driven him off?"

"Not yet."

"Emma—" She inhaled. "Never mind. Keep an eye on him tonight?"

"Always."

Mark was quiet; his silence was not comfortable. Emma was generally comfortable with silence—it was one of the reasons she'd so liked Nathan. He didn't *need* her to fill silence in order to be at ease. But this silence was different, and she knew it. It was a veneer over things that couldn't be said, even if words were roiling beneath it.

She hated Mark's mother. Hated her, despised her, wanted to see her hauled off to jail to answer for what she'd done. Not just the death, but everything that had led up to it. No one had forced her to become a mother.

But saying this out loud wouldn't help Mark. It wouldn't change anything. Hating his mother had zero effect; it didn't offer him either comfort or support. She almost reached out to take his hand but remembered that he found touch uncomfortable—at least while he was alive. He was dead, but that didn't mean what it meant to her father. Or to Nathan.

She inhaled. Exhaled. What did she want from this evening? Why was she quietly following her father's reluctant lead to take a severely unwanted child home to the mother who had murdered him?

Because the child wanted to go there. This wasn't about Mark's mother, in the end; not to Emma. It was about Mark. It was about the dead child. Any mistakes he made here couldn't harm him further; he'd suffered the worst already.

But his mother had gotten away with murder. When she should have been caring for and about her son, she had abandoned him to die, instead—and no one knew. Everyone thought she was the grieving, bereaved parent. If Emma did nothing, said nothing—where was the justice in that? How was that fair to Mark?

"Emma," her father said.

She looked up, as apparently her feet had gotten really interesting.

"That's the house."

It was about the same size as the Hall house, and if Emma remembered correctly, it also lacked a father. It didn't lack siblings, but it lacked anything as fundamental as a mother, in Emma's opinion. She inhaled, held her breath, and then turned to Mark, who was staring at the front door.

Eric said, quietly, "Are you certain this is wise?"

"I'm certain it's not," she replied. "Mark, is my father right? Is that the house?"

Mark nodded, never taking his eyes off the front door. Emma tried to imagine what it would be like to stand in front of her home in the same context. How would she feel if her mother had killed her?

She failed, because she couldn't imagine it. In her worst nightmares—the ones that involved her mother—her mother had either died or disappeared. She had never tried to kill her.

"You don't have to do this," Emma said, aware that she was partly speaking to herself. But the alternative—breaking her word to Mark—had seemed worse. It didn't seem worse now.

Mark frowned. "I don't have to do this," he repeated, as if trying to make sense of the words.

Michael, who couldn't see Mark, said, "He wants to do this."

Mark looked at Michael. To Emma he said, "Michael is your friend." It was a question without the intonation.

"Michael is my friend," she agreed.

"Why?"

"If you mean why do I like him, there are a bunch of reasons."

"He's not normal."

She hated that word more than she'd ever hated it before. "I'm not normal, either."

He frowned.

"I'm a Necromancer. I can see—and talk—to the dead. Michael doesn't hate me just because I can do these things. Michael finds it hard to deal with strangers. He finds it hard to talk to people he doesn't know. He finds it hard to talk to people he *does* know if they're speaking about something he doesn't really understand. But he's direct, he's honest, and if he says he'll help you, he will. Michael's easy to trust."

"Is trust important?"

"Very. At least to me." Petal shoved his nose into her gloves. She dropped a hand to his head; he was warm enough that she could feel the heat rising off his fur. She should have left him at home. But she'd needed a reasonable excuse to give her mother, and walking the dog was an all-weather, all-season necessity. Mark's home wasn't the place for him.

It wasn't the place for Mark, either.

"Can we talk to my mother now?"

Emma nodded. "It's late," she added.

"She's awake."

"You're certain?"

"That's her window."

"Awake doesn't always mean someone will answer the door."

"She'll answer the door," he replied. "Because it might be an emergency. She always answers the phone, too—even when it's late."

"Michael, can you stand on my right? Mark will be standing on my left, and I'll be holding his hand." She handed Michael Petal's leash.

Michael nodded, his expression as neutral as Mark's.

"And I'm chopped liver?" Eric asked, with just the barest trace of humor.

"No. Chopped liver is disgusting." Emma walked up to Mark's front door and stood beneath the fake lamp that encased the porch light. She carefully removed her gloves; her fingers were already cold, and her breath came out as mist. "Ready?" she asked, as she held out her left hand.

He smiled. It changed the entire cast of his face.

She reached out with her free hand and pressed the doorbell.

Mark's mother was, as Mark predicted, awake. She didn't answer the door immediately, but the door was thin enough that the thump-thump-thump of feet hitting stairs that little bit too fast could be heard. If she rushed to reach the door, she didn't rush to open it; it opened slowly, revealing just a thin strip of her face and body. She was wearing rumpled, dark clothing and no makeup; she had probably been ready for sleep.

And it looked like she needed it; the lower half of her eyes were shadowed by dark semicircles, and she was pale. "Can I help you?" she asked, in obvious confusion.

"Yes," Emma replied. "We found your son." She lifted his hand, and his mother's gaze drifted down to his upturned face.

Her hand fell away from the door, which swung inward to reveal a woman who was just a shade taller than Mercy Hall but much, much skinnier. To Emma's eye, she looked almost anorexic. Her eyes sported such dark circles she looked like she'd been hit in the face.

Emma hated her. But what she felt, for just that moment, wasn't hatred. Michael moved to stand on the other side of the boy, one step forward, as if to ward off any blows his mother might aim at her child. She didn't appear to notice. Her eyes were fastened to her son's silent face.

They rounded, exposing the ring of white around brown irises. The hand that had held the door rose to cover her open mouth. Her knees gave slowly—or she knelt, it was hard to say which. "Mark!" Her hand fell away from her mouth.

Emma looked down to Mark. Her hand was not yet numb enough; it hurt.

"Mark, oh, god, Mark. Where have you *been*?" She reached out for her son, her palms up and open. Her son took one hesitant step forward, but he was anchored by Emma's hand.

Mark's mother moved, fully opening the door. "Mark?"

He looked up at Emma. The questions he wanted to ask had deserted him, as had the rest of his words. Emma swallowed. "Mark," she said quietly. "Should we go in?"

"Mark?" his mother whispered. She lowered her hands.

"Mom?" A voice called down from the top of the stairs. "Who is it?"

"It's Mark!"

"Mom," the voice said, both gently and with apprehension, "it can't be Mark." It was an older boy's voice. Not a teenager's, but not far off. Emma looked up to see Mark's brother descend the stairs. He turned and hollered back up. "It's just a neighbor!" before he caught sight of the door.

He froze, his eyes widening just as his mother's had. His expression was just as hard to look at. "Mark!" Unlike his mother, he noticed Emma, Michael, and Eric.

He hesitated, the way a child would, which made Emma revise his age downward.

"Hi, Phillip," Mark said, his eyes just as wide as his brother's. He lost years—and he looked young for his age to begin with—as he smiled. He had a heartbreakingly open smile.

Phillip looked at Emma. "Let go of his hand," he told her. "He doesn't like to be touched."

"It's okay now," Mark said quietly. "It doesn't feel bad anymore."

"Mom," Phillip said, in a quiet voice, never taking his eyes off his brother. "You're freezing the house. If we're going to let them in, let them in and close the door."

Mark's mother was still on her knees, but the sound of her older son brought back the rest of the world. She rose—unsteadily—and nodded. "Come in," she said, as if seeing Emma, Michael, and Eric for the first time. "It doesn't hurt when she holds your hand?" she asked her son.

Her dead son.

"Not anymore."

Phillip's surprise at seeing his brother shifted, as if he could read the truth that no one had yet put into words in his brother's expression. "Why?" he asked.

"I'm dead," Mark replied, in a tone that suggested his state was self-evident.

Emma was watching Mark's mother, although it was hard to look away from Phillip. She saw the moment the woman's expression shattered, but it had been so fragile to begin with. Eyes that were circled and dark seemed to sink into the hollows made by sharp cheekbones and stretched skin; tears added reflected light to her face—the only light that touched it. This was the face of a murderer, and Emma knew she would never forget it.

This was what her father had been trying to tell her.

Phillip stepped between Mark and his mother—or between Emma and his mother. Emma wasn't certain which. What she knew was that Phillip was afraid. Afraid and determined.

"You're dead?" he demanded. "You're sure?"

"Yes." He looked at Emma. "Emma heard me. Emma promised she would bring me home. Emma," he added, before she could stop him, "is a Necromancer."

She felt like one as she stood, her arm numb, Mark by her side. His brother was staring, his eyes wide and unblinking; his mother, half-hidden by her older son, was—was weeping.

Emma had wanted monsters. Monsters could kill their own children. And this woman *had*—but if she was a monster, monsters were broken, shattered, pathetic things that were to be pitied. Emma did not want to pity a murderer. She'd been so angry, listening to Mark. She could stir the ashes of that anger now, but it provided no warmth and no heat.

She couldn't accuse the woman of killing her own son—not when her other son stood between them. Because then he'd know. It couldn't break Mark's mother any more than she was already broken; it could injure Phillip in a way that simple cold couldn't.

Why had she even come here?

Because she'd promised.

Emma stepped into the hall, and Mark followed because he was attached. He didn't seem to be aware of her—not the way Phillip was. Someone closed the door; she thought it must be Eric. Her dog stayed more or less near her legs; he was generally well behaved in other people's houses. Something about Emma stopped him from sniffing around strange legs and hands, looking for food.

Phillip glanced at the stairs, and Emma remembered that Mark had

had two siblings, both of whom were, in his opinion, normal. Whatever that meant. "Mom."

When his mother failed to answer, Phillip briefly closed his eyes.

Mark's hand tightened in Emma's. "Why is she crying?" he asked his brother.

"She's been crying on and off since the funeral." He spoke in a quiet, matter-of-fact way, as if his mother weren't present. "She went out to look for you—" He inhaled, held his breath, and smoothed the worry off his face, which made him look older. "Do you want to see your room?"

Mark shrugged. "Not really. Did you change it?"

"No. It's the same mess it always was." He paused and then added, "I beat your high score, though."

Mark yanked his hand free of Emma's and ran up the stairs. He ran through his brother, whose eyes were widening.

Emma tried to massage feeling back into her hand.

"Where did he go?"

"If I had to guess, he went to his room to look at the high score list. What game?"

"Tetris. It's ancient, but he liked it."

"You didn't beat his high score."

Phillip shook his head. "It's not possible. He's a monster Tetris player. It's like he's hooked directly into the machine. I tried, though. I can't see him, now."

"No."

"Will my sister—"

"No. Unless he comes back downstairs and takes my hand, she won't see him either."

Phillip swallowed. He slid an arm beneath his mother's arms and guided her toward the living room doors. "Can you—"

Emma crossed the hall and opened one of the two glass doors that led to the living room, and Phillip walked his mother in.

*   *   *

Michael was staring at his feet, or at the floor beneath them, when Emma turned. Eric passed them both, and offered Phillip the help that Emma, hands numb, couldn't. She couldn't hear what Eric said to the boy; she could hear the broken syllables of Phillip's response, but not clearly enough to make sense of them.

"I don't understand," Michael said.

"I don't understand, either."

"She left him to die," he continued, as if Emma hadn't spoken. "She must have *wanted* to leave him." Before Emma could answer—and it would have taken a while, because she had no words—he said, "Why is she crying?"

Emma was surprised to find her throat tightening. Without thought, she reached out for the other dead person in the hall. Michael didn't even blink when her father coalesced at her side.

"I'm not Mark's mother," her father said, although to Michael this was self-evident, "but if I had to guess, I would say she made a mistake."

"But Mark *died*."

"Yes. Some mistakes can't be undone. I don't know why she took him to the ravine. I don't know why she left him there and told him to wait. I don't know if she meant to abandon him to the cold."

"But she *did*."

Brendan Hall nodded. "Yes. Maybe she thought it would make her happy. Maybe she was having the very worst day of her life and she couldn't deal with any more stress. Maybe she meant it to be an hour or two. I don't know, Michael."

"But she's crying. And she—"

"She was happy to see him."

Michael swallowed but didn't deny it. "I thought she would be afraid. I thought she would scream or hide or try to lie—"

"You thought she would be like the guilty criminals on TV."

He nodded, blinking rapidly. "Why did she ask him to come in? She knows he's dead. She *knows*. I don't understand."

"No. People—even people we know well—are sometimes impossible to understand or predict. I don't think Mark's mother has accepted Mark's death."

"But she *caused it*!"

"Yes. And sometimes the mistakes we make ourselves are the hardest for us to face and accept. I know Emma felt Mark's mother got away with murder."

"She did," Michael replied, voice low.

"Did she?" He nodded toward the living room. "We should go in. Mark's coming back."

"What was he doing?" Emma asked.

"Playing a game."

"A game?"

"I think he's making certain that Phillip will never be able to beat his high score," her father replied, with just the touch of a rueful smile. "He's only eight, Em."

"My sister's not sleeping," Mark said, as he drifted through the floor. He'd automatically taken the stairs on the way up.

"What is she doing?" Emma asked, glancing up those stairs; if his sister joined them, she couldn't do it the way Mark just had.

"She was watching me play Tetris."

"She can't see you." But Emma's stomach felt like it dropped two feet. His sister couldn't see Mark, no. But she could see the computer.

"I think she's coming downstairs," Mark added, in a much smaller voice.

And she was. She was walking, wide-eyed, her arms level with the banister. She stopped at the top of the stairs and looked down to see two strange teenagers—and a rottweiler—in her hall.

"What's her name?" Emma asked.

"Susan. She doesn't like to be called Sue," he added. "I don't know why people do it."

"Your brother is not going to be happy."

Mark looked down. "I'm sorry."

She didn't tell him it wasn't his fault. "It doesn't matter. After tonight, she won't be able to see you again, and she might want to say something."

"What?"

"Good-bye."

"Oh." He hesitated for a moment as Emma looked up the stairs at the girl who stood by the banister.

"Hello, Susan. Your mother and Phillip are in the living room. My name's Emma and I'm a—a—" She hesitated as Mark held out his hand. Without a pause, she took it and watched as the girl's eyes widened.

"Mark?"

Mark said, "Hi, Susan." He looked very guilty.

"You *were* playing Tetris!"

"Phillip said he'd beat my high score."

Susan snorted. "Phillip is such a liar." She looked older than Mark, although she wasn't much taller. She also didn't appear to be surprised. "Has Mom seen you?"

Mark nodded.

"She's been a mess since you died." Susan then added, "Why is that girl holding your hand?"

"It doesn't hurt."

"That's not what I asked." She walked with much more confidence down the stairs. "Who are you?"

"Emma."

"I heard that part. Why do you have that dog?"

Emma blinked. "He needed to go for a walk. He doesn't bite people, and he doesn't usually destroy furniture." Petal headed obligingly toward Susan. "She doesn't have any food, Petal."

"Petal?"

"His name."

"That's a stupid name for a big dog." Stupidly named or not, Susan hesitantly patted his head. "But who *are* you?"

"Emma's a Necromancer," Mark replied. "Was Mom really mad at me?"

"At you? God, no. But she's been mad or sad about everything. Tell her you're okay," Susan added. It was delivered as if it were a royal command and Susan were the Queen.

"I'm dead."

"I *know* that." Susan reached out to take Mark's other hand. The fact that Mark didn't like to be touched—at least when alive—was something she'd forgotten. Or, given her personality, something she'd ignored.

Mark didn't seem to be surprised or upset, but Susan wasn't thrilled when her hand passed through his. "Why are you holding *her* hand?"

"Because you can't see me if I don't."

"Oh. Well, that's okay then." She gave Emma another look and then headed toward the closed doors of the living room. "Are you coming, or what?"

Mark's mother's name was Leslie. She was sitting in the corner of a long, leather couch, a drink in her shaking hands. Emma eyed its contents with some suspicion. Susan eyed its contents with loathing, which confirmed Emma's suspicion; the girl did not, however, march over to her mother and take the drink away.

"Susan, why are you awake?" It was Phillip who asked.

"Mark woke me up," she replied, casually tossing her younger brother to the figurative wolves.

He knew it, too, but accepted it. ". . . I was playing Tetris," he mumbled.

"Yes, because *someone* told him he'd beaten the high score," Susan added, punting fault back into Phillip's corner.

Both Emma and Michael were only children. Sibling interactions had always been a bit mystifying, if sometimes viewed with envy.

"Have you tried to touch him?" Susan asked her brother. "Look." She shoved her hand through Mark's chest, and then waved her arm around. Mark was looking down at her hand, his eyes slightly rounded.

"That's pretty cool," he told his sister.

"Yeah. Cool and creepy."

"Susan likes horror," Mark told the room.

Phillip, far from looking horrified, now looked embarrassed. Emma wasn't certain on whose behalf, but suspected it was theirs: Emma's, Eric's, and Michael's. "She's always like this," he said.

Emma thought she understood why as she turned to face Mark's mother. Her eyes were still red, her lips swollen; she had crumpled tissues in her left hand.

"So," Susan said, and Emma realized suddenly that Susan was like a miniature version of Amy, "Why did you come home? You didn't *need* to put up a new high score; Phillip's too much of a klutz to beat the old one." She snickered and added, "He's been trying, though."

She had asked the question that Phillip and Leslie couldn't. Or wouldn't. But they listened for the answer just as apprehensively as if they had.

"I wanted to come home," Mark told her. He turned toward his mother, who sat frozen, like a cornered mouse trying to avoid a large, hungry snake in a small glass aquarium. "I wanted to ask Mom why she left me in the ravine."

Emma had come here for Mark. For Mark. She reminded herself, because she needed the reminder. Phillip's face shuttered. His mother's couldn't crumple any further. Susan, however, lost some of her childish directness, but she didn't look surprised by Mark's statement. She turned to look at Phillip; her glance seemed to take in everything in the room that didn't include her mother.

Phillip was silent. He opened his mouth and closed it. Emma thought he wanted to deny the truth in Mark's words and realized that on some level, he'd known. He'd known. But he knew his brother, probably better than Emma knew Michael; he knew that empty words of comfort or denial would change nothing.

She saw the same thing in Susan's face and realized a second thing: Mark was, unintentionally, asking them to make a choice between himself and their mother. Mark was dead. Their mother was alive.

And her father was right: Mark loved his mother, even if she had killed him. Susan and Phillip loved her as well. She had done something monstrous—but to them, she wasn't a monster. Monster or no, they failed to look at her. They looked at Mark and then looked away.

Mark didn't notice. He looked at his mother and then tugged Emma's hand. She followed where he led in silence, although she could no longer feel that hand; it was numb. He stopped a yard away from where his mother sat, drink in her hand like a useless shield. The liquid shook.

"Mom, why did you leave me in the ravine? Did you forget about me?"

"I didn't—I didn't leave you in the ravine."

Emma couldn't even feel outrage at the lie.

"You did." The words themselves were all of the accusation his voice contained; he was stating fact and stating it inexorably, the way Michael sometimes did. "You left me in the ravine. You told me to wait for you. You told me not to move."

"Mark, baby—" She swallowed. Drank.

Never drink when you're angry, Sprout. Never drink alone. She glanced at her father, remembering his words, and remembering as well the sharp, acrid taste of his drink. She couldn't recall how old she'd been at the time, and his words hadn't made a lot of sense then; they made sense—as so many of his words did—now.

This, Emma thought, watching, was what she had wanted. She had wanted Mark's mother to face her crime. She had wanted his mother to know that people knew. But she felt no sense of triumph, and looking at Mark, she realized he didn't either. He was standing in place awkwardly, stiff with anxiety; he looked—at the moment—like a very young Michael.

He blamed himself.

Michael had often blamed himself. God, she hated this. "Leslie."

Mark's mother looked up at her, as if she were drowning and Emma herself was a life buoy that had been tossed just out of reach. Emma swallowed. She had come here for Mark. Not for Leslie. Not for Phillip or Susan. But Mark didn't need Emma's anger. He didn't, she understood, need his mother's pain, either. What he needed—and what Michael needed almost by osmosis—was to understand.

Not to forgive. Not to judge. Simply to understand.

CHAPTER
FIFTEEN

SHE LET GO OF HER ANGER, or at least untangled it. The wreck of the woman curled defensively on the couch in front of her helped. It had always been hard to stay angry at Petal when he lay, belly to floor, his eyes wide, his voice pitched in a pathetic whine.

She's not your dog, Emma.

No.

"Leslie," she said again, in a gentler tone. "Mark isn't here to judge you. It's not what he does. What he needs—right now—is to understand why things happened as they did." She exhaled. "He needs to know that it wasn't his fault. He needs to know that it wasn't punishment for something he'd done." And it couldn't be, Emma's voice implied. "You can't bring your son back to life."

"No one can do that," Mark told Emma.

"Believe that I know that," Emma replied, never taking her eyes off his mother. "You can't bring him back. You can't undo what's done—it's done. It's over. It's in the past. What you *can* do is give him a measure of peace. You can answer his question. It's the only answer he cares about, now.

"You took him to the ravine. It was freezing outside. You asked him to stay there. He tried to do what you asked of him, even if he didn't understand why. He needs to understand why you asked it." She glanced, then, at the living children.

They were watching their mother. Phillip looked tired or weary; Susan was a wall. They knew what their mother had done. Mark seemed oblivious to anything in the room that wasn't his mother. Even Emma, her entire arm now numb, was like a shadow.

"Mom?"

"I went back for you," his mother said, her voice breaking. "I went back. You were—" She looked at her empty glass, and handed it blindly to her older son. "I called the police. I told them you'd gone out and you hadn't come home. I didn't mean to leave you there to—" She looked at her two living children.

"But why did you tell me to wait there?"

She closed her eyes. Opened them. They were bloodshot, ringed, and almost without hope. Emma thought she would lie. A lie—if it was believable—might be a kindness. But Leslie had passed beyond the point where a lie had any meaning to her. She couldn't protect herself, and Emma realized, watching her, that she had given up trying.

"I was never a good enough mother for you," she told her son. "I don't mean that you thought I wasn't good enough—I *wasn't*. I was only barely good enough to handle Phillip and Susan. You needed someone patient. You needed someone consistent. I—I tried."

Phillip took a step toward his mother; Susan caught his arm. They exchanged a silent glare, but their mother didn't notice. She was staring at her dead son as if—as if she could engrave the sight of him into her vision so that she never lost it again.

"But it was hard for me. I'm *not* logical. I'm not mathematical. I've always reacted emotionally. Before you went to school, it was easier. If I didn't understand you, I understood how to work with you. I knew our routine.

"But school changed that. The other kids changed it. The other mothers." She shook her head. "They'd look at you, and then they'd look at *me*, like it was my fault you weren't—"

Emma said, "Please do not use the word normal."

Mark glanced at her for the first time since he'd entered this room.

"What word would you like me to use instead?" Leslie replied, with more heat and less pathos.

"Try 'like their children.'"

Leslie closed her eyes. "Mark was never like most of the other children."

"No. But he didn't have to be."

The eyes shot open. "He did if he wanted to have any friends! He did if he wanted to be left alone instead of being bullied. If he could have fit in—" She exhaled sharply. "He was lonely. He felt isolated. You probably have no idea what that's like."

"I understand lonely," Emma replied.

"No, you *don't*. Don't tell me you've ever lacked friends. I won't believe it."

"My father died when I was eight," Emma shot back. "My boyfriend died this past summer. I *know* lonely."

"You don't know it the way someone like my son does, and you never will."

Emma started to speak; Michael interrupted. Mark looked up at Michael, too. "I'm not like other children—or other people. I'm like Mark."

Mark's mother blinked.

"I don't know how to be like other people. I know how to be like me. But I have friends. I'm not always lonely."

"And people are never mean to you?" Mark's mother demanded.

Michael thought about this. "Some people are mean to me," he told her. "Some people are mean to everyone. It's impossible for me to like everyone," he continued. "I don't know anyone who likes everyone. So it's impossible for everyone to like me. There will always be people who can't."

Leslie opened her mouth, but Michael hadn't finished.

"If I learn to pretend—if I pretend to be someone else—the people who like me won't like *me*. They'll like what I pretend to be. That's not the same as being liked. Those people wouldn't be my friends because they wouldn't know me at all."

Mark's brow furrowed as he worked his way through Michael's words.

"Are you lonely?" Michael continued.

Leslie blinked. After a long, confused pause, she nodded. She held out her hand for the empty glass in Phillip's hand. Phillip kept it.

"Are you normal?"

"Yes."

"And you're *still* lonely. Being normal hasn't made you happier. If it hasn't made you happier, and you're the adult, why did you think it would make Mark happier?"

"Because," Phillip said, coming once again to stand between his mother and Michael, "she thought Mark would be happier if people liked him more. And he would have been."

"Maybe he wouldn't be dead now, either."

Phillip's jaw set. He couldn't see the way his mother flinched—but he didn't have to. Love was complicated. It was never all one thing or the other. But when he met Emma's eyes, he flinched, his expression shifting into almost open pain. Phillip hadn't killed his brother. Emma thought, if he'd known where Mark was, she wouldn't even *be* here tonight; Mark would. And he would be alive.

Phillip knelt, surprising Emma. He knelt in front of Mark to bring their eyes to the same level. "The day Mom took you for a walk, two things happened."

Mark nodded, waiting.

"Jonas broke up with her."

Mark glanced at Susan, and Susan nodded.

"And her boss sent her home from work with a warning."

"But—why?"

"Because she had to leave work in the middle of the day twice that week. Do you remember?"

Mark wilted. "To come get me."

Phillip nodded. "At school. The school called her. She had to leave. Her boss told her she wasn't committed enough to work."

"But she—did she lose her job?" Clearly work meant something to Mark.

"No," Susan said, joining both of her brothers and their conversation. "Because you died. Her boss wasn't very understanding about the school stuff, but she wasn't a monster. I think she felt guilty, after."

Oh, the words. This is what her father had meant. Monsters—no. People were people. They were capable of monstrous actions, yes. But they were still people.

"Did Jonas break up with her because of me?"

Phillip and Susan exchanged a glance. "Not just because of you," Mark's brother said. But Susan said, "Yes." When Phillip's eyes narrowed in her direction, she folded her arms across her chest. "What? Mark's different, but he's not an idiot. He's never been completely stupid."

"Mom?"

Mark's mother said nothing. Mark moved, dragging Emma with him.

"Mom, was it because of me?"

Emma saw the yes lurking in his mother's eyes. And she saw the no his mother wanted to replace it with. They were in perfect balance for just a moment. "I came home from work. Jonas called. We had an—an argument. I couldn't—I can't—afford to lose my job." She was crying now, but the tears trailed down her face like an afterthought. "He loved me. He said he loved me. But he needed to know that he was the most important thing in my life. That we had the same goals.

"He asked me to send you to your father."

Mark flinched. "Just me? Not Phillip or Susan?"

"He told me," his mother continued, "that I'd done enough for you. I'd done all the hard work. I was going to *lose my job* if I didn't turn things around. Ian had gotten off easy. It was Ian's turn. And Ian has a new wife. He has someone else to help him around the house and to help with kids."

"She *has* kids," Susan said.

"Well, so does your father."

"I don't *have* a father," her daughter shot back. "And I don't *need* one." She turned and leaped onto the couch and put her arms around her mother. Emma wanted to cry, because Emma remembered almost *being* Susan. And saying the same things to her mother, to Mercy, in the early years. But her father had died. In no other way would he have left them. Susan's father was still alive, somewhere. Alive and no part of his children's lives.

Emma looked across the room at her father; he was watching Leslie and her daughter as if—as if he wanted to step in and join them, to offer the comfort that an ex-husband and absentee father had probably never offered them.

"Why didn't you say yes?" Mark asked. Mark was probably the only person in the room who could.

Michael opened his mouth, reminding Emma that her count was off by one. But he closed it without letting words escape.

"What was I going to tell your brother and your sister?" his mother answered, putting an arm around that sister and drawing her close. "Jonas—wasn't happy. He pointed out that I do earn more and that if we—if we were going to set up house, he needed me to be employed. He—" she laughed. It was not a happy sound. "He needed a sign of commitment. From me.

"And I knew—I knew he was leaving. He was already gone." She closed her eyes. Opened them. "I couldn't—" she exhaled. "When you came home, I couldn't deal with my life. I couldn't look at you and not see the thousands of ways in which I've failed at everything. I just—I needed alone time. I needed the space." She swallowed. "I took you out for a walk. And I left you there.

"I didn't mean to leave you there forever. I didn't mean—" She pulled away from her daughter and rose for the first time since Emma had entered the room. But she didn't walk away; she walked toward Mark. "I fell asleep, Mark. I—"

"You were drinking." It wasn't a question and it wasn't—quite—an accusation.

"After my day? Yes. Baby—I'm so *tired* all the time. I'm so tired of doing it alone when I'm *no good at life*. I'm terrible at it. I never make the right choices. I never make the right decisions. I—" She came to stand beside her older son, rather than behind him. "You were my biggest failure. If I had been any good at being a mother, you'd've been happy. It killed me to see you cry. To see the way the world treated you. The way other mothers looked at you, as if you were stupid or alien. The way they looked *at me*.

"I worried *all the time*. I was always worried. I never knew when the school would call, when something else would hurt you. I never knew how to make it *stop*. If I'd been a good mother, if I'd done the right things—" She lifted her hands, palm up, as if offering to take her dead child into her arms.

And Emma saw the look on Phillip's face.

"But I didn't. I didn't. I tried to talk to your father."

Phillip said, "She didn't ask him, Mark. She thought about sending you away, but in the end, she didn't ask."

"Why?" Mark asked.

Phillip rolled his eyes. "Because she loves you. She loves us all."

"But she took me—"

"Yes," his mother said, voice low. "All I could see that day was failure. Everywhere. I couldn't . . . I wanted a few minutes of quiet. I wanted a few minutes when everything I saw didn't remind me of how useless I really am. I thought—"

"If I were different. If I hadn't been born." Mark had no mercy, but there was no anger in the words. His mother flinched anyway.

But Phillip said, "Sometimes we just—we want a different life. We can't *have* it," he added. "And we don't want it all the time. But sometimes we *all* feel that way. Even you."

Mark looked confused. "You think that?" he asked his brother.

Phillip shook his head. "Of course I do. So does everyone in the world. Except maybe Susan. When Mom woke up she ran out of the house. She barely put on a coat. It was dark. We didn't know where you were." Phillip's gaze hit the carpet. "Susan woke her up. Susan said, 'Mark's not home.' And, Mark? If *I'd* woken her up—if I'd woken her up *earlier*—you wouldn't be dead.

"But I knew about Jonas. I heard her talk about work, and what her boss said. I knew—I knew she needed to sleep. And I *let* her. So it's not just Mom's fault. It's mine, too."

Susan got up off the couch and came to stand on Phillip's other side. "Are you mad at us?" she asked Mark.

Mark looked confused.

"Are you mad at Mom?"

"I think I was. I think, before Emma brought me home, I was angry. But I was more afraid."

"Of what? You're already dead."

Phillip and Leslie flinched. Mark, of course, didn't.

"I don't know. I thought it was my fault. It was my fault I was dead. I thought I had finally done something so bad I deserved to be dead. If I were normal—"

"We agreed we're not using that word," Emma told him.

"I didn't." He turned to his family. "But now I know Mom was having a really, really bad day. The worst day ever."

Leslie began to weep. Mark reached out to touch her, the movement awkward and hesitant, as if he seldom offered comfort to anyone. His hand passed through her, of course.

"And it was my fault," Mark continued. "I didn't do anything on purpose. But—it was my fault."

His mother was shaking her head. "It wasn't—it was me. It's always been me. I'm not strong enough—"

"But it will be better now," he continued, and Emma realized he was *still* trying to offer comfort. "Because now I'm not here all the time. Jonas could come back."

"Jonas," Susan said, in a voice that was both ice and fire, "is *never* coming back. I'll stab him in his sleep. Through his eyes."

"Susan—" Phillip began.

She turned an unquelled murderous gaze on her brother, who thought better of the correction and fell silent.

"And your boss—"

"Mark," Emma said gently. "Your mother was having the worst day ever. If she could take it all back, if you could *be here* and be alive, it would suddenly be the best day ever." And she realized, murder or no, accident or no, it was the truth. It wasn't what she'd expected to find when she'd knocked on Mark's door. But it was true.

"Yes, but then she would have bad days again. The same bad days."

And that, Emma thought, was the truth as well.

"You lied to the police," Mark continued, his voice dropping as if lying to the police were the larger crime.

His mother nodded. "I didn't know what else to do. I couldn't tell them that I—that I killed you."

"But you didn't mean to kill me."

"Baby, sometimes what you mean to do doesn't matter. If telling the truth would have brought you back, I would've told them the truth. Telling the truth would've landed me in jail. I would have lost the job, possibly the house, and Phillip and Susan would have had nowhere to go." She blew her nose and straightened her shoulders. "I'm sorry, Mark."

Mark smiled. It was genuine, and even peaceful. "Then it's okay," he told his mother. As if he were a child. As if apologies somehow made everything better. Emma only vaguely remembered being that child; it seemed so far away. He turned to Emma. "I would like to stay here."

"Can he?" his mother asked.

Emma nodded. She couldn't tell his mother there was nowhere else for him to go. She didn't want to explain the complications the dead faced to someone for whom life was probably not a whole lot better. "He won't be able to talk to you. You won't be able to actually see him unless I'm here."

"Yes, we will," Susan said. "He can play Tetris!" she shoved her hands through her brother's chest, laughed, wiggled her fingers and then said, "Come on. Phillip!"

Phillip rose. He turned, hugged his mother that little bit too tightly, and then allowed himself to be dragged off by his sister and the once again invisible ghost of the brother whose absence had haunted this house since his death.

NATHAN

NECROMANCERS CAN SEE THE DEAD, but they have to be looking. Emma hasn't been looking. She hasn't seen Nathan once tonight at Mark Rayner's house. Nathan has done nothing to make himself visible, though. It's a trick he's learned, and he didn't learn it the hard way—which would be the way Emma's father did.

The dead don't always see each other, either. Mark would never have seen Emma's father without some prompting on Emma's part. Mark doesn't see Nathan.

Emma's father does. He says nothing, does nothing, makes no sign. He's never interfered in their relationship, not when Nathan was alive and not now. But he's worried.

And he should be.

Emma brought Mark home. Nathan didn't want her to do it; neither did her father. Eric was practically spitting bullets. People don't think of Emma as strong. No, that's not true—Allison does. But mostly, they think of Emma as *nice*, as if nice implied weakness. Truth is, Emma is kind. She hates to cause pain. All that Hall guilt works like a tunnel; she can't climb the walls and doesn't even see them most days.

She saw them tonight. She saw them, but she'd made a promise to a child. The fact that he was dead didn't matter. Or maybe, Nathan thinks, it mattered more. She was terrified, but the promise was more important than the dread. Emma doesn't generally make promises. But it won't stop her from making promises like this one. Emma sees the dead as people. She sees the living as people. The dividing line is so thin, Nathan wonders if she's consciously aware it exists.

He doesn't have the right to be proud of her; he didn't raise her, he didn't guide her, he didn't shape her. He spent the happiest months of his life by her side—but she was already herself.

Emma was afraid. She came anyway.

Nathan knows how angry she was when she arrived. He understands how much she hated Mark's mother before she'd even approached his front door. He felt the same way.

But what happened in the living room of Mark's home wasn't about anger or hate. It was about fear, and failure, and love; it was about loss, about the way pain can cause the losses people most fear.

Nathan goes upstairs to where Phillip and Susan are bunched around Mark's computer, watching the screen come to life as if it were a bridge between the living and the dead. Nathan can see Mark; his siblings can't, but they know he's there.

Mark, however, isn't aware of Nathan.

Emma isn't, either. Nathan knows when to leave her alone. It's harder, though. She was his world while he was with her—but there were always things to do when she needed space for thought. Now there's almost nothing.

"You shouldn't be here."

Nathan turns. He doesn't recognize the voice. He doesn't recognize the woman it belongs to. But something about her tone and the texture of her words makes it feel like the heart of winter in this small room.

Mark looks up, frowning. He looks through Nathan. He doesn't look past the old woman.

To Nathan's surprise, she smiles at Mark, the many lines around her lips and eyes transforming her expression. She doesn't look terrifying when she smiles.

"I live here," Mark says.

"In a manner of speaking," Nathan adds.

"And this is my room," Mark continues, soldiering on.

"Yes, of course it is. But I wasn't speaking to you."

Mark's frown deepens. "They can't hear you."

The old woman pins Nathan down with a wordless glare that manages to make clear exactly what she wants him to do. He steps through the bedroom door as Mark begins an explanation of Tetris to a woman who was probably chiseling stone tablets when she was his age.

It's no surprise that it takes her a while to finally join him in the hall.

"You shouldn't be here," she says again, as the smile falls away from her face, leaving only the ancient behind.

"I don't have anywhere else I need to be."

If she has a sense of humor, she's not sharing it. "She sent you."

Nathan says nothing.

"She sent you to Emma."

"Does—does Emma know?"

"I don't know. Young girls in love are often blind and willful."

It's a typical thing for the old and bitter to say, but there's an edge to her voice that implies personal experience. "Were you?"

She smiles. Her smile is less barbed than anything else she's directed his way. "I was young once. A long time ago. All pain was new, then. All grief was sharper, harsher. All loss was the end of everything. But you learn that you survive what seems fatal."

He can't imagine her ever being in love. He can't imagine the courage it would take to love her; she seems so cold and harsh.

"Emma's seen you."

Nathan nods.

"When?" The question is cutting.

Nathan shrugs. He doesn't want to admit that he has trouble keeping track of time, not to this woman. He settles on: "Before tonight."

The woman falls silent. "Does Emma know," she finally asks, "why you're here?"

"I'm here," he replies, with more heat, "because I *want* to be here. I want to be with her."

"You're here because you were sent here."

He shrugs. It's the truth. But so is what he said. "She didn't tell me why."

"No?"

It's one of his biggest fears. It's not the only one, but being on the other side of death has made most of the others irrelevant. It's not as restful as it sounds. "If I understand being dead, this is where I would have ended up eventually. Emma said she was waiting."

"Emma probably didn't know where to find you," is the bitter answer. "There's far too much that girl doesn't know."

He slides hands into pockets out of habit; it's not like they can hold anything else. "How do you know Emma?"

"You ask about your Emma and not your Queen?"

"She's not my Queen."

"You don't call her Queen in her presence?"

Nathan is silent for a moment. "What we call her doesn't matter. She's what she is."

"Oh? And what is that, boy?"

"The Queen of the Dead. She's an old-style Queen. She might as well be a god."

"A bitter, small god indeed."

"A lonely god," Nathan replies. He's not certain why. Maybe it's the empty throne that's always by her side when she sits in her courtroom. It's not a lesser chair. It's not set back. It's beside hers, and to his eye—to his dead eye—it's equal. But empty. Always empty. An image of the man she would make King hovers there, but he's more of a ghost than Nathan or any of the rest of the dead.

The old woman says nothing for a long, long moment. When she speaks, she surprises Nathan. "Tell me about your Emma."

"She's not mine."

The shape of the woman's brow changes. "Not yours?"

"She's a person. Romantic words aside, we can't actually own each other. We can be responsible for another person if the person is a child, but even then, we don't own them."

She snorts. "Just the work?"

"Something like that." He shrugs. He doesn't like the old woman, but that's no surprise; she's hard and bitter.

"Tell me about the Emma you know," she says, giving ground. That's surprising.

"Tell me why you want to know," he counters.

"I took a risk with that girl. I took a risk I've never taken."

"What risk?" he asks, in spite of himself.

She glares at him. "You'll tell your Queen if she asks. You'll tell her everything."

He thinks it's true. But he's never tried to hide from her; he's never tried to lie. He doesn't argue. Instead, he looks at his feet. When he looks up, she's watching him, her glance no less harsh but mixed with appraisal.

"You understand what she wanted, sending you here?"

He doesn't.

"Your Emma sees the living. She sees the dead. She doesn't understand that they're not the same. The closest she's come was this evening, when she brought that boy home."

Nathan nods.

"She didn't want to bring him," the woman continues. "It was a foolish act. I almost told her as much—but I wanted to see how she handled herself. I wanted to see what choices she made, given all of the facts she amassed. Given," she continued, voice softening, "her anger."

"Emma has a temper," Nathan says quietly.

"Yes. She does. But so do we all. Do you understand her anger?"

"Who wouldn't?"

The old woman nods. "Walk with me, boy." She drifts through a wall, and Nathan follows because he can't think of a polite way to say no. Apparently manners still matter, even when he's dead.

She doesn't speak. She doesn't stop. He's almost afraid to follow her when the streets bank and end in a jagged line, as if half the city has been cut away by a madman with a gigantic ax. But the line, if jagged, has the quality one finds in dreams. There is no rubble, there are no bodies; there's just an uneven break.

"It is the memory of a city," the old woman says. "If you let go of yours, you will see a place that spans all the lives of the people who have ever lived here. You'll see open fields and plains and heavy forests; you'll see old log homes and the ghosts of small homes that were destroyed to make way for larger ones. You'll see streetlamps, streetlights, dirt roads, footpaths—and they overlap, shifting from one step to the next."

"Sounds like a good way to get lost."

She nods, as if the words were profound. "But you are lost, all of you. You hold tightly to the lives you once lived, although they're no longer yours. What do you see now?"

Night. Night sky. Nathan thinks it's an open plain with edges of mountain or forest, but he can't tell; it never quite coalesces. He squints, frowning. "Night," he finally says.

"Just night?"

"There's not a lot of light here. Maybe it's because I'm dead."

"No. It's outside of your experience, and perhaps that's as it should be. This," she added, "is where I stay." She doesn't say "where I live."

"Your Emma can't see this place yet."

Yet. Nathan stiffens.

"But when she brought that boy to his mother, she saw the edges of it. She doesn't realize what she sees. She doesn't understand what it means; that much is obvious."

"And you'll tell me?"

The old woman grimaces. "I've been here a long time." She shakes her head. "Love is a tricky thing. It strengthens us and weakens us; it binds us and it liberates us. It makes us hold on too tightly; it colors everything we see.

"But the dead aren't bound in the same way."

Thinking about Mark—never mind Mark, thinking about *himself*—Nathan shakes his head.

"That boy doesn't understand that he's dead. He doesn't understand what it means. What you saw—what you still see, if I had to guess—he *doesn't* see. He would have been lost had Emma not found him. The wonder, to me, is that she *did* find him.

"Understand that there were always those, among the dead, who were lost. The light that beckons you, that beckons Emma's father, that devours the young Necromancer—Mark couldn't see it. He couldn't leave the literal forest in which he'd been told to wait, and had Emma not found him, he would still be there decades from now. Waiting."

"Would that have been much worse?"

"In my lifetime, yes. It would have been. In a way that most of the living don't understand, it would have been a tragedy. Now, there is only tragedy. The Queen of the Dead doesn't *see* the dead; she doesn't serve them. She offers no guidance; she does not lead them home.

"Emma has had no training. She has learned nothing. But she *sees*. What she did for Mark was forbidden in my time. Not finding him," she adds. "Not leading him out of the forest. But taking him home."

"Why?"

"Because we were already feared. The dead do not meet the living if the living can't see them and speak to them on their own. There have been no guides—not since the Queen of the Dead. Now, those who might learn the art are taught other things. They look inward always;

they are strapped and bound by their knowledge of their own lives. They can't—and won't—look beyond them."

"And Emma did."

"Emma did. Without guidance."

Nathan shakes his head. "Emma doesn't judge."

"We *all* judge. It's part of the human condition. But it is not a part of the human condition that serves the guides of the dead well."

"Is there no hell?"

"I don't know," the old woman replies. "But if there were, it would look at lot like this. Life blinkers us. It is difficult to see beyond the walls of our own experiences. Emma is certain that she would never be Mark's mother. She was angry—she was more than angry—when she arrived. She had already decided what she felt—and thought—of Mark's mother.

"I don't know if that's changed," the woman adds. "But I do know this: In the end, it didn't matter. The child mattered. The dead mattered. What she needed to do to ease his transition, she did. She may have wanted justice. She may have wanted retribution. These are natural desires. They are human desires.

"But she chose. And I do not think she was unmoved, in the end, by what she heard. I have put the only power that remained to me in her hands. But I am an old woman. Older by far than you will have the chance to be; older by far than Emma. Fear is a constant companion, and hope is bitter, it is prone to so many failures.

"Emma has now made choices that seem promising to me." She turned, in the darkness, to face Nathan. "All but one."

Nathan swallows. "Me."

"You. You are now the heart of my fear, boy. I understand why she loves you. But I fear what that love presages. You should not be here. She is *not ready* for you, not yet. She is discovering—against all hope—the limitations of her power."

"She doesn't even understand her power yet."

"You will find that she does. She doesn't understand how to use it the way the Queen and her people do, but what she did for Mark tonight, they could not do. If she holds to that, she will be the first to do so since the end of all our lines so many years ago; she will be the only person born with her gift that has some hope of unseating the Queen and her Court.

"But what she did for Mark, she could do within the bounds of mortal compassion. What she sees when she sees you is the enormity of her own loss—and the enormity of yours. What she feels for you is tied in all ways to the interior of the life she lived—and wanted. That life is over, boy."

Nathan says nothing.

"And she has not yet accepted it. Seeing you here, seeing you *almost* in the flesh, seeing the boy she loved as if he had never died, she won't accept it. And if she can't, then there is no hope."

CHAPTER
SIXTEEN

SILENCE.

The silence of cars, of snow against streetlamps. The impersonal sound of wind in branches, the constant friction of leash, the rising white clouds of dog breath. Moonlight. Stars.

Emma looked at the time; it was almost 11:30. She hadn't lied to Michael's mother; Eric had brought his car. He just hadn't driven it to Mark's house.

"Your mother's worried about you," she said to Michael.

"I know."

"Do you think you'll be okay now?"

He exhaled and turned to her as if he'd lost ten years. She could see the echo of Mark's face in his. "I don't understand people."

"Do you understand what happened to Mark?"

Michael nodded slowly. "She didn't mean to kill him."

"No."

"But he died anyway."

"Yes."

"He shouldn't have died. It's not fair." He closed his eyes and stopped walking; Emma stopped as well. Her hands ached, but some feeling had returned to the one that had been Mark's anchor. "You're going to tell me life's not fair."

"I don't have to," she said, her voice soft. "I don't need to tell you things you already know."

Michael's nod was stiff. "There's no justice in the natural world." He said it without bitterness, as if stating fact. "Justice is a human construct."

"And humans aren't perfect." It was an old conversation. Old, familiar, and, tonight, painfully true.

"But if we don't keep trying, there's no justice at all." He inhaled, opened his eyes. "Thank you for taking Mark home. Thank you for taking me with you."

"I promised," she said. "But if I don't get you home, your mother's not going to be very happy."

Petal nuzzled Michael's hand, and Michael turned his attention to the dog. Emma did as well, but the sound of Eric's phone drew it away.

"Are you going to answer that?" Emma asked.

Eric grimaced; he was already fishing the phone out of a pocket. "I hate these things," he said, as he looked at the phone. His grimace froze in place. "It's not the old man."

Emma froze as well. She glanced at Michael, at Petal, and then back at Eric.

He answered his phone. "Hello?" Pause. "Amy?"

At the sound of Amy's name, Michael rose, his hand still attached to Petal's head as an afterthought.

"You're where? Now?"

Emma fished her own phone out of her jacket pocket; her hands were shaking. It was off. She'd turned the phone off before she'd entered Mark's house. It took her four tries to turn it on, and as she fumbled, her father appeared by her side.

"Dad—"

"I'll go to Allison's," he told her, understanding the sharp edge of her sudden fear.

"Can you get there—" but he was already gone.

Michael didn't carry a phone. His mother had tried to give him one. Or, more accurately, three. He'd lost each and every one. Emma checked hers. There were four missed calls, all of them from Amy.

Eric wasn't doing a lot of speaking—but he was on the phone with Amy, and in general, Amy did the talking when a phone was involved. "Where will you be?" Eric finally asked.

The tone of his voice made Emma want to grab the phone out of his hand.

"No, there were too many people, from the sounds of it, to be Necromancers." Eric sucked in air. "Yes, they're capable of hiring people—but it doesn't generally end well for the people they hire. Look—you're all right? Your family is—" He inhaled sharply again. Emma couldn't hear what Amy said, but she could hear Amy.

"Emma and Michael are with me. Emma just turned her phone back on. No, we weren't someplace where a phone would have—yes, I'll ask her not to turn it off again until we're all in the same place. Have you spoken with Allison?

"Okay. Meet us at my place. We'll head there immediately. Hello?" Apparently, Amy had hung up.

Emma was so cold she felt like warmth would never reach her again. "What happened?"

"We need to get to the car," Eric replied.

"We need to take Michael home."

"We can't."

"We need to—"

"Phone Michael's house," Eric told her, his voice that little bit too tight.

"Emma?" Michael said.

Emma turned to Michael and handed him Petal's leash. He looked at it as if it were entirely foreign.

"Emma, what happened to Amy?" Michael's voice was softer.

"Amy is fine," Eric said, voice tight.

"And my mother?" Michael asked, voice rising at the end.

No, Emma thought. *No, no, no.* "I need to go home," she whispered.

"It won't help. If your mother is fine—if nothing's happened—and you go home, it probably won't stay that way." Eric stared at his phone and cursed under his breath.

"Where's Chase?" Emma all but demanded.

"Good question. He's not answering his phone."

"I'll call Allison."

"She's not answering her phone, either. Not according to Amy."

No.

Emma called Michael's house. She called before she'd planned out what she might say if someone actually answered the phone. Michael was rigid with anxiety, and because he was, Emma couldn't afford to be. She almost cried with relief when his mother picked up.

"I'm glad you called," his mother said. "I was beginning to worry. Someone came to the door to speak with Michael about fifteen minutes after you left."

"Who?"

"I didn't recognize him. He said he's a friend of Michael's. He left homework for Michael. Michael's homework," she added. "He said he'd borrowed it. He apologized for being so late to get it back."

Emma wanted to tell her to burn it. Most homework was done electronically; it didn't *need* to be returned. In person. By a stranger. She covered the mic with her hand. "Your mother's fine. She's worried about you," she added, "but you kind of expect that from mothers."

"Michael is not going home," Eric said.

"Michael doesn't exactly do sleepovers. What do you want me to tell her?"

"Whatever you need to tell her." He turned to Michael. "Can you talk to her without explaining too much?"

Emma knew the answer, but she looked to Michael anyway. He was less rigid than he had been, his unvoiced visceral fear for his mother's safety giving way to a more common fear. Michael was not one of nature's liars. He was practically the anti-liar.

"Are any of us going home?" she asked softly.

"No." Eric exhaled as they reached his car. "I'm not going to kidnap you. Either of you. You know what's at stake. You know who your enemies are. If you insist on going home, I can't stop you. But, Em—I can't protect all of you either. There are too few of us."

"Could you protect Michael and his family if I don't go home? Could Michael go home?"

Michael said, "I'll stay with Eric. I'll stay with you, Emma."

"But your mother—"

"She's still on the phone," Eric reminded her.

Michael frowned. "I think she knows that." To Emma he said, "I don't want to make my mother worry. I don't want to scare her. But I don't want her to die. If I tell her—if she knows—she'll call the police. She'll call the school. If she calls the school, the Necromancers will know she knows.

"I don't think they kill people randomly."

Thinking of Allison's brush with death, Emma disagreed. "I don't think they care."

"They do, or they wouldn't have to kill people who know about them."

"Can I suggest," Eric said, unlocking the door and opening it, "that this is not the time for this argument?"

Michael frowned. "We're not arguing."

Eric slid behind the driver's wheel. Michael opened the back passenger door. "Can I talk to my mom?"

Eric stiffened. Emma said, "Of course," and handed Michael the phone. She didn't tell him what to say—or what not to say. His entire posture made it clear that he knew what was at risk. He probably saw it more clearly than Emma did; he had the ability to be both terrified and observant at the same time.

"Mom," he said, while Eric's jaw clenched, "I won't be coming home tonight. Something is happening. I can't explain it. But Emma needs me to be here. She'll be with me. I don't want you to worry. I'm okay. But we have to figure out what we need to do." He fell silent, listening. Emma couldn't hear what his mother said to him and was grateful. "I need you to trust me," was Michael's reply. "No, I can't explain—it would take hours, and even then it would be hard.

"But I *will* explain it, when it's over. I promise. I have to go. No, everything's not okay—if it were, I'd be coming home now. But it would be worse if I did." He hesitated and then handed Emma's phone back to her, which she'd been dreading.

"Emma, what's happening?" Mrs. Howe demanded.

"I can't explain it. What Michael said is true. It would take hours, and even then—it would probably take more hours on top of that. I won't let him out of my sight." She started to say, *I won't let anything bad happen to him*, but she couldn't. Instead, she said, "The only thing Michael's worried about right now is you. And me, a little. He needs you to be okay."

"Where are you going? Where are you going to be?"

"We're—" She shook her head. "If I can, I'll call you and let you know. Everything's up in the air."

"Emma—"

"—I'm sorry, I have to go." She hung up.

"She's going to worry," Michael said, with quiet confidence.

"Love," Emma replied, "makes worriers of us all. Yes, she'll worry."

"Are you going to call your mom?" he asked.

Emma compromised. She tried to call Allison.

There was no answer.

Amy was at Eric's when they arrived—or at least her SUV was. They walked past it; Eric hadn't chosen to park in front of the house. Petal was antsy; it was clearly past Emma's bedtime, which meant it was past his. She let Michael handle the leash and handed him the last of the Milk-Bones that served as dog bribery.

Eric didn't lead them directly to the house, either. He didn't exactly skulk—something bound to cause suspicions in anyone who happened to look out their window at the wrong time—but he walked with purpose in the wrong direction, dragging Emma and Michael in his wake.

"Em."

She turned at the sound of her father's voice. The world was all of night, and the single syllable he'd made of her name made it too cold, too harsh.

"Ally?" she asked. The word made almost no sound.

Eric slowed. Michael couldn't see her father—but he could see her. He stopped. Petal wound the leash around Michael's legs.

"Allison's alive. She's with Chase. Chase," he added, looking briefly at Eric, "is also alive."

"And the rest of the Simners? Her brother? Her parents?"

Silence.

"Dad? Dad!"

"Her brother was shot."

"Is he—"

"Emma, I'm not a doctor. I don't know. Emergency crews are on the way."

"How do you—"

"The neighbors. You don't shoot guns in that neighborhood without raising alarms." His hands slid into his pockets; they were fists. He hesitated, then said, "you'll have to tell Allison about her brother. She wasn't there when they broke into the house."

"How do you—"

"I found her. Chase got her out. Allison heard the gunshot, and she tried to go back. Chase . . . wouldn't let her. I wouldn't want to be that boy if her brother dies."

"Was Chase hurt?"

Her father nodded. "Not by Allison, not yet. I think he meant to bring her here."

"Where are they now?"

"Chase didn't drive."

Eric cursed. "Can you take me to them?"

Her father nodded.

Eric turned to Emma and Michael, who were so silent they might not have been breathing. "Stay here. Go inside, and do whatever the old man tells you to do. Don't argue with him. Don't argue with me."

"If Necromancers are there," Emma began.

"If?" Eric said, with a laugh that was worse than his swearing. "You don't have the training. I do. Chase does. Go into the house, Emma. Amy's probably waiting, and we can't afford to have her kill the old man. I'll bring them back."

CHAPTER
SEVENTEEN

ALLISON COULDN'T BREATHE.

It wasn't the running—although she wasn't much of a runner, and her sides had been cramping on and off for the last half hour. It wasn't the cold; she was numb enough now that the air no longer chilled her or shocked her when she drew it into her lungs.

She couldn't hear her own breath. She couldn't hear Chase.

She could hear the echo of the gunshots. She could hear them over and over again, shattering the quieter noises of a normal night in a neighborhood that saw violence on television, contained in a frame, made distant because it was meant to be entertaining.

She knew Chase was bleeding. She'd asked him why; he hadn't answered. He was a redhead; his skin was normally pale. Tonight it looked ashen, his eyes too dark.

He had come to save her life.

She *knew* he had come to save her life. She was certain that he probably had. And she hated him for it. Right now, right in this moment, fear had turned any gratitude she might have felt to ash. Her face bore the mark of his open hand; his bore the smaller mark of hers—and a scratch that had welted.

It was silent. It was too silent. If she broke the silence, she'd scream. Or she'd cry. Or both. And even if she hated herself for her cowardice—because that's what it was, this running, this silence, this abandonment—she *wanted* to live. Another thing to hate about herself.

Chase checked her coat; he checked the heavy necklace she'd been given what seemed a lifetime ago. His lips were almost white. He said nothing, but she knew what he feared: not men with guns, but Necromancers. He was certain they were here, somewhere. He was certain that they were hunting.

The snow didn't help. Its pristine, untouched surfaces held on to footsteps like accusations; there was nowhere they could walk—or run—that didn't leave an immediate, obvious trail. Only the sidewalks had been cleared, and Chase wanted to avoid them.

So did Allison. If they were seen—if their neighbors saw them, if anyone tried to help or interfere, there would be more deaths. No. No, not *more*. Not more. Please, god, not more.

She shook. In any other circumstance, she would have pretended she was cold; it *was* cold. Her hand was stiff; it was locked in Chase's, as if he didn't trust her to follow, as if he thought she'd turn and go home at any moment.

He had taken the lead. This was the neighborhood that had been home for all of Allison's conscious life, but Chase knew it too. He knew it at least as well—on a night when the world had gone insane—as she did, but saw it differently. The houses were obstacles; the driveways, the backyards, the cars parked in the street or the fronts, were cover for changes in direction.

Chase carried a mirror; he used it, instead of sticking his head out or up, where possible.

And he led them, in the end, toward the cemetery and the ravine. Allison knew there was no safety in numbers, but she felt exposed. Even the sounds of passing cars—and the intermittent whiteness of passing headlights—dwindled. Here, she could hear Chase breathe.

It was labored, almost as labored as her own shallow breaths. She stumbled twice. Her feet were numb.

"I don't care if you hate me," Chase whispered. "You probably will. There's nothing you could have done at your house except die."

She wanted to argue but couldn't—it was true. It didn't making running feel any better or any more justified. His grip tightened briefly, and then—for the first time since he'd slapped her, or maybe since she'd slapped him—he let go of her hand. Instead of his hand, she found herself holding the hilt of a knife; he'd placed it in the palm of her gloves, and her hands were so stiff she almost dropped it.

"I know you don't know how to use it," he said, looking over her shoulder, his eyes constantly scanning the shadowed trees. "You're not meant to kill here. If someone or something grabs you, stab it or cut it and run away."

"Chase—"

"I mean it."

"You're—"

"No, I'm not. I'm fine." He smiled. It was a lopsided expression; it contained a world of pain and very little warmth. "I'm not afraid of Necromancers. They'll kill me, one day. I'll kill them until that day. It's been the whole purpose of my life. Of what was left of my life.

"I know how you feel. I know why you hate me. I can't honestly tell you it's going to stop any time soon. The only thing I wanted on the day I didn't die—" He inhaled. Exhaled. "I shouldn't be talking. Stay here. Keep your back to the tree, breathe into your sleeve."

"Where—where are you going?"

"I need to put a few things on the ground. We're going to stay here, within this area, until they find us. Or until they give up. I'm hoping for the latter. Stay here. I won't be far."

She nodded. She didn't ask what she could do to help—he'd just told her. She could stay out of his way. She could be as silent and invisible as possible. She could breathe into her sleeve so her breath didn't rise in telltale, visible mist. Invisibility was something that came naturally to Allison, at least in her normal life.

But invisibility wasn't the same as inactivity. It wasn't the same as huddling in silent fear. She bit her lip, held her breath. She examined the knife Chase had pushed into her hands. It was simple, its edge notched in at least two places; the hilt was rough and worn. This had been made by hand by people who didn't have the time to prettify their work.

People like Chase. Maybe Chase himself. He probably knew how to slit a man's throat. He certainly knew how to kill. She closed her eyes. He'd killed Merrick Longland. But Merrick Longland hadn't *stayed* dead.

Allison had no doubt at all that she would.

That her parents, if killed, would. That her brother would never open his eyes and speak again. No. No. No. She took a deep breath and forced herself to exhale slowly into her sleeve; it was damp. She felt the tree at her back as if it were the hand of a friend. She could hear Chase moving across brittle snow. She could feel the ghost of a tendril wrapped around her throat; could hear the echo of an equally brittle apology for her coming death.

And she could hear Emma's voice. The panic in it. The pleading.

She swallowed, bowed her head, and lifted her chin. If she died here tonight, it wouldn't be because she had just given up. She couldn't fight; it was true. It wasn't a skill that she'd ever felt a pressing need to learn. Reading about fighting—and she'd done a lot of that—wasn't the same. She was on the outside, looking in.

She promised she'd learn. If it came to that, if she survived, she'd learn.

A shadow cut across the snow. Chase had returned. He glanced at the knife in her hand and grimaced.

"It'll cut through anything but the fire," he told her softly.

His hands, she saw, were empty. She knew whose knife she carried.

She tried to give it back, but he ignored it. "Do you know why I like you?" he asked. She blinked. It wasn't the question she expected.

"No. I always wondered."

"You remind me of home. Of the best things about home. I didn't appreciate them enough when I had them, and when I lost them—" He shook his head. Smiled. It was the first real smile that had touched his face since it had appeared at her bedroom window, hanging upside down.

"We don't get a chance to do things over. Things happen. They're in the past. We can see them—over and over again—but we can't touch them. We can't change them. I *need* you to survive. I need you—just you, I don't give a damn about anyone else—to make it out of here alive. If you do—if you can do that for me, if I can even ask it when I know what it'll cost you—then I'll feel like surviving myself had some purpose. Not dying won't be the end of my life. It won't be the worst thing about it."

She swallowed.

"You're solid. You won't turn your back on your friends. You won't lie—I honestly doubt you know how. Don't try on my account," he added, grinning. "It'll just be humiliating. You're not like Emma. You're not like Amy. People don't stop in the street to give you a second look."

It was true. People seldom really gave her a first one. "I don't need it."

"No. You don't. But the thing is, Ally, I don't need it either. I don't give a shit what people see when they look at you. I don't care what they miss. In my life—in the life I've lived since I lost my family—it's pointless. Most people would run screaming. They'd hide in a corner. They'd forget what they'd seen."

"It's safer for them. After tonight, you'll understand why." He turned away, and then turned back. "I hate that you're not one of them. But I like you because you're not one of them. You can't fight. You don't understand Necromancers. You really don't understand what we're facing."

"But even if you did, you'd still be here."

"And getting in the way."

He nodded. "And getting in the way." He reached up and brushed her cheek with his fingers; they were cold, but she felt them as if they were burning. "I'm sorry I hit you. My father would've killed me if he'd been alive to see it."

"I hit you first."

"I couldn't let you go back. I'm sorry. I couldn't. I never wanted you to be here. I wanted you to be safe. To be safe, to be an echo of the things home used to mean to me, where the rest of my life couldn't touch or destroy it. I hated your best friend."

"Do you hate her now?"

"Yes. Yes—but I understand why you don't. And I understand, when I try to be fair—and it's work, so don't expect too much of it—that she sees and loves what I see—and love. You're not superficial. You're not trying to be something. You're not trying to impress me or Emma or even random strangers. I can't expect her to walk away from you when she's known you for most of your life; I can't walk away, and I've known you for weeks."

His face was so close to hers. It was dark, but she could see his eyes, could see his expression. "If someone comes, if I'm not here—remember what I said. There's almost no binding magic that you can't cut through. You cut—and you run."

"Chase—"

"Please. Please, Allison. Promise." He hesitated and then said, "If you die here, it will kill Emma. It will break her. If you can't promise for my sake, promise for hers."

"That's—"

"Unfair?"

It was. It was so unfair.

"Maybe we haven't been formally introduced," he said, grinning again, his face pale. "I'm Chase Loern. Unfair is my middle name. I've been accused of worse when it comes to getting what I want." The smile fell away from his face. "They're coming."

Allison could hear nothing but Chase, yet she didn't doubt him. He stepped back, stopped, grinned again. Before she could speak, he kissed her. He was out of reach before she could react.

"If you want to slap me," he whispered, "you'll have to stay alive."

She would have stuttered if she'd had voice for words. Before she could find that voice, she saw a pale green light illuminate the snow on either side of the tree at her back. The Necromancers had arrived.

CHAPTER
EIGHTEEN

THE DOOR OPENED BEFORE Emma could touch it, sliding in toward an ordinary looking front hall. Ernest stood three yards back; his eyes were dark, his jaw set. "Don't stand there like gaping tourists," he snapped. "Get in."

Michael obeyed instantly. Petal started to growl. Emma looked once over her shoulder and obeyed, stepping forward as if she were walking around the corner into a nightmare landscape. It wouldn't have surprised her at this point to see Ernest sprout horns, fangs, or guns.

Amy appeared in the hall at his back. Given the expression on her face, horns, fangs, and guns would have been gratuitous.

The door shut behind them. No one had touched it.

"Allison's still not answering her phone," Amy said, first up.

Emma nodded. "I don't think she has it with her. I turned mine on," she added quickly.

"Where's Eric?"

"He's gone to find Ally. And Chase." Emma closed her eyes. "Ally's brother was shot."

"So was my father," Amy replied. "They mostly missed."

"Your mom?"

"She's terrifying the police."

"She knows you're—"

"No. I told her I was going to Nan's. I had hysterics and told her I couldn't deal with the police." That was not—in any alternate universe Emma could think of—a remotely believable lie. Sometimes she wondered at the optimism of parents. "There were no Necromancers at my house. There were guns, possibly knives, and a lot of noise—but no Necromancers. If Allison's someplace without her phone, I think the timing is a bit coincidental for a random, armed break-in."

Ernest said, quietly, "We warned you. This isn't a game."

"Michael's mother seems to be okay for now. But they know Michael's not at home," Emma said, speaking past Ernest to the most dangerous person in the hall.

Amy nodded. "I took the liberty of packing." She turned and headed into Ernest's living room while Ernest shut his mouth. "I don't have much that'll fit Allison, though."

Michael opened his mouth.

"I raided Skip's closet," she told him. "You're not the same size; he's fatter. But it'll do."

"Where are we going?" Michael asked. It was the sensible question.

"Someplace else." Amy exhaled as she remembered who she was speaking to. "I borrowed keys and a pass card from my dad's office. We've got cottages and small chalets a couple of hours outside the city in a bunch of different directions. Inside the city isn't safe at the moment; if they want us, we'll make them work for it. They're not going to be able to pillage our information from the school records."

"And our parents?"

"I don't think they care whether or not our parents live or die," Amy replied. "It's just us they're gunning for." She grimaced. "At least that's the hope."

"Your parents—"

"Yes. My parents are probably safe. My father can afford to hire a small army, and has the smarts to figure out how to do it legally."

"My mother can't," Michael said quietly.

Amy didn't argue. "I'd tell my father," she finally said, "who to look out for. But to tell him that, I'd have to tell him pretty much everything *and* make him believe it. And he won't leave it alone if he does. He'll go to the police. He'll go above the police. It'll be all over the place inside of a week." She glared at Ernest, who had come to stand behind a suitcase the size of a small fridge. "This is the best I've got. I'm willing to entertain suggestions. From you guys," she added, pointedly excluding the man in black.

And he was in black. He had shed the old-fashioned tweed look that made him seem older than he was; to Emma's eye, he now looked like a lived-in version of Chase. She grimaced. Chase was not the person she wanted to be thinking about now.

But Chase had gone for Allison. He had, according to her father, saved Allison's life. He might be keeping it safe even now—something Emma had no hope of doing on her own.

"Earth to Emma," Amy said.

Emma shook herself. Amy's implied criticism was deserved. There were decisions that she could help make, things she could do. Better to do them than to become paralyzed by the things beyond her grasp. "It's going to look suspicious if we all disappear together."

"We're not. We're going on retreat together to an unspecified location. I'm obviously so shattered by an armed break-in into my own home that I needed the time away to put myself back together."

Michael frowned. Amy looked angry; she didn't look shattered. "We're supposed to help you . . . recover?" he asked.

"Exactly. I'll call my mother before we leave, and I'll tell her that I'm heading out of town for a few days because I don't feel safe at home." She folded her arms. "I'll tell her I need my friends with me. My mother can call your parents first and get their permission. Would that work?" She was mostly looking to Michael. She assumed everyone else could just *make it* work.

Amy wasn't above telling Michael what to do—she was Amy, after all. But she didn't particularly enjoy his version of panic, and she understood she'd be facing it soon if he wasn't handled with care. Amy's version of care, but still.

Michael turned to Emma. Michael, who had already called his mother.

Emma swallowed. "My mother would buy it if your break-in hits the news. She won't be thrilled—we'll be skipping school—but she'll understand it. I think Mrs. Howe would be worried—"

"Duh. Mother," Amy snapped.

"—But I think, if your mother talked to her, she'd actually be relieved. Michael's already phoned to tell her he isn't coming home." She exhaled and fell silent.

"You're not telling me something," Amy replied, voice flat the way the side of a knife was.

"Allison didn't answer her phone because she didn't have it with her. She's not at home."

"And?"

"Yours wasn't the only home that was targeted tonight. Chase— Chase somehow got Allison out of hers, but he didn't take down the people who were targeting her family. Her brother was shot. Unlike your father, whoever shot him didn't mostly miss. Ally's mother is probably out of her mind with worry—for Toby *and* Ally. I don't think your mom's going to be able to talk her down if she doesn't know where Allison *is*. And if she knows that your place was hit as well . . . she's not stupid. She might decide that the timing isn't coincidental."

"How? You *know* the timing wasn't coincidental. How is her mother going to know that? The two probably look entirely unrelated." Amy frowned. "Let me think about this. We're going to have to sell it differently." She swore softly and added, "Ally's not going to want to leave the city if her brother's really hurt."

Emma nodded, but added, "She'll go. If she understands that her brother was in danger because she was there, she'll go anywhere you tell her to go. I just think her mother will have a harder time with it, because Toby will be in the hospital." *If he survives.* She couldn't bring herself to say this.

Amy as a force of nature was a fact of life for the teachers in Emery; she was for the parents of her many acquaintances and friends too. If Amy wanted you to do something, you did it. Unless, Emma thought, you were Michael. Michael's sense of reality often collided with Amy's sphere of influence.

But he wasn't arguing now. He was nodding. He was nodding a little bit too quickly. Hall guilt asserted itself. She should never have gotten Michael involved. She should have taken Chase's advice—his bitter, heated advice—and left town when she could, without dragging all of her friends into isolation with her.

"You know," Amy said, "you should have been Jewish."

Emma blinked.

"You're so good at guilt, you don't need a mother reminding you of all the reasons you should feel guilty. If you feel guilty for dragging me into this mess, spare me. No one makes me do anything I don't want to do. And no one stops me, either." She glanced at Michael. Opened her mouth. Closed it. "We'll need clothing for Allison. I think she'll fit some of Skip's stuff—width-wise, at least. I've got money. I've got credit. I've got a car—I don't know if we want to ditch it or not.

"But we're going to have to decide what we do going forward. I for one don't intend to let some random Queen of invisible dead people dictate the course of *my* life. I don't intend to let her kill me or my friends.

"She needs to go."

*　　*　　*

"You make it sound so simple," Ernest said, his voice dry as kindling in winter.

"It *is* simple," Amy replied, folding her arms. "The logistics might be more difficult. I don't know how many of you there are. I assume all of you aren't here, in my city. I assume you've thought of all this before, and you've never managed to take her out. I even sort of understand why.

"Doesn't change the fact that she has to go."

"You are all schoolchildren," Ernest replied, folding his arms in the exact same way Amy had, although Emma didn't think the mimicry deliberate. "You can't fight. You don't understand Necromancy. You can't—without Emma's help—talk to the dead. You have nothing to contribute to the mission you so cavalierly dictate."

She lifted a brow and then turned back to Emma and Michael. "We'll need to talk to Eric. And Chase, if he makes it back."

Ernest's lips thinned; so did his gaze.

"I understand that you think we're useless," Amy said—without bothering to look at him. "Understand that we're not. We won't approach things the way you do—we can't. Doesn't mean we can't do anything. The first thing we're doing is getting out of the city for a bit. You can come with us, or you can stay here. I personally prefer that you stay here. We're going to take Eric and Chase with us."

Margaret said, "I like that girl." She had materialized—at least in Emma's view—beside the fireplace, between where Ernest and Amy stood, bristling at each other. "Her manners leave a little to be desired, but these days, it seems everyone's do. You understand that Ernest is not wrong?"

Emma nodded. "But neither is Amy."

Margaret smiled. "We forget that our world is not *the* world. We couldn't predict you—yet here you are. You opened the closed door, dear. The dead see you as clearly as they see the Queen. You carry our hope with you, but I think that hope will falter if you're forced to carry it alone—or forced, by circumstance, to carry it our way. Ernest," she added, although Ernest had not once looked in Margaret's direction, "we've tried for decades, and we've failed. Perhaps it's time to consider different methods or different avenues of approach. If I understand events correctly—and I frequently do—the greatest risk we face has already been taken."

"It was taken without consultation," he replied, every syllable spoken as if he disagreed with the decision.

"Of course it was. The decision was never yours—or mine—to make. But it's been made. We're committed, whether we like it or not."

He turned to Margaret. Amy, frowning, turned to Emma. "If the other half of this conversation has anything to do with us, I'd like to hear it."

Emma nodded and held out a hand to Margaret. Margaret glanced at it and shook her head. "That will not be necessary, dear," she said, smiling at the tail end of the endearment. "I don't require your hand. I'm bound to you; you hold me. If you desire it, I can appear at any time."

"Do you need my permission?"

"Yes. But permission is not a legal contract. It's not a ritual. You don't have to say the words if the words themselves trouble you." She turned, once again, to Ernest—but this time she also had Amy's attention.

Allison watched the pale green light grow brighter; her sleeve covered her mouth and nose, but it wasn't doing any good—she was only barely breathing. Chase, across from her in the shadow of the nearest tree, nodded brief encouragement before his gaze went elsewhere. He drew two knives from the folds of his jacket. They were longer and slimmer than the blade he'd given her, but reflected no light at all.

She closed her eyes.

This wasn't the first time she'd faced Necromancers, and at least this time there was no baby involved. She didn't have an infant to worry about; she didn't have responsibilities to fail. There was only Allison.

Why was it so much easier to fail yourself?

The light on the snow brightened, and the snow began to melt. No, she thought, watching, breath held. It wasn't melting; it was sinking and breaking, the crystals across its hardened surface surrendering territory to familiar, burning vines. Those vines shed light, and the light cast shadows. None of those shadows bore the familiar, attenuated shapes of people.

She lifted the dagger, remembering the way the vines had wrapped— like tentacles—around her exposed throat. She wore a necklace now that might protect her from the worst of it. She wore a jacket that would have her on the outs with Amy for six months under any other circumstance—not that she was ever "in" with Amy—that might stop the soul-fire from instantly devouring her.

Neither of these was armor. Neither of these was skill.

She listened. She glanced at Chase and saw an odd expression cross his face, just before she heard the first evidence of actual people. Someone screamed. Someone shouted a warning.

Someone laughed.

None of these voices were familiar. One woman, by the sounds of it, two men. How many Necromancers had Chase and Eric said there were? Three? Four?

As if he could read her mind, Chase held up a hand in the darkness. Four. He lowered two fingers. She'd heard three distinct voices. At least one could use Necromantic magic. The snow broke again, as if it were glass; small crystals fanned outward in a cold spray. The vines began to move, creeping along the ground and breaking snow as they traveled. Breaking it and melting it.

The sickly green fire did nothing to stem the chill of the winter air in any other way.

The voices drew closer. "We can't move at this speed. The ground's trapped."

"I noticed," the woman replied.

Chase slid away from his tree, gesturing for Allison to stay put. He couldn't move silently, but their enemies were making enough noise it probably didn't matter.

"Don't approach the areas where the vines have withered. It's the only safe place for our enemy to stand."

That, Allison thought, had to be the Necromancer, or at least one of the two. Her fingers curled around the knife Chase had given her; she could barely feel it. She hesitated, then removed her right glove, shoving it into her pocket. The air was cold.

The vines spread as green fire encased their circular, twisting forms. But they spread in a narrow line that seemed to travel straight ahead. As they did, they began to gain height. Watching in silence as she breathed into her sleeve, Allison realized they were forming a wall. A wall, a hedge of burning fire and thorns. She'd seen this before, and understood that they meant to enclose the area.

The area and everyone who was trapped within it.

"Come out," a male voice said. "Come out and I may choose to spare your lives. All we want at the moment is information."

She wanted to believe him. She wanted to believe that this might end without death—either hers or Chase's.

All she loses is a few years. A few years, in the existence of the dead, is nothing.

She couldn't. Fear was a horrible pressure against her chest and the insides of her throat—but it couldn't make her stupid enough. And if she were, Chase wouldn't be. Chase would walk out of here alive, or the Necromancer would—not both.

Voices drifted closer and then veered away. She pressed her back into the tree, willing herself to be invisible. The green light the vines shed made it harder, and Allison knew, as she watched them grow, it would soon be impossible. She'd be seen.

She checked the necklace at her throat. *Think.* One of the men had given instructions to avoid the areas where the vines had withered.

Something Chase had done—something he'd planted, iron maybe—
had killed the vines being powered by Necromantic magic.

By the dead.

She heard another curse—a woman's voice. It was followed by two
gunshots. At this range, they sounded like firecrackers, but louder,
fuller. "Longland," the woman said, as the reverberation died into silence. "You go ahead."

"I don't have your vision."

"You won't need it. You're already dead. If they damage your body,
it doesn't matter; it can be fixed."

Longland was here.

"Those weren't the Queen's orders," Longland replied. After a longer
pause, he added, "And I can't breach the barrier."

"The Queen's not here. *I* am. Go in. The ground's contaminated;
cross in the contaminated zone; it shouldn't stop you. If the hunter tries
to leave, he'll be leaving through those gaps; we're unearthing the iron
we can find." The gun fired again, and this time, Longland cursed.
"Your job was to find the kids. Ours was to clean up. Find them."

Eric stopped at the edge of the ravine. The snow was newly broken in
several places; the air was cold, the night clear. Trees loomed like the
broken pillars of ancient walls. From between those broken pillars
stepped Brendan Hall, his eyes silver, like contained stars.

"They're here," he said.

Eric hadn't asked Brendan Hall to scout ahead, but he was grateful for
his presence. He could see more or less what Emma's father could see: The
ground was glowing a faint, sickly green, and the sky above the ravine was
paler than it should have been at this time of night. "How many?"

"Two Necromancers."

"They did this with two?" He didn't ask Emma's father how long it
had taken; the dead did not have a concrete sense of the passage of time.

Emma's father nodded. "Chase is wounded."

"Badly?"

"Not enough to stop him immediately."

Eric cursed. "Allison?"

"Frightened. Bruised, but otherwise whole." He hesitated.

"You went in?" Eric's brows rose.

"Chase had time to salt the earth. There are gaps in the barrier. I don't know how long they'll last. I can slide through them, with some effort—but if I breach the barrier, the Necromancers will know."

"If anything breaches that barrier, they'll know if they're paying attention." Eric looked into the darkness from which no sound escaped. *Hang on, Chase. I'll be there soon.*

Snow, rain, safe houses that changed from one minute to the next—these had been Chase Loern's life. He didn't have a home. He hadn't for a long time. If you asked him on the wrong day, he didn't have friends, either; he had enemies. He had a mission.

He glanced over his shoulder at a tree.

He'd learned a few things since he'd lost his home, his friends, and the life he'd taken pretty much for granted. He'd stepped into a world of kill or be killed, and he was fine with that. Killing? He'd make the bastards pay. They'd left him alive. They'd regret it, right up until the time they got lucky or he got careless.

Until then? He'd fight.

He'd learned how to do that. No sweat. He'd learned how to kill Necromancers. If he'd known then what he knew now—but no. No.

What he'd learned, the most important lesson, was that the world was a harsh, bitter place. You had to get its attention. It didn't negotiate with a man on his knees; no point. It had you where it wanted you.

Chase didn't beg. He didn't plead. He didn't pray. He'd tried that once, and he'd learned. He knew that the person with the power got to dictate the terms—any terms. Life or death. In Chase's world, power meant one thing.

But he glanced at the tree again, knowing who sheltered behind it.

In his old life, he wouldn't have noticed her. That was the truth. She was plain. She was surrounded by people who weren't. She was quiet; she didn't demand attention, and she didn't reach out—the way Amy did—and grab it with both hands, shaking it until she got what she wanted. She would never have crossed his path.

But the first night he'd seen her, she'd almost slapped him. She had been practically quivering with indignant rage. She was willing to say what her best friend wouldn't: He had come to kill Emma. The fact that Emma was demonstrably not dead didn't change her fury one bit. The fact that Emma didn't *want* her anger or the confrontation it would cause hadn't changed it either.

Among the hunters, tempers frayed. Life on the edge did that. It was all about the fraying. He'd seen temper before; he'd see it again. But not Allison's temper. Not Allison's rage. It wasn't for herself. It wasn't for her loss. She'd known what was right—and what was wrong. And Chase was wrong.

He wouldn't have raised a hand against her if she *had* slapped him. He wouldn't have raised his voice. For a minute—for just a minute—he could see the world as she saw it. And it felt familiar. It felt like—like home. Like the home he'd lost. Like the home he'd never tried to build again.

It was *stupid*. It was *wrong*. His entire life had proved that. Tonight would prove that to Allison. It would open her eyes.

And he didn't want that. He wanted her to live in the world she saw. He wanted her to have what he'd lost—what he should never have lost, if the world were sane. Because he thought Allison could somehow defend her corner of the universe. Not with knives. Not with cold steel, or silver, or guns, or weapons; those weren't her particular strength. She might be able to learn them; Chase had.

But even armed as she stood, sanity—angry, furious sanity—had roots that were deep enough, strong enough, to weather the storms that surrounded her.

He had no home. It was better to have no home; he'd only have to leave it. But he knew now that some glimmer of it had remained dormant in him, and she had touched it.

He couldn't pray. He couldn't beg. He couldn't plead. But what he wanted now depended on the things he had learned since the last time he'd tried. With his own hands, with his own power, he intended to protect the things he loved.

Allison looked for the gaps in the growing wall. She looked for the places where vines had, as the unseen speaker had claimed, withered. The tree she was sheltering behind was no longer good cover; green light had become too bright. She hesitated. Chase had told her to stay put. He knew Necromancers. He knew their powers. He'd given her the knife she held in a shaking hand, and he'd told her to cut and run if necessary.

But running with no destination was a disaster in the making. She didn't know where the Necromancers were, but their voices had drawn closer. She could see the wall of risen vines; it towered above her in the distance. As she narrowed her eyes, she could see gaps in that wall. The vines at these locations were brown and dark; the fire didn't burn around them. They were almost evenly spaced, and they weren't wide—but they were there. If she could make it that far, she should be able to push through them; they were just about wide enough.

She inhaled, held her breath, and then crouched, peering at half-height around the cover of the tree's trunk. She couldn't see Chase; she couldn't see anything but green and white.

She exhaled into her sleeve, although visible breath was fast becoming a nonissue. Chase had told her to remain where she was. But he'd also told her to cut and run if necessary.

"Over there!" The woman shouted.

Allison froze. She didn't have to hide her breath; she stopped breathing for a long, agonizing minute. But the voice was followed by footsteps—and the footsteps led away from the tree. Away from her hiding place.

She had no idea what Chase could do. She'd spent one afternoon with Ernest—and Michael—and all she'd learned was how to run. How to kick someone so she could run. How to hit them. How to cause enough pain to get away. She'd learned that she needed to wear a thick, ugly necklace that rode a little too high on her neck; she'd learned that iron links could be sewn into coat linings. She'd learned that silver was useful.

She hadn't learned why—and Michael had asked.

She knew that Chase could fight. Chase could use knives. He could use guns. He could use—in a pinch—crossbows. But she knew that Chase could do more than that; if she needed proof, she only had to look at the hedge wall.

She even understood—and hated herself for it a minute later—why he hunted Necromancers before they came into their power. Against people like that—against people who were *almost* normal, she might stand a chance. Against people who had magic, almost none.

She heard another curse, more shouting; she took a deep breath, bit her lip, and headed in a straight line toward a gap in the fire that limned the wall. She held the knife clenched in one hand, and it made running harder, somehow, but she knew it could cut through the Necromantic magic anyone was likely to spare for her.

And she knew, as she reached the dead vines that couldn't support fire, that she should push them out of the way. She did that, cutting in places. She made a gap for herself; she'd be scratched, but whole, when she came out the other side.

But she didn't push through the hedge. She did the stupid thing. She turned. She looked back.

Chase was facing two Necromancers. She could see the red shock of hair that made him visible no matter how many people surrounded him. She could see fire—green fire—enveloping his body like a bubble.

She knew he was struggling. His movements were slow; the fire had trapped him. It hadn't stopped him; it hadn't killed him. Without help, it was only a matter of time. She wasn't the help he needed. Running back to him wouldn't save his life; it would only end hers. She suffered no illusions and no false sense of her own abilities.

She turned back to the hedge, and then turned again.

She suffered from no illusions.

She wasn't brave. She wasn't kind. She worried about herself and her own needs far too much. She had been jealous of Nathan. She had wanted him to *go away*. And then, sickeningly, he had. She could spend the rest of her life making up for that one selfish thought—and it probably wouldn't be enough.

Jealousy is natural. If you hate yourself for being jealous, you're going to spend a lot of time hating yourself. But now that you've said it, *how do you feel?* She could still see her grandfather's teasing smile, and his voice was so clear he might have been standing beside her.

Terrible.

Jealous?

Afraid. Afraid that I'll lose Emma. Afraid that I *deserve* to lose her.

Fear is natural, too. Your mother's not here, so let me put this the crudest way possible. Going to the bathroom is natural. If you never do it, you die. He held up a hand. *Yes, you won't die if you never experience jealousy, but that's not the point of the analogy. You need to go to the bathroom. When you're an infant, you go anywhere. Your parents clean up after you. When you're a toddler, you're not supposed to drop your pants and pee on the sidewalk.*

But you've seen children do it. You even laughed.

Because they're *children.*

Yes. But they're doing what comes naturally. They have to learn *that there's a time and place to express what's natural. This is not about what you* feel. *What you feel is natural. It's understandable.*

This is about what you do. *Fear's the same. It's not about the feeling. It's natural. It's human. It's about what you* do.

Her grandfather was gone, but his voice came back to her as she stood, frozen, by the hedge wall.

We all want to be good people, her grandfather said. *But no one starts out that way. When we're infants, we're greedy little creatures. The only things that exist are our wants and our needs. We're not much better as toddlers. Becoming the person you want to be isn't an accident. It's not something that just happens.*

We choose. We live with our choices. We make better choices. We learn to judge others less harshly when we understand the costs of our own mistakes. So here's my advice for the day.

Do your best to make the choices that will lead to you becoming the person you want to be. Accept the fact that you're human. Accept the fact that you'll fail when the days are long and harsh. And never knowingly make a choice that will make you think less of yourself. Make choices that will make others think less of you if you have to—but don't make choices that lead to self-hate.

There's enough hatred in the world. Don't add to it.

CHAPTER
NINETEEN

ALLISON LOWERED HER HANDS. For just a moment she could see everything so clearly it might have been noon. She could see Chase. She could see his scorched hair. She could see blood on his hands and steam rising from the snow beneath his feet. The woman was almost within his reach, but she no longer had a gun; the man was ten yards away from him, his hands spread in a fan at the level of his chest. He was the source of the fire; she was certain of it.

She had no illusions. She didn't need them, now. She wasn't going to run away while Chase fought. She wished—how she wished—she had taken her phone with her when she left the house through her bedroom window; it was on her desk. She had no way of calling for help; screaming probably wouldn't cut it.

But she wasn't helpless. There was no one holding her back except herself. Herself, her lack of experience, her fear. And if she gave in, Chase would die. Allison sometimes hated what Emma's sense of guilt did to Emma—but really, was her own so different?

She pulled back into the tree cover. She used what little of it there was. She crouched, which made movement agonizingly slow. Slower than Chase's. And she headed around him, as if her life depended on it.

She didn't give much for her chances if she caught the attention of both Necromancers now.

Chase had it.

Chase had it, and she needed him to keep it while she edged her way around them to the man who was standing out of his range, controlling the fire.

And when she reached him—if she did—what was she going to do? She didn't look at the knife in her hand; it was the only weapon she carried. The "if" was big enough she was willing to concentrate on one problem at a time.

She heard the woman curse and demand more power from, presumably, the man; he didn't reply. But his focus was on Chase; Allison rounded a tree, forgetting to breathe into her sleeve, and she was ten yards from his back.

His exposed back. He wore a wool coat that fell past the back of his knees; it was either dark gray or black. She couldn't see his hands; she could see fabric stretched across taut shoulder blades. His boots were invisible, his legs ending in snow.

But he wore no hat. She doubted very much that he wore a necklace similar to her own. She ducked behind the tree again. She would have to run if she couldn't move silently. She wasn't certain how much attention the Necromancer's partner was actually paying to him—and wasn't certain if they had taken the time to trap the ground, as Chase had done. She was pretty certain they hadn't.

But what did she know?

Chase was in trouble. She needed to do something. She had a knife. She could stab the Necromancer with it—but probably only once; twice if she was lucky. She needed to make it count. And she needed to make it count in a way that still left a knife in her hands.

It was hard to breathe. If she messed this up, she was dead. They were both dead. But if she didn't try at all, Chase was.

The worst thing that ever happened to me? Not dying.

She hadn't understood it, when he'd said it. But the gunshot—at her house—made it real in a way she'd never really considered. She could imagine Chase as a younger boy. She could imagine how powerless he'd felt; she felt powerless now, but she wasn't. She had a knife. She had silence. She had a Necromancer who was concentrating on the only person he thought might be a threat.

She had *something*. She had hope, a bitter chance. She intended to use it, because she didn't *want* to become Chase.

Allison Simner had never stabbed a man. She'd only hit one once, if you didn't count her brother. She hated causing pain. Even angry, she tried to avoid it. But she moved toward the back of a stranger she now hated, and she held on to hate, sharpening her fear rather than surrendering to it.

The Necromancer was taller than she was. His hair was dark, but snow dusted where he'd come too close to branches. More than that, she couldn't tell. She practically crawled across the snow toward his exposed back. She couldn't see Chase at all.

She was almost in touching distance of the Necromancer when he turned, his hands dropping as she raised the knife to press it against his throat. "Stop the fire," she told him, her voice steady.

His eyes were gray light. Emma had told her that meant he was using power; she tightened her grip on the knife and drew it across his exposed skin. The blood that welled there was more of a shock to her than it was to him, judging from his reaction.

"Or what, little girl?"

"Allison!"

"Or I'll kill you." It was cold. It was *so* cold.

He smiled. That was the worst of it. He smiled. He was bleeding. She'd cut him. But not enough. If he was afraid at all, it didn't show. And she knew that she had to do more, do it quickly; that she had to make him bleed in earnest. She knew where the dagger had to cut.

But she froze.

The woman screamed; the Necromancer who faced Allison stiffened. She saw his eyes begin to glow as her hand shook, and she knew that her moment was passing. Maybe it had passed. But she also knew that Chase was free. Chase who wouldn't have bothered with threats. Chase, who wouldn't have wasted the one chance he was given, if he was given one at all.

She moved her arm before the Necromancer could grab her wrist; she held the knife. She wasn't surprised when his hands became gloved in the white brilliance of fire; this close, the fire wasn't so much tendrils of flame as the pointed, solid light of acetylene torch. And it was aimed at her.

She cut it with the knife—it was so much easier to use the knife that way. Fire didn't bleed. It separated, as if it were an extension of his hands; it fell away, as if it were solid. But it didn't bleed. It didn't kill. She backed away. *Cut and run.*

But she couldn't run now. She couldn't turn her back on the man. The air was dry; the walls of her throat clung together, making breathing hard.

And then she was hit across the face and her knife hand by something warm, and she looked at the underside of the Necromancer's chin—and the sudden, gaping wound where his neck had been. She froze, but her knife was nowhere near the open wound; it was nowhere near slick enough, or red enough.

"You really are a stupid girl," a horribly familiar voice said. The Necromancer toppled to one side, reaching for his neck as if to close what had been so brutally opened. Her hands shook and she forced the knife up, to point it at Merrick Longland.

He showed no more fear than the Necromancer had. "You've already made clear that you've no intention of using what you wield." He stepped toward her; she stepped back. "Your hunter had better be less squeamish than you are." He turned his back on her.

"Why?" she asked. Back exposed, she could have stabbed him. But she knew, now, that that was a wish, a dream. Whatever it took to knife a man in the back, she didn't have it. Not yet. Maybe not ever.

He didn't pretend to misunderstand, although he didn't turn to look back at her. Instead, he folded his arms across his chest; she could see small mounds of snow moving just above his feet, and realized he was tapping his left foot, as if impatient.

"Your Emma has something I need. She values you enough that saving your life might put her in my debt." He cursed and added, "I'd hoped my former colleagues would be competent enough to do away with the hunter by now. If you'd stayed where you were, I wouldn't be saving his life as well."

Chase.

Chase had killed Longland.

"I recognize him," Longland said, as if she'd spoken out loud. Maybe she had. She began to shake. It was cold. It was just so cold. "It's his fault that I'm here now. It's his fault that I'm powerless." He turned on her then, and she saw the knife he carried, saw the blood that darkened every crease in his exposed hand. "I don't intend to kill you, but I'll need you to stand between us for a few minutes."

When she blinked, he grabbed her arm and dragged her around—as he'd done once before. This time she wasn't carrying a baby. She was carrying a knife. And the knife was just as helpful in the end as the baby had been.

Chase was sprinting across the snow. He was bleeding; there was a cut across his forehead and his left cheek. His hair, which had barely recovered from the last bout of green fire he'd been forced to endure, was singed and blackened. He carried two knives, and the woman he'd been fighting lay facedown in the snow. The fire that burned around the hedges dimmed; the hedges themselves began to wither.

Longland lifted his knife to Allison's throat, and she let him. He didn't explicitly threaten her; the gesture was enough to stop Chase dead.

"I resent having anything to do with the preservation of your life," Longland said, in his chilly, even voice.

Chase looked above her head at Longland's face. With the guttering of the fires—both white and green—Longland stood in shadow, Allison his shield.

"Not half as much as I do," Chase replied. "Let her go."

"Put down your weapons."

Chase knelt and placed the daggers in the snow, where they became less visible with passing seconds. He rose. "Let her go."

"When we've finished our negotiations. I don't intend to harm her unless you attempt to harm me. If I'd wanted her dead, I wouldn't have intervened." She couldn't see Longland's face and didn't try; she watched Chase. "I wanted you dead."

"The feeling's mutual."

"You're not dead, I note; given the nature of your injuries, you're unlikely to die immediately. And given the risk the girl took, I doubt I could kill you without harming her first, which would defeat the purpose. I won't harm her if you—"

"If I what? Give you my word I won't try to kill you?" Chase laughed. Longland didn't. "Yes."

"You know what that's going to be worth." Chase spit. "As much as yours would have been in similar circumstances."

"I'm already dead," Longland replied. "Which you understand, even if the girl doesn't. If you destroy my body, there's nothing keeping me here; I'll return to the City of the Dead at the command of my Queen, and I'll reach her side instantly. Nothing I know—*nothing*—will be hidden from her."

"You're hers—"

"I'm hers, but I'm not bound the way the dead are; I can't be and be reanimated in this fashion. You know this," he added again, his voice sharpening. "I don't wish to inform the Queen that I took a personal interest in preserving the lives of the people she ordered killed. I have a measure of freedom if you don't damage me so badly I have no physical anchor. And I assume you have an interest in keeping the knowledge of tonight's events contained for as long as they can be."

Chase hesitated.

Merrick glanced at the corpse to one side of his feet. "He didn't see who killed him." He nodded in the direction of the woman. "She didn't see anything but you. They can tell the Queen only what they witnessed—and only when she summons them."

"She summoned you."

"Not exactly. She found me. But I could be more easily found when I was not reanimated. I'm not alive; I exist in a half-world between the living and the dead. If she calls me, and I am compelled to return, I must resort to pedestrian means: planes, cars, trains. If you attempt to destroy me -and you succeed—I will be at her side instantly."

"Why did you interfere?" Chase asked. Some of the rage and the fear drained from his face, although he didn't exactly relax.

"Emma values this girl. I preserved her for that reason."

"And if—"

"What Emma did once, she can do again. I want her to open the gate. I want to escape this place. Without Emma, we don't stand a chance."

"We?"

Longland laughed bitterly. "The dead. You don't understand what it's like. The Necromancers who died tonight didn't. They will now," he added, with a strange mixture of both malice and pity. "To do what she did the first time, your Emma—"

"She is *so* not my Emma."

"Emma, then—she gathered more power than the Queen of the Dead has ever held. And what did she do with it? If rumor is to be believed, she used it all to pry open a door for a few precious minutes. Not to make herself immortal. Not to consolidate her own power in the face of her rivals; not to better her position in Court.

"I don't understand her. I try—but I don't. And it doesn't matter. What she did once, she might do again, and if she does, I want to be there. I'll give her everything I have—everything I've managed to retain—in order to be the smallest part of the lever she uses to open that door again.

"I'll kill if I have to. I'll save lives—even yours—if that's what it takes to convince her that I'm worthy of that privilege. I'll return her friend to her. I'll tell her everything I know, teach her anything I've learned—"

"She doesn't need to learn anything you learned," Allison said, breaking into their discussion for the first time.

Longland stiffened; Allison thought he would argue. But in the end, he didn't. "Maybe you're right. I wouldn't have survived my first week at Court if I hadn't learned some of it. But this isn't that Court, is it? And it *can't* be that Court, or I'll never be free. I have nothing else to offer," he continued, speaking once again to Chase.

"What were they planning to do to the rest of them?" Chase countered.

"The Necromancers came to this girl's house because they knew she knew."

Chase cursed.

"The others are in less danger."

Allison was frozen for one long moment. "What do you mean, less danger?"

"There are no Necromancers with them."

"But people were sent—"

"Yes, they were sent. You do not want our existence made public; you will force the Queen's hand. If pressed, she can usher in a new dark age. It's not without risk," he added, as Chase opened his mouth. "And it's possible she'll fail—but hundreds of thousands will perish before she does, with no guarantee that she'll be stopped."

Allison swallowed. "My family—"

"Most of your family is unharmed. They weren't concerned with your family; they wanted you. And the hunter, when they realized he was present."

Most. *Most* of her family.

Longland shook her and then let her go. He stepped back. "I don't understand you," he said. "You survived. There was *nothing* you could do there but die."

She glanced at Chase. "There are worse things than death."

"If you're dead, there's no chance at all that you can make people pay for what they've done to you."

Allison turned to Longland, but before she could answer, he lifted a hand. His expression was hard to read. She didn't try for long. Instead, she turned to Chase. He hadn't moved. His shoulders had relaxed, but he was watching Longland; he made no move to retrieve his weapons. Allison did; Longland didn't tell her to stop.

"I told you to run," Chase said, voice low.

"I know."

"Why didn't you do it?"

"Because I couldn't make myself believe there was nothing I could do." She lowered her gaze. "But you were right. There was nothing I could do. I couldn't—" She bit her lip. "I couldn't kill him. I couldn't just stab him without warning. I—"

He exhaled. "You'd better clean up before you see Emma again, or she'll kill me."

"You? Why?"

"You are covered in blood, and she's going to assume it's yours."

"But that's not your fault—"

"No, it's not. Fault isn't going to matter much." He reached out then and pulled her into his arms; he rested his chin on the top of her head, emphasizing the difference in their height. "I didn't tell you to kill and run. Not even I would be that stupid.

"You're not a killer. You're not Eric. You're not me. You're halfway Emma and your ridiculous friends."

"But not Amy?"

Chase chuckled. "Amy could have killed him."

Allison didn't laugh. "I don't think even Amy could have just slit his throat."

His arms tightened. After a moment he said, "No, probably not."

"You could have."

"Yes. I learned. I don't want you to have to learn what I did. I don't want you to need it the way I needed it."

"Why?"

"Because if it didn't break you, it would change you. I happen to like who you are right now."

"Even if I do something stupid."

"Even then. Maybe especially then. And you were right, for the wrong reasons. I'm not dead. They are."

"Chase—"

"We need to find the old man. We need to get back to Eric's."

"I want to go home."

He released her. "Old man first. I don't know if there were other Necromancers."

"There weren't," Longland said, in a tone that implied he should have asked. "But I wouldn't say it's safe. If I didn't think she'd go with you, I'd send you."

"I wouldn't let him go alone," a familiar voice said.

Allison turned, as Eric stepped around the trunk of a tree. He was carrying a gun. Not surprisingly, it was aimed at Longland.

Allison was shaking. It wasn't the cold. "He saved my life," she said.

"I heard."

"So please don't kill him."

He looked past Allison to Chase, and her gaze followed his. Chase grimaced but nodded.

"Amy is not going to like this."

"We don't have to tell Amy," Chase countered, which made clear just how little he knew about Amy Snitman.

"No problem," Eric said. "But she's at our place."

". . . Our place? The old man let her in?"

"I think he'd've been happier not to, but she's Amy." Eric glanced at Longland. "You have somewhere you need to be?"

Longland shrugged. "I have someplace to go. It won't last."

"Were they sending reinforcements?"

"Not yet. The two you killed a few nights ago weren't high in the hierarchy; the two you killed tonight were more significant. She'll call them home."

"The way you were called." It wasn't a question.

Longland nodded. He watched Eric for a long moment as Eric turned back to Chase. "Emma and Michael are also at our place."

"What the hell?"

"Allison's wasn't the only home hit."

Allison froze. Had this been the nightmare she desperately hoped it was, this is the moment that horror and adrenaline would have forced her to wake. Her heartbeat was a physical sensation, it was beating so quickly, but she was still standing in the snow in a ravine that was now up two corpses.

"Was anyone—was anyone hurt?" Allison managed to ask.

"We don't know," Eric replied. "But we know who their actual targets were. You're not going home," he added. "I'm sorry. Amy apparently packed a suitcase the size of a small freezer; we're leaving town."

"But our parents—" Allison swallowed. Her parents. Gunshots. Guns.

Chase slid an arm around her shoulder; she couldn't tell if he meant to hold her up or not. "I'm sorry." His voice was soft at the edges. It was cold at the core. "Their best chance of survival is your absence. Even if they worry. Even if they go out of their minds with worry. Even if they call the police and report you missing—it's better than going back. For them."

He didn't add, *This is why I told you not to get involved.* She was grateful for that. To her surprise, he said, "It's not your fault. Never believe it is."

"You warned me."

"Yes." He surprised her. He smiled. His teeth were slightly red—with blood. His. He didn't seem to notice. "But a question for you, and I want an honest answer."

"I'm not a liar."

"Not a good one, no."

"What's the question?"

"Knowing what you know now, what would you do differently?"

She was silent.

"Think about it in the car," Eric told her. "If these are the last two Necromancers, we've bought ourselves a bit of time—but not a lot."

The car was warmer than the air, but not by much, at least not for the first few minutes. Longland sat in the back—beside Chase. Chase had opened the front passenger side of the car and all but pushed Allison into it. He didn't trust Longland, but that was fair; Eric didn't trust him either. Allison was surprised that they'd chosen to take him along with them.

But she knew what Chase would say if she asked: Better to know where he is and what he's doing. Better to have him in easy reach; if necessary, we can kill him at any time. Even if, she thought, what he'd said about being dead was true. He didn't look dead to Allison; he didn't sound dead.

She met Chase's steady gaze in the mirror and looked down at her lap. What could she have done differently? If she'd known about the break-in, she could have started a fire and forced her family out of the house in time. Maybe. But that wasn't what he meant, and she knew it. She couldn't control what the Necromancers chose to do. She couldn't control what they wanted.

The only thing she could have done differently was take his advice at the very beginning. Walk away from Emma. Abandon her best friend.

She hadn't. She didn't know if all of her family was unharmed. *Most of your family is unharmed.*

Had she traded one of their lives for her friendship with Emma? Is that what she'd done? And if she had, and she could somehow go back, would she preserve that life and turn her back on friendship?

If a man had held a gun to her mother's head and offered her the choice, in *that* moment, she could have done it. *Speak to Emma again, and your mother is dead.*

She closed her eyes.

And opened them again. "No," she told Chase. "I wouldn't."

He was silent.

"Love is a weapon."

"Yes. In other people's hands. It's a weapon. It's a weakness."

"But, Chase—without it, what's the point? If love can be used to force us to abandon everything we value, what do we become, in the end? If we turn our backs on our friends, on our beliefs, on anything else we also love—what does that make of us? Cowards?"

"Survivors."

She was silent, thinking of the Necromancer—the man she couldn't just kill. Cowards, she thought, and survivors. "It's a stupid question."

"They're my specialty."

"I can't change the past. I can't change my decisions."

"I only wanted to know if you would."

"Why?"

He shrugged and looked out at the passing night. And then he smiled. He looked tired. He was always pale, but his eyes were dark, and his skin looked slightly sunburned. Or windburned. "Because I don't want you to give up on me."

"We were talking about Emma."

"Yes, and I was thinking about hypocrisy. I'm—I've been—angry at her for putting your life at risk. But if she didn't—if she hadn't—I wouldn't have met you, either. I don't want any more regrets. But I don't want you to be saddled with regrets like mine."

"People have regrets all the time, Chase. It's just—it's just a people thing. People who regret nothing have probably never tried anything. In their lives. Does this mean you'll stop hating her?"

"I won't hate her any more than I hate myself."

"So that's a no?"

Eric chuckled. "Hold out for something better than that," he advised.

"Pay attention to your driving," Chase shot back. "Or the entire discussion will be moot."

"It might be moot anyway. Amy wasn't happy."

This time, Chase didn't ask why Amy's happiness was a concern.

EMMA WAS ALREADY ON HER FEET when she heard the front door open. Ernest was seated; he glanced up at the sound, but not in a way that made it a threat to anyone in the room.

She held her breath; if Ernest didn't rise to greet whoever was making an entrance, she couldn't; it wasn't her house. But she listened for the sound of voices. She heard footsteps instead.

And when Allison—when Allison, spattered in blood—walked into the living room, she almost wept with relief. Margaret was in the middle of saying something to a less and less happy Ernest when Emma cut her off and ran across the room.

Allison said, "I'm *fine*."

And Emma replied, "Yes, but are you okay?"

Allison laughed. "No, not really." She let her forehead drop until it rested on Emma's shoulder, and then, she shook. She might have stayed that way for a long, long time, but Michael had come to stand to their left, and he was agitated—if silent—while he waited.

"It's not my blood," Allison told him, without lifting her head. She knew him well enough to know why he was panicking. She also knew him well enough to know her brief comment wouldn't stop him.

"If the two of you could have your huddle someplace other than the door, the rest of us could enter the room," Chase told them.

"I'm not sure that would be a net positive," Amy replied. She started to say more, then sucked her breath in; the sound had so much edge it might have killed a lesser person. Emma looked up and met the eyes of Merrick Longland.

Allison disengaged. "He saved my life," she said, with a trace of defiance, knowing what had caught Amy's attention. She caught Michael's arm. "A Necromancer was about to kill me, and he—he killed the Necromancer before I died."

Michael was blinking. Emma sympathized; she was blinking as well. But she caught Michael's other arm, and she and Allison retreated to the fireplace, taking him with them. There, she took a deep breath. "Ally, come let me help you clean up?"

Allison glanced at Michael, but nodded.

You'll need to tell Allison about her brother.

Emma wondered, as she walked up the stairs at the side of her best friend, if this is what Nathan's mother had felt when she'd phoned Emma to tell her about Nathan's accident. She knew only what her father had told her: that Allison's brother had been shot. She didn't know if he'd survived. And she knew it would be the first question Ally asked.

But Allison said, "Chase knocked on my window. He practically broke it. I was studying with headphones on." She was watching her feet. "I opened the window; Chase was on the roof. Well, the part of him that wasn't in front of the window. He told me we had to leave— and we had to leave now. He didn't tell me why." She swallowed. "I didn't even grab my phone. I climbed up on the desk and he dragged me up to the roof. You don't want to know how we came down." They reached the second floor and made a beeline for the bathroom, where Emma picked up a face cloth and soaked it in hot water.

"Stand still," she told Allison, who obliged. Mostly. "You came down the old tree?" She began, carefully, to wipe the blood from her friend's face, pausing to dump her glasses into the sink; they needed at least as much cleaning.

"I almost missed it. I saw them from the tree," she added, her voice dropping again. "I saw them open the front door. I heard shouting." She closed her eyes. "We climbed down the tree—I was better with that—and Chase started to move us.

"I heard a gunshot. I tried to go back."

"Chase wouldn't let you."

Allison shook her head. "I was so afraid. So afraid. For my family. For myself. I don't know who was shot—" she stopped, meeting Emma's eyes in the vanity mirror. After a long pause, she said, "You know."

Emma swallowed. "Toby."

"Tobias was shot?"

"Yes. I don't know more than that. We were leaving Mark's mother's house—I promise I'll tell you all about that later—and Amy called." She ran hot water again to rinse the towel out. Steam rose in silence, like mist. "People broke into her house. Her father was shot. He's alive and he's mostly fine, according to Amy. Amy was enraged."

"And you—"

"She couldn't reach my phone; I'd turned it off. She couldn't reach yours either. And when Eric said you weren't answering—" Emma closed her eyes. Opened them again. "I asked my father to go to your house and tell me—tell me—" Her smile broke. "And tell me whether or not you were alive. He told me you were. But he said your brother had been shot, that emergency vehicles—and the police—were on the way."

Allison's hands were like ice as Emma set the cloth down and caught them in hers. "Amy has a car, a suitcase full of clothing from various members of her family, credit cards and keys to a number of her family's various cottages. We're leaving with her.

"Ernest thinks, if we disappear, our families will be more or less safe."

"Have you—have you talked to your mom?"

"Yes. Before you arrived. There was a break-in at Amy's house; Amy's father was shot. They mostly missed him—I don't know how. Amy staged a breakdown."

"Staged?"

"She pretty much came up with a reason that most of us can skip school for a few days. Or more. She flipped out and told her mother she was so terrified she couldn't be in the house."

Allison snorted, and they both managed a smile; parents could be so naive.

"I phoned home to tell my mother about Amy's break-in and Amy's subsequent breakdown. I said I was at Nan's, with Amy, and that Amy was hysterical."

"Your mother bought that?"

Emma nodded. "Enraged people are often hysterical; I didn't mention the rage part. My mother assumed she was justifiably terrified. I told my mother I needed to be with Amy and that I probably wouldn't be coming home for a couple of days."

"She was okay with that?"

"Not the first time—but she talked to Mrs. Snitman, and that seemed to help."

"Michael's mother?"

Emma bit her lip. "I'm going to phone her when Michael's sleeping, because I have to lie to her, and he's already so wound up it'll be messy." She exhaled. "It's your mom that we can't get around. Amy's terror at armed men showing up in her house makes perfect sense to all of the parents who *didn't* deal with the same.

"But your mother—"

Allison swallowed.

"I can ask my father to check in on Toby. I think he can do that from wherever it is we're going. But it won't be the same as being able to see him for yourself, and we won't know——" She stopped and closed her eyes. "We won't know how bad the injury was. We won't know. If he's——if he's dying, you won't be able to be there. Not with him and not with your mother."

Allison closed her eyes. Eyes closed, she said, "It's my fault he was shot. It's my fault any of my family was in danger at all."

"Funny, I was thinking the exact same thing. It's *my* fault that your brother was shot. It's *my* fault that any of your family—even you—were in danger at all."

Allison's eyes snapped open. Emma wasn't smiling.

"They're not going to kidnap us. If you choose to stay home, Chase will have a coronary, but no one's going to knock you out and dump your unconscious body in Amy's car. My dad didn't tell me how bad Toby was—but it's bad. If it weren't, I'm sure he'd've said so. Amy wants us all to leave—but she understands what's at stake for you. We're going to one of Amy's getaways. Chase and Eric will come with us; I'm sure Amy's telling them that right now."

"And Michael's okay with this?"

"He's as okay as the rest of us."

"Which means no."

"Which means mostly no. But none of us are exactly calm. I think you're about as clean as you're going to get if you can't take a long shower. Here, have a comb—there's dried blood in your hair; I think I got most of it. I can head downstairs if you need time to decide—and I can make sure people give you that time."

"Even Amy?"

Emma didn't smile. "Even Amy."

Allison fished her glasses out of the sink. "Can you ask your father to check now?"

"He's not here right now."

"No," a familiar and beloved voice said. "But I am."

Emma turned toward Nathan.

"Em?" Allison said; she had taken a dry towel to the surface of her glasses before she deposited them across her ears and nose.

"Nathan's here," Emma replied. Her voice came out as a whisper. Allison couldn't see him. Emma lifted a hand and held it out to Nathan—and Nathan dropped both of his hands into the pockets of his jeans, shaking his head. "Allison can't see you if I don't touch you."

"I know."

There was so much finality to those two words Emma let her hand drop to her side. "Ally," she finally said, "can you give us a couple of minutes?"

Allison nodded, opened the door and walked into the hall. Then she walked back in and said, "You might want to have this conversation in a room that isn't the bathroom, given the number of people in the house."

"Good idea."

Nathan was never a person to fill a silence, even when it had gone past the point of awkward into nearly painful. Emma could—but not with Nathan. She knew how to find small, daily things interesting when she needed to. But days when she could cheerfully do this didn't generally including two shootings and the near death of her best friend.

"Where are you going?" she asked.

"Back," he replied. "To the City of the Dead."

She nodded, as if this made sense.

"If I stay, I'll follow you. If I follow you, I'll know where you are. I might not be able to tell the living how to get there—but I'll know. And what I know—" he stopped abruptly. "You've been avoiding me."

She started to lie. Stopped herself. This was *Nathan*. Lies had never really been necessary, before. She couldn't quite make herself believe they were necessary now. No, she thought, feeling the cold of all kinds of winter, that wasn't true. But she hadn't been lying to Nathan—not directly.

Only to herself. And those lies were just as harmful, in the end. She exhaled. "Yes."

He didn't seem to be surprised; his expression rippled as he closed his eyes and waited, his *Why?* unvoiced, but nonetheless loud.

"You didn't find me on your own," she said, voice almost a whisper.

His eyes widened, and this time he looked away. But he answered. "No."

"You didn't find your way home on your own, either. My dad said it would take a couple of years before you could—" She swallowed. "Before you could tear yourself away from the door. But it didn't."

He said nothing, but he met her gaze; he didn't hold it for long, but to her surprise, the faintest hint of a smile touched his lips.

"She sent you."

He nodded.

"Do you understand why?"

After a long pause, Nathan asked, "Do you?"

Emma closed her eyes. Opened them again. "Yes." She wanted to look away from his luminescent, oddly colored eyes, but she didn't. "When I saw Merrick Longland, I was afraid. We were all afraid. Because we'd all seen him die.

"I wasn't there when you died," she added. "But it must have been just as messy, just as painful. I never expected to see Longland again. But, Nathan—until October, I never expected to see you, either, except in dreams."

"Or nightmares?"

"Or nightmares. But when I saw Longland again—it wasn't just the fear. It was the hope—" She had to look away. "It was the *hope*, Nathan. Longland was alive, and if Longland could come back to life—so could you." When she turned to face him again, he was watching her; his eyes were shining. It was a light that looked familiar to Emma, although she couldn't immediately say why. "I was angry. I was angry with Eric, because he must have known. He didn't even look surprised. He didn't react as if it was impossible."

"No," Nathan said, voice grave. "He wouldn't."

"Necromancers are supposed to raise the dead. We're Necromancers. He knew it was possible."

"Emma—"

She lifted a hand to her mouth, mute for a moment because her voice was becoming so quavery, and she hated that. "It was everything I *wanted*. If I could learn how to use this power—this power that I didn't ask for and didn't want—I could bring you back. You could be *with me*. I could hold you. I could hold your hand without losing all sensation. I could—" she stopped. For a long moment, she struggled with breathing, because breathing right now was too close to tears, and she was still Emma Hall. "But Longland isn't alive."

His eyes widened slightly.

"He's—no one living would be able to tell the difference, but Longland said it's different. He's not alive; he's dead, and he's trapped in a body that's not really his. He can interact with the world. He can pretend to be alive."

"But he's dead. He's cold. And the only thing he now wants—"

"That is *not* all I want from you."

She turned to face him. "Isn't it?" she whispered. "Can you tell me, honestly, that if I could somehow open that door—or remove the impenetrable glass from that window—you'd even be standing here now?"

Nathan had never, to her knowledge, lied to her. He was therefore silent. It was a silence that stretched and thinned, and Emma was almost afraid of what would happen if it broke. But conversely, she wanted it to break. People were just like that.

"No." He looked down at his feet. "If the way had been open, I would have gone almost immediately. I didn't know where I was. I didn't understand—not completely—what being dead meant. I was cold, Em, yes. And it's warm there. Don't ask me how I know—I can't explain it. I don't think even your dad could. I didn't think of going home after I—after. I didn't even think of moving. I didn't think of moving on, either—I was lost.

"And when I did see the light—and I realize how melodramatic that sounds—I walked toward it. I knew it was where I belonged. I wanted to go there, I wanted to be there. But I never tried."

"Why?"

"Because when I got close enough, I could hear the screaming. The wailing. The sobs. I knew—I knew if I tried, I'd join them, and I could probably howl there like a lost toddler for too damn long."

"How did you get back?"

"She found me."

"She?" But Emma already knew the answer. The Queen. The Queen of the Dead. She frowned, then, and approached Nathan. He stood his ground, but stiffened—and that surprised her. It also hurt a little.

"Why do you think she sent me back?"

"The same reason," Emma replied, looking at his hands, at his face, and then, eyes narrowing, at the center of his chest, "that she sent Longland."

"Em?"

And she closed her eyes. Closed them, because even closed, she could see Nathan. She had always been able to see him with her eyes closed, because while he was himself, he was also some huge part of her hopes and her dreams. Her daydreams. Only his death had plunged him into nightmares—and even in nightmares, it was his sudden, inexplicable absence that caused her to wake, crying.

She could no longer see the narrow halls of an older Toronto home. She couldn't see the white doorframes that had clearly been painted half a dozen times. She couldn't see the carpet, which was so neutral a beige she might not have noticed it at any other time. She could see Nathan.

And at the center of his chest, glowing faintly, the links of a slender chain. She lifted her hand, and she knew as she did, that Nathan was bound and that she did not hold him. Her hands closed in fists.

She opened her eyes. Nathan was standing before her, but the world reasserted itself around him, as much as it could.

"She sent you because she knew."

"About you?"

"About me. About—" She exhaled. "She knows how I feel about you."

"And Longland?"

"He's an offer."

Nathan's smile shifted. He looked tired, to Emma. She didn't know whether or not the dead usually experienced the exhaustion that comes from too much fear, too much stress—but Nathan clearly did. "People always underestimate you. I had no idea why she sent me. She didn't ask me to do anything. She didn't ask me to say anything or learn anything. She didn't tell me to watch you. She just told me—to come home."

"She knew—she had to know—that I would want to see you," Emma continued. "But it's not that—it's Longland. He was meant to be proof that I could—" she couldn't say it.

"You could bring me back."

Emma nodded. "But I don't know *how*. I don't understand the power I have. I don't know how to use it. I see the dead—but it's not a struggle. I don't *try*. It happens. It's like weather. Or breathing." Her voice dropped. She looked up at him.

When they'd first met, she hadn't really noticed him. He was one of a dozen people who drifted in and out of class. He played computer games. He read. He tinkered in the science labs.

But he was friendly—and entirely without condescension—to Michael. That had caught her attention. Held it a little bit too long. He

wasn't classically gorgeous. He wasn't daydream material. But her daydreams were wild and incoherent; you couldn't build a life on most of
them, because they couldn't bear weight.

Nathan could. While he was alive, he could. He could listen. That
was a gift. But better, he could accept her. Not just the good bits. Not
the parts other people might find attractive. She wasn't a trophy girlfriend, although she could have been. He was a quiet space. A quiet,
accepting space. He saw her as she was, good and bad.

There weren't many people who saw her. Not as she saw herself; if
he'd done that, he would have walked away as quickly as he could, especially on the bad days. But as she actually was. He surprised her with
the small things he noticed. He surprised her by noticing things about
her she hardly noticed herself.

She had never lied to him, not deliberately. If she didn't want to talk
about something, she said exactly that: I can't talk about this right now.

"I don't think she thought Longland would actually speak to me. I
don't know if she understands what it does—and doesn't—mean to
him, to be half alive. And, Nathan—it would have worked if he hadn't."

"Em, don't —"

She lifted a hand, a signal between the two of them that he needed
to let her finish, because she wouldn't be able to if he interrupted her.

"It would have worked. I know myself. Even now—if you asked me,
if you said it was what you wanted, I'm not sure I could say no. Because
even knowing what I know, it's what *I* want." She saw his expression,
then, and before he could speak—and he wanted to—she closed the
distance between them, put her hands on either side of his face, and
kissed him.

It was not a short kiss. The shock of cold numbed her lips and the
palms of her hands. Everything about the gesture caused pain. She let
him go and saw that his eyes were closed.

Eyes closed, he said, "I would never have asked." And he smiled as
he opened them. They were bright. Shining. She was sure hers were as

well, but for entirely different reasons. "I know you mean it. I know you think you couldn't say no. I know what my dying meant to you—I left. I did worse than leave.

"But to do what was done to Longland, you'd have to become like the Queen of the Dead. Like Longland himself, before he died. You'd have to learn to see the dead—all of them—as sources of convenient power. You'd understand that power is necessary, because without it, you couldn't maintain what you'd built for me.

"You can't learn all that without changing something fundamental. The Emma who still walks Michael to school is not the Emma who could build me a body for her own convenience. Or even for mine. You'd do it because you love me.

"Because I love you. And it would change the nature of what love means to both of us. I didn't plan to die. I didn't want to die. I never wanted to be a source of loss and pain to the people I loved—the people who loved me." He looked past her shoulder for just a second, and then his gaze returned to her face, as if anchored there. "But I was. I was. I would change it in a heartbeat if I could—but not that way."

Emma placed a hand on his chest, her fingers splayed wide. It was solid. It was even warm.

He hadn't finished. "When I'm with you now, I don't see the exit. I don't long for it. I'm not drawn to it. I see you. I could spend the rest of your life seeing you, and I'd be happy. Believe that.

"I have to go soon. She's calling."

"You're bound to her."

His smile was slow and sweet. "Yes."

She reached into his chest, then. She reached for the slender links she could only barely perceive, curling her palm around them. Warmth became sudden heat; she could have flattened her palm against a live stove element with the same effect. She cried out, her hand jerking open.

"Don't worry," he told her. He lifted a hand and then let it drop. "I'm already dead. Nothing worse can happen to me." He was fading as she watched. She tried to grab the chains at his heart's center again. She didn't care if they burned. She had held onto fire before.

But her palm passed through them. She tried to grab his hand; it was no longer solid. "Nathan!"

"I'm sorry."

She tried to throw her arms around him. To keep him. She knew— she knew this was an echo of dying for Nathan. He didn't want to go; he didn't choose to leave. But choice or no, he vanished.

She was left—as she had been left the first time—holding nothing. But this time she knew, for certain, that Nathan was out there some-where. She knew who or what had taken him. She had told herself for months now that death was impersonal, because it was.

But the Queen of the Dead? There was *nothing* impersonal about her. Emma clenched her hands, and she turned to head down the hall.

Her father was waiting.

"How do I get him back?" she demanded. She had no doubt that he'd seen everything.

He didn't answer the question. Instead, he said, "Amy's packed the car. She's waiting. Allison and Michael are with her."

Emma swallowed. She didn't want to go downstairs yet; she knew what her face looked like. She had to work to bring rage—and the pain at its core—under control; she had to stop her hands from shaking so much.

And that would take time, and it was time they didn't have. "Dad?"

"I'm sorry, Em."

"She won't send him back," Emma whispered. "I didn't do whatever it was she wanted me to do. She won't send him back."

"I don't think so, no."

She made it halfway down the stairs, stopped, and turned again. "Allison's brother?"

"He's alive. No—don't. He's alive, but he wouldn't be if it weren't for machines. They're not certain he's going to pull through; he hasn't regained consciousness."

Emma closed her eyes. She balanced a moment between guilt and anger, and to her surprise, anger won. "Amy's right," she said, as she continued down the stairs.

"She frequently is."

"The Queen of the Dead has to go."

NATHAN

THE QUEEN IS NOT IN HER THRONE ROOM. The Court is not in session. The dead line the halls like rough statues; without the Queen's command, there's almost nothing for them to do—and nothing they dare to do. They don't speak. Not like Emma's dead.

Not like Brendan Hall.

Not like Mark.

Certainly not like Margaret.

These people have forgotten the life they lived; life might not have happened, for them, at all.

Nathan walks among them, avoiding them as if they were physical presences. As if he is. He knows he could walk the straight line through them, and through the walls themselves; nothing prevents it.

But the Queen doesn't care for it.

He walks the long way. She's not dead; she uses the halls. Many of the people who live in this great, fanciful edifice aren't dead either; they use the halls too. Her knights. Her Necromancers.

Some of the dead gathered here belong to them, but they don't wander the halls like handless puppets; they are hidden, invisible even to Nathan's eyes, until the moment the Necromancers choose to show their power. In the throne room, they take out their dead, displaying them like trophies or status symbols. No Necromancer of note or worth in the Queen's Court is ever without them.

The Queen alone doesn't choose to do this—but her power is absolute and unquestioned. She is never without it. If she died, this city would crumble—probably instantly. But he can see her in the distance. The stone walls do nothing to bank the brilliance of her light. He cannot imagine that she will ever die.

He didn't lie to Emma. He didn't tell her all of the truth.

But he didn't tell the Queen all of the truth either.

"Nathan." She is sitting in her outer chamber, on a chair as unlike the tall-backed official throne from which she rules as chairs can get. She is dressed in long, flowing robes, but they are looser and far less confining; her hair is unbound and falls in one long, glistening sheet down her back and over her shoulders. She wears no crown in this room.

She wears one ring.

He kneels before her, because she demands respect, no matter where she might be found. She doesn't stop him, but she tells him to rise almost immediately, and when he looks up, he meets her steady gaze. Her eyes are clear and shining; they are so much like Emma's eyes, it is hard to meet them. But once he has, it's impossible to look away.

"She saw you," the Queen says.

Nathan nods.

"She saw you and she attempted to take you from me."

He nods again.

"Do you wish to go to her?"

He does, and says, nothing.

The Queen rises. "I did not expect her to attempt to break my binding."

He knows that Emma almost succeeded. The Queen walks from the room, indicating that he is to follow; he does. She opens tall, wide doors and leaves the confines of the palace for a grand balcony that is longer than Nathan's former home. And wider. Above her, the sky is gray; beneath her, the sky is gray.

"Merrick Longland has not returned to me." She stands, back to Nathan, and gazes up, and up again, and Nathan knows what she is looking at: the only light that is bright enough, at this distance, to rival her own. He looks as well, but he schools his expression; all of the dead do. What they long for, what they yearn for, is beyond them; acknowledging it only annoys her.

"Is he dead?"

"No," Nathan replies.

"Ah." She seems amused; he can't see her expression. Amusement is no safety when it's in her voice. "Has she seen him?"

"Yes."

She turns, then, her expression haunted. "Did she speak to you, Nathan? Did she offer to resurrect you?"

He says nothing for as long as he safely can; he doesn't want to answer this question. And what he wants, in the end, doesn't matter. "No." Before she can speak, he adds, "She doesn't know how."

"Not yet. Not yet." The Queen smiles. It is cold. "You are certain, in the end, that she did love you?"

He says nothing.

She walks toward him, stopping six inches from his chest. She touches it with the flat of her palm; her hand is warm. It is the only warmth in the Castle. The only warmth he's experienced that is not Emma's. It is bloody hard to be cold all the time.

"Yes."

"And did she tell you that she loves you?"

He closes his eyes. It doesn't make a difference; he can still see her clearly. Eyes closed, she is the only thing he can see. "Yes."

"And you believed her."

"Yes."

"Then she will come, Nathan. She will come to me. I have not yet decided what I will do with her when she does." She looks at his face again. "You wanted to see her." She caresses his cheek. He meets her gaze without flinching because her touch doesn't make him flinch. It is warmth. It is life.

"Do you want to be able to hold her? To touch her?"

"Yes." Even more than he wants to crawl out of this conversation into painful oblivion. Love is not something to be pulled apart and dissected, not like this. Not by outsiders. There is no joy in it; there is a rough, painful voyeurism.

Her hand falls, and her eyes narrow. "Why?"

It is not the question he expects. And he knows he will have to answer it because the compulsion is almost painful. He doesn't have the words for it. He starts to say, *because I love her*, but he understands that this is not the answer she's seeking. And he understands that he doesn't have that answer, because in the end, the question has nothing to do with Nathan.

He has become so used to fear that he is almost too numb to feel it. "Because," he says, "she's alone." He can't look away. "She once made me promise that I would let her die first, when we were old. So she wouldn't have to face losing me."

"And you promised?"

"It was a stupid promise. I didn't want to make a promise I couldn't keep. But I know—I know what my death did to her. I know what it did, and I'd take it back in a second if I could. I want to be able to hold her when she cries—because she does cry, but only when she's alone. Only when no one living can see her."

It is all true. And he knows, looking at the Queen's face, that the Queen has also cried, and that she never cries where anyone living can see her. It is not safe for even the dead to bear witness to her weakness.

"Come," she says. "What your Emma is too unschooled to do, I will do."

His eyes widen, then.

"Yes, Nathan. I will resurrect you. I will bring you back to Emma alive and in the flesh."

ABOUT THE AUTHOR

Michelle Sagara lives in Toronto with her husband and her two sons, where she writes a lot, reads far less than she would like, and wonders how it is that everything can pile up around her when she's not paying attention. Raising her older son taught her a lot about ASD, the school system, and the way kids are not as unkind as we, as parents, are always terrified they will be

Having a teenage son—two, in fact—gives her hope for the future and has taught her not to shout, "Get off my lawn" in moments of frustration. She also gets a lot more sleep than she did when they were younger.